Quest for the Holey Snail

Rob Johnson

XERIKA PUBLISHING

QUEST FOR THE HOLEY SNAIL

Published by Xerika Publishing

Cover design and all illustrations by Penny Philcox.

First published 2016 by Xerika Publishing
10 The Croft, Bamford, Hope Valley,
Derbyshire S33 0AP

ISBN 978 0 9926384 6 7

http://www.rob-johnson.org.uk

For my brother, Ian.

I think you would have liked this one.

ACKNOWLEDGEMENTS

I am indebted to the following people for helping to make this book better than it would have been without their advice, technical knowhow and support:

Helen Gilhooly; Alex McGillivray; Penny Philcox; Dan Varndell; Chris Wallbridge; Cynthia Wallbridge; Cathy Whitton; Nick Whitton; Heidi, Louis, Patrick and Robyn Woodgate.

Many thanks also to retired West Yorkshire Police Inspector Kevin Robinson for technical advice on British police procedures.
https://crimewritingsolutions.wordpress.com/

And finally, my eternal gratitude to Penny Phillips for her unfailing support, encouragement and belief. Rather less grateful for all the beetroot. I'm really not sure it helped that much.

ILLUSTRATIONS AND COVER DESIGN BY PENNY PHILCOX

Very special thanks to Penny Philcox for the original artwork and cover design. Such an amazing talent and seemingly inexhaustible patience in the face of my frequent requests for alterations.

DISCLAIMER

This book contains no historical or mythological accuracy whatsoever.

No snails (holey or otherwise) were harmed during the making of this book.

1

There are times in most people's lives when they would give their eye teeth for one of those Swiss Army knives with their vast array of handy little tools and gadgets. This exchange is rarely achieved, however, because very few people actually have eyes with teeth in them, unless of course they have recently been attacked by some wild beast or other which has tried to bite their face off. Fortunately for him, Horace Tweed had not been subjected to such an assault, but *un*-fortunately for him, this meant that he was lacking in any eye teeth to trade for a Swiss Army knife, which he so desperately needed at this particular moment.

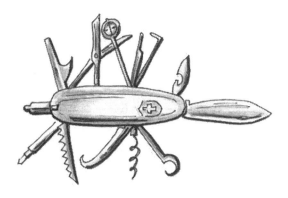

And even if he had been in possession of the requisite number of eye teeth, there was no-one in the immediate vicinity to trade them *with*, given that the only current occupants of Flat D, 221b Mortuary Street were himself and a Staffordshire Bull Terrier called Zoot, who Horace knew for a fact was not the proud owner of a multi-tool of any description.

The handy little tool or gadget he was most in need of right now was the one for unpicking the end of a roll of Sellotape which some idiot (very possibly Horace himself) hadn't bothered to fold back neatly or even scrunch untidily the last time they'd used it. The reason he was in such urgent need of accessing the end of the Sellotape was as follows:

1) An important-looking letter had dropped through his letterbox earlier that morning.

2) The aforementioned Staffordshire Bull Terrier called Zoot had immediately ripped the important-looking letter to pieces.

3) Each attempt to reassemble the important-looking letter from its constituent parts ended in failure because of either:

a) a gust of wind through the missing pane in the kitchen window (four times);

b) a sudden and involuntary fit of sneezing (twice).

Some kind of fixative was therefore essential to the task in hand except that it was proving exceptionally difficult to release the end of the Sellotape, not only because Horace was seriously lacking in the Swiss Army knife department, but also because his obsessive nail-chewing habit had left him entirely lacking in the fingernail department too.

'Damn and buggeration,' he said, finally giving up on the tape and hurling it across the room, where it ricocheted off the chipped nose of a life-size plaster of Paris bust of Timothy S. Leatherman (inventor of the eponymous Leatherman multi-tool device) and out through the missing pane in the kitchen window of his third floor apartment.

* * *

The last thing anyone expects when out for a morning stroll along Mortuary Street – or any other street, road, avenue or lane for that matter – is to be struck on the top of the head with an economy size roll of Sellotape, hurled (albeit inadvertently) through the missing pane of a third floor window and travelling at a speed in excess of 83.7 miles per hour. Mr Dikgacoi was no exception, although he may not have agreed that this was the *last* thing he would have expected.

'Ouch!' he said, and his hand flew to the injured part of his skull, unprotected as it was by even a single productive follicle.

Still massaging the top of his head, he stooped to pick up the offending projectile and was surprised to find not one but two rolls of tape lying side by side on the pavement.

'Hmm,' he said as his double vision began to correct itself. 'That's the third to last thing I would have expected.'

'You don't see that sort of thing very often, even in my line of work,' said a passing solicitor who specialised in no-win-no-fee personal injury litigation. 'Are you okay?'

'I think so,' said Mr Dikgacoi. 'But it looks like whichever idiot last used this tape didn't bother to fold the end neatly or even scrunch it untidily.'

'Any double vision? Headache? Mild concussion? Palpitations? Deep vein thrombosis?' asked the solicitor and then glanced at Mr Dikgacoi's totally bald scalp and added, 'Sudden hair loss?'

'Vision was a bit iffy, but it seems to be fine now.'

'You can't be too careful where head injuries are concerned, you know. Not in my experience.'

'Have you had one then?' said Mr Dikgacoi.

'One what?'

'Head injury.'

'No, but I happen to be a solicitor who specialises in no-win-no-fee personal injury litigation and I think you have a very strong case.'

'Case?'

'Against whoever wilfully hurled this roll of Sellotape at you with malice aforethought and very possibly murder in mind.'

'Well, I'm not sure about that,' said Mr Dikgacoi, smiling politely. 'Anyway, there's no real harm done.'

The solicitor fished inside the top pocket of his waxed cotton Armani suit jacket and produced a business card, which had coincidentally been manufactured from recycled waxed cotton.

'My card,' he said, thrusting it between the palm of Mr Dikgacoi's hand and the scalp he was still massaging with it. 'In case you change your mind. Like for instance if you develop brain damage at a later stage as a direct result of the impact.'

Mr Dikgacoi thanked him and pocketed the business card at precisely the same moment as something else happened which nobody would have expected. (Well, perhaps not "nobody".) A massive explosion was heard from just around the corner at the top end of Mortuary Street, and a huge ball of fire illuminated what would have been the night sky if it hadn't been eleven o'clock in the morning.

The solicitor glanced at his watch. 'Damn. Ten minutes early.'

He gave Mr Dikgacoi a freemasonly handshake and scurried off in the direction of a potentially large number of new and seriously injured clients.

'Don't forget to get in touch before amnesia sets in,' he called out over his shoulder as he went. 'You can always come crying to me, you know.'

* * *

Despite its relative proximity to Flat D, 221b Mortuary Street, Horace Tweed was totally oblivious to the sound of the explosion on account of the fact that he was currently on his hands and knees with his head inside the bottom cupboard of a Welsh dresser in search of a Pritt stick which he seemed to recall putting there on 15th January 2007 after having completed the finishing touches to his Halloween costume in plenty of time for the big day.

'Double damn and buggeration,' he said as he added a decapitated Action Man to the growing pile of long forgotten "stuff" that was threatening to engulf both his ankles. 'I'm sure it's in here somewhere.'

A spoutless teapot bearing the image of a three-legged goat and the words "Prestatyn Welcomes Careful Drivers" joined the pile at precisely the same moment as the flat's doorbell went "*bing-bong*".

'Ouch!' went Horace, who had forgotten he was half inside a cupboard when he attempted to stand, thereby whacking his head against the underside of the drawer above.

Zoot the Staffie, who had withdrawn to his bed under the kitchen table when Horace had shouted at him over the shredding-of-the-important-looking-letter incident, now leapt into action and hurtled towards the door to see who the unexpected visitor might be. However, due to the highly polished nature of the bare floorboards, the hurtle turned into a high speed slide which culminated in a resounding "*thump*" at the base of the door and a temporary loss of consciousness.

Horace, who was well aware of the slipperiness of the floor, joined him at a considerably slower pace, massaging his injured scalp and then inspecting the palm of his hand to ascertain whether a bump had started to form. With his other hand, and with some difficulty due to the additional weight of Zoot's bulk, he pulled open the door and surveyed his visitor from head to toe and back again.

This took fractionally longer than it would have done with someone of average height because the man was improbably tall despite the complete absence of any hair whatsoever. His camel hair duffel coat was about three sizes too small for him and was sufficiently untoggled to reveal the central section of a faded maroon T-shirt beneath and its partially visible image of a giant sea turtle.

'Is this yours?' said Mr Dikgacoi.

Horace examined the economy size roll of Sellotape in the man's hand.

'Poss-ib-ly,' he said after a pause of several moments, not wishing to commit himself too early in the exchange for fear of self-incrimination.

'Perhaps it would help you to identify the item if I were to tell you that the last idiot to use it let the end of the tape go back without so much as folding it neatly or scrunching it untidily.'

'I see,' said Horace, gently rubbing the now throbbing injury to the top of his head.

'It hit me on the head,' said Mr Dikgacoi, gently rubbing his own cranial injury.

Horace paused for even more moments than the last time.

'I don't suppose you happen to have a Swiss Army knife about your person, do you?' he said at last, subtly shifting the focus of the conversation away from his personal culpability in the matter.

'I do as a matter of fact,' said Mr Dikgacoi.

Horace beamed. 'And would it include the little tool for unpicking the ends of Sellotape amongst its array of handy little tools and gadgets?'

'Of course,' said Mr Dikgacoi, looking rather affronted that he could be taken for someone foolish enough to possess a Swiss Army knife *without* such a handy little tool or gadget.

'Excellent,' said Horace, his beam instantly switching from dipped to full. 'Would you care for a cup of tea?'

'I would, yes. Thank you very much.'

* * *

After an hour and nine minutes and two cups of tea, the important-looking letter was finally reassembled from its constituent parts with the aid of several inches of Sellotape, the end of which was now safely and neatly folded back onto itself.

During the lengthy reassembly process, Horace had explained to Mr Dikgacoi why he believed that the letter was quite as important as it made itself out to be. 'I'd eat my hat if it's not a reply to the advertisement I placed in a national and moderately well respected periodical not two weeks ago,' he'd said.

'What advertisement was that then?' Mr Dikgacoi had not unreasonably asked.

'I'll show you,' Horace had said and then rummaged in the top pocket of his pyjama jacket before producing the advertisement which he had previously clipped from the aforementioned periodical:

WANTED

GAINFUL EMPLOYMENT OF AN ADVENTUROUS NATURE BUT WITHOUT RISK OF PERSONAL PHYSICAL HARM.

CAN PROVIDE OWN TIME TRAVEL MACHINE IF REQUIRED.

PLEASE CONTACT ETC., ETC.

15

And this is what the important-looking letter said when it had finally been reassembled from its constituent parts:

Dear Mr Etc., Etc.,

Re your recent advertisement in the latest edition of "Practical Adventuring", please visit me immediately for a foregone-conclusion interview re employment of an adventurous nature. We can discuss the personal physical harm issue at the time. If you do not possess a Swiss Army knife (minimum twelve handy little tools or gadgets), bring someone with you who does. The employment of an adventurous nature is top secret. Tell no-one else except the tall fellow with the Swiss Army knife who's standing next to you.

Yours sincerely,

A Wellwisher

P.S. Finger buffet provided, but please bring your own croutons and/or nut allergy antidote if required.

'Blimey,' said Horace. 'That sounds pretty exciting.'

'What's croutons?' said Mr Dikgacoi.

'Never mind that now,' said Horace, who wasn't entirely sure what croutons were either but had an idea it was another word for mad people. 'This calls for a minor celebration.'

'More tea?'

'Not *that* minor a celebration. I was thinking more in terms of a glass of mildly alcoholic ginger beer.'

'Splendid,' said Mr Dikgacoi, who really wasn't at all keen on ginger beer but certainly preferred it to tea, which he hated with a vengeance. 'But shouldn't we get going? The letter does say "immediately" after all.'

'We?'

'Well, I do have a Swiss Army knife, and to be perfectly honest, I too have recently been seeking gainful employment of an adventurous nature.'

'Really? What an amazing coincidence.'

'It is, isn't it?'

2

On their way to the address which was printed at the top of the important-looking letter (not shown in above facsimile), Horace suddenly realised he didn't even know his new companion's name.

'So what's your name then?' he said.

'D-I-K-G-A-C-O-I,' spelt Mr Dikgacoi.

Horace frowned. 'Deeeyekaygeeayceeoheye? That's a very long and unusual name if I may say so.'

'No, that's just how you spell it.'

'So how do you pronounce it then?'

'No idea.'

'You don't *know*?'

Mr Deeeyekaygeeayceeoheye shrugged. 'Never seen the need really.'

'But what if someone asks you your name? Like I did just now.'

'I spell it out. Like I did just now. I think it's pronounced "Jacky". Or something like that anyway.'

'What did your parents call you?'

'Nine.'

'Nine?'

'We were a very big family. My parents couldn't remember all the names, so they called us all by numbers. The order we were born in. It was a bit confusing with the twins though. Seven A often thought *she* was being called when in fact it was Seven B and vice versa.'

'Yes, I can see that might have been tricky,' said

Horace and then pondered the awkwardness of pronouncing "Deeeyekaygeeayceeoheye" for several seconds, staring out of the train carriage window as he did so and chewing on what little still remained of his badly bitten fingernails. "Jacky" didn't suit Mr Deeeyekaygeeayceeoheye at all, and "Nine" sounded far too impersonal.

'I know,' he said at last as he spotted an advertising hoarding on the platform of the station where the train had been waiting for the past eighteen minutes due to a stray Wrigley's chewing gum wrapper on the line. 'What about Christian?'

'What about them?'

'No, not Christians, plural. Christian as in Christian Dior. As your new name. Deeeyekaygeeayceeoheye is far too much of a mouthful, and Nine sounds a bit... impersonal.'

'Christian?'

'Yes.'

Mr Deeeyekaygeeayceeoheye looked doubtful. 'I'm not sure, to be honest. If anything, I tend to see myself as more of a humanist really, and—'

'Okay then,' Horace interrupted and scanned some of the other advertising hoardings. 'How about Persil?'

Mr Deeeyekaygeeayceeoheye shook his head.

'Kelloggs? ... Birdseye? ... Always Ultra? ... MacNugget? ... Texaco? ... Exlax? ...'

Mr Deeeyekaygeeayceeoheye shook his head with increasing vigour after each of Horace's suggestions and then suddenly pointed through the carriage window. 'There,' he said. 'What about that?'

Horace followed the direction of his pointing finger. 'Mr *Ladies*?'

'No, no, no. *Next* to the toilets. The big sign there.'

Horace shifted his gaze to the sign in question. 'Yes, I see what you mean. It's certainly got a ring to it.'

* * *

Fifty-seven minutes and twelve seconds later, when their train finally arrived twenty-nine minutes and eighteen seconds behind schedule at their destination station, Horace Tweed and Norwood Junction hurried along the platform, eager as they were to meet their new employer for the very first time.

Perhaps if they hadn't been quite so eager, they might have noticed the man with the deep scar which ran from just below his left ear to almost the middle of his chin, narrowly bypassing the corner of his mouth. Dressed in a broad-brimmed, dark black hat and almost floor-length, dark black coat, he was leaning against the station wall, pretending to read an upside-down copy of *Lurkers Monthly*. He followed their progress with his eyes through a pair of dark black wraparound sunglasses, and the moment Horace and Norwood left the station, his feet followed them as well in a pair of red and white baseball boots.

And if the man in the baseball boots hadn't been so intent on keeping his quarry in sight, he might have noticed the man in the off-grey, almost floor-length hooded robe and Union Jack flip-flops who tossed his copy of *Unusual Footwear* into the nearest litter bin and set off after *him*.

* * *

Horace was beginning to regret not having invested in a moderately priced *A-to-B* at the station kiosk as Norwood Junction had suggested. For his part, Norwood Junction (né Mr Dikgacoi) – or Norwood for short – was beginning to regret having unquestioningly accepted Horace's assertion that he was genetically blessed with what he termed "an innate sense of direction".

'That's not the same one, is it?' said Horace as the two prospective adventurers stood side by side, staring at the long, low building on the opposite side of the moderately busy high street.

'Same what?' said Norwood.

'The same station that we left not an hour and six minutes ago.'

Norwood studied the long, low building with its grey slate roof, its mustard yellow brickwork and its iron-framed glass awning, noting inwardly that the geraniums in the hanging baskets looked in serious need of a good watering.

'It certainly looks very… stationy,' he said.

'Do stations often move then? Like it's been following us around or something?'

Norwood briefly considered the possibility and then dismissed it as unlikely before the penny dropped and he realised the cause of the misunderstanding.

'No,' he said, turning towards his companion with a knowing smile which some might have incorrectly construed as mildly patronising. 'I said "stationy", not "stationary".'

'Oh, I see,' said Horace and paused lengthily before adding. 'Is there such a word as "stationy" then?'

'Yes indeed,' said Norwood. 'Of course it's not much in use nowadays, but it was all the rage back in the day.'

DIGRESSION ONE: ON THE COMING OF THE RAILWAYS AND WHETHER THERE REALLY IS SUCH A WORD AS "STATIONY"

PLEASE NOTE: *This is the first of a handful of digressions to be found at random intervals throughout this book. To be honest, they don't really add much to the story itself, so you can skip them if you like or maybe come back to them later. It's entirely up to you of course.*

* * *

By the annoying and totally meaningless phrase "back in the day", Norwood was referring to: "the period during the reign of Queen Victoria when the entire public transport system was revolutionised by the coming of the railways". Indeed, it was the monarch herself who was directly responsible for this revolution by offering a prize to anyone who could devise a means of travel which didn't involve horses (Royal Proclamation 871). This wasn't because she was some kind of namby-pamby, anthropomorphising, vegan eco-warrior who was on some kind of soft-in-the-head mission to liberate the entire equine species from its traditional role as an oppressed beast of burden. Not a bit of it. In fact, she loved nothing better than sitting on them, being pulled around in carriages behind them and occasionally even eating bits of them too.

And here's another fact. It is only relatively recently that historians have discovered a clue as to the real reason why the Queen Vic was quite so keen to find an alternative to horsepowered travel, and it materialised in the form of a letter unearthed from a heap of undelivered post at a Royal Mail sorting office in Billericay. The letter – somewhat ironically undelivered due to "Insufficient Postage" – was written in Her Royal Monarchness's own hand and addressed to her faithful servant and Scottish comedian, Arnold "Billy" Brown. In the letter, she describes in particularly graphic detail how she'd been strolling along Prince Regent Street the day before to "check out the bargains in the January sales" when she'd slipped on a massive pile of steaming horse doo-doo and gone flying bustle over crown to the obvious amusement of a bunch of nearby proletarians. Tellingly, she concludes her letter with the now famous invocation, "Who will rid me of this turbulent horse shit?".

Grovelling royalist sycophant as he was, Brown would of course have been straight onto the case before you could shout "The Duke of Saxe-Coburg-Gotha's yer uncle", but since he never received the letter, he did naff all about it, which probably explains why Victoria had him beheaded as a "disobedient Scottish git".

So, despite Brown having failed her in her hour of need, the Queen took matters into her own hands and issued Royal Proclamation 871. Spurred on by the generosity of the royally offered prize (two tickets to a gig at the Albert Hall), engineers – both amateur and professional – laboured night and day to try to devise a means of public transport which didn't involve horses. There were many failures and a smattering of not-quite-successes. One such of this latter category was the invention of an external combustion engine by a part-time cobbler named Thadeus Boatbuilder. The creation of this remarkable means of propulsion made it almost inevitable that he would win the coveted prize until the day arrived when the initial prototype was to be put to the test.

In the absence of real guinea pigs in those days, Thadeus assumed the role himself but with disastrous results. Having securely strapped a four-wheeled external combustion engine to the underside of each of his feet (which incidentally made him appear twenty-seven inches taller), he fired up the first of the two engines, and a serious design flaw became immediately apparent. Thadeus had overlooked the necessity for some kind of dual ignition system which would start both engines simultaneously, and as a result, his left foot shot forward at an alarming rate while his right foot remained firmly planted to the ground. Tragically, this meant not only that his invention was consigned to The Dustbin of Silly Ideas (until rediscovered and substantially modified by Henry Ford many years later), but also that two funerals had to be held in order to bury both halves of Thadeus's body.

The months turned into even more months, and Queen Victoria began to despair that a horseless public transport system was little more than a whimsical royal pipedream.

'Cheer up, old thing,' said Albert Hall, the Prince Recent, over breakfast one day. 'I've been hearing some jolly exciting stuff about this new railways thingummywotsit.'

'Railways?' said the Royal Wifeness. 'What on earth are *railways* when they're at home?'

'Great long strips of metal tied together with planks. They can put them almost anywhere apparently.'

'And their point *is*?'

As it happened, Albert hadn't the slightest idea what these so-called railways were supposed to be for, so never mentioned the "R" word again from that day until quite some fortnights later when an astonishing announcement was announced. According to the newspapers, some bright young spark by the name of Stephenson had finally figured out what to do with the massive network of rusting strips of metal that now covered the entire country. Having grown bored with writing books about pirates and blind people called Pew, he had turned his attention to designing what he called a "Railway Carriage" (later to be renamed "Pullman" after some other writer chap). Unfortunately, this invention wasn't going to win him any prizes – royal or otherwise – on account of the fact that the carriage remained completely motionless unless towed by an awful lot of horses. However, not to be thwarted, Stephenson returned to the proverbial but nevertheless real drawing board and quickly invented a "Train" (or as it has come to be known in more recent times, the "Delayed Seventeen-Ten From Carshalton Beeches").

And the rest, as they say, is "The History of British Public Transport Systems Through the Ages" except for one small detail. Delighted though Queen Victoria and her subjects were with Stephenson's brilliant new invention, it soon became clear that something was missing. Although a growing fleet of Trains and Carriages had been happily criss-crossing their horseless way the length and breadth of the country, there wasn't one single place where they could stop so that people could get either on or off them. These "Passengers", as they were known at the time but later renamed "Customers" for some bizarre reason, grew ever more frustrated as they waited patiently beside the Railway only for a Train and its Carriages to whizz past and cause them to miss all kinds of important meetings and appointments.

Something had to be done – and quickly. But just as frustration was threatening to turn into all-out revolution, a certain Mrs Gwendoline Terminus hit upon the extraordinary idea of inventing specially designed buildings which she called "Stations" after her son, Derek. So thrilled was Her Royal Victorianess with this simple but highly effective solution that she instantly rewarded Mrs Terminus with the specially created honour, Keeper of the Royal Off-Peak Season Ticket. At the same time, the Queen issued Royal Proclamation 893, in which she decreed that the very first Station to be built should be named "Victoria" and that all future Stations should look pretty much the same (i.e. "stationy"), although not necessarily as big.

2
(Continued)

'I'm afraid all stations look pretty much the same to me,' said Horace, back in the present. 'But if it *is* the same one we left an hour and six minutes ago, that means we've been—'

'Walking in an enormous circle,' Norwood interrupted.

They continued staring at the station for several seconds, both wondering how to turn a bad situation into a better one, when their attention was suddenly diverted by the sound of screeching tyres. Instinctively, they turned towards the noise to see a large, dark black van with normal-sized, dark black tinted windows hurtle sideways from around the nearest corner and onto the wrong side of the road. The sound of screeching tyres was immediately amplified to eardrum-piercing proportions as the drivers of half a dozen vehicles on the correct side of the road slammed on their brakes to avoid a collision. This was followed by the hooting of numerous horns and several gestures of a sexually explicit nature as the van narrowly managed to maintain a semi-upright position and then mounted the pavement only yards from where Horace and Norwood were standing.

But the van showed no signs of slowing and, if anything, seemed to increase its speed as it bore down on the prospective adventurers.

'Look out!' someone shouted helpfully, but neither

Horace nor Norwood had time to even wet their pants, let alone get out of the way, so they resorted to the age-old defence mechanism of shutting their eyes.

There was yet another screech – much closer this time – and then the sound of van doors being thrown open.

Horace and Norwood both opened their eyes at exactly the same moment to see three enormous figures leap out of the van, the front of which was now a matter of inches from where they stood. The three were dressed identically in dark black from head to foot, including matching ski masks, and were clearly in a hurry.

Horace and Norwood stepped back to let them pass, but the sheer weight of the massive hands which grabbed hold of them was sufficient indication that they had utterly misread the situation. Innocent by-gawpers watched in horror – and several took photographs or videoed the scene on their mobile phones – as the tall, bald stranger and his shorter and even stranger companion were swept off their feet (not at all in the romantic sense) and bundled unceremoniously into the back of the van.

'Well, that was a bit unceremonious,' tutted a woman by-gawper, continuing to film the van as it made an even louder screech than all of the previous ones put together and sped off on the legally designated side of the road.

One of the only two people who were not photographing or videoing the hasty departure of the dark black van was a man in a broad-brimmed, dark black hat and almost floor-length, dark black coat. Apparently, he had no interest whatsoever in recording the event for posterity — or even for a few quid from the media — and jumped into the nearest taxi instead.

The only other person who wasn't photographing or videoing the hasty departure of the dark black van was a man in an off-grey, almost floor-length hooded robe and Union Jack flip-flops who immediately clambered into

28

the nearest-but-one taxi.

'*Tune Latine loqueris*?' he asked the cab driver.

The cabbie shot his passenger a glance in the rear-view mirror but was unable to make eye contact due to the hiddenness of the man's face inside the cowl of his robe.

'Sorry, mate,' he said. 'Don't speak Latin. Where you wanna go?'

'*O me miserum*,' said his passenger (which is actually Latin for "Oh bugger") and then followed up with, '*Sequere illud vehiculum*!' and repeatedly jabbed his finger in the direction of the hastily departing dark black van.

3

In all her years on the force, Detective Chief Inspector Harper Collins had worked with plenty of cops who liked nothing better than a good fresh corpse to get their teeth into. Not literally, of course, although there were a fair few who shared some of the more unpleasant personality traits of a demented werewolf or half-crazed vampire. But she wasn't one of them. Almost by definition, murders were messy affairs, and the scene of the crime itself was invariably awash with blood and other unmentionable secretions as well as the occasional detached body part.

After a particularly gory double homicide a few months earlier, she'd seriously considered applying for a transfer to Traffic, but then it struck her that the life of a traffic cop wasn't just about giving out parking tickets and breathalysing pissheads. They had their fair share of maimed, mangled and occasionally decapitated motorists to deal with when it came to multi-vehicle pileups on the motorway – very probably a whole lot more vomit-inducing than any murder scene she'd ever had to attend.

But as murder scenes went, even DCI Collins had to admit that this one really wasn't so bad after all. The immaculately tidy master bedroom of a suburban semi and not so much as a pinprick's worth of blood in sight. Male victim – late sixties or early seventies – bare-chested and flat on his back near the foot of the bed with his arms still attached to the torso and stretched out at right angles. The legs straight and together and also attached. Almost as if he'd been fixed to an imaginary horizontal crucifix. The expression on the man's face was almost peaceful, and if it hadn't been for what looked like the deliberate positioning of the body, it might well have appeared that he'd died from natural causes. But whoever the killer was, they'd made no attempt to conceal the fact that this was a murder.

By contrast to Harper's relief at the almost sanitary condition of the murder scene, her youthful and disturbingly casual detective sergeant was patently disappointed.

'Not much blood then,' said DS Maurice Scatterthwaite as he squatted beside the body and shovelled another plastic forkful of curry-soaked chips into his already over-crammed mouth, his normally hollow cheeks expanding alarmingly to cope with the additional onslaught.

Harper didn't respond. Stating the obvious was one of Scatterthwaite's many irritating habits. Another was his constant snacking and how he never seemed to put on an ounce of fat however much he ate.

'So if there's no blood,' the sergeant went on, 'that's a pretty good indication he must have been murdered elsewhere.'

'Well, no,' said Harper from her own squatting position on the opposite side of the victim. 'I'd say that the absence of blood is more likely an indication that there aren't any holes in his body. Other than the standard anatomical quota, that is.'

Scatterthwaite sniffed and chewed on another forkload while he considered the theory, apparently unable to think with his mouth closed.

'Could be,' he said, wiping a drip from his nose on the back of his latex-gloved fork hand, an action which resulted in a dollop of curry sauce disengaging itself from the fork and ending up on the corpse's bare chest.

'Christ almighty,' said Harper as her sergeant produced the paper napkin thoughtfully provided with the takeaway and began dabbing at the gobbet of sauce. 'What do you think you're doing?'

'What's the problem? He's dead, isn't he?'

'I'm not talking about offending the guy. I'm talking about this being a crime scene. You know? Forensics and stuff?'

Harper stood up and looked around the bedroom for the photographer, realising she needed some decent shots of the symbols on the victim's chest before Scatterthwaite obliterated them altogether with his paper napkin. There were a couple of SOCO guys dusting for fingerprints and generally poking around in the room's various nooks and crannies, but neither of them seemed to have a camera. She went out onto the landing and spotted the photographer at the far end, half leaning out of an open window. She called out to him, and he swung round, dropping his Nikon to chest height.

'What's so interesting out there?' said Harper.

'Sunset. Don't see one like that very often.'

'And this sunset has a bearing on the crime scene *how* exactly?'

The photographer mumbled something down at his camera.

'Right then, David Bailey,' said Harper. 'Arse in here. Now.'

She nodded towards the open bedroom door behind her, and the photographer slouched along the landing, head down as if he'd just been summoned to the headmaster's office.

'But I've already done in here,' he said as he passed.

'Really? Well, I'd like to watch this time.' She pointed to the corpse. 'Victim. Close-ups. Lots. And make sure you get some crystal clear shots of the symbols on his chest – what's left of them.'

She folded her arms and studied the symbols again while the photographer clicked away, her brow knotted in concentration as she struggled to decipher their meaning. Forensics would have to do a proper analysis, but as far as she could tell, the marks had been made with a blackish-red shade of lipstick. The two-inch high characters looked like a string of Roman numerals except that the first 'X' was about half the height of the others, and the penultimate character was a right-angled cross:

$$\underline{\text{III}}_x\text{XX}_+\text{X}$$

But what if the right-angled cross was meant to be a plus sign? If that was the case, then maybe the small "X" was actually a multiply sign. Three times twenty plus ten. Seventy. Okay, so why not just write "70" or even "LXX" if the murderer had some kind of thing about Roman numerals? And why did the whole thing have a diagonal line drawn through it?

$$\underline{\text{III}}_x\cancel{\text{XX}_+\text{X}}$$

Maybe whoever drew the symbols changed their minds and decided to cross them out afterwards, but then why not just wipe them off? After all, Scatterthwaite had managed to erase part of the final "X" with his paper napkin without even trying.

He was still squatting beside the body and was now licking the last vestiges of curry sauce from the Styrofoam takeaway carton. She contemplated asking him what he thought the symbols might mean, but instantly dismissed the idea as being a complete waste of breath. Besides, the photographer had just asked him to move away from the body so he could get some clearer shots, and she knew that simultaneous motor and mental activity were well beyond the sergeant's capabilities. He stood up, brushing some chip residue from his white forensics overalls onto the victim's chest, and was about to take a step back when there was a faint crunching sound. He lifted his plastic-clad foot to see what it was he had trodden on and then bent down to inspect the carpet immediately next to the corpse.

'Hello. What's this then?' he said, poking at something with his finger.

'Whatever it is, don't touch it,' said Harper and quickly moved to his side of the body so she could see for herself what evidence he'd destroyed. But by the time she got there, Scatterthwaite already had whatever it was in the palm of his hand.

'Yuk,' he said. 'What the hell's that doin' here?'

Harper peered over his shoulder to examine the object of his revulsion, her weight mainly distributed onto her back leg in case she needed to jump back in a hurry. And for once, she was forced to agree with him. What indeed was a now crushed and presumably once whole snail doing in the middle of an otherwise pristine bedroom carpet?

4

Everything was dark black behind his blindfold, and Horace's wrists and ankles were getting really rather sore from the constant chafing of the ropes which bound them together. Then there was the bruising matter of rolling this way and that across the plywood-lined floor of the van every time it took a bend at centrifugally inadvisable speeds – which was far too bloody often for Horace's liking. Rolling in the "that" direction was, however, marginally preferable to the "this" direction since the latter brought him to a bone-crunching halt against the hard steel wall of the van, whereas the former was somewhat cushioned by the considerably less rigid surface of Norwood, who was identically bound and blindfolded in a horizontal position.

'Ouch,' said Horace after a particularly jarring roll in the "this" direction.

'Be quiet,' snapped one of the two enormous figures who had been given orders by the enormous-figure-who-appeared-to-be-in-charge to "Whack 'em if they give you any trouble".

Quite apart from the physical pain, Horace was suffering badly in the psyche department as well. Not only because of the terrifyingness of the ordeal itself or even the unknowingness of what the outcome might be, but also because of his desperate need on such occasions of heightened anxiety to have a good old chomp on what little remained of his fingernails. Currently prevented from connecting teeth to fingernails himself, he wondered if he could somehow jiggle himself into a position where Norwood could do the job for him, but since he'd only ever chewed his own nails before, he couldn't be certain that he'd derive the same degree of satisfaction. Was it the act of chewing or the fingernails' sensation of being chewed which was most beneficial to alleviating feelings of anxiety? Perhaps he could try both. A kind of controlled experiment. If Norwood doing the chewing failed to do the trick, he could try chewing Norwood's fingernails instead. Then he wondered if it was possible to get themselves into such a position whereby both activities could be carried out simultaneously, and if so—

'And you can stop that wondering an' all,' said the second of the enormous figures, the voice much deeper than the first's.

'I need to pee,' said Norwood.

'Well, you'll just have to wait,' said the enormous figure with the higher voice.

'Till when?' said Norwood.

'Till we get where we're going.'

'And where's that exactly?'

'Never you mind.'

'Well, I do mind, as it happens, and I have to say that—'

'No you don't.'

'Don't what?'

'*Have* to say anything. And if you *do* say anything else, I'll have to whack you like the EFIC told us.'

'EFIC?'

'Enormous Figure In Charge.'

Norwood fell silent, and Horace tried desperately not to do any wondering at all, which was really rather difficult in the circumstances. So, instead of wondering, he tried *imagining* what it would be like to chew the claws of a two-toed sloth in the hope that imagining

36

wasn't a whackable offence like speaking and wondering obviously were.

But by a strange quirk of apparently arriving at their destination (signified by a slowing of the van, a marked reduction in rolling across its floor and then the sound of tyres on gravel for several minutes, followed by the squeal of brakes and then a complete stop), there was little time left for speaking, wondering, imagining or whacking of any kind.

'Right then,' said the lower voiced enormous figure. 'Let's be 'avin' you.'

'Letsby Avenue?' said Horace. 'Is that where we are?'

'No,' said Lower Voice.

Horace felt a hand on one of his ankles and then the sensation of someone cutting through the rope that bound it to the other one.

'That wouldn't be a Swiss Army knife you're using by any chance?' he said.

'What of it?' It was Higher Voice.

'How many handy little tools and gadgets has it got?'

'Fourteen.'

Horace exhaled a whistle through his teeth. 'Impressive,' he said. 'You both got the same?'

'Standard issue in this job.'

'What?' Norwood chipped in. 'Are you in the Swiss Army then?'

This was greeted with what sounded like the death throes of an ancient and overworked steam boiler in stereo, but which Horace surmised was the two enormous figures chuckling.

'Yeah, right,' said Lower Voice.

Horace was about to ask what organisation they did work for that was so generous with its multi-tool employee benefits and whether they got an additional handy little tool or gadget with every year of service when the back doors of the van were flung open and a blast of fresh, cold air smacked him in the face. The next moment, he was hauled to his recently unfettered feet and then passed bodily from one enormous pair of hands to another pair, which were approximately twenty-eight inches below the first. And the very next moment after that, he felt a sharp stabbing pain in the side of his neck that was rather like a wasp sting, but unlike a wasp sting, the pain lasted for less than half a second, so Horace didn't even have time to say "Ouch!".

With one enormous hand now gripping him by the elbow, he was marched across what felt like Grade 89 pea gravel and then up a flight of twelve stone steps. The clank of a heavy iron latch and the Dracula's-castle-type creaking of a large – possibly oak – door were followed by the slip-slap of his Airwair rubber soles on a tiled – or maybe even polished marble – floor.

The slip-slapping continued for a distance of what Horace estimated to be about thirty-one yards (with a slight deviation to the right at roughly the halfway stage) before the hand on his elbow brought him to an abrupt halt and then steered him through a ninety-degree right turn.

'Come in.'

The sound of the deep and somewhat muffled voice was immediately followed by the unmistakable "*knock knock*" of knuckles on adjacent door, the order of which two sounds Horace found to be a source of some perplexity. The slight creak (less Dracula's castle and more Frankenstein's en suite bathroom) of the knuckle-stricken door and then a bit more slip-slapping before a softer surface and then another hand-on-elbow enforced halt.

A lengthy pause was followed by an even longer one, its faint echo indicating to Horace that whatever room he was now standing in was pretty-damn-big-I-can-tell-you.

'Silence!' barked the deep but now unmuffled voice

which had said 'Come in' just now. 'And what the Jesus Jones have they got those things on for?'

'Er…?'

It wasn't much to go on, but Horace thought the erring on the side of him came from the higher voiced enormous figure.

'Those… wadjemacallits,' continued the "Come in" voice. 'You know. Over their eyes. Earwigs.'

'Earwigs, sir?'

'Blindfolds. I meant blindfolds, dammit. Take 'em off this instant before they suffocate.'

Horace, who believed himself highly adept at assessing a person's character and even appearance merely from the sound of their voice, quickly made the following assessment of the person who'd said "Come in":

- a bit of a grump-box;
- weak understanding of the human anatomy;
- male;
- aged between thirty-seven years four months and thirty-seven years and five months;
- creeping baldness discreetly covered by a jauntily angled beret (won from Pablo Picasso many years ago in a bet about the reproductive capacities of the nematode);

- one unblinking Cleethorpes-grey eye, its erstwhile neighbour now missing and the empty socket discreetly covered by a black-rimmed monocle which had been painted with a large red arrow pointing in the direction of the functioning eye and bearing the inscription: "THIS ONE, IDIOT!";
- massive black beard obscuring a once strong but now bedoubled chin with, at its centre, a cavernous dimple which he used to tell people he'd won off Kirk Douglas many years ago in a bet about—

But Horace had no time for further surmising. His blindfold having been removed, he blinked at the sudden ingress of light, which he had been entirely deprived of for the previous two hours and nineteen minutes. Blink by blink, his eyes gradually became accustomed to the sudden undarkness, and he briefly scanned his surroundings. If anything, the room was even larger than he'd estimated, being approximately 27.6 times bigger than the whole of his own apartment. The furniture was a lot more expensive too with Louis Quince this and Chippingdale that and Hepplegripe something else in every direction. Also unlike his own apartment, the ceiling was high-vaulted, multi-chandeliered and festooned with gold leaf and paintings of golden-haired, chubby kids with wings.

Next, his gaze travelled towards the occupant of a high-backed crimson armchair a little to one side of a vast inglenook fireplace, wherein roared a blaze of Guy Fawkes Night proportions. A hasty glance around the massiveness of the room assured Horace that this must be the person who'd said "Come in" since there was no-one else present apart from the two enormous figures in dark black ski masks and his co-adventurer Norwood (now also unblindfolded). He permitted himself a grin of self-satisfied smugness at having correctly deduced the voice owner's gender and the ocular deficit/monocle with the arrow, but the grin was almost instantly supplanted by a pout of disappointment when he realised that he'd been completely wrong about every other aspect of the man's physical characteristics. Clearly aged between sixty-nine years ten months and sixty-nine years eleven months, there was a full head of ginger toupee where Picasso's beret should have been and absurdly large muttonchop whiskers (of a similar but not identical ginger hue) instead of a black beard. Nor was there any sign of Kirk Douglas's dimple in the long and pointed, crone-like chin which—

'What in the name of all that's impertinent do you think you're staring at, you half-dried whelk dribbler?' snapped Monocle Face, rhythmically stroking an imaginary white cat on his lap.

'Er...' erred Horace, inwardly congratulating himself that at least he'd been right about the grump-box bit.

'I still need to pee,' said Norwood.

'We'll have tea when I say we'll have tea,' said Monocle Face, 'and not a moment before.'

'No, I said *pee*. You know. Spend a penny. Visit the little boys' room.'

The monocle slipped from Monocle Face's face as his features drifted into blank incomprehension, and he looked from one to the other of the enormous figures. 'What in Nietzsche's biscuit barrel is he blathering on about?'

The higher voiced enormous figure cleared his throat. 'Begging your pardon, sir, but I believe he needs to take Mr Squirrel on a picnic by the lake.'

'Well why the Millwall Supporters' Club didn't he say so in the first place? Show him to the place that dares not speak its name before he does a jubilee on the Persian.'

'Thank you,' said Norwood and then raised his still

41

bound wrists to chest height. 'But unless someone wishes to provide some "hands on" assistance, perhaps…'

Instead of finishing the sentence he gave a slight downward nod in the direction of his own hands and possibly even further south.

'Yes yes,' flustered Monocle Face. 'It is precisely for this kind of emergency that I provide all my employees with Swiss Army knives. Well get on with it, Enormous Figure One. What are you waiting for? And you may as well deal with the other one while you're at it.'

With a couple of swishes of keenly honed stainless steel, both Norwood and Horace's hands were free, and Norwood was escorted from the room.

Monocle Face fixed Horace with a stainless steely glare through his one good eye. 'And now perhaps you will explain the reason for your sudden and unbidden intrusion into my home.'

Horace opened his mouth to speak before the realisation struck him that he hadn't the slightest idea how to respond. Hadn't he and Norwood been on their way to an important appointment when they'd been kidnapped and brought here against their will by a bunch of enormous figures in dark black? And if this man with the absurdly large side-whiskers and the imaginary white cat hadn't ordered their abduction, then who had?

'I see,' said Monocle Face. 'The old name, rank and serial number ploy, eh? Well let's see if a few turns on the rack won't loosen your tongue, shall we? Take him away, Enormous Figure Two.'

Horace's still open mouth widened to the size of a small dinner plate, and his eyeballs popped to match. Overall, a more than passable impression of how Edvard Munch's model must have looked when posing for *The Scream*. Once again, he felt the firm grip of an enormous hand on his elbow, and in that moment he knew there was only one chance to save himself. He had to blurt, and he had to blurt fast.

And so it was that he blurted everything that had happened to him since he'd placed the advertisement seeking employment of an adventurous nature, and he completed the blurt by producing the important-looking letter which he had received in reply.

Several silent seconds followed, during which Horace's teeth sought out not one but four different fingernails, and Monocle Face continued to stroke the imaginary white cat on his lap.

'Let me see that,' he said at last, beckoning to Horace with the hand that wasn't stroking the imaginary white cat.

Horace stepped forward to give him the important-looking letter, and Monocle Face rested it on the back of the imaginary white cat while he wiped his monocle on his sleeve. Replacing the monocle in its eyeless socket and holding the letter first at arm's length and then almost touching the tip of his nose, he studied it minutely. Then, presumably disturbed by the to-ings and fro-ings of its master's non-stroking arm, the imaginary white cat bit him on the very real finger, and he swept it to the floor with a curse of unprintable dimensions.

Sucking his injured digit, he looked up at Horace and said, 'Jo bis dis doo, gibbet?'

'Pardon?' said Horace, unable to discern a single word due to the presence of the man's finger in his mouth. (The man's own mouth, that is, and not Horace's.)

Monocle Face tutted and rolled his one functioning eye before trying again without the oral-digital impediment. 'So this is you, is it? Mr Etc Etc?'

'Well, no. Actually my name's Horace Tweed.'

'Oh?' The monocle dropped out again. 'So you're not the person I sent this letter to then?'

'Yes, I am, but—' Horace interrupted himself as

43

realisation dawned. 'So you're "a wellwisher" then?'

'Of course.'

'So what's your real name?'

'A. Wellwisher. Alexander Wellwisher if you must know.'

'Oh, I see,' said Horace at precisely the same moment as Norwood re-entered the room with Enormous Figure One.

'And who's he?' said Wellwisher, brandishing the important-looking letter in Norwood's direction.

'That's Norwood,' said Horace. 'Norwood Junction.'

'Unusual name,' said Wellwisher.

'His real name's Mr Deeeyekaygeeayceeoheye,' said Horace.

'Well, I can certainly see the need for the alias,' said Wellwisher, flinching slightly as the imaginary white cat leapt back onto his lap. 'And while we're on the subject of introductions, this is Enormous Figure One and Enormous Figure Two.'

Norwood snorted a snorty kind of laugh. 'So I'm not the only one with an alias then, eh?'

Wellwisher's features frowned in puzzlement. 'Those are their real names,' he said and then added by way of apparently necessary explanation, 'They're twins. Or, more precisely, triplets if you count Enormous Figure Three, who is probably more familiar to you as Enormous Figure In Charge.'

Horace and Norwood ran their respective gazes up and down the two identically clad enormous figures from dark black boots to dark black ski masks and back again.

'They certainly look very alike,' said Horace, which reminded him of a very important question he needed to ask. 'But why did they kidnap us when we were coming to see you anyway?'

Wellwisher then explained that "a man in my position" had to be extremely careful not to let any old hoi polloi know his whereabouts and hence the need for all the kidnapping and blindfolding malarkey.

'So how come your address is clearly printed at the top of the letter then?' said Norwood.

'Is it?' said Wellwisher with seemingly genuine astonishment at this revelation, and he perused the important-looking letter once more, paying particular attention to the top bit. 'Well, slap my chops with a flat-footed gerbil, so it is. Better do something about that in future.'

There was another lengthy silence as he continued to stare at the important-looking letter, all the while stroking the imaginary white cat on his lap. Horace and Norwood exchanged glances, but it was unspokenly recognised that Norwood's glance was, on that occasion, worth fractionally more than Horace's, so Horace got to do the throat clearing thing to attract Wellwisher's attention.

'Ahem,' said Horace.

Wellwisher was shaken from his reverie. 'What's that?'

'Um,' Horace began, 'now that we've established who we all are — well sort of anyway — we were kind of wondering what exactly you had in mind vis-à-vis the gainful employment of an adventurous nature but without risk of personal physical harm.'

'Excellent point,' said Wellwisher, sitting bolt upright in his chair and slapping his palms down heavily on top of its arms. This caused his monocle to drop out again and the imaginary white cat to bite him on the same finger as before. This time, however, he didn't seem to notice the wound, and instead of uttering a curse of unprintable dimensions, he gave a barely perceptible and almost encouraging smile and said, 'Come on then. Why don't you tell me all about it?'

Horace attempted to stifle a sigh of such

diaphragmical origin that the resulting noise sounded more like a hearty belch. He chewed at what little remained of the index fingernail of his right hand. This was going to be a very *very* long day.

5

The room was getting hot. So hot in fact that even her eyeballs were beginning to sweat. Harper Collins got up from behind her desk and went to open a window. But it wasn't in its usual place. She checked the other three walls of her office. Not there either. What was more, the door seemed to have disappeared as well.

She took several deep breaths and tried not to panic. But the deep breaths started to turn into hyperventilation, and she began to feel giddy, so she sat back down again and placed her palms squarely on top of the desk. It began to vibrate. Slowly at first and then gathering momentum as if in the early stages of an earthquake. The tremors spread up through her arms to her shoulders and then down through her torso until her entire body was seized with convulsions.

She snatched her hands from the desktop and her shudders subsided, but the desk itself continued to vibrate with an even greater intensity. Any second now and all her neatly arranged files, her computer, her phone, her— Shit. Where the hell were they all? The desk was completely bare except for a single sheet of white paper marked with a curious arrangement of symbols in bright red ink:

$$\text{III} \times \text{XX} + \text{X}$$

She snatched up the paper to examine the symbols more closely, but as she did so, the characters slid down the page and merged into a single stream of wet ink which dripped onto her lap. No, not dripped. Oozed. She dabbed at it with her finger. Jesus Christ. Blood.

Hurling herself backwards, she overturned her chair as she stood and felt something crunch beneath her feet. She looked down. The floor was covered with a dense, pulsating carpet of blood-spattered snails. *Crunch. Crunch.* It was impossible to avoid them as she sought out the nearest windowless wall with her back and pressed herself against it. This too was trembling violently and appeared to be… moving. Slowly but relentlessly towards the centre of the room. Harper shot a glance at each of the other walls. All three were also on the move and gathering pace. The middle of the desktop began to rise, curved upwards by the encroaching walls, groaning and creaking as it threatened to split itself in two at any moment. Something was pressing down on the top of her head. She tried to look up, but the weight of the descending ceiling prevented her. The scream died somewhere deep in her throat.

The sound of a telephone ringing. But where the hell was the phone? Then a voice. A man's. Familiar but distant. The words incomprehensibly reverberating inside her skull. Screw that. If I can hear *him*, then maybe he can— But her cry for help glued itself to the roof of her mouth.

By now, she could almost touch the wall in front of her with her outstretched arm, and the ceiling had forced her into a crouching position amongst the snails, several of which had begun to slime their way up her legs. She thrashed at them with her hands, but others instantly took the place of any she managed to dislodge.

The man's voice again. Louder this time but the words still nonsense. Or was that her name being called? Concentrate. She had to concentrate. She tried to close her eyes, only to discover that they were already tight shut, so she opened them instead.

A face above her, inches from her own. Dim. Out of focus. A firm hand on each of her shoulders. Her arms and legs thrashing wildly. A phone ringing.

'Harper?'

The voice again. But closer. Much closer.

'You okay?'

Jonathan?

Feature by feature, the face above her began to take shape. Her husband's. Gingerly, as if in fear of doing herself physical harm, she used her no longer flailing limbs to ease herself into a sitting position against the headboard of the bed.

'You having a nightmare?' said Jonathan, easing a hank of sweat-sodden hair from in front of her eyes.

'Something like that,' she said and then registered that the phone had stopped ringing. 'Who was it calling?'

Her husband reached across her and took the cordless phone from her bedside table.

'Huh,' he grunted when he'd checked the caller ID. 'Only Scatterbrain.'

Harper grinned. 'Scatter-*thwaite*,' she corrected.

'You gonna call him back?'

'What time is it?'

'Bit after four.'

'Better had, I suppose. Must be pretty important for Mr Conscientious to call me at this time of night.'

Jonathan handed her the phone and kissed her on the cheek.

'I suppose you know you're absolutely wringing with sweat?' he said.

'Perspiration. Men sweat and women—'

'Yeah, yeah. Whatever.'

He switched on the lamp on his side of the bed, and Harper squinted at the sudden blaze of light.

'You want me to run you a bath or something?' he

said, swinging his feet down onto the floor.

'Cuppa would be good too.'

Jonathan let out a theatrically heavy sigh and padded across the bedroom carpet towards the open doorway. Harper hit the reply button on the phone and focused on the tautly rippling muscles of his buttocks as he went.

'Nice arse,' she called out, and he gave his bum an extra little wiggle before disappearing out onto the landing.

'Pardon?' said the voice on the other end of the phone.

'Er, no. Not you. I was talking to er… someone else?' The rising inflection in her voice made the statement sound more like a question.

'Pity.'

Harper felt the blood rush to her already flushed face and decided that irritation was the best form of defence.

'So what's so bloody important you have to call me at four in the morning?'

'Looks like we've got number two,' said Scatterthwaite.

'What?' She sat forward, launching herself away from the headboard, and ran a hand backwards through her soaking wet hair.

'Another murder. Same MO. Same everything by the sound of it.'

'Same markings on the chest?'

'So they say.'

'You're not there yet then?'

'Do me a favour. Bastards only just woke me up.'

Harper switched the phone to her other ear and threw back the duvet. 'So where is it?'

'What, the stiff? Couple of miles from your place as it happens.'

'Okay, pick me up on the way, yeah?'

She was halfway to the bedroom door and was about to hang up when a thought occurred to her.

'What about snails?' she said, but all she got back in return was the dial tone.

6

'Snails?' said Horace, almost choking on his tea.

'Ah yes,' said Alexander Wellwisher, beaming from ear to there. 'But not just any old snails. Goodness me, no. Not by a long slime trail.'

He laughed heartily at his own "joke" while Horace and Norwood smiled politely.

Wellwisher seemed to have only two settings – grumpy and hyper – between which he appeared to be able to switch at any given moment. Right now, he was about as hyper as a five-year-old kid who'd just scoffed an entire bucketful of bright blue food colouring.

'In fact,' he went on once he'd calmed down enough to speak again, 'the "*helix pertusa*", to give it its correct title, has one particularly remarkable property which sets it apart from every other pulmonate gastropod. – Or "had" I should say because the little blighter is believed to have become extinct round about the middle of the twelfth century.'

Norwood sat forward on the vast settee which he shared with Horace and set his cup and saucer down on the table in front of him. 'And what exactly is this particularly remarkable property?' he said.

'Yes indeed,' said Wellwisher. 'Sets him head and antennae above all the other gastropods if you get my drift.'

'I think what my friend here wants to know,' said Horace, smartly pre-empting another outburst of unbridled guffawing, 'is what's so special about the *helix…* er…?'

'*Pertusa.* Oh, didn't I say? It possesses the secret of eternal youth.'

Horace and Norwood looked at each other for a moment while they considered this revelation, and then Norwood said, 'So how come it became extinct?'

Horace nodded, believing this to be a not unreasonable question, but Wellwisher clearly thought otherwise and flipped back into grumpy mode again.

'Not for the *snail*, you idiot. For *people*,' he said and then added, 'Human *beings*' as if he assumed further explanation was necessary.

'Ah,' said Horace and Norwood in unison, giving the impression that this was a perfectly satisfactory answer. In truth, however, they both still thought it was a bit weird that this snail knew all about eternal youth but was apparently unable to prevent the demise of its own species.

'Of course,' said Wellwisher, 'you couldn't just go up to a *helix pertusa* and ask it to *tell* you the secret of eternal youth. Dear me, no. You had to make a special kind of soup using the Holey Snail as the main ingredient.'

'*Holy* snail?' said Norwood. 'You mean it's like a saint kind of thing?'

'Ho-*lee* Snail,' said Wellwisher, giving him the father of all patronising smiles. 'The common name for the *helix pertusa*. So called because it has hundreds of tiny holes all over its shell.'

'Ah,' said Horace and Norwood in unison again, both wondering what evolutionary purpose lay behind such a seemingly pointless development but neither of them daring to ask.

Wellwisher tipped a saucerful of tea from his cup into his saucer and slurped. Then he smacked his lips in apparent satisfaction, although he can have derived little real benefit since half the tea was absorbed into his absurdly large muttonchop whiskers through capillary action, and the other half splashed onto the back of the imaginary white cat on his lap through the force of gravity. Fortunately on this occasion, the cat didn't seem to notice.

'So what do you say?' said Wellwisher, stroking the imaginary white cat and then inspecting his palm in puzzlement as to how the imaginary white fur had become quite so wet all of a sudden.

'Er… thank you?' said Horace, having not the slightest idea how to interpret the question but recognising that some form of verbal response would be considered less impolite than a blank stare and a shrug.

'No, you donkey, I'm talking about the gainful employment of an adventurous nature. Are you up for it or not?'

There then followed a lengthy bout of glance exchanging between Horace and Norwood, which ended in a draw when both unspokenly agreed that neither of them had a clue what the "it" was they were supposed to be up for or not. However, concurrence was also reached on the likelihood that Wellwisher would instantly crank up the grumpy mode if they didn't exercise a certain degree of tact when seeking clarification.

'The thing is…' ventured Horace.

'…we're not exactly sure…' continued Norwood.

'…exactly what it is…' added Horace.

'…you want us to do,' concluded Norwood.

Or at least he thought he'd concluded until Horace appended another "...exactly" as if further emphasis of the word would forestall the expected outburst of extreme grumpiness.

But whether it was the additional "exactly" which did the trick or not, the anticipated tirade failed to materialise, and Wellwisher even apologised for not having made himself clear. He then went on to explain in some detail that the employment of an adventurous nature he had in mind for Horace and Norwood was that they should locate the precise whereabouts of *helix pertusa* – and whenabouts with regard to the period prior to its extinction – and bring back as many of the little blighters as they could manage.

'Consider it as a kind of quest,' he said.

'For the Holey Snail,' said Horace, thinking that the phrase sounded vaguely familiar, but he couldn't quite place where he'd heard it before.

'And if we undertake this quest, what would you propose to do with the snails?' asked Norwood.

'...Exactly?' added Horace, believing that the word had done a pretty good job so far, so why not stick with it.

Wellwisher's eye widened and so did the empty socket, which caused his monocle to drop out once more. 'Haven't you been listening? Look at me for goodness' sake. Is this a young man you see before you or an ageing, one-eyed crock with an irritatingly unpredictable bladder?'

He spread his arms wide as if to give them a better view, and then a thought seemed to occur to him, and he leaned forward in his armchair, replacing his monocle and narrowing his one functioning eye firstly at Norwood and secondly at Horace. 'You *are* in possession of a means of transport capable of travel through time, I take it?'

'Yes indeed,' said Horace with undisguised pride. 'As I said in my advertisement.'

Mentioning the advertisement reminded him that he'd also specified that the employment of an adventurous nature would not involve risk of personal physical harm, and he raised the point without further ado.

But just as Wellwisher opened his mouth to speak, the door to the massive and opulently furnished room burst open, and both Horace and Norwood were also left open-mouthed when they turned to see who had entered. Aged in her mid to late twenties and a touch above average in height, she was without doubt the most stunningly beautiful young woman that either of them had ever clapped gawping eyes on. Her long blonde hair fell in shimmering tresses over the perfect curves of her upper body, which was clad in an impossibly tight, pale yellow leotard with matching tights. She quickly crossed the floor towards where the three men were seated, the movement being far more of a glide than a walk.

'Sorry I'm late,' she said. 'I was trying a new yoga position that I hadn't done before, and it took me ages getting out of it again.'

Horace and Norwood immediately leapt to their feet, mouths still gaping like the twin openings to the Dartford Tunnel.

'Better late than dead,' said Wellwisher, who had remained seated and whose own mouth appeared to be carrying out its duties perfectly normally. 'Allow me to introduce my cousin, Vesta Swann.'

'Niece,' corrected the vision of gorgeousness, 'but at least you got my name right for a change.'

She smiled at Wellwisher with palpable affection and kissed him lightly on the top of his ginger toupee before turning to Horace and proffering a small but immaculately manicured hand in his direction. He wasn't sure whether he was supposed to shake it or kiss it and, in his confusion, managed to carry out a fumbling and rather bizarre combination of both.

'Nice nails,' he said for want of anything better to say and only speaking at all because he recognised the need to get his mouth moving again.

By contrast, Norwood was spared the consternation of having to decide between kissing or shaking since Vesta high fived him instead and then assumed an elegant, legs crossed position in the middle of the vast settee. Horace and Norwood sat down either side of her – with unnecessary proximity, given the space available – each of them only pretending to try and avoid thigh contact.

'This brings me to an important proviso of your employment,' said Wellwisher, 'which is that Vesta will be accompanying you on your quest, and I shall brook no demur on this issue.'

Although neither Horace nor Norwood had the slightest idea what a "demur" was and certainly wouldn't know how to brook one even if they fell over it in the street, it took them less than half a nanosecond to consider their response.

'Fine by us,' they chorused with a level of enthusiasm normally associated with young children who've just been asked if they'd like an extra helping of chocolate sauce on their ice cream.

'Excellent,' said Wellwisher, clapping his hands together.

Obviously disturbed by the sudden movement, and with painful inevitability, the imaginary white cat bit him on the finger – a different one this time – and he swept it onto the floor with a roar of leonine proportions. In fact, so loud was the roar that the faint, throat-clearing "Ahem" from the doorway of the room almost escaped unnoticed. Almost but not quite.

Horace couldn't tell whether it was Enormous Figure One or his twin brother who was politely trying to gain their attention, but whichever it was seemed to have shrunk slightly since their last encounter. The dark black clothing appeared to hang in unfamiliar folds and creases here and there, whereas previously it had been stretched almost to seam-bursting. Even the ski mask looked as if it had sagged a little, and he'd swapped his dark black boots for a pair of red and white baseball boots.

'Dinner is served,' said the somewhat less than enormous figure in a butlerish tone and with a servantly nod of his ski-masked head.

'Splendid,' said Wellwisher, springing to his feet in a surprisingly springy way for a man of his age. 'But I rather think we can dispense with the ski mask now, don't you, Enormous Figure One?'

'As Mr Wellwisher wishes,' said Enormous Figure One – for apparently it was he – and with slow deliberation, reached up and grasped the little red bobble on top of the mask. Then, in one swift movement, he snatched it from his head to reveal a leering grin and a deep scar which ran from just below his left ear to almost the middle of his chin, narrowly bypassing the corner of his mouth.

Wellwisher gasped and fell back into his armchair. 'Who the devil are you?' he said. 'And where is Enormous Figure One?' (for apparently it was not he after all).

The less than enormous figure merely chuckled in response and from somewhere behind his back produced a gun which was far bigger and scarier than any weapon Horace Tweed had ever seen in his life.

7

Early indications were that death had occurred between 7 a.m. and 11 a.m. the previous day, but the body hadn't been discovered until almost midnight when a couple of uniforms had finally got round to responding to a call from a concerned neighbour. The victim had lived on his own, and the neighbour had raised the alarm after he'd failed to turn up for the birthday dinner she'd prepared for him that evening and there'd been no answer when she'd rung his doorbell. There'd been a further delay in contacting Harper — or, more precisely, Scatterthwaite — before somebody at the station had eventually joined up the dots and realised that the murder bore some remarkable similarities to the one they were already working on.

Once they'd gathered all the information they could at the murder scene, Harper and Scatterthwaite had headed back to Nelson Street nick, grabbing a quick breakfast on the way. But the moment they'd walked in through the main entrance, the desk sergeant had informed them that another murder had just been reported and off they'd set again.

Everything about this third murder was almost identical to the first two. There was the same cruciform layout of the body on the floor. The complete absence of blood. The same markings on the chest:

Harper crouched down to take a closer look and brushed away some flakes of pastry from the Ginsters pasty that Scatterthwaite was currently munching on.

'Looks like we've got a serial killer on our hands,' he said, spraying more crumbs over the corpse.

Ignoring her sergeant's entirely superfluous remark, Harper wandered over to the log-effect electric fire and picked up one of a dozen birthday cards from the mantelpiece, taking great care to hold it by the tip of one corner even though she was wearing her standard issue latex gloves. The design on the front was a particularly tasteless cartoon involving Viagra and a Zimmer frame with the words "Happy 70th Birthday" emblazoned across the top. She put it back and scanned the others, most of which made some reference to a seventieth birthday.

'These his?' said Harper over her shoulder.

'Guessh sho,' said Scatterthwaite through a mouthful of pasty.

She turned to face him. 'You want to find out?'

The sergeant shrugged. 'If you like.'

'I do like,' said Harper. 'The wife's in the kitchen, isn't she?'

As if on cue, there was a grief-stricken shriek from the next room.

'Doesn't sound like the plods are doing much of a job consoling her,' said Scatterthwaite as he headed for the door.

When he'd gone, Harper resumed her squatting position beside the body and studied the symbols on the chest again. Okay, so she'd already worked out that it was probably a simple mathematical formula that added up to seventy, and the seventieth birthday cards were surely not just coincidence, but why hadn't the killer just written "70" or even "LXX"? And why the crossing out?

'Yep,' said Scatterthwaite as he came back into the

room. 'Seventy today, the missus says. Bang on the old three score years and ten, eh?'

Harper was so deep in thought and so used to ignoring his generally inane prattling that she almost missed the significance.

'Three score years and ten,' she repeated to herself, not realising that she'd spoken the words aloud.

'It's from the Bible,' said Scatterthwaite.

'Yes, I know where it's from,' said Harper and silently read the symbols again.

Three times twenty – three twenties – three score – plus ten. Three score years and ten. It certainly seemed to fit, and the Roman numerals gave a definite biblical slant to the formula.

'Do we know exactly how old Murdoch was?' she said.

'Murdoch who?' said Scatterthwaite, wiping the last of the pasty crumbs from his mouth with the back of his hand.

'The first victim? From yesterday?'

'Late sixties probably.'

'And the one this morning?'

'About the same, I'd say.'

Harper ran through both of the previous crime scenes in her mind's eye. There'd been birthday cards at both, but she couldn't remember if any of them mentioned a specific age.

'Well there's another little job for you then,' she said as she got to her feet. 'Find out their exact ages, and while you're at it, chase up what's happening with Murdoch's postmortem report. And don't let them fob you off with any nonsense about being too busy. I know for a fact they've hardly got anything on at the moment.'

'Ah,' said the sergeant. 'Only one problem with that.'

Harper waited for an explanation, which came in the form of a mobile phone he produced from his pocket.

61

'Battery's dead,' he said, giving the phone a shake as if some kind of visual clue might be necessary.

She held his gaze without speaking until he worked out the solution for himself.

'Tell you what,' he said eventually. 'I'll use the radio in the car.'

Harper mentally gave him a heavily sarcastic round of applause, and thankful to be shot of him for a few minutes, went back to her examination of the victim. There was something else she needed to check.

Down on her knees and one elbow with her cheek almost brushing the carpet, she ran her eyes along the left side of the body where it met the floor. Finding nothing, she repeated the operation on the other side and found what she was half expecting, close to the bottom of the ribcage. This time, the snail was still intact.

8

The less than enormous figure in the doorway gestured with his bigger than enormous gun that Horace, Norwood and Vesta should sit down, all of them having sprung to their feet the moment the intruder had revealed himself to *be* an intruder. Conversely, Wellwisher – who had been standing at the time – had slumped back down into his armchair. Norwood and Vesta instantly obeyed the unspoken instruction, but Horace – who appeared to have completely misinterpreted the gun waving gesture – took three steps to his right and stood on one leg, covering one eye with one hand and one ear with the other.

'God dammit,' said the less than enormous figure. 'What's the matter with you? Do you not understand simple gun gesturing?'

With his uncovered eye, Horace stole a peek at Norwood and Vesta and decided that sitting down seemed to be the less than enormous figure's preferred option, so he joined them on the vast settee.

'Thank you,' said the less than enormous figure, but not really *sounding* very grateful at all. What he did sound like was very American though.

'And what in the name of Billy Butlin's bumcrack do you mean by bursting in to my home without so much as a by your… by your…' Wellwisher struggled to find the right word.

'Leave?' Norwood offered tentatively.

'Hey, nobody leaves without I say so,' said the

American (for thus he transpired to be).

With that, he pulled up a straight backed and lavishly upholstered chair and straddled it in the wrong-way-round kind of way that American people are sometimes wont to do, especially in cowboy films. He propped the butt of the huge gun on his thigh so that the muzzle pointed up towards the ceiling, his finger still on the trigger as if to indicate to the assembled company that he was more than ready to blow their goddamn heads off if they so much as twitched an eyelid. For now, however, he simply sat there and beamed at each one of them in turn and then began the whole process all over again.

After the fourth round of silent beaming, Wellwisher's mounting grumpiness got the better of him.

'Are you just going to sit there all day beaming at us,' he said, 'or are you going to tell us what you're doing here?'

'Interesting question,' said the American, pensively fingering the deep scar which ran from just below his left ear to almost the middle of his chin, narrowly bypassing the corner of his mouth. 'And I guess we could all ask ourselves the same thing. What *are* we doing here? What is the point of existence? In fact, is there any point at all, and is it by chance or design that we—'

'No, no, no,' interrupted Wellwisher. 'I'm not talking about all that philosophical existentialist twaddle. I'm asking you what you are doing *here*. In my house. You.'

'Huh,' said the American with a snort of disdain. 'And they say us Yanks are shallow.'

Wellwisher opened his mouth to speak again, but the American waved him to silence.

'Okay, grandpa, keep your wig on and I'll tell ya,' he said. 'The reason I'm here is because my employer understands you have something he wants.'

'Oh?' said Wellwisher. 'And what might that be exactly?'

Horace noted that the use of the word "exactly" seemed to be catching on and allowed himself a faint inward glow of self-congratulation for its earlier and repeated introduction until he remembered the potential danger of their current situation, and the glow turned into a fear-induced bout of rampant indigestion.

'In a word,' said the American. 'Snails.'

Wellwisher told him he'd no idea what he was talking about and continued to deny all mollusc related knowledge even when the American read out the scientific name (*helix pertusa*) from a small scrap of paper he'd previously secreted about his person as an aide memoire. The American then got quite grumpy himself and accused his reluctant host of "shitting him". This in turn provoked Wellwisher to up the grumpy stakes by several notches and flip into a hitherto unwitnessed really bloody angry mode (even though he wasn't at all sure what was involved in shitting someone). But when the American jumped up from his back-to-front sitting position, walked round behind the settee and pointed the incredibly long barrel of his gun at the back of Vesta's head, Wellwisher felt obliged to furnish him with the requested information – such as it was.

'And since I don't have any *helix pertusa*,' he concluded, 'I can't give you any *helix* bloody *pertusa*, now can I?'

The American didn't seem particularly surprised by this revelation nor even entirely disappointed. 'But you're looking for them, aren't you?' he said.

Wellwisher folded his arms across his chest and grumped by way of response.

'Swell,' said the American. 'So I'll just have to take this purty little granddaughter of yours away with me until you *do* have them.'

'Cousin,' corrected Wellwisher.

'Niece,' Vesta corrected further.

Horace, who had been contemplating doing something brave ever since the intruder's arrival, had so far failed to formulate a plan of action that was anything less than dangerously foolhardy or very probably downright suicidal. But this latest development was too much to bear. This scarfaced desperado in the red and white baseball boots was about to abduct the vision of gorgeousness who sat beside him on the settee. And who knew what terrible suffering she might be forced to endure at the hands of such a monster during her captivity? No, the time had come to act and act decisively. A derring-do deed of selfless courage without a moment's thought for his own safety or even survival. It was now or never.

He stole a sideways glance at the American's gun, which appeared to have grown in size since the last time he'd looked at it. Now or never... All of a sudden, the "never" option was beginning to hold a far greater appeal than its "now" alternative.

Horace extended his sideways glance beyond the gun and as far as Norwood to see if he might also be considering an almost certainly suicidal act of selfless courage, but if the rabbit-in-the-headlights trance was anything to go by, it was highly unlikely.

Then something happened which astonished Horace to the core of his astonishment circuits. As if from nowhere, he heard a cracked and faltering voice saying, 'Take me instead.'

His eyes shot around the room to see who it was that had spoken.

'Pardon me?' said the American.

'What, are you deaf as well as stupid? I said take me instead.'

There it was again. The disembodied voice. A little more confident this time. And somehow strangely familiar.

Horace's gaze ranged around the room once more until the realisation struck him like a huge speeding bullet from a ridiculously enormous gun. Everyone was staring at *him*.

Oh hell, he thought. Surely it can't have been me who just said—

'Take you instead?' said the American, and there was no doubt whatsoever who he was addressing.

Horace gave the slightest of shrugs and cleared his throat. 'Er, yes, I suppose so.'

The American studied him for several moments and then laughed like a hyena in urgent need of exorcism.

'Dude,' he said when he was finally able to subdue his laughter. 'I gotta hand it to you Limeys. When it comes to worn out, tired old clichés, you guys sure do take the biscuit.'

Horace was about to point out that "take the biscuit" was a tad on the cliché side itself when he felt a firm but gentle hand squeeze his upper thigh. He almost recoiled in horror until he remembered that he was sitting next to Vesta and not Norwood, and he looked down to confirm that the thigh-squeezing hand did indeed belong to the vision of gorgeousness herself.

'Thank you,' he heard her say in a soft, low voice, and his eyes travelled upwards to meet her iris blue irises. They were smiling, and perhaps there was even the faintest hint of... No, probably not.

'Yeah, all very touching I'm sure,' said the American. 'Come on, sweetpea. Time you and me were on our way.'

Nobody's ever called me "sweetpea" before, thought Horace, but realised the American was actually talking to Vesta when he gave her a prod between the shoulder blades with the barrel of the gun. She uncrossed her legs and rose slowly to her feet while Wellwisher spluttered some protestations and threw in a threat or two, Norwood continued to maintain his rabbit-in-the-headlights trance, and Horace chewed at his severely depleted fingernails. The American edged towards the door, and Vesta followed but then came to an abrupt halt after only half a dozen paces.

'Wait,' she said. 'I'm not going anywhere till I've changed out of my yoga togs.'

The American laughed, although a little less demonically hyenic this time. 'No time for that now, sweetcheeks. Besides, you look purty fine to me just as you are.'

Horace thought there was more than a hint of lasciviousness in his tone and strongly disapproved. Silently but strongly.

'Well I'll need to pack a bag then,' said Vesta. 'How long do you expect we'll be gone for?'

'Depends entirely on your grandpa there,' said the American.

'Cousin,' said Wellwisher.

'Niece,' said Vesta and then corrected herself. 'Uncle, I mean.'

The American's features suddenly switched from leering grin to really rather cross. 'Okay, that's it,' he said. 'I've had about as much as I ca— ca— ca—'

He let out a Richter scale sneeze that rattled the windows and nearly blew out the fire in the inglenook fireplace.

'Jesus,' he said, wiping his nose with the back of his hand. 'You got cats in here?'

A few seconds earlier, Horace had in fact spotted the imaginary white cat twining itself in and out of the American's ankles, an activity which it appeared to find eminently satisfying.

'What of it?' snapped Wellwisher.

'Cos I'm— cos I'm— cos I'm… aller—tchooo!'

If anything, this second sneeze was even more explosive than the first.

'Allertchoo?' said Wellwisher. 'What in the name of all that's polyester and cotton is the man blithering about?'

'I think he means allergic,' said Norwood, the initial sneeze having evidently shaken him from his trance.

'Aa— aa— aa—tchoo!'

This time, there was an entire series of nasal explosions which were so severe that the American was bent double, and he inadvertently pulled the trigger of the enormous gun. The bullet utterly obliterated a priceless, life-size statue of Isambard Kingdom Brunel and embedded itself in the wall behind, a mere seven-sixteenths of an inch from an original oil painting of *The Flying Scotsman*. Wellwisher, Horace and Norwood all clapped their hands to their ears to protect their auditory faculties from decibel poisoning as the brain-rattling din of the gunshot reverberated around the vastness of the room. Vesta, however, instantly seized the opportunity to take the three strides between her and the American and smashed the edge of her hand down onto the back of his exposed neck, karate style.

Another involuntary gunshot left a gaping hole in the ceiling where the cherubic face and winged torso of one of the flying chubby kids used to be, and the American crumpled to the floor. Vesta grabbed the still smoking gun and pressed the muzzle into the small of his back while Wellwisher, Horace and Norwood slowly uncovered their ears, each wearing a similar expression of stunned admiration.

'Impressive,' said Norwood.

'Very,' said Horace.

'Is he dead?' said Wellwisher.

'No,' said Vesta. 'Out cold though by the look of him.'

Horace stood up and approached with considerable caution. 'So what do we do now?'

'Tempting to have the blighter flayed alive and then boiled in his own juices,' said Wellwisher, 'but I suspect that might be construed as unlawful. Have a shufty through his pockets and see if you can find out who he is and who he works for.'

Vesta backed off with the gun just far enough to give Horace and Norwood room to roll the American onto his back and search through his pockets. Finding nothing of any interest, the realisation dawned that he was wearing Enormous Figure One's clothes and not his own, and a brief foray out into the hallway resulted in the discovery of a pile of dark black clothes including a broad-brimmed, dark black hat and a long, dark black coat. Next to this, they found the bound and gagged figures of Enormous Figure One and Enormous Figure Two, who they released with the aid of Norwood's Swiss Army knife.

Back inside the room, Horace handed Wellwisher a batch of business cards he'd retrieved from an inside pocket of the dark black coat. Each one was exactly the same and looked like this:

WORSTHORNE PHARMACEUTICALS INC.

Kenny Bunkport
Public Relations Executive

Tel: 020 7946 0500
Email: bunkport@worsthorne.com

'Interesting take on public relations,' said Horace.

Wellwisher brandished the business cards at nobody in particular. 'And what in the name of Marcel Proust's pet donkey is Worsthorne Pharmaceuticals?'

'Inc,' added Norwood helpfully, but Wellwisher

ignored him.

There was a strange moaning sound from the head end of the prone American, and he began to stir.

'I think our Mr Bunkport's coming round,' said Vesta.

A brief discussion then followed, and Wellwisher was all for keeping him captive and interrogating him with menaces, but he eventually accepted that Bunkport wasn't the sort who was likely to tell them any more than they knew already, however much they tortured him. Besides, as Wellwisher himself pointed out, Mrs Gaviscon, the cook, would be seriously miffed if she was told at such short notice that there'd be an extra mouth to feed at dinner. And so it was decided that Enormous Figure One and Enormous Figure Two should tie the man up and then drive him to some barren wasteland in the middle of nowhere and dump him.

While Stage One of this plan was being conducted (the tying up bit), Wellwisher announced that the mention of dinner had reminded him he was "ravenous enough to eat the face off a hind leg". He therefore instructed Enormous Figure Two to temporarily postpone implementing Stage Two of the plan (the driving to some barren wasteland in the middle of nowhere bit) and to make all speed to the kitchen to ascertain "how much longer that vicious old harridan of a so-called cook intends to keep us waiting".

'I just hope there's nothing involving snails on the menu,' Horace whispered to Norwood.

'Quite,' said Norwood, *sotto voce*. 'Especially as I'm allergic to shellfish, and I imagine that snails might have a very similar effect.'

'You two stop your damn whispering and start making plans,' said Wellwisher. 'You've got a quest to fulfil, and you'll be setting off the minute you've had your after dinner mints.'

'Ah yes,' said Horace. 'The quest for the Holey Snail.'

His attempt to inject enthusiasm into the words was singularly unconvincing, but truth be told, he could think of several other things to quest after that would be far more exciting than some multi-perforated mollusc. But then again, Horace was not blessed with the gift of clairvoyance and so had no way of knowing quite what lay in store for him and his co-adventurers. If he had, he would almost certainly have settled for something a lot less likely to cause personal physical harm than questing after the Holey Snail.

9

The stink of ammonia was almost unbearable, but even that was preferable to having to listen to Scatterthwaite's inane witterings. The end cubicle of the Nelson Street police station's toilets was like her second office, and DCI Harper Collins spent almost as much time in there as in her real office. So much time in fact that most of her colleagues assumed she had some kind of unspeakable bowel disorder. But everyone needed a quiet place where they could do some serious thinking, and this was hers. And at that particular moment, she had plenty of thinking to do.

Sitting fully dressed on the closed plastic lid of the toilet, she took a sip of vending machine coffee and opened the buff-coloured folder on her lap. The postmortem report on the first murder victim had finally arrived, and she read it through word by word for the third time that morning to make sure she hadn't missed anything.

Stanley James Murdoch had died from potassium chloride poisoning, and the presence of a tiny puncture wound on his arm had led the pathologist to deduce that the poison had been injected directly into the bloodstream. The snail which was found wedged in the victim's windpipe had not — as initially believed — caused death by asphyxiation since it was later discovered to have been inserted post mortem. Toxicology tests also revealed that the victim had inhaled a small amount of a fentanyl-derived gas prior to death which was of a sufficient quantity to induce a state of unconsciousness for anything up to thirty minutes.

Harper leaned back against the low level cistern, the back of her head resting against the wall above it, her eyes closed.

What was it with these bloody snails? One next to the body and another rammed down the throat. She'd have to wait for the postmortem reports on the second two victims to find out if they also had snails wedged in their windpipes, but there had certainly been a snail next to each body in much the same position as the one Scatterthwaite had stomped on at the first murder scene. There could be little doubt that all three murders were the work of the same person, so she could only assume the snails were intended as some kind of calling card. But what the hell was their significance? Serial killers who left calling cards usually did it to taunt the police — to let them know that the same person was committing the murders and how clever they were for not being caught. But generally there was some kind of link between the calling card and the killer's motive.

Okay, so what do I know about snails? she thought. They're slow, they carry their homes with them, and they leave a trail of slime. Harper had to admit that this was about the extent of her knowledge and really didn't get her very far. Maybe she'd mug up about them on the Internet later, but in the meantime, she'd focus on how the murders were actually carried out.

The postmortem report said that the first victim had died from a lethal injection of potassium chloride. So how did the killer get close enough to administer it? All the evidence suggested that the murder took place inside the victim's home, but there was no sign of a struggle or forced entry. Did Murdoch let his killer in? If so, perhaps he knew him — or her — personally. But then there was the gas he'd inhaled. The murderer could have blasted him with it as soon as he opened the door and knocked him out cold on the spot. Then it would be a simple case of injecting the poison, shoving the snail down his throat and arranging the body in the shape of a crucifix.

Harper took a sip of her coffee. The case was certainly intriguing, but so far she had very little to go on other than her educated guess that the symbols on the dead men's chests had something to do with the biblical reference to "three score years and ten". The house-to-house enquiries she'd ordered in the vicinities of all three of the victims' houses had drawn a complete blank. Nobody had seen anything out of the ordinary apart from one batty old woman who said she'd seen someone wearing a monk's habit and Union Jack flip-flops entering Murdoch's house at about the time of the murder. It had seemed like a promising lead at the time until a background check on the witness revealed that she regularly complained to the police about a variety of matters, including Arnold Schwarzenegger stealing underwear from her clothesline and little green men from outer space setting up home in her dustbin.

The wife of the third victim hadn't been much help either. She'd still been too much in shock to offer them anything that might have proved useful to their investigation, and any answers she *had* given were almost entirely unintelligible through the constant sobbing. But maybe she'd calmed down a bit by now, and if so, it was definitely worth another try. After all, it wasn't as if there were a whole bunch of other leads to be followed up, except of course for some extensive snail research on Wiki.

Harper drained the rest of her tepid coffee and tossed the plastic cup into the bin beside the toilet. She got to her feet and unbolted the cubicle door, wondering as she did so if there was any way she could sneak out of the station without Scatterthwaite noticing.

'Anything at all you can remember could be vital for us to find your husband's killer,' said Harper, leaning forward in her chair and resting her forearms on the edge of the kitchen table.

'Well, it was all a bit of a blur really,' said the recently widowed Mrs Daphne Wadd, 'on account of me being unconscious on the floor for most of the time.'

'Perhaps you could begin with that then,' said Harper. 'How you came to be unconscious in the first place.'

Mrs Wadd chewed at her lower lip and ran a liver-spotted hand over her neatly set, blue-rinsed hair but without actually making contact with it. 'Now, let me see…'

Harper resisted the urge to drum her fingers on the table while she waited for an answer, but DS Scatterthwaite's patience was on a hair trigger.

'Come on, woman,' he said. 'It was only yesterday, for God's sake.'

Harper shot him a glare as he reached for another Garibaldi biscuit from the plate in the centre of the table. His inappropriate use of the good-cop-bad-cop routine was just one of many reasons why she'd tried to give him the slip when she'd crept out of the police station earlier, but he'd spotted her from the canteen window and was on her before she'd even got to her car.

'Birthday card,' said Mrs Wadd, who seemed not to have noticed Scatterthwaite's outburst. 'That was it. It was when he opened the birthday card.'

'What was?' said Scatterthwaite.

'It was his seventieth birthday, you know,' Mrs Wadd went on, 'and he'd had quite a few cards considering quite a few of our older friends are dead now and Janet — that's our youngest daughter, you know — well, she hardly ever remembers — not even at Christmas — but

76

then she's in Australia now and since Shane left her with the four kids to bring up on her own, not to mention a four-hundred-acre sheep farm to run single-handedly, well it's not really surprising when you come to think about it...'

While Mrs Wadd continued to chunter on, Harper found herself involuntarily drumming her fingers on the edge of the kitchen table after all and decided that a gentle interruption would be preferable to Scatterthwaite launching in again.

'So was there something special about this birthday card?' she said.

Mrs Wadd instantly abandoned her detailed explanation of why their *eldest* daughter probably hadn't sent a card because she was still suffering from complications that had arisen due to a recent operation on an ingrowing toenail and stared blankly back at Harper for several seconds before the penny dropped.

'Oh, I'm sorry, dear,' she said. 'Barney always used to say — Barney was my husband, you know — he always used to say I could talk the hind legs of a... a... Oh, what was it now?'

'The birthday card?' Harper prompted.

'No, no, that wasn't it. It was some kind of—' She broke off with a self-conscious chuckle. 'Oh, I see what you mean. Yes, well, one reason it was unusual was that it was delivered by hand. We knew that because there was no stamp on the envelope, you see?'

'No shit, Sherlock,' Scatterthwaite muttered through a half-chewed chocolate digestive and yelped when Harper kicked him under the table.

'And the picture on the front was a bit odd too,' Mrs Wadd continued.

'Oh?' said Harper. 'In what way?'

'Well, it was a great big snail and it had this great big cross sticking out of its shell — like a crucifix, you

77

know? Like it had been stabbed with it, sort of thing. And in big red letters, it said "HAPPY 70TH BIRTHDAY" coming out of the snail's mouth like in one of those speech bubble things. But the "70TH" bit had been crossed out and somebody had written "LAST" instead. "HAPPY LAST BIRTHDAY". All rather horrid really.'

Mrs Wadd bowed her head and sniffed back a tear.

Harper reached out and placed a hand on her arm. 'You okay to carry on?'

'Yes, I'll be fine, thank you, dear,' she said, tearing a sheet off the roll of kitchen towel in front of her and dabbing at her eyes. 'But I dare say another cup of tea wouldn't go amiss.'

'I wouldn't say no,' said Scatterthwaite, thrusting his empty cup and saucer towards her. 'Few more biscuits would be good too.'

Mrs Wadd took his cup and saucer and the empty biscuit plate and began to fill a kettle at the kitchen sink.

'So was anything written inside the card when you opened it?' Harper asked.

'Well, that's the thing of it, you see. I haven't the slightest idea.'

'Oh?'

'No, because I was looking over Barney's shoulder when he opened it and all of a sudden, "*pifff!*".'

'Pifff?'

'That's what it sounded like, yes. And then there was this little cloud came out like steam and a rather odd smell — sort of like gone-off Stilton with a hint of japonica blossom after the rain. But that's all I can remember till I woke up on the floor here and went into the lounge to find Barney...'

Her already quavering voice tailed off completely, and she tore off another sheet of kitchen roll.

Harper stood and put an arm round Mrs Wadd's

heaving shoulders. 'I'm sorry to put you through all this, Mrs Wadd, but I hope you understand how important it is for us to find out everything you know about your husband's— Could I have a look at the birthday card?'

Mrs Wadd blew her nose and shook her head at the same time. 'I'm sorry, dear, but it doesn't seem to be here any more.'

She dropped a teabag into the china teapot, and Scatterthwaite twisted round in his chair. 'Pop a couple in this time, will you, love? Last one was a bit on the weak side.'

Another withering glare from Harper. 'I hope you're taking notes of all this.'

'How to make a cuppa tea?'

'Mrs Wadd's evidence.'

'All up here, boss,' said Scatterthwaite, tapping the side of his head with his index finger.

Harper was highly doubtful that he'd even been *listening* to what had been said, never mind actually remembering it, but she knew she'd be wasting her breath to tell him so.

'There was one other thing, now I come to think of it,' said Mrs Wadd as she took a new packet of chocolate digestives from the cupboard above the sink.

Harper spun round to face her. 'Oh yes?'

'Of course, I could have imagined it, being a bit hazy when I came round, you know, but just for a moment, out of the corner of my eye, I thought I saw...' She shook her head and chuckled softly to herself. 'No, it's silly really. I must have been... whatchamacallit... illucinating, being as I was only just waking up, sort of thing.'

'But what was it you *thought* you saw?' said Harper.

'Well, promise not to laugh, but it looked a lot like the chap from that programme on the telly about monks and there's all these murders and stuff. At least one a week usually. Murders, I mean. Not programmes. They're only on once a week. Anyway, there's this one monk who solves them all and... Ooh, what's it called? Barney used to watch it regular as clockwork. He always said the main monk — the one who solved all the— Cadbury. That was it. Brother Cadbury. — No, wait a minute, I'm getting my wires crossed. Brother Cadfael. I remember now. Anyway, and like I say, I might have imagined it, but I just caught the tail end of him going out the back door there.'

'Oh right,' Scatterthwaite snorted. 'So all we need do is put out an arrest warrant for Derek bleedin' Jacobi, do we?'

Harper, who very rarely watched television, had no idea what they were talking about. 'Let me get this straight,' she said. 'Are you telling me you saw somebody dressed as a monk leaving the house when you came to?'

'With one of those big pointy hood things, yes. Oh, and a pair of flip-flops on his feet.'

'Flip-flops?' Harper could scarcely believe what she was hearing. 'I don't suppose you happened to notice whether they had some kind of pattern on them, did you? Like a Union Jack, I mean.'

Mrs Wadd thought for a moment before answering. 'Now you come to mention it, I did see a bit of red and blue — and some white too, I think. I bought some for Barney once when we were on holiday in Llandudno. Not Union Jacks of course. Flip-flops. But he refused to wear them. Said they made his toes itch.'

Harper wandered over to the open door on the far side of the kitchen, which led out onto the back garden. 'And you saw him leave by this door, you say?'

Mrs Wadd nodded and placed a full plate of biscuits down onto the middle of the table.

'Tell me, Mrs Wadd,' Harper went on. 'Do you

always leave the door open like this?'

'Oh yes, dear. Barney always said we needed the fresh air, what with his asthma and whatnot. Course, we always locked it when we went to bed. Not that we really needed to. Hardly ever any crime round here, you know.'

There was the briefest of pauses before Mrs Wadd reached for the kitchen roll once again.

For his part, Scatterthwaite reached for the plate of biscuits and said, 'What? Run out of Garibaldis now, have we?'

10

The room was shaped like the inside of a railway carriage, except only about half the length. The walls and curved ceiling were of random stone, giving it the appearance of a medieval dungeon, but it was much warmer and drier than one of those awful places. There were no windows (which would have been fairly pointless anyway, considering that the room was several feet below ground level), and the only source of illumination was half a dozen flaming torches fixed at regular intervals along each of the long walls.

A huge and rather ancient-looking mahogany table filled the entire room with scarcely enough space between its perimeter and the stone walls for the twenty-seven high-backed wooden chairs which surrounded it. So large was the table in relation to the size of the room that the only access was via a heavy oak door at one end which slid back and forth on metal runners. The door had originally opened inwards but had had to be adapted after the table had been built in situ and it was discovered that the gap between door and table was so small that nobody could get either in or out. This had resulted in the tragic demise of two carpenters and a French polisher, who died from starvation before someone figured out that a *sliding* door was the only possible solution to the problem. For some unknown reason, the alternative method of changing the hinges so that the door opened outwards had not been considered.

It was through this very door and at that very moment

that a stooping figure in an off-grey, almost floor-length hooded robe entered the room and said, 'Sorry I'm late, everyone, but the thong thing on my Union Jack flip-flops broke — that bit that goes between your big toe and the one next to it — and it took me forever to fix the damn thing.'

The "everyone" to whom the hooded figure had apologised consisted of eleven other identically hooded figures seated along the long sides of the mahogany table. A twelfth hooded figure sat at the far end of the table opposite the sliding oak door. His chair was somewhat bigger than all the others and had arms as well, and he said, 'Yes, yes, Brother Herring. Just get to your place as quickly as possible, will you? We have much business to discuss.'

There then followed a good three or four minutes of commotion as three of the hooded figures had to climb onto the table to make room for Brother Herring to pass them and take up his designated seat. Once he'd accomplished this, the others clambered back down onto their chairs amid much muttering and cursing due to the inherent difficulty of climbing on and off tables whilst wearing almost floor-length hooded robes.

By far the most upset of the assembled company, however, was the little marmoset monkey whose job it was to wheel a small, three-tiered trolley up and down the top of the table with its cargo of drinks, snacks and other delicacies for the as-required refreshment of those present. Dressed in his own scaled-down version of a floor-length hooded robe, he was jumping up and down, clapping the sides of his head with the palms of his tiny hands and producing a constant series of shrieks which reverberated ear-splittingly around the narrow confines of the room. This, as any primatologist would have recognised immediately, was an unambiguous demonstration of his distress at having the rhythm of his trolley-wheeling disrupted by the sudden ascendance of three hooded figures onto his tabletop.

'Brother Simeon!' yelled Chairbrother Lemonsole (the hooded figure in the big chair at the end of the table). 'Enough now!'

Brother Simeon (for such the monkey was known since the strict laws of the Society forbade any non-human member from assuming the name of any kind of fish whatsoever) completely ignored the command and continued jumping, slapping and shrieking until the hooded figure who was closest to him — a Brother Turbot — seized a banana from the bottom shelf of the trolley, peeled it and thrust it into the little marmoset's hand. Instantly, Brother Simeon began chomping contentedly on the banana, and peace was at last restored.

'Thank you,' said Chairbrother Lemonsole. 'And now perhaps we can get on?'

Each of the hooded figures around the table seemed to nod their agreement, although it was difficult to tell exactly because their heads were almost entirely concealed within the cavernous depths of their hoods.

'Good,' said Chairbrother Lemonsole, consulting the agenda on the table in front of him. 'Item One. Any Other Business.'

'Point of order, Brother Chairbrother.'

Lemonsole glowered at the hooded figure halfway down the left side of the table whose hand was thrust so perpendicularly into the air that the voluminous sleeve of his robe had fallen back almost to his armpit, revealing a thin white arm not unlike a prizewinning stick of celery.

'Yes?' said Lemonsole in a very tired voice. 'You wish to say something, Brother Anchovy?'

'Isn't it a bit... unorthodox to *start* a meeting with "Any Other Business"?' said Anchovy. 'I mean, if we haven't had any business, how do we know what's *other* business?'

There was some general muttering of the "hear hear" variety, and even Brother Simeon clapped his tiny marmoset hands.

'In my experience as chairbrother,' Lemonsole explained, '"Any Other Business" is always the item on the agenda that takes the longest to get through, and we usually run out of time before we get to the end of it, so it makes perfect sense to start with that and get it out of the way first.'

Apart from the perpetual "*squeak squeak*" from the unoiled wheels of Brother Simeon's trolley, there was complete silence for several seconds while the assembled brethren considered the wisdom or otherwise of their chairbrother's pronouncement. This was followed by another round of hear-hearing and a ripple of muffled applause — muffled because most of the brethren had their hands buried inside the opposite sleeves of their robes, which made it very difficult to applaud convincingly.

'Good,' said Chairbrother Lemonsole and once again checked the agenda in front of him. 'And the first item under "Any Other Business" is a status report from Brother Pilchard on what progress has been made in our mission to foil a certain Mr Wellwisher's quest for the Holey Snail.'

He sat back in his big chair, and Brother Pilchard stood up from his smaller one, ostentatiously clearing his throat before beginning to deliver his report. *'Salve, Fratres. Ut institutum est, i secuti quidam generosum—'*

He broke off abruptly at the sudden barrage of boos, jeers and such shouts as "Speak English!", "Damn showoff!" and "Bloody classicist!", and order was only restored when Lemonsole banged his chairbrother's gavel so hard on the table that Brother Simeon's trolley was momentarily airborne to a height of almost two inches.

'Brother Pilchard,' said the chairbrother. 'Whilst your knowledge of Latin and other ancient languages is to be commended, there are many here who lack your sophisticated education — myself excluded of course — and I would therefore urge you to continue your report in the common tongue of English.'

There was a deep grumping sound from within the dark recesses of Brother Pilchard's cowl, and he cleared his throat for a second time. 'Brother Chairbrother. My dear brethren. Thou hast charged me with thy most earnest task that I should sally forth from this hallowed hall with intent most pressing to seek out—'

'Modern English, I think, Brother Pilchard,' said Lemonsole, stifling the rising tide of groaning and muttering from the assembled company.

Brother Pilchard grudgingly obliged and gave a lengthy and often tedious account of how he had learned of Mr Wellwisher's quest to find the Holey Snail and how Wellwisher had replied to an advertisement placed by a Mr Horace Tweed, who happened to be seeking gainful employment of an adventurous nature. Pilchard had then followed Tweed and his companion — a Mr Norwood Junction — to the imposing residence of the aforementioned Mr Wellwisher where, immediately prior to their entry into the house, he had fired his blowpipe at Tweed and thereby managed to implant a microscopic tracking device in the subject's neck.'

'Tracking device?' queried Lemonsole.

'Yes indeed, Chairbrother,' Pilchard replied chirpily. 'Not only does it tell us the exact whereabouts of the subject at any given moment, it also tells us his whenabouts.'

'His whenabouts?'

'It is my understanding that — concomitant to the specific needs of the aforementioned quest for the Holey Snail — it will be incumbent upon Mr Tweed to travel not only through space — in the strictly geographical and earthbound sense of the word — but also through time as well.'

'So you mean you can still follow the chap however far he travels through time?' said Brother Mackerel, whose voice was at least an octave higher in pitch than all of the brethren that had spoken so far and made him sound like a woman, which, as chance would have it, she was.

'Precisely,' said Brother Pilchard, a complacently triumphant grin lurking somewhere within the dark depths of his hood.

'And do we possess the physical means whereby to travel through time ourselves?' asked Brother Whitebait.

'Indeed we do. *Hawking 3* is having its three thousand year service as we speak.'

Brother Pilchard concluded his report with several extraneous and unnecessary details, and when he sat down, a spontaneous round of applause rippled through the room, although it was just as muffled as the round of applause earlier.

Chairbrother Lemonsole then opened the floor for any other "Any Other Businesses", but there were so many of them and the discussions so lengthy that they took several hours to complete, meaning that time ran out before the meeting could discuss Item One on the main agenda ("Motion to censure Brother Simeon for stocking past-their-sell-by-date Wagon Wheels on his trolley").

MEETING CLOSED AT 04.37.

11

Horace Tweed's time machine didn't look much like a time machine at all. In fact, it looked a lot more like a battered old VW Transporter camper van, which is hardly surprising since that's exactly what it was apart from a few essential modifications to enable it to travel back and forth in time.

'It doesn't look much like a time machine,' said Norwood Junction when Horace had backed the van out of the rented lockup garage and switched off the engine.

'What's a time machine supposed to look like then?' said Vesta, circumnavigating the van and giving it a thorough inspection.

Norwood shrugged. 'I'm really not sure, but I thought it'd have a lot more... chrome about it and all sorts of cogs and wheels and levers, etcetera.'

'There's a bit of chrome round these headlights,' Vesta pointed out.

Horace couldn't help but feel a little aggrieved that his co-adventurers seemed so unimpressed with his pride and joy. 'Lack of chrome's a design feature,' he said. 'Makes you a lot less conspicuous.'

'Still,' said Vesta, who was sensitive enough to pick up on Horace's indignation, 'I expect it's all very different on the inside. Much bigger than it looks from the outside, for instance.'

She and Norwood looked at Horace expectantly while they waited for his answer.

'Actually, it's exactly the same size as it looks from

the outside,' he said.

'Nicely kitted out though,' said Vesta, peering in through a side window in another attempt to soothe Horace's feelings. 'It's got all kinds of cupboards and a cooker and a little fridge and all sorts.'

Horace followed her gaze and rallied somewhat. 'And if you lift that worktop thing, there's a little sink underneath it. It's got an electrically operated mixer tap and everything.'

'Well, fancy that,' said Vesta brightly. 'That'll certainly come in handy.'

'Is the sink chrome?' asked Norwood.

'Stainless steel,' said Horace, expecting another negative response from his male co-adventurer but was favourably surprised when Norwood nodded sagely and said, 'Yes, much more practical in my experience.'

Horace checked his watch. 'We ought to get going really or we'll miss the time portal.'

As if understanding his master's words, Zoot, the Staffordshire Bull Terrier, who had been quietly sniffing around the interior of the now empty garage and occasionally marking parts of it as his territory, came bounding over and began barking excitedly at the sliding door on the side of the van. Obligingly, Horace opened it, and Zoot leapt inside, followed rather more sedately by Vesta, Norwood and then Horace himself.

Since returning to Horace's apartment from Mr Wellwisher's house the evening before, the three adventurers had stayed up for most of the night, not only admiring the state-of-the-art Swiss Army knives that their new employer had issued them with, but also making plans and preparations for their journey through time and space in search of the Holey Snail. Although Wellwisher had told them that this particular gastropod had become extinct round about the middle of the twelfth century, it was unanimously agreed to apply some judicious bet hedging and travel much further back in time to a period when it was known for certain that the Holey Snail was alive and well and thriving nicely. This in turn had led to a lengthy discussion as to precisely which era to aim for as well as which geographical location. Entire countries and historical periods were dismissed for a variety of reasons but generally on the grounds of the potential risk to the adventurers' health and wellbeing (e.g. areas and decades where excruciatingly debilitating diseases were epidemic, endemic or, most especially, pandemic; and the Viking invasion of Britain and its aftermath were also a complete no-no of course). Eventually, however, and after many hours of debate and research on the Internet, Horace had confessed that:

a) He had only ever used the camper van once in Time Travel Mode and this was only for two hours into the future because he couldn't wait to find out the result of the League Cup fourth round match between his beloved Crystal Palace and Manchester City.

b) This maiden voyage itself had not been entirely successful since he had not only travelled backwards in time instead of forwards, but he had found himself in ancient Pompeii in 79 AD moments before the eruption of Mount Vesuvius and had only just managed to get himself out of there and back to the present with seconds to spare.

c) It was therefore clear that setting the controls in Time Travel Mode was hardly what you might call an exact science, so they may as well just select some preferred parameters and hope for the best.

'So how do we actually set the controls then?' said Vesta.

'Well,' said Horace, crouching down in front of the small built-in oven opposite the sliding door, 'first, we set the temperature gauge on the oven to the time zone required.'

'78 AD then,' said Norwood. 'A whole year before Vesuvius erupted and right in the middle of the longest most peaceful period in the history of the world.'

'Yes, but as I said, it's really not that accurate,' said Horace. 'All I've got on the temperature gauge is a picture of a very small flame and a picture of quite a big flame. The big flame indicates that you want to go a very long way back in time, and the little flame is for just a few hours or so.'

'So it's all or almost nothing then,' said Vesta.

'Oh no,' said Horace with a hint of indignation. 'You can go to all points in between, depending on where you set the dial between the big flame and the little flame.'

'But what if you want to travel into the future?' asked Norwood.

Horace pushed himself upright and flipped open the hinged worktop above the oven to reveal a stainless steel sink, a three-ring gas hob and a grill. 'You just turn the grill full on and then the time settings on the oven gauge work in reverse. That's what it says in the handbook anyway.'

There was a longish pause while Vesta and Norwood eyed the grill, the oven and the temperature gauge with what could only be described as deep suspicion mingled with a heavy dollop of mounting apprehension.

'One thing that does slightly bother me,' said Vesta, breaking the silence and stroking her perfectly proportioned chin.

'Yes?' said Horace.

'If it's as inaccurate as you say—'

'Oh, it is. It is,' said Horace with inappropriate pride.

'—how do we know we can get back to the present? The here and now, I mean.'

'Piece of cake.'

'What, you have to cook one in the oven?'

Horace roared with laughter, but instantly nipped his guffaw in the bud when he spotted Vesta's pained expression.

'No, no,' he said. 'All you do is set the trip meter back to zero, and off you go. The Back To The Present setting works perfectly.'

Vesta's expression switched to one of intense relief, and Norwood's did much the same.

'So then,' said Horace, clapping his hands together and rubbing them vigorously. 'Let's get going, shall we?'

'No time like the present,' said Norwood, who hadn't meant it as a joke, but they all laughed anyway.

Horace crouched down again and turned the oven's temperature gauge approximately four degrees towards the picture of the big flame. Then he opened a full-length cupboard to the side of the oven and took out an open-face motorcycle helmet, which he handed to Vesta, and a fluorescent orange bicycle helmet, which he gave to Norwood.

'Might get a bit bumpy,' he explained and placed a stainless steel colander on Zoot's head, securing it in place with string under the dog's snout and buckling him into a specially made harness on the back seat of the van.

With Norwood safely belted up on the seat beside Zoot, and Vesta likewise in the front passenger seat, Horace strapped a leather flying helmet (complete with goggles) onto his own head and climbed into the driver's seat.

'One other thing,' said Vesta as Horace reached for the ignition key. 'How do you set the location? The place we want to go to.'

'Excellent point,' said Horace, who had completely forgotten this crucial aspect of setting the controls, 'although I'm afraid it's no more accurate than selecting a time zone. Basically, you only get to choose one of the seven continents and then it's pot luck really.'

'So how do you do that?'

'It's all down to a specific combination of switches. Pass me the handbook from the glove box, would you?'

Vesta opened the glove box in front of her knees, had a quick rummage and then passed him a battered and grease-stained handbook. Horace leafed through the pages until he came to the required section.

'Best stick to Europe, I think,' he said and gave a running commentary as he followed the instructions in the handbook. 'Hazard lights — on. Windscreen wipers — intermittent wipe. Headlights — dipped beam. Heated rear screen — off. Fan strength - two. Cassette radio - off. Ashtray - closed.'

'Ashtray?' said Vesta.

'Certainly,' said Horace. 'We don't want to end up in Antarctica, do we?'

He passed her the handbook, and she returned it to the glove box.

'Right then,' he said. 'Time to hit the road.'

'The road?' queried Norwood.

Horace explained that the van had to be travelling at

precisely twenty-seven-point-three miles per hour in order for it to launch itself through the time portal, and so saying, he fired up the engine and headed out onto the main road. Two minutes later, when he was almost certain that he'd been keeping the van at a steady twenty-seven-point-three miles per hour for nearly half that time, nothing out of the ordinary had happened apart from a growing queue of traffic behind them. The analogue speedometer couldn't be relied upon for its accuracy of course, so he alternately increased and decreased his speed by the merest of fractions. Three miles further on, the queue of traffic had more than doubled in length, but still the van failed to launch itself through the time portal.

'Something's not right,' he announced to his co-adventurers, but no sooner had the words left his mouth than he realised he'd forgotten the most important control setting of all — the control to switch from Normal Mode to Time Travel Mode.

'Of course,' he said and slapped his forehead with the palm of his hand. 'Sorry about this, Norwood, but I need you to put us into Time Travel Mode.'

'Okay,' said Norwood, 'and how do I do that exactly?'

'You need to lift the worktop and turn on the sink tap full blast.'

'The sink tap?'

'Yes.'

'To select Time Travel Mode?'

'Yes.'

Horace slowed the van almost to walking pace while Norwood unstrapped himself from his harness, stood up, lifted the worktop and turned on the sink tap full blast. Horace waited until he'd sat back down again and was safely re-harnessed and then accelerated to what he believed to be a steady twenty-seven-point-three miles per hour. Almost immediately, there was a sound that was not unlike the clanging bells on a pinball machine, which exponentially increased in volume and rapidity of clangs until there was an explosively loud "*bang!*" and a flash of intense violet — or possibly even ultraviolet — light.

Then everything went black.

12

It certainly wasn't the first time, and it was highly unlikely to be the last, that Harper Collins had had to battle against an almost overwhelming urge to give her detective sergeant a good, hard slap. And if he said "More haste, less speed" or "Patience is a virtue" once more, she very much doubted that she'd be able to resist. They'd been stuck behind some beat-up old VW camper van for the past five minutes or so as it dawdled along at less than thirty miles per hour, and her impatience gauge was rocketing.

As soon as they'd returned to the car after their interview with Mrs Wadd, she'd radioed the police station that all officers should be on the lookout for anyone dressed in a monk's habit and wearing Union Jack flip-flops, but she had serious reservations that anything much would be done about it until she got back to the nick herself.

'Come *on*,' she said, changing down to second gear as the van slowed almost to a crawl.

'Maybe we should pull him over and book him,' said DS Scatterthwaite.

'For driving too slowly?'

'Well, there must be *something* we could do him for. Look at the state of the thing for a start. Bound to have something faulty on an old banger like that.'

'And spending the next half hour checking over the van and writing him a ticket is going to help us get back to the station quicker, is it?'

'Just saying,' said Scatterthwaite and bent his head over the task of unwrapping his second Mars bar of the journey so far.

Harper glanced across at him and scowled, and when she returned her gaze to the road ahead, the camper van had completely disappeared. Vanished into thin air.

'What the— Did you see that?'

'See what?' said Scatterthwaite, taking a large bite out of his Mars bar as he looked up.

'The camper van. One minute it was right there in front of us and then all of a sudden... gone. Vanished.'

'Probably just turned off.'

'Where though? There hasn't been a turning since—'

Harper didn't bother to finish the sentence, realising that it was pointless trying to engage Scatterthwaite in any form of mental process while he was eating. As she knew from experience, this amounted to multi-tasking as far as he was concerned, and this wasn't an ability that featured anywhere on his pathetically impoverished list of skills. But the van's disappearance was curious to say the least. There was no way she'd imagined it and no way it could have turned off the road without—

The blaring of half a dozen vehicle horns from behind her interrupted Harper's train of thought and reminded her that she was still travelling at less than thirty miles an hour, so she stepped on the gas and changed quickly up through the gears.

* * *

Harper had got no more than two paces inside the police station when the desk sergeant called out to her that the superintendent wanted to see her the moment she got back.

'Oops. Sounds like somebody's been a naughty girl then,' said Scatterthwaite.

Harper ignored him and took her time climbing the stairs to the top floor. A summons from Superintendent Leopold was never a welcome prospect, particularly when it was as urgent as this one, and when she got to his outer sanctum, his secretary told her to go straight in. Also a bad sign. Normally, he'd keep you waiting for half an hour or more if it was something routine and fairly unimportant.

'Where the bloody hell have you been?' he said before Harper had even closed the door behind her.

Although Leopold was only a couple of years older than her, he always spoke to her like she was a wayward teenage daughter. He was one of those fast-track, graduate types who believed that arrogance and smugness were part of the job description. He was also something big in the Freemasons, so he'd had little trouble slithering up the greasy pole despite having demonstrated a minimal talent for police work.

'Doing my job?' said Harper, having realised long ago that pissing him off wasn't going to make a blind bit of difference to her chances of promotion.

'Not well enough, apparently,' Leopold snarled, prodding a spidery thin finger at the buff-coloured folder on the desk in front of him. 'Since you've been gadding about God knows where, there's been three more.'

'Three more?'

'Murders. Same MO, same bloody symbols, same bloody snails. All committed within a couple of hours of each other and spread over an area of twenty-odd square miles.'

Leopold sat back in his fancy leather-bound chair and folded his arms across his narrow chest, staring up at Harper with his deep-set, gimlet eyes as he waited for her response. She had plenty of responses to this latest bombshell but none that she felt inclined to share with Big Chief Leopold.

'Well, you know what this means, don't you?' he went on, wielding the buff-coloured folder for some kind of dramatic effect.

Harper shrugged, deciding to play dumb and wind him up with a typically Scatterthwaitean answer. 'Our serial killer has a very fast car?'

Leopold slammed the folder back down onto the desk. 'It means that there must be more than one of them.'

'Sir?'

'More than one murderer, for Christ's sake.'

'Oh.'

'Yes, "oh". And not only that, but one of the victims is none other than Dicky Double himself.'

'Who?' Harper was obviously expected to recognise the name, but this time she wasn't acting dumb deliberately.

'Dicky Double,' Leopold repeated. 'Don't tell me you've never heard of Dicky Double. He's hardly been off the telly for the best part of fifty years.'

'I don't really watch TV.'

Leopold's eyes popped as if she'd just told him she was pregnant with Elvis Presley's lovechild.

'What?' he said. 'You've never seen Double Trouble? Dicky at the Double? Dicky Takes the Micky?'

Harper shook her head. From the titles alone, it didn't sound like she'd been missing very much.

'He's a national institution, for heaven's sake,' said the superintendent, seemingly taking her ignorance of popular culture as a personal affront.

'Was,' said Harper.

'Excuse me?'

'*Was* a national institution. Didn't you say he'd been murdered?'

Leopold's cheeks glowed incandescent. 'Which is precisely why I need to know you're making some kind of progress on the case. I mean, it's bad enough that

100

we've got a bunch of serial killers on the loose, but now that one of the victims is a famous bloody celebrity, the press are going to go apeshit, and I've got a press conference this afternoon, and I need to be able to tell them we've got some leads we're working on or they'll bloody well crucify me.'

Harper resisted the temptation to tell him that "famous celebrity" was in fact a tautology and that using words like "crucify" might be considered insensitive, given the positioning of the victims' bodies. Instead, she said, 'We do have one lead we're following up.'

'Oh?'

Harper explained how two separate witnesses had spotted someone dressed in a hooded monk's habit and Union Jack flip-flops at two of the earlier murder scenes and that she'd requested all officers to be on the lookout for anyone fitting that description.

'A monk in Union Jack flip-flops?' said Leopold. 'And you expect me to pass that little nugget of information on to a slavering pack of newshounds, do you?'

'It would certainly help to circulate the description as widely as possible, yes.'

The superintendent glared at her and spoke in a chillingly measured tone which rapidly rose in both pitch and volume to a crescendo of crimson-faced apoplexy. 'Listen to me, Chief Inspector Collins. Unless you want to find yourself back on traffic duty before you can say "defective brake lights", you'll get back to me by three o'clock this afternoon at the latest with something I can give the press which doesn't make me sound like I've been seriously overdoing the magic bloody mushrooms!'

Harper deliberately failed to close the door on her way out of his office and headed straight for the women's toilets via the coffee vending machine. There thinking to be done.

13

Following precisely the opposite sequence to when Horace, Norwood, Vesta and Zoot had set off in their time-travelling camper van, there was a flash of intense violet — or possibly even ultraviolet — light, an explosively loud "*bang!*" and a sound that was not unlike the clanging bells on a pinball machine, which exponentially decreased in volume and rapidity of clangs until there was almost complete silence.

'I was expecting a much bumpier landing than that,' said Norwood.

'Yes, the landings are often quite smooth,' said Horace even though he'd only ever made the one brief trip in the van in Time Travel Mode.

'Any idea where we are?' said Vesta, removing her open-face motorcycle helmet and shaking loose the shimmering tresses of her long blonde hair.

'Or when?' added Norwood, removing his fluorescent orange bicycle helmet and rubbing his hand over his entirely bald scalp.

'Neither where nor when unfortunately,' said Horace. 'This is what the salesman at Time And Again told me was an "entry level" model, so it doesn't have all the extra bits and bobs like a whenometer or a whereometer.'

'Time And Again?' said Vesta.

'Place where they sell second-hand time travel machines.'

'All looks a bit kind of... red,' said Norwood, peering

out through the window next to his seat at the back of the van and simultaneously removing the stainless steel colander from Zoot's head.

'And dusty,' said Vesta.

Horace looked through the driver's window and was forced to agree that their immediate surroundings did indeed appear to be rather red and very dusty. There were no buildings, no trees, no grass — in fact, nothing but a mostly flat expanse of reddish-coloured dust.

'Perhaps we've landed on a beach,' said Vesta with a cheery hint in her voice.

'Or in a desert,' said Norwood, somewhat more gloomily.

'Only one way to find out,' said Horace, throwing open the driver's door and jumping down onto the reddish-coloured dusty ground.

Vesta, Norwood and Zoot joined him, and they all stood silently scanning the area until Vesta shouted, 'Look! What's that over there?'

Her co-adventurers followed the direction of her perfectly manicured pointing finger to discover that the object of her attention was a peculiar-looking vehicle with six wheels and some kind of box mounted on a long vertical pole which was fixed to its roof.

'Reminds me of one of those things they sent up to Mars to take pictures and collect samples and stuff,' said Norwood.

There was a lengthy pause while each of them considered the implications of Norwood's remark in the context of the reddish and dusty ground beneath their feet.

'Oh, good grief,' said Vesta at last. 'We've only gone and landed on Mars.'

'But that's impossible,' said Horace, 'unless Mars has suddenly become a member of the European Union.'

'The EU's accepted stranger places,' said Norwood.

'Maybe we've ended up thousands of years into the future,' said Vesta, 'and who knows who the EU might have let in by then?'

'We can't have travelled into the future though,' said Horace, 'because, if you remember, the van can only go forwards in time if the grill is turned on full, and it was definitely off when we left. Besides, if this really *was* Mars, we'd all be dead by now.'

'Ah, yes,' said Norwood, nodding sagely. 'Not enough oxygen.'

'So where are we then if we're not on Mars?' said Vesta.

'Well, we're not on a beach,' said Horace, failing to observe any indication of sea via any of his sensory organs.

'Desert then,' said Norwood with more than a dash of told-you-so in his tone.

'Could be,' said Horace. 'Perhaps we should explore the—'

But the rest of his sentence was drowned out by a deafening roar which appeared to be rapidly approaching the very spot where they now stood. The adventurers snapped their heads round and saw amid a burgeoning cloud of reddish dust, thirty or forty figures racing towards them, each brandishing a knife, an axe, a heavy club or some other implement capable of inflicting severe physical damage.

'Well, this is certainly not what I signed up for,' said Horace, recalling the capitalised and unambiguously worded phrase from his advertisement: "WANTED - GAINFUL EMPLOYMENT OF AN ADVENTUROUS NATURE BUT *WITHOUT RISK OF PERSONAL PHYSICAL HARM*" [Horace's italics].

As the howling mob came closer, the adventurers could make out that all were dressed in torn and filthy rags that were heavily streaked with blood, and as they got closer still, it became abundantly clear that they were not at all in the best of moods. Black-rimmed eyes were suffused with fiery crimson, and yellow, broken teeth snarled and gnashed at the air. Some had a bloody gash where an ear, an eye or a nose once was, and all sported hanks of grease-sodden hair that looked like it hadn't seen a comb or a brush in goodness' knew how long.

'Crikey,' said Vesta, 'they look a bit like—'

'Zombies?' said Norwood, an unmistakable quaver in his voice.

'The undead, yes,' said Vesta. 'Living corpses. And they seem to be coming for *us*.'

14

Her usual cubicle in the women's toilets was occupied, so Harper had been forced to sit at her own desk to ponder the facts of the case and try to develop a strategy for solving it. Mercifully, she was spared the perpetually irritating presence of DS Scatterthwaite, who was no doubt stuffing his face with yet more carbohydrates in the canteen. In front of her was an A4 pad covered with doodles and the occasional scribbled note. The doodles were mostly of an abstract nature, but others were more discernible as, for instance, a faceless figure in a monk's habit and flip-flops, a badly drawn snail with a cross piercing its shell, and a stick person lying on the floor and arranged in the shape of a crucifix. In the centre of the page was a large figure "70", which Harper was currently converting from one dimension into three.

It was clear from what they'd learned so far that there was some kind of religious theme to the killings. The cruciform shape of the victims. The birthday cards with the snail and its cross. The biblical Roman numeral format of the three-score-years-and-ten symbol drawn on each of the victims' chests. And then of course there was the monk in Union Jack flip-flops that two witnesses had spotted, although now it seemed they had more than one killer on their hands.

It was also no coincidence that all six of the victims had been murdered on their seventieth birthdays. Until now, all of them had been men, but two of the latest three were women, the only difference being that neither of these had been stripped to the waist and the symbols had been written on a piece of paper and pinned to their clothing. How very considerate of the killer to spare the corpses' blushes. But she still didn't have a clue as to the significance of the snails. Her Internet searches had revealed little more than that some snails live on land, some in the sea and some in fresh water, and some have gills and the rest have lungs. Not exactly a great help in working out their relevance to the murders.

Harper pushed her face into her hands and considered the possibility of keeping surveillance on anyone in the area who was due to turn seventy in the next day or so. Leopold would obviously kick up a stink about how they were overstretched already and there was no money for overtime, but he was the one who was leaning on her to get a result.

'Excuse me, ma'am.'

Harper looked up into the cherubic features of a uniformed male constable. 'Yes?'

'There's been a sighting, ma'am.'

'Of?'

'Your monk bloke in the flip-flops.'

'Hardly *my* monk bloke, Constable,' said Harper, grabbing her mobile phone and car keys from the desktop. 'Where is he?'

The constable checked the memo clutched in his hand. 'Mortuary Street.'

'Who's on it?'

'Sergeant Noble and PC Barnes,' said the constable, almost trotting to keep up with her as she hurried out into the corridor.

'Tell them not to collar him but don't let him out of their sight. You seen DS Scatterthwaite around?'

'Canteen, I think, ma'am.'

Harper rolled her eyes and seriously contemplated trying to give him the slip again but decided that brawn rather than brain would probably be more necessary on this occasion, so he might be of some use after all.

15

'Quick!' shouted Horace. 'Everyone back in the van!'

But no sooner had he and his co-adventurers turned their backs on the almost-upon-them zombie horde than another voice megaphoned its booming way through the dense cloud of reddish dust and stopped them in their tracks: 'Cut! Cut, for God's sake!'

The zombie horde skidded to a halt and a short man with glasses, a bushy beard and a wrong-way-round baseball cap pushed his way into the small gap between the adventurers and the front row of slavering undead.

'What in hell do you think you're doing?' he yelled at the nearest adventurer, who happened to be Horace.

'Er...' said Horace, who was having great difficulty making sense of what *anyone* was doing. 'Running away?'

'You know how long it's taken to set up this shot?'

'Somebody's been shot?' said Norwood.

The man snatched the wrong-way-round baseball cap from his head and whacked it against his thigh, causing a small explosion of reddish dust. 'No, dammit, nobody's been shot. Not till the end of this scene — if we ever get that far.'

'Scene?' said Vesta.

'Yes, scene,' said the man and slapped the baseball cap back onto his head. Realising that it was now the right way round, he irritably twisted it through a hundred and eighty degrees so that it was the wrong way round again and added, 'I'm trying to make a movie here in case you hadn't noticed.'

Of course, none of the adventurers *had* noticed or they wouldn't have been about to cack their pants at the prospect of being viciously slaughtered by a pack of flesh-eating zombies.

'So this isn't actually Mars then?' said Horace, beginning to assimilate this latest piece of information.

The man took a step forward, his eyes less than six inches in front of Horace's. 'Are you completely insane? Of course it's not goddamn Mars. It's a goddamn movie set, you moron.'

'Well, that's a relief, I must say,' said Vesta. 'For a moment there I thought we'd landed ourselves in some serious trouble.'

'Lady,' said the man, who was presumably the director of the movie, 'you *have* landed yourself in some serious trouble. And if you don't get your goddamn arses and that goddamn piece-of-shit camper van outta here in the next five seconds, I'm gonna call security and get them to throw you out.'

'There's no need to take that kind of tone,' said Norwood.

The director's face looked like it was about to explode and send tufts of bushy beard flying like hairy shrapnel in every direction across the reddish-coloured dust, but instead, he grabbed a walkie-talkie from somewhere round his hip area and yelled into it, 'Get me security. Now!'

'Okay, okay,' said Horace, his palms spread towards the man in a gesture of surrender. 'We know when we're not welcome.'

'And get that fleabag mutt of a mongrel away from my zombies!'

For the first time, Horace became aware that Zoot had disobeyed his instruction to stay behind in the van and was now lying on his back, waggling his little legs in the air in ecstasy while four of the undead crouched around him, one of whom was massaging the dog's upturned belly with an apparently fingerless hand. Once again, Zoot was oblivious to his master's commands, and Horace quickly admitted defeat, taking him by the collar and gently but firmly leading him back towards the van.

'Just before we go,' he said as he passed the director. 'Could you tell us what year this is?'

The director's mouth hung open. 'Uh?'

'It's a perfectly simple question.'

'Nineteen seventy-eight. Don't you *know*?'

'It's rather a long story,' said Vesta, 'and I was under the impression you wanted us to get our "goddamn arses" out of here toute suite. But if you're really that interested, it all began when—'

But she got no further with her story because the director had snatched a long-bladed knife from the hand of the nearest zombie and was pointing it at her in a distinctly threatening manner.

'Very nice,' said Norwood, leaning forward to inspect the knife more closely, 'but rather primitive. Seems to be a single blade and totally lacking in any additional handy little tools and gadgets.'

'Not at all like a Swiss Army knife,' said Vesta.

'Not in the same league at all,' agreed Norwood.

The director made some swishing movements in the air with his mono-bladed knife. 'I ain't gonna tell you again,' he said.

'Oh good,' said Norwood, 'because you were starting to get irritatingly repetitive. Incidentally, you don't happen to know anything about snails, do you?'

'What?'

'Snails. Especially holey ones. You see, my co-adventurers and myself are on a quest to—'

The interruption on this occasion was due to the arrival of three extremely large men who were almost as enormous as Enormous Figure One and Enormous Figure Two. All were dressed in dark blue uniforms with the word "SECURITY" printed in big letters on the backs of their jackets, and they instantly obeyed the director's barked instruction to 'Get this bunch of goddamn morons into their goddamn piece-of-shit camper van and get them the hell outta here.'

'Nineteen seventy-eight, eh?' said Horace once all of the adventurers were back inside the van. 'There must be a lot less Time than I'd realised.'

Then he crouched down in front of the gas cooker and turned the temperature gauge through a lot more degrees than the four he'd originally set it to.

When Norwood had opened the sink tap full blast and the adventurers were safely helmeted and harnessed in their seats, Horace switched on the ignition and eased the van forward. The horde of slavering zombies parted to let it through, and Vesta called out to the director through the open passenger window, 'By the way, what's the name of this movie you're making?'

'Not that it's any of your goddamn business,' he snarled, 'but it's *Attack of the Zombie Warriors from Mars*.'

'Yeah, I thought so,' said Vesta. 'I saw it on the TV a year or two ago. It was rubbish.'

Horace hit the throttle and accelerated to a speed of precisely twenty-seven-point-three miles per hour. Almost immediately, there was a sound that was not unlike the clanging bells on a pinball machine, which exponentially increased in volume and rapidity of clangs until there was an explosively loud "*bang*!" and a flash of intense violet — or possibly even ultraviolet — light.

Then everything went black.

DIGRESSION TWO:
DIARY OF A ZOMBIE

Little is known about what it is really like to be a zombie other than from fictionalised accounts in such films as *Attack of the Zombie Warriors from Mars* and *Seven Brides for Seven Zombies*. However, the recent discovery of a personal journal has provided some extraordinary insights into the day-to-day existence of the living dead. What follows are selected extracts from this diary:

Tuesday, 14th July

Turned up to work as an extra on *Attack of the Zombie Warriors from Mars*, only to be told by the director that I didn't look "zombie enough" so had to spend best part of an hour being plastered with makeup. After they'd done, I looked a lot less like the living dead and a lot more like Edna Everage after fifteen rounds with Muhammad Ali. You could tell that none of the other extras were real zombies by their rubbish howling and the way nearly half of them went for the vegetarian option at lunchtime. Managed not to attack any of them (just), although the movie would probably have benefited from me turning a bunch of them into proper zombies! All in all, a pretty crap day, but the cash will come in handy.

Saturday, 25th July

Miriam still not returning my calls. Maybe she was more upset than she let on when a bit of my nose fell off into the casserole she'd spent ages cooking. Has she been having me on all this time when she's claimed she doesn't care about my appearance and loves me for what's underneath the putrid, rotting skin? Perhaps we'd get on better if I gave her a good bite and turned her into a zombie as well. Conversation's a bit on the stilted side most of the time, so at least we'd have something in common to talk about.

Monday, 27th July

Unbelievable! Idiots at the Benefits Office told me they're cutting my disability benefit because "living dead" has been taken off the list of criteria due to cutbacks. I mean, how much more disabled can you get? Still, at least the Benefits Officer will get the opportunity to find out first-hand what a zombie has to put up with. Took an almighty chunk out of the bugger's neck before I stormed out. Ha bloody ha.

Thursday, 30th July

Bit of light relief last night when a couple of Jehovah's Witnesses came a-calling. Daft sods asked me if I'd found God, so I told them it probably wouldn't be such a great idea if I did because I'd probably eat him. The look on their faces — priceless!

Sunday, 2nd August

Called round to Miriam's flat earlier but no answer. Fairly sure she was in so think she must be avoiding me. The big silver cross fixed to her front door is new. Surely she hasn't got religion all of a sudden? Or is she trying to tell me something but doesn't know her vampires from her zombies?

Wednesday, 5th August

Just when I thought things couldn't get any worse, it seems I've now been banned from the local swimming pool. Manager said there'd been complaints about various body parts being found in the water and the trail of blood I left behind me after my fifty-metre butterfly against the clock. Told her it was no worse than kids peeing in the pool, but she wouldn't have it.

Tuesday, 8th August

Thought a visit to the weekly meeting of Zombie Club at the church hall might cheer me up but, if anything, made me feel more depressed than ever. There's only so much incomprehensible moaning and groaning I can take, so I left after half an hour. Can't believe how unutterably boring the living dead can be at times. Scabby Gordon behaving like a total dick as usual. Am I the only one who doesn't find his *Shaun of the Dead* Simon Pegg impersonation hysterically funny? If I could, I'd rid the world of him for good, but I'm not that great a shot, and even at point blank range, I'd probably miss his lentil-sized brain.

Saturday, 19th September

Ran into a bunch of anti-zombie vigilantes tonight on my way home from the Millwall game. You'd think they'd have worked out by now that the only way to kill a zombie is by destroying its brain. Instead, I ended up with a shitload of bullets in the chest and elsewhere, which totally ruined a brand new shirt and pair of jeans. Got my own back, though, by dragging one of the idiots back home with me for supper. Should last the week if I make curry, soup, etc. Always make a point of eating most of each body I get. Don't want the place overrun by even more zombies ruining the neighbourhood.

Wednesday, 23rd September

Utterly miserable. Email from Miriam banging on about not seeing any future for us. It's her, not me. Wants us to still be friends, blah, blah, blah, blah. Had leg soup and went to bed.

Monday, 12th October

Decided to write a pros and cons list about being a zombie. Plenty of cons, but the only pro I could think of was that, unlike mortals, zombies can never really die unless their brains are blasted to hell. But then I started to wonder if that shouldn't go under the cons heading as well. I mean, what's so great about being undead? You've got bits dropping off you all the time, you stink to high heaven regardless of how many showers you take, and it's almost impossible to get a girlfriend, never mind keep one (e.g. Miriam). Not only that, but even though being a zombie isn't actually illegal itself, eating people definitely is, so that's one big paradox there to start with. Besides, what's the big deal about eating humans when it's perfectly acceptable to eat virtually every other animal on the planet? And how about the contribution us zombies make towards solving the problem of overpopulation? Living death is so unfair!

Saturday, 7th November

Against my better judgement, went on a Zombie Club outing to see *Attack of the Zombie Warriors from Mars*. Wish I hadn't bothered. Film was the biggest load of tosh I've ever seen in my undead life and couldn't have been more inaccurate about what it's like to be a zombie if it had tried. Never mind being an extra, they should have hired me as a technical adviser. I was only on screen for about three seconds, but of course that was more than enough for the others to rip me to shreds over it. Not surprisingly, Scabby Gordon got his rocks off in the pub afterwards by doing what everyone else thought was a hysterically funny impersonation of me. One day, I swear I'll eat the little toerag just to shut him up. Only thing is, the first rule of Zombie Club is we don't eat other zombies. But who gives a toss? I'm getting way past caring about all that crap.

Thursday, 17th December

Bloody Christmas almost here again. Think I'll give the Zombie Club Xmas party a miss this year. All the moaning and groaning even more incomprehensible than normal after they've all got a few pints inside them. And what *is* the point of a Secret Santa when you know damn well that it's just going to be some human body part or other? And how come Scabby Gordon always seems to end up with the liver?

Friday, 1st January

Oh great. Another year to look forward to, which will no doubt be as bloody awful as the last one. Xmas card from Miriam arrived day before yesterday. Repeated all the cobblers about still wanting to be friends and then the real bombshell. She's only getting bloody married because she's bloody well pregnant! Hoped I'd understand and assured me the kid wasn't mine. Course it's not bloody mine! Stupid cow.

Monday, 4th January

Felt a bit more cheerful this morning when I heard there were some professional zombie hunters operating in the area. At least this lot should be a bit more clued up about how you actually make the undead well and truly *dead*. But to be on the safe side, I got a magic marker and drew a dirty great target on my forehead, right where the frontal lobe is. Off out now so may not be writing any more if all goes to plan. In any case, it's been getting harder and harder to hold a pen properly with hardly any fingers left.

16

By the time Harper and Scatterthwaite got to Mortuary Street, the monk had walked on for another half a mile and was now sitting in a greasy spoon café on the corner of Paradise Road and Glib Street. Sergeant Noble and Constable Barnes had parked almost opposite, and Harper and Scatterthwaite slid into the back seat of their marked police car.

'Not exactly what I'd call discreet,' said Harper.

'Nobody said anything about "discreet", ma'am,' said Sergeant Noble, eyeballing her in the rear-view mirror.

'Missed the class on surveillance techniques at training college, did you?'

'Haven't lost him though, have we... ma'am?'

The slight pause before the "ma'am" wasn't unfamiliar to Harper as a clear indication of how most of her male colleagues felt about taking criticism from a higher-ranking female, but as on so many other occasions, she chose to ignore it.

'How long's he been in there?' she said.

'Half hour maybe.'

Harper squinted through the grimy glass front of the café across the street and focused on the hooded figure sitting at a table close to the window. His head was tilted forward over a mug, which he held clasped between both hands, and his features were totally obscured by the overhang of his cowl. On the table in front of him was an empty dinner plate.

'Any minute now and he'll be coming out,' said

Harper. 'Soon as he's through that door, I want him nicked, okay?'

'Knock yourself out,' said Sergeant Noble.

'What's up, Sergeant? Afraid a little old monk'll get the better of you?'

Noble twisted round in the passenger seat and fixed her with the unblinking stare of a cobra that was about to strike. 'No, it's because I don't want to spend the next God knows how many hours filling in a lot of useless bloody paperwork... ma'am.'

'And anyway,' said PC Barnes, 'who's to say he *is* a little old monk? I saw this film once called *Rasputin: Dark Servant of Destiny* and he was some kind of monk, and he wasn't old *or* little. In fact, he was really big and he—'

'Little or old or not,' Scatterthwaite interrupted, 'if he's the geezer we're after, then he's also a serial killer, so he's hardly gonna be harmless.'

'Yes, thanks for that input,' said Harper. 'I can always rely on you to—'

She broke off as she noticed the monk get to his feet, but instead of walking to the door, he headed in the opposite direction towards the back of the café. Of course, he might just be going to pay his bill, she thought, or on the other hand...

'Is there a back way out?' she said.

Noble shrugged. 'Search me. We were only told to keep an eye on him.'

Harper threw open the back door of the car. 'Right then. Shift your arses.'

Stepping out onto the pavement, she glanced back over her shoulder and saw that none of the other three had made the slightest move to follow her.

'That means all of you. Now!'

She sent Noble and Barnes down a side alley to cut off any potential escape route from the back of the café

120

while she and Scatterthwaite charged in through the front door. The place was empty apart from an elderly couple at a corner table and a flame-haired woman in a grubby floral apron behind the counter at the far end who was lethargically drying a chipped white mug with an equally grubby tea towel.

Harper flashed her warrant card at her. 'Where'd the monk go?'

The woman picked up a smouldering cigarette from a glass ashtray on the counter and took a drag. 'The what?'

'Get a lot of monks in here, do you? — Long robe. Big hood. He was sat at the table by the window.'

The woman took another drag and screwed up her face as the smoke drifted into her eyes. 'Jakes probly.'

'What?'

'Bogs,' said the woman, jabbing a thumb behind her.

Harper passed through the gap between the wall and the end of the counter and turned sharp right. Immediately on her left were two doors, each with a handwritten note pinned to the peeling lavender paintwork — "LADYS" and "GENTS". She glanced in through the half-open door of the women's cubicle and took in the tiny washbasin and the broken plastic lid of the toilet bowl, recoiling at the stink of stale urine.

'Must be in this one then,' said Scatterthwaite with a nod at the closed door of the Gents, and before she could stop him, he smashed the sole of his size nine boot smack into the middle of it.

The jarring sound of splintering hardboard was accompanied by a muffled shout from inside the cubicle and the disappearance of Scatterthwaite's boot and part of his leg almost to the top of his calf. The remainder of the door had resolutely refused to budge.

'Bollocks,' he said, hopping on his other foot and flailing his arms wildly to maintain his balance.

'What the hell did you do that for?' said Harper,

instinctively grabbing him by the arm to prevent him from falling.

'Element of surprise?'

'Yes, well I think you've achieved that quite successfully,' said Harper and then shouted through the cubicle door. 'You all right in there?'

Her question was met with complete silence apart from Scatterthwaite's moaning and groaning as he attempted to free his firmly lodged foot.

'Do you think you could open the door?' Harper shouted again.

'Yeah, but before you do that,' Scatterthwaite added, 'maybe you could take my boot off so I can get my bloody foot out.'

Still there was no response.

''Ere, what you done to my bleedin' door?'

It was the flame-haired woman from behind the counter, who appeared to be still drying the same mug as before.

'Police business,' grunted Scatterthwaite.

'We have reason to believe there's someone inside who's a suspect in a murder investigation,' said Harper with a half-hearted stab at a conciliatory smile.

'Well, why didn't you just open the bloody door then 'stead of smashin' it to buggery like that?'

'It's not locked?'

'Course not.'

'How do you know?' said Harper and reached for the door handle.

''Cos it never 'as been. Least, not since a few years back when some old bloke 'ad an 'eart attack in there and croaked. 'Ad to break the door in ourselves then so's we could get 'im out. Never again, we thought, so off comes the lock for good 'n' all.'

By the time the woman had finished speaking, and with Scatterthwaite tottering and hopping to keep up,

Harper had opened the door as far as it would go, which was only a little more than half way. There was something on the inside that was preventing it from opening any further, but the gap was more than enough for her to lean in and discover the cause of the obstruction. The monk's upper body was slumped forward over the toilet bowl, his arms hanging limply on either side and his legs stretched out behind him so that both feet were wedged against the bottom of the door. Judging by the thin, vertical streak of blood on the lavender-coloured tiles beneath the high-level toilet cistern, he must have been propelled forward by the impact of Scatterthwaite's boot in the middle of his back, whacked his head against the wall and instantly lost consciousness.

Harper bent down to ease the monk's feet away from the door so she could open it fully but froze the moment she took hold of his ankles.

'Oh Christ,' she said. 'I don't believe it.'

'What's up?' said Scatterthwaite, craning his neck round the edge of the door.

'Look at his feet.'

Scatterthwaite craned a couple of inches further and his eyes popped. 'Shit, I see what you mean. Brown leather sandals and white socks? Unbelievable bad taste even for a monk.'

'No,' said Harper. 'I mean they're not Union Jack flip-flops, are they?'

17

Following precisely the same sequence as when Horace, Norwood, Vesta and Zoot had made their unscheduled and rather alarming stop on the set of *Attack of the Zombie Warriors from Mars*, there was a flash of intense violet — or possibly even ultraviolet — light, an explosively loud "*bang!*", etcetera, etcetera... until there was almost complete silence. Almost, that is, apart from a faint tapping noise not unlike the sound of someone rapping their knuckles against a metal surface.

'Is that someone knocking on the outside of the van?' said Vesta, her perfectly proportioned nose pressed up against the passenger window as she squinted back along the side of the van in an attempt to answer her own question.

But at exactly the same moment, her head recoiled in shock at the sudden appearance of a face on the outside of the glass. It was the face of an old man with very long, straggly grey hair and an equally long but even stragglier grey beard. He appeared to be smiling, but it was hard to be sure through all the grey hair, which was almost constantly smeared across his face by a strong breeze.

'Perhaps we should ask him where we are,' said Horace.

'And *when* we are,' Norwood added, unbuckling himself from his safety harness on the back seat.

'He looks friendly enough, I suppose,' said Vesta, 'although it's hard to tell through all that hair.'

She slowly wound down her window but only by an amount sufficient to allow conversation, yet leaving nowhere near enough of a gap to provide the old man with the opportunity to reach in and throttle her to death if that turned out to be his intention.

'Hello,' she said.

'Greetings,' said the old man. 'Have you travelled far?'

'Not sure, to be honest. Depends where we are really.'

'You don't know?'

'We're not in Italy, are we?'

The old man probably smiled. 'No, fair lady, this is Greece.'

Vesta turned to her co-adventurers with a flattered grin and mouthed the words "fair lady". Horace thought that the old man was being overly forward after such a brief acquaintance but recognised that he seemed harmless enough and suggested they all got out of the van to stretch their legs.

Once outside, he surveyed their surroundings. A barren, rocky landscape with the occasional lonely shrub as far as the eye could see — which wasn't very far since the whole area was almost completely ringed by rather large mountains. Then, Horace surveyed the old man himself. They still had no idea what time period they'd landed in, so he couldn't know whether anorexia had been invented yet, but if it had, this poor man certainly looked as if he'd been severely afflicted by that awful disease. Bones jutted and prodded at the inside of his slack, sun-scorched skin, the only invisible area of which was covered by a tattered loincloth that hadn't seen the inside of a washing machine for many a long year — if ever.

The old man introduced himself as Thestor.

'Fester?' said Norwood, whose hearing was still somewhat impaired from the din of all the pinball clanging when they'd landed.

'*Thes*-tor,' the old man enunciated.

Once all of the introductions had been completed, Thestor invited them all to his cave for some light refreshment.

'Cave?' said Horace. 'You mean, like a hole in the rock?'

'Well, it's quite a big hole actually,' said Thestor, clearly affronted. 'Cool in the summer and mostly quite dry in the winter.'

He was certainly right about the "big" part. In fact, it would have been better described as somewhere between huge and massive, although Thestor had made it appear almost cosy with some innovative *trompe l'oeil* techniques involving animal skins and plenty of black and terracotta paint. He ushered his guests to a pile of such skins in the middle of the floor, and when they were seated, rubbed his hands together enthusiastically and asked them what they would like to drink.

'Cup of tea would be nice,' said Vesta.

Thestor screwed up his face in apology, his features now perfectly visible since he'd come in out of the wind. 'Sorry.'

'Coffee?' suggested Norwood.

This time, Thestor's expression was much more of the "no-idea-what-you're-talking-about" variety.

'Perhaps you could tell us what you *do* have,' said Horace, not intending to sound irritable at all but quite possibly coming across as if he was.

'I've got this,' said Thestor, picking up a large earthenware jug that was decorated in black with pictures of naked men taking part in what looked like a variety of sporting events.

'Lovely,' said Vesta. 'What is it?'

Thestor gazed into the jug and scratched his head. 'Not sure what you'd call it exactly.'

'How about "approximately"?' said Norwood.

'It's my own recipe, you see,' said the old man. 'Never felt the need to give it a name as such. Didn't seem to be a lot of point really when I hardly ever get a single visitor from one year to the next.'

'Maybe you could tell us what the ingredients are then,' said Norwood, who was the sort of person that always read the ingredients list on food and drink items before deciding whether to buy them or not.

Thestor gave a kind of half shrug, which was achieved without any movement of the shoulder of the arm of the hand that was holding the earthenware jug. 'Mostly berries really. Funny thing is, if I drink too much of the stuff when I've kept it for a while, it makes my head go a bit weird.'

'Really?' said Vesta.

'I see,' said Norwood.

Judging by the hesitant tone in both of their voices, it was plain to Horace that his co-adventurers were about to decline Thestor's offer of liquid refreshment, but he had begun to feel sorry for the old man and his lack of visitors, so he said, 'Sounds delicious.' Then, with what he hoped was a steely-eyed glare at Vesta and Norwood, added, 'We'd all love some, wouldn't we.'

Vesta and Norwood nodded with an abundantly evident lack of enthusiasm.

Thestor beamed with abundantly evident delight. 'The only thing is, you'll have to share, I'm afraid.'

So saying, he picked up a solitary earthenware bowl and filled it to the brim with a reddish-blue liquid from the earthenware jug. Passing the bowl to Vesta, he next poured a generous quantity of the liquid into a hollow in the rocky floor of the cave so that Zoot could also drink his fill.

* * *

'This may sound like an odd question,' said Horace, taking a third sip of Thestor's home-concocted-but-not-at-all-unpleasant liquid refreshment, 'but could you tell us what year this is?'

'I could indeed,' said the old man. 'It's 1323 BC, give or take a year or so.'

'BC?' said Norwood.

'Before Christ,' Thestor explained.

'Yes, I know what BC means, but how do *you* know about the birth of Christ happening thirteen hundred years in the future?'

'You're not the first time travellers to have come this way, you know. Not by a long chalk.'

Up until then, Horace had been wondering why the old man had appeared to be so little surprised by the arrival of a VW camper van as if from nowhere, but now he had his answer.

'And some of them tell me things,' Thestor added. 'Stuff about what happens in the future — like the baby Jesus and whatnot. But I'm also a seer myself of course.'

'A seer?' said Vesta.

'A soothsayer. An augur. A predictor of things to come. Except I'm not really, but everyone thinks I am, and that's how all my troubles began.'

Thestor then told them the story of how he'd come to be living in a cave in such a desolate wilderness and clad only in a tattered loincloth. The story went like this:

'My father was one of the best seers in the land in his day and even got to be Chief Soothsayer to King Moros the Unpleasant himself. That was after Moros had had his previous Chief Soothsayer boiled alive in vinegar for falsely prophesying that the following Tuesday would be warm and dry when it turned out to be pouring with rain and distinctly chilly. So, as you can tell, being Chief Soothsayer to the King was a bit of a precarious position.

'Fortunately, though, my dad was brilliant at foretelling the future and never once got any of his prophecies wrong. But it was genetic, you see. His father had been a top class seer and so had his father before him and his father before him and so on and so forth. A whole line of top notch soothsayers going back for generations, almost to the time of King Whatshisname the Unmemorable.

'And so when I was born of course, it was just assumed that I'd inherit the same ability to see into the future and be able to continue the family tradition once my father had popped his sandals. But there was one little detail that nobody except my mother knew about. My dad wasn't actually my dad. My real father was an apprentice carpet beater from somewhere up north, and the only genes I inherited from him were the ones whereby I could instinctively identify and differentiate between several hundred types of dust. Not much use when somebody pays you money to find out who's going to win next week's *episkyros* final.

'I didn't find out who my real father was until I was

about ten years old and I'd just come home from school after receiving the latest in a series of beatings from my schoolmates — on this occasion, for inaccurately predicting the questions that would come up in an important exam. While my mother tended to my wounds, she was presumably overcome with a fit of guilty remorse because she suddenly started sobbing and then blurted out the awful truth about my progeny.

'I was shocked at first, but in a way, I also felt a strange sense of relief to discover the real reason why I was so rubbish at soothsaying. On the other hand, my mother swore me to absolute secrecy on the subject. No-one — and least of all my father — should ever learn of her shameful indiscretion with the apprentice carpet beater from somewhere up north.

'Needless to say, my life as an unwillingly fraudulent seer went from worse to downright dreadful. Having barely survived the numerous beatings from my schooldays, I was put to work for a certain unscrupulous moneylender by the name of Butacidas. My duties were mostly of the office-cleaning-and-general-fetching-and-carrying variety, but the main reason Butacidas had employed me was for my supposed skills as a seer, which, like everyone else, he assumed I had inherited from my father and forefathers.

'What he wanted me to do was assess each of his prospective clients by looking into the future to determine whether they would repay the loan at all, and if so, how long it would take them to settle the account. Not surprisingly, being utterly devoid of the necessary prophetic abilities, I relied almost entirely on guesswork to make my assessment — although I did occasionally factor in such physical characteristics as how close the clients' eyes were to each other and whether they blinked a lot. But even by guesswork alone, I believed I should have been able to achieve somewhere in the region of a fifty-fifty success rate at least on the question of their general creditworthiness, but, alas, this did not prove to be the case. Due to the inherent wobbliness of statistical probability, eight out of ten of the prospective clients that I "approved" ended up defaulting on their loans, either partly or in full, and after receiving countless beatings from Butacidas, he finally kicked me out of the door for good.

'My father — who still entertained the false impression that he *was* my father — was in despair at my complete ineptitude as a soothsayer and was at a loss as to how I would ever be able to make my own way in the world. Eventually, however, and because he was still Chief Soothsayer to the King, he managed to wangle me a job at court as Royal Soothsayer (Third Class). Moros was no longer the king at that time, having recently died as the result of a bizarre discus accident, and he'd been succeeded by his nephew, Eupolos the Underwhelming.

'For the first few months, and with a great deal of help from my father, I actually achieved some degree of success with my prophesying, but this was mainly because third class royal soothsayers were rarely given anything particularly taxing to foretell about the future. "What will Cook be serving up for supper tonight?" "Will these socks shrink in the wash?" "Will it be Thursday or Friday tomorrow?" That kind of thing. I even began to develop a sense of pride in my work, but that's when everything started to go horribly wrong. If there's one thing that irritates the gods more than anything else, it's when us humans show signs of getting a bit up themselves, and in many ways I became a victim of my own success.

'Despite my father's objections — for he alone knew the truth about my shortcomings — I was promoted to Royal Soothsayer (Second Class) and was therefore expected to perform my soothsaying duties at a much higher level than before. From that moment on, almost every prediction I made turned out to be totally wrong, and matters came to a head one day when my father and all of the other senior soothsayers were laid low with the Macedonian flu. This meant that responsibility for any and all prophesying that the king requested would have to fall on me. And as bad luck would have it, it wasn't long after I took on the role of Caretaker Chief Soothsayer that he came up with the most challenging question he'd ever posed during the entire period of his reign so far.

'It so happened that the mighty army of the Aspirinians was at that exact same time massing within our borders and threatening to attack and lay waste the capital city itself.

'"So, young Thestor," King Eupolos said to me when he'd summoned me to the throne room. "Tell us what it is you foresee and advise us on our wisest course of action. Do we attack the barbarian horde or do we sue for peace?"

'Well, how in Hades was I supposed to know? He might just as well have tossed a coin for all the advice I was going to be able to offer him. Still, I went through the motions, pretending to go into the usual trance and doing plenty of moaning and wailing and arm waving, and after about ten minutes of that, I said in a kind of spooky monotone voice, "The common potato has eyes but cannot see, your majesty."

'"And what's that got to do with anything?" said the king.

'A bit more moaning and wailing and then "Without water and nutrients, even the humble runner bean plant must surely wither and die."

'"I don't suppose you could be a bit less cryptic, could you?" said the king. "I mean, it's a perfectly simple question. Do we attack them or not?"

'I trotted out a few more pseudo-wise aphorisms, mostly involving different varieties of fruit and vegetables, but as the king got more and more irritated, I realised there was little point in stalling for time any longer. I was never going to get even the slightest glimpse of the future to inform the advice I gave him, so I decided to err on the side of caution and said, "A slug may attack a cabbage, but far better for the brassicas who remain within their net."

"Brassicas?" said the king. "What tribe is this? I've never heard of them."

'I explained that brassicas weren't actually a tribe at all but members of a particular genus of plant, and he pondered my words for a good couple of minutes.

'"So your advice is that we shouldn't attack but sue for peace instead?" he said.

'I gave a heavy shrug, as I'd seen real soothsayers do when finding themselves in a tight spot, and said, "It is not for me to interpret the sayings of the gods, your majesty."

'The king seemed to accept that this was the best he was going to get and immediately sent an emissary to the Aspirinian camp to invite their top brass to the palace to discuss terms for peace. Less than an hour later, the emissary's horse returned to the city with the emissary's head tied to its saddle and was closely followed by the entire Aspirinian army. Their soldiers then proceeded to burn half the city and slaughter nearly three-quarters of its population before riding off with every scrap of gold and silver they could find.

'I myself managed to evade their murderous attention by hiding in the palace dung-heap while the king avoided capture by concealing himself inside a secret vault beneath the royal bedchamber. Once he was sure the Aspirinian horde had departed, he emerged from his hiding place and immediately summoned "the useless idiot of a so-called bloody soothsayer" to his presence. I assumed he probably meant me, so I dutifully — but bum-squeakingly — attended him in the throne room to learn the precise nature of the terrible and agonising death which no doubt awaited me.

'Perhaps with some justification, the king was in a right royal rage and blamed me and me alone for the fact that he'd lost half his city and three-quarters of its population. To be perfectly honest, I thought he was pushing it to claim that it was *entirely* my fault, but I was hardly in a position to argue. Fortunately, however, King Eupolos had inherited none of the vicious bastard tendencies of his predecessor, King Moros, so instead of having me boiled alive in vinegar or torn apart by wild horses, he banished me from the city to live out the rest of my days in extreme poverty and abject hermitry.

'And that, folks, is how I ended up living in a cave in this gods-forsaken wilderness and dressed only in a tattered loincloth that hasn't seen the inside of a washing machine for many a long year — if ever.'

And it was at this precise moment when Thestor finished his tale that Horace, Norwood, Vesta and Zoot took yet another sip of his home-concocted-but-not-at-all-unpleasant liquid refreshment and instantly lapsed into a state of deep unconsciousness.

18

The interview room was small and windowless and a tribute to minimalism, furnished only with a table, set at right-angles halfway along one wall, with two chairs on either side of it. DCI Harper Collins and DS Maurice Scatterthwaite were sitting next to each other and staring at the hooded man opposite them — the monk that Scatterthwaite had knocked out at the grubby little café a couple of hours earlier.

Once he'd regained consciousness, they'd taken him to the nearest hospital, where it was diagnosed that his injuries were nothing more serious than an impressively large bump on the forehead and a broken nose. But they were serious enough as far as Harper was concerned. The monk would be perfectly within his rights to press charges, and not only could she do without the extra hassle right now, it wasn't hard to imagine what Superintendent Leopold's reaction would be when he picked up his newspaper and read the banner headline: "COPS BEAT UP HOLY MAN" or "IS POLICE BRUTALITY BECOMING A HABIT?".

So far, though, the monk hadn't even mentioned the possibility of pressing charges. In fact, he hadn't said a single word about anything. Not a word. From the moment he'd come round at the café, all they'd got out of him was the occasional grunt or groan, and even these were few and far between apart from when he was having his nose repositioned at the hospital. As soon as he'd been patched up, Harper had politely asked him if he wouldn't mind accompanying them back to the police station, and he'd nodded his agreement. The fact that he wasn't wearing Union Jack flip-flops was hardly proof of his innocence of course, but she had one of her gut instincts that he wasn't a killer, and her gut instincts had rarely let her down before. On the other hand, taking him in for questioning had meant that she'd got Leopold off her back for the time being at least, since he could now tell his imminent press conference that they were currently interviewing a potential suspect.

But if she was right that the monk really was innocent, she needed to soft-soap him into abandoning any thoughts he might have about making an official complaint. To this end, she'd made sure he was kept well supplied with hot, sweet tea and chocolate Hobnobs despite Scatterthwaite's insistence that scaring the shit out of the guy with a variety of unpleasant threats would be a far more effective strategy for ensuring his silence. But even with Harper's infinitely less draconian approach, the monk's silence was exactly what they'd got.

Harper checked her watch. Nearly fifteen minutes in the interview room, and they still hadn't had a peep out of him. She'd kept her questions light and straightforward, assuring him at frequent intervals that he wasn't facing any charges and he was only there to help with their enquiries, but he hadn't so much as told them his name or even if he preferred his Hobnobs to be milk or plain chocolate. Hedging her bets, she'd ordered a PC to fetch a packet of each, but the monk hadn't touched either of them. Scatterthwaite, however, had already polished off half of the milk chocolate packet and was just starting to get stuck into the plain.

'You know what I really like?' he said.

Harper couldn't have cared less what he liked, but she knew he was going to tell her anyway. Scatterthwaite abhorred a silence like Nature abhors a vacuum.

'What I really like,' he went on through a mouthful of plain chocolate Hobnob, 'is when you get a couple of these and you put a Rich Tea biscuit in between. Like a Rich Tea chocolate Hobnob sandwich, yeah?'

'Perhaps you'd like to pop out and get a packet of Rich Tea then,' said Harper, partly regretting she'd said anything which might encourage him to continue with his moronic babbling and partly almost wishing he'd fail to spot the sarcasm in her tone and really would bugger off out to the shops.

'Yeah?' he said, scraping back his chair and getting to his feet. 'I might as well, I s'pose. I mean there's naff all happening here, is there?'

Harper bit her lip. It was so tempting to let him go, but then why should he be the one to go off on a jolly when it was entirely down to him that the monk was here in the first place?

'Sit,' she said, clearly enunciating the word as if she were training a dog — which, in a sense, she was.

'Uh?' Scatterthwaite was clearly struggling to make sense of even this simple command but finally cottoned on and slumped back down onto his chair.

'Waste of time if you ask me,' he said and helped himself to a couple more Hobnobs.

'I didn't,' said Harper, aware of the sulky pout from his voice alone and a marked increase in the volume and rapidity of his chomping. Weirdly enough, it was almost a welcome relief from the otherwise deathly silence in the room, and she had to admit he was right about something. This was indeed a complete waste of time. She checked her watch again. Another five minutes and she'd let the monk go. — Let him go? The guy could walk out of there whenever he liked, but she'd rather hoped to have at least found out where he lived so that one of the uniforms could give him a lift home. But unless he told them where, that particular element of the soft-soap routine was a non-starter.

She eased herself down in her chair by a couple of inches to try and sneak a better look at his face, which was almost totally obscured by the downward tilt of his head and the dark shadow cast by the overhang of his cowl. Apart from a bushy, black beard and a splash of white from the dressing over his nose, there was nothing to be seen. But maybe that was odd in itself. Almost as if he was deliberately keeping his features hidden. Had she been too hasty in relying on her gut instinct and assuming his innocence purely on the grounds that he wasn't wearing Union Jack flip-flops? And what about his silence? In her experience, keeping shtum was a fairly good indication that a suspect was guilty, so why did this monk insist on keeping his trap shut when he hadn't even been accused of anything? Why didn't he just— Hang on a minute. "Trap" — "monk" — Trappist monk? Vow of silence? Oh Jesus.

Harper leaned forward and rapped her knuckles on the table to attract his attention. The monk lifted his head by the merest of fractions, and from her lowered position, she was just able to make out his eyes. It was impossible to see them clearly in the deep shadow of his cowl, however, so she couldn't even tell what colour they were, never mind read his expression.

'You're not a Trappist, are you?' she said.

A barely perceptible shake of the head.

'Some other order that takes a vow of silence then?'

This time, the monk reacted like one of those nodding dogs in the back window of a car, and Harper thought she detected the trace of a smile. She sat back and, remembering the need for the softly-softly approach, suppressed an urge to shout "Why the bloody hell didn't you say so before?". Well, not "say" of course, but surely he could have mimed something or written it down somewhere. Preferably, he should have had some kind of ID card like those deaf people who come knocking on your door, selling dishcloths and tea towels and whatnot.

She snatched the notepad and pen from in front of Scatterthwaite and pushed it across the table towards the monk. 'You are allowed to write, I suppose?'

Another nod, but with considerably less enthusiasm.

'Could you write down your name for me then?'

The monk picked up the pen and held it close to his face, turning it this way and that while he appeared to examine it for a full five seconds before smoothing the top sheet of paper with the edge of his hand. Then he rolled up the sleeves of his habit and bent low over the notepad as he began to write. At least, that's what Harper assumed he was doing since his cowl had fallen so far forward, the pad was completely obscured from view.

'Why didn't he just *say* he couldn't speak instead of wasting all this time?' said Scatterthwaite, bringing the side of his head down almost to the level of the tabletop to try and get a look at what the monk was writing. 'Can't understand all this vow of silence business though, can you? I mean, what's the point? I suppose it's *possible* that God might be able to hear you when you're prayin' inside your head, like, but what about all the hymn singin' and that? How'd they go on about that, eh? Just stand there miming or what?'

He took another couple of Hobnobs from the plain chocolate packet and added, 'Can't imagine doing that meself. Takin' a vow of silence? No chance.'

'Pity,' said Harper, beginning to wonder what was taking the monk quite so long to write his name.

'Must be a bloody long name,' said Scatterthwaite as if reading her thoughts.

Once again, Harper leaned forward and rapped on the table. 'May I see what you've written?'

The monk hesitated and then slid the notepad towards her. She turned it the right way round, and all that was on it was a very elaborate "B", decorated with half a dozen flowers weaving in and out of the two loops of the letter.

'Yes, that's very nice,' said Harper, 'but we're a bit pushed for time, so do you think we could skip the fancy calligraphy stuff for now and hurry things along a little?'

Another hesitation before the monk took back the notepad, scribbled furiously and passed it back to her.

'Brother Bernard?' said Harper, squinting to interpret the spidery scrawl, which was in extraordinarily stark contrast to the ornately detailed "B".

She took his failure to respond as confirmation and asked him to write down what monastic order he belonged to, where he lived and what his movements were around the times of the murders.

According to what he wrote, this was his first visit into town in over a month and he'd only come in today to run a couple of errands for the monastery, which was about five miles out in the sticks.

She'd have to check his story of course, but in the meantime, there was no reason to detain him any longer. Besides, he'd shown no indication that he wanted to make a complaint about Scatterthwaite's assault, so Harper wanted him out of there before he changed his mind. Getting Scatterthwaite to apologise to the monk was a battle she could have done without, but when she eventually dragged it out of him, she told him to arrange for a car to take Brother Bernard back to his monastery.

Alone in the interview room, Harper's gaze drifted towards the monk's scribblings on the notepad while she contemplated her next move. Amazing how different his almost illegible handwriting was compared to the meticulously ornamented "B" with its interwoven flowers and the— She turned the pad through ninety degrees so that the letter lay on its back with the two loops uppermost. Was it her imagination or did that look a lot like a couple of snails humping?

19

When Horace, Vesta, Norwood and Zoot had all regained consciousness, it was early morning and their host was nowhere to be seen. This was of some moderate concern to the adventurers, but far more disturbing was the realisation that their hands and feet had been tied together with thin strips of animal hide.

Horace shifted his weight from his left buttock to his right and then back again to try and gain some relief from the numbness inflicted by the hard stone floor of the cave.

'I'll have to have words with your uncle the next time I see him,' he said.

'Words?' said Vesta. 'What kind of words?'

'Harsh ones, I'm afraid.'

'Oh, he won't like that at all.'

Horace shuffled round to face her, or at least as far as his bound hands and feet would allow him. '"Without risk of personal physical harm". It was a condition that I clearly stipulated in my advertisement.'

'It's not so bad,' said Norwood. 'A soft, fluffy cushion wouldn't go amiss, and my wrists and ankles are chafing a bit from the strips of animal hide being rather too tight, but other than that, it could be an awful lot worse.'

'I'm not just talking about chafed wrists and numb bums, Norwood. I'm talking about whatever horrors this Ancient Greek fellow might have in mind for us whenever he gets back from wherever he's gone.'

Zoot was the last to regain consciousness and, failing

to register that his front and back paws were bound together, attempted to stand but abruptly fell over again with a whimper of complaint.

'I hardly think we can blame Vesta's uncle,' said Norwood. 'After all, he couldn't have predicted that we would—'

'Ah, so you're awake at last, are you?' interrupted Thestor, their erstwhile host and current captor, in an annoyingly chirpy tone.

The adventurers swivelled their heads to see him silhouetted against the bright sunlight in the mouth of the cave. He was carrying something glinty, but it was impossible to tell what it was until he took a few steps inside, at which point it became abundantly clear that it was an enormous, double-headed axe.

'What's that for?' said Horace, trying to suppress the wobbliness in his voice but not doing a very good job of it.

'Breakfast,' said Thestor. 'I'm absolutely starving.'

'You're going to eat an axe for breakfast?' said Norwood.

Thestor threw back his head and laughed a laugh which, as Horace silently observed, was not without a hint of the demonic.

'Dear me, no,' he said when he'd calmed himself down sufficiently to speak. 'Something much tastier than that.'

So saying, he looked at each of the adventurers in turn with a leery sort of grin that also had a touch of the demonic about it.

'Oh my God,' Vesta whispered hoarsely. 'He's going to eat us.'

'So who'd like to give me a hand?' said the Ancient Greek, rather disturbingly running his thumb across the blade of the axe to test its sharpness.

'And he's going to start with our *hands*,' Norwood croaked, his eyeballs popping, and he pressed his back as hard as he could against the wall of the cave as if he were attempting to force himself through it.

'Now, look here,' said Horace, deciding that the prospect of ending his life being slowly dissolved in the old man's gastric juices was impetus enough to start getting assertive. 'I'd always believed that you Ancient Greeks were a civilised lot, and I certainly had no idea that you ever resorted to this kind of behaviour.'

'Eating breakfast?'

'Eating *people*.'

Thestor stared at him for several seconds. Then he stared down at the axe. Then he stared back at Horace again before tossing back his mane of straggly grey hair and letting rip with a guffaw of laughter, which, mercifully on this occasion, had scarcely a whiff of the demonic about it at all.

This time, he didn't bother to calm himself down before starting to speak, which was a pity because it was really quite hard to understand what he was saying through all the spluttering. The gist, however, appeared to be that he was not — nor never had been — of the cannibalistic persuasion, and it was a source of great amusement to him that the adventurers should have thought that he was about to cut them up and eat them. On the contrary, there had been a gross and highly regrettable misunderstanding, which had been caused in no small part by an unfortunate ambiguity of language. What he had intended to convey was that he had been out hunting and had returned with a carcass that was far too large to fit onto his meagre spit. Accordingly, he had fetched his axe in order to cut the meat into more manageable proportions, and as for his reference to someone giving him a hand, this was simply a request for assistance in carrying out the task.

'That's all very well,' said Horace in the belief that it would be premature to relinquish the high-horsey approach just yet, 'but how were we supposed to help you with our hands and feet tied?'

'Well, obviously I would have untied you first. In fact, I can untie you all now if you like.'

'Excellent,' said Norwood and stretched his bound wrists out in front of him.

Thestor came towards him with the enormous, double-headed axe.

'Er, you wouldn't happen to have anything a little smaller, would you?' said Norwood, attempting to push himself even further back into the cave wall.

'Good thinking,' said Thestor, and he set down the axe and took a vicious-looking hunting knife from somewhere within the folds of his tattered loincloth.

'That looks rather dangerous,' said Vesta.

Thestor examined the blade of his knife. 'Not as dangerous as the axe, I think.'

'No, I meant keeping it... you know... down there.'

Vesta nodded somewhat coyly in the general direction of his loincloth, and Thestor grinned.

'I'm very careful how I sit down,' he said and proceeded to cut through the strip of animal hide around Norwood's wrists.

'So how come you tied us up in the first place if you're just going to cut us free now?' said Horace.

'Only because I didn't want you disappearing off while I was out hunting. You'd have missed breakfast otherwise.'

'Very thoughtful of you,' said Vesta. 'But what about knocking us all out with your home-concocted-but-not-at-all-unpleasant liquid refreshment?'

'Ah yes, I'm sorry about that,' said Thestor, handing Norwood the hunting knife so he could cut the animal hide around his ankles himself. 'I tend to forget quite how potent it is when you're not used to it.'

'So it was never your intention to render us incapable and keep us as your prisoners?' said Horace.

Thestor clapped a grubby, bony hand to his grubby, bony ribcage in the approximate position of his heart. 'May the gods strike me down, disembowel me and hold up my steaming entrails before my dying eyes.'

'I'll take that as a "no" then, shall I?'

'Although...'

'Although what?'

'Well,' said Thestor with a glimmer of contrition, 'apart from not wanting you to miss breakfast, there was one teeny-tiny matter I wanted to have a little chat with you about before you left.'

Horace, Norwood and Vesta raised an eyebrow each, and Zoot rolled himself onto his feet and immediately fell over again.

'A sort of proposition, as you might say.'

Horace, Norwood and Vesta lowered their eyebrows and raised their other ones instead. Zoot stayed where he was, lying on his side and panting heavily from his latest exertion.

'The thing is, I was wondering if we might be able to help each other out in some way,' Thestor went on. 'A kind of quid pro quo arrangement, if you follow my Latin.'

'Explain,' said Horace.

'Quid pro quo? It means that—'

'Yes, I *am* familiar with the term,' Horace snapped. 'I mean what is it that you have in mind?'

Apparently, Thestor didn't appreciate being snapped at because he gave Horace quite a grumpy look before launching into his explanation.

'I believe I already mentioned that you're not the first time travellers to have passed this way,' he said, 'and in my experience, none of them travel through time for the sole purpose of broadening their minds. They've all been after something of a more material nature, and I'd hazard a guess that you people are no different.'

He paused for effect, and the effect was that the adventurers exchanged furtive glances while Horace — and very probably Vesta and Norwood, although perhaps not Zoot — wondered if the old man was much better at reading thoughts than predicting the future. Either way, none of them said a word, and they all waited for Thestor to get on with his explanation, which he did by jumping ahead to the what-was-in-it-for-him part of the proposition.

In short, he was fed up to what remained of his back teeth with his life as a hermit and with living in a cave in a gods-forsaken wilderness, dressed only in a tattered loincloth. He was desperate to return to the royal court, and now that King Eupolos the Underwhelming had died in a bizarre orgy accident, he saw his chance to worm his way back in and be reinstated as a royal soothsayer. The new king, Amnestios the Lenient, had — perhaps not surprisingly, given his name — built up a reputation for leniency during the few short weeks of his reign and had already pardoned dozens of those who had been banished, incarcerated and/or boiled alive in vinegar by his predecessors. But Thestor wasn't content with simply being allowed back to live in what was left of the city after its sacking by the Aspirinians. He wanted his old job back and all the perks and privileges that went with it.

'And that's where you come in,' he said.

'We do?' said Vesta, who, along with Horace and Zoot, had now been freed from her bonds by Norwood and the hunting knife.

'I need to curry favour with the new king, you see.'

Horace wondered if curry had actually been invented by 1323 BC, and if it had, whether the Ancient Greeks would have known about it, but he let the matter pass.

'I need to convince him of my amazing abilities as a soothsayer,' Thestor continued. 'Make prophecies that actually come true for a change, and since you people *know* what happens in the future, you can give me all sorts of stuff I can predict.'

'We can?' said Norwood.

'It would have to be things that will happen very soon of course. Other time travellers who've come this way have told me about lots of things that happen in the future, but they've all been hundreds of years from now, so they're no good to me as prophecies because no-one can know whether I'm right about them or not. If I'm to impress the king, I really need you to tell me things that are going to happen in the next few days.'

'That's very specific,' said Horace. 'I mean, this is 1323 BC, and not even Wiki is that precise about dates when it's this far back in history.'

'Wiki?' said Thestor.

Horace briefly outlined the wonders of Wikipedia, which inevitably led on to succinct descriptions of Google, the Internet and all manner of other technological innovations, including, somewhat tangentially, the popularity of the Moog synthesiser among various rock bands of the 1970s.

'This is all very fascinating,' said Thestor an hour and a half later, 'but I could really do with something a bit closer to the here and now if you can manage it.'

Horace scratched his head and so did Vesta and Norwood. (Their own heads, that is, and not Horace's.) Zoot licked his unmentionables. (Most definitely his own and not Horace's.)

'Like I said,' said Horace. 'It's not that easy, I'm afraid. We'll have to give it some serious thought.'

'Perhaps a spot of breakfast might help?' said Norwood, the question in his tone adding a little more weight to the already heavy hint.

Thestor clapped a grubby, bony hand to his grubby forehead. 'By all the gods, I completely forgot. What a terrible host you must think me. But if one of you could help me cut up the... the... Well, to be perfectly honest, I'm not at all sure what kind of beast it is, but it's certainly big.'

So saying, he picked up his enormous, double-headed axe and shuffled out of the cave, closely followed by an obliging and very hungry Norwood Junction and a probably equally ravenous Zoot.

Their exit was even more closely followed by a bellowing roar, which sounded not at all unlike a distressed and very angry animal of about the size of an adult hippopotamus, and the rapid reappearance of Zoot, his eyes wide and his tail firmly between his legs.

'It would appear that our breakfast isn't quite dead after all,' said Horace.

20

If anyone coming out of Thestor's cave had bothered to look in the approximate direction east, fourteen degrees south, they would have seen nothing but the same barren, rocky landscape and occasional lonely shrub that were visible in every direction, including that one. However, a passing bird — if it had bothered to look down — might well have spotted two off-grey shapes lying flat on the ground and about fifty yards from the cave's entrance. And if it had bothered to swoop earthward to make a closer inspection, the bird would have realised that each of these shapes was in fact a human being, clad in an off-grey monk's habit with the hood concealing the whole of the back of its head. Hopping round to the front of them, the bird would have observed from what little was visible of their faces that one was male and the other female — if indeed the bird had the ability to distinguish between human genders, which is admittedly doubtful.

One thing that the bird would definitely not have known was that the male was called Brother Herring and the female, Brother Mackerel. Also unknown to the bird would be that their reason for lying face down behind a low rock was to avoid being seen from the cave whilst having a perfect view of its entrance themselves.

'How's the neck?' said Brother Herring.

'Better, thanks,' said Brother Mackerel. 'Got a bit of whiplash from the landing, that's all.'

'Yes, I'm sorry about that. I've only ever time-travelled on *Hawking 2* before. This new model's going to take some getting used to.'

'Quite a comfy ride though. Considering.'

Brother Herring raised an eyebrow, which was meant to convey a question along the lines of "Considering what?", but Brother Mackerel failed to spot it on account of the heavy shadow cast by Herring's cowl that obscured almost all of his face. So, after waiting fruitlessly for a response for several seconds, he tried the verbal communication approach and said, 'Considering what?'

'How far we've come,' said Mackerel. '1323 BC according to the annometer, so that's... three thousand, three hundred and thirty-eight years.'

'Yeah, I know. Long way to come for a few snails, isn't it?'

'Not just any old snails, Brother Herring.'

'No, of course not.'

'Snails which possess the secret of eternal youth.'

'Yes, quite,' Brother Herring agreed, and the two monks fell into silence until Brother Mackerel said, 'Incidentally...'

'Yes?'

'Is it okay if we drop the "Brother" bit? Now that it's only the two of us, I mean.'

Brother Herring thought about it, but before he'd finished thinking, Brother Mackerel said, 'Makes me a bit... uncomfortable, you know?'

'On account of you being a woman, you mean?'

'Well, yes, it does rather. I know it's a rule of the Society and all that, and don't get me wrong, I think it's great that women are even allowed to join, and I'm really grateful for that, but I still feel a bit... you know.'

'Uncomfortable about being called "Brother" when you are in fact a woman.'

'Yes.'

Brother Mackerel thought about it some more and then said, 'Okay then, but it'll have to be our secret, yeah?'

'Of course,' said the monk formerly known as "Brother Mackerel", and Brother Herring detected a definite smile in her voice.

Another silence descended, during which Mackerel fell into a deep sleep until Herring woke her up, saying, 'Wake up, Mackerel. Something's happening.'

The "something" in question was the appearance from inside the cave of a bony old man dressed only in a tattered loincloth, a chunky-looking black dog and an improbably tall, bald man wearing a camel hair duffel coat that was about three sizes too small for him. As soon as they'd stepped out of the cave, the old man went over to what appeared to be a large, black rock and prodded it with the handle of an enormous, double-headed axe. Judging by the mighty roar which emanated from the rock, it wasn't a rock at all but some kind of living creature that wasn't happy about being prodded with an axe handle — or probably any other implement handle for that matter.

The bony old man jumped back, and the creature reared up on the hindmost pair of its six legs. Apart from the extra legs and what appeared to be the neck and head of a goat growing out of the middle of its back, the creature looked not unlike a heavily maned lion of about the size of an adult hippopotamus. Its front four sets of massive claws thrashed at the air, and the bright sunlight glared off the dazzling white of its fangs as it blasted out its bellowing rage. A second later, the beast swiped at the bony old man and swept him high off the ground, dangling him by his tattered loincloth little more than a foot above its gnashing teeth.

'Rather him than me,' said Brother Mackerel.

'Quite,' said Brother Herring.

21

'So I says, "Constable," I says. "If you wanna make it as a detective, you gotta know one thing, and that's this. Once you've got a suspect in custody and they decide to clam up on you, get 'em down to the cells quick as you can and well out of the way of all that video and tape-recording nonsense. That's where the real detective work's done," I says. And d'you know what he says to me, this wet-behind-the-ears plod of a constable? Only starts bangin' on about human bloody rights violations and all that code of ethics bullshit. I mean, I ask you, there I am trying to give the little toerag a bit of friendly advice and...'

DS Scatterthwaite continued his mindless chuntering while Harper Collins attempted — but ultimately failed — to block the noise from entering her consciousness. The only respites she'd had during the last hour and a half were when Scatterthwaite had briefly paused to bite off another chunk of pie, cake, sandwich or whatever else he happened to be stuffing his face with at the time. By rights, someone of her rank shouldn't have had to be doing surveillance work at all, but Superintendent Leopold had been adamant that he couldn't spare any more officers for the job. Three squad cars were all she'd asked for, but he'd point blank refused to give her any more than two. And this was the man who'd been breathing fire down her neck to "get a result pretty damn sharpish or I'll have your guts for garters".

Harper had argued that this was the perfect

opportunity to catch the murderer — or murderers — since all of the victims so far had met their deaths on their seventieth birthdays and all but one lived on their own, and on this particular day, there were only three such potential victims within an area of about ten square miles. But the superintendent still hadn't budged, which was why Harper was now sitting in an unmarked car thirty yards down the street from one of the three addresses with Scatterthwaite annoying the hell out of her — as usual.

She was well aware of course that, over and above Leopold's innate pig-headedness, there'd been another reason for his refusal. Sheer blistering fury at having been made to look an utter fool over his precious press conference. Minutes after he'd left the room, and having told the assembled hacks that a suspect was being interviewed at that very moment, he'd discovered that Harper had released the monk without charge. Her gut instinct had been right, however, and Brother Bernard's alibi that he hadn't left his monastery at the times of the murders had been confirmed by none other than the abbot himself and half a dozen other senior monks — none of whom had been wearing Union Jack flip-flops.

'Run the details by me again,' she said, not because she didn't know them already but because it was the only way she could think of to interrupt the constant flow of idiotic chatter that was pouring out of Scatterthwaite's pie-hole.

'What?' said Scatterthwaite, clearly unhappy at having his monologue on "How to Be a Great Detective" so abruptly curtailed.

'The subject?' said Harper. 'The potential victim?'

Scatterthwaite made a big show of flipping open the notebook on his lap. 'Howard Peter Ledley. Age, sixty-nine. Address—'

'Seventy today, I think you'll find.'

There was a brief pause while Scatterthwaite processed the relevance of this information, and then he said, 'Oh yes' and got as far as 'Address, twenty-seven, Brooke—' before Harper interrupted him again.

'That house right over there in fact,' she said, pointing through the rain-smeared windscreen at the two-up-two-down terraced house they'd been watching for the past ninety minutes.

Scatterthwaite followed the direction of her finger and gave a chuckle of what might have been embarrassment except that he didn't really *do* embarrassment.

'Oh yes,' he said again and pulled a King Size Twix from his jacket pocket. 'You want a finger?'

'Pardon?'

'Twix,' he said, waving the gold and red packet in front of her as a visual clue. 'There's two fingers in every packet.'

'Really?' said Harper, packing as much feigned amazement into the word as she could.

'It's one of the things I like about a Twix. You can have one finger and then—'

'No thanks.'

'Diet, is it?' said Scatterthwaite, ripping open the packet with his teeth. 'You women and your figures, eh? I was reading this article the other day when I was at the dentist. Blimey, that was a session, I can tell you. Bloody root canal. Nightmare. Anyway, what it said in this article was that most women...'

And as he launched into a detailed and utterly misinformed analysis of female eating disorders, Harper spotted a figure at the far end of the otherwise empty street, and it was coming in their direction.

'Does that look like a monk to you?' she said, speaking more to herself than seeking confirmation from Scatterthwaite.

But he responded anyway by turning on the ignition

and giving the windscreen wipers a dab.

'Could be,' he said, leaning forward and peering through the early morning drizzle.

Harper felt her body tense as the figure came steadily closer, but it was evidently in no great hurry to get where it was going. Definitely a monk's habit, but the figure was still too far away to make out what it was wearing on its feet. There was no way Harper was about to make the same mistake twice.

'This might well be our man,' she said.

'Shall we grab him then?'

'No, Sergeant, we don't "grab him". We sit tight for now and see what happens.'

And what happened was that the monk appeared to be checking house numbers as he continued along the terraced street and then came to a halt in front of number twenty-seven. Swinging open the low wooden gate, he took the few short paces to the front door and stooped in front of it. Presumably pushing something through the letterbox, Harper thought, and if her suspicions were correct, it was a card wishing the occupant a happy seventieth — or last — birthday.

The monk stood upright and retraced his steps to the gate, which he left hanging open, and then carried on down the street in the same direction as before. As he passed their car on the opposite side of the road, Harper eased herself lower in her seat and focused hard on his feet, but the habit was too long for her to catch more than an occasional glimpse. She was almost certain, though, that there was a flash of red and possibly blue.

'We just gonna let him get away?' said Scatterthwaite.

'The last time I checked, it wasn't actually a crime for monks to deliver birthday cards.'

'Yes, but—'

'If I'm right, he'll be back soon enough, and I'll be inside waiting for him,' said Harper and opened the passenger door.

'So what do I do?'

'Keep watching and be ready to dive in when I call you.'

'Call me?'

Harper waved her walkie-talkie at him, then closed the door and hurried off across the street. The last thing she wanted was for the birthday boy to have passed out before he had a chance to let her into the house.

22

Horace raced out of the cave, closely followed by Vesta, to see a hippopotamus-sized creature with six legs rearing up on the hindmost pair and dangling Thestor by his tattered loincloth less than a foot above its gnashing fangs.

'I really don't want to be around if that loincloth comes off,' Vesta whispered.

'Me neither,' said Horace.

Thestor was screaming for help, and Norwood was staring up at the beast and ineffectually shouting, 'Put him down. Put him down this instant. Do you hear me?'

'He prod me with stick, I eat him,' roared the creature from its lion-like head.

'But there's no meat on me,' said Thestor. 'It'd hardly be worth the bother.'

'That's okay,' said the lion-head. 'I've already had breakfast, so I only need a snackette.'

'Fair's fair,' said the goat, whose head and neck seemed to grow out of the middle of the creature's back. 'You were going to kill *us* with that double-headed axe thing.'

'No, I wasn't,' said Thestor. 'I was trying to find my breakfast, and I thought you were lying on top of it.'

'What did it look like?' bleated the goat.

'What did what look like?'

'Your breakfast.'

Thestor made an attempt at a shrug, but it wasn't a gesture that was easy to achieve from his present position of being dangled several feet in the air by his loincloth. 'Four legs. Bit of a tail. Deer sort of thing.'

'That's rather a vague description, isn't it?'

Thestor stopped wriggling for a moment while he thought about it and then said, 'You ate it, didn't you?'

'Not me. I'm a herbivore,' said the goat and jerked its head towards the lion-like head at the front. 'She's your meat eater.'

The lion-head twisted round to glare at the goat. 'Oh, that's right. Grass me up as usual, why don't you?'

The goat rolled its slit-pupilled eyes. 'I hardly think Mr Bag O'Bones here is in any position to beat you up over it.'

'That's not the point. You know very well you're always trying to drop me in it every chance you get.'

'Not listening,' said the goat in a singsong kind of voice, turning its head away and closing its eyes tight shut.

'Oh, and when did you *ever* listen to anything I said?'

The lion-head then launched into a scathing diatribe which largely consisted of a list of occasions when the goat had grassed her up, dropped her in it, or otherwise got up her nose. Fortunately for Thestor, she was unable to talk and gnash at the same time, and not only that, but it seemed she'd forgotten his very existence and, inch by inch, he was being lowered back down to the ground.

'And what exactly do you contribute to this relationship, eh?' the lion-head was saying. 'Nothing. That's what. Doodly squat. All you ever do is moan and complain all day long and get me to stand under some damned tree or other so you can gorge your stupid goat face with leaves for hours on end.'

By now, Thestor's feet were almost within tiptoe reach of the earth, but at that very moment, the lion-head whipped round and shot him a look of venomous fury.

'And where do you think you're going?' she roared.

Thestor ignored what was undoubtedly a rhetorical question anyway, and instead, he stared with knotted brows at the enormous fleshy pad of the beast's offside middle paw.

'I'll bet that hurts,' he said.

'What does?'

'That paw. Is it supposed to be green like that?'

The lion-head let out a sigh so powerful that Horace, Norwood and Vesta were nearly knocked off their feet by the blast.

'It's infected,' she said. 'Hurts like ruddy Hades if you must know.'

Thestor brought his face to within a foot of the paw to examine it more closely. 'Looks like you've got something stuck in it. Some kind of... piece of bone maybe?'

'How do I know what it is?' snapped the lion-head. 'All I know is it's been stuck in there for weeks, and if I put any pressure on it at all, the pain is excruciating. If I didn't have five other legs, I'd fall over every time I tried to walk. Course, goat-face back there doesn't feel a damn thing. Different pain receptors or somesuch. I dread to think how much moaning and whining I'd have to put up with if—'

'I think I might have some balm for that,' Thestor interrupted.

'Some what?'

'Balm. It's a sort of ointment that will clear up the infection and ease the pain.'

The lion-head paused while she considered the prospect. 'Won't get rid of the goat as well, will it?'

'I'm afraid not,' said Thestor, 'but we'll also need to get that bone out somehow.'

The heavy frown which accompanied the "somehow" was a clear indication that removing the deeply embedded piece of bone from the creature's paw was going to be a far trickier operation than simply slapping on a load of ointment. Horace, Norwood and Vesta exchanged glances, and as soon as they'd finished, they all took a step forward.

'I think we might be able to offer some assistance in that department,' said Norwood as each of them brandished a very shiny and absolutely-top-of-the-range Swiss Army knife (all supplied by Mr Wellwisher as a perk of their employment).

Of Thestor, the lion-head and the goat, only the goat failed to gaze upon the multi-tool device in awe and wonder because he'd fallen asleep and was snoring loudly.

'These are absolutely-top-of-the-range models of the Swiss Army knife,' Horace announced, 'and are therefore equipped with a multitudinous array of handy little tools and gadgets, including one for extracting fragments of bone from the paw of a... a, er...'

161

Horace wasn't at all sure what name to give the creature in front of him, but of all the handy little tools for removing foreign objects from the paws of a whole range of animals, he was certain that at least one of them would do the job perfectly.

'Well,' said Norwood helpfully, 'even though there may not be a handy little tool or gadget for removing fragments of bone from the paw of a mythological beast *per se*, I'm confident that—'

'Hey,' interrupted the lion-head. 'Who are you calling "mythological"? You see me, don't you? With your own eyes? Right here in front of you?'

'Yes, of course, but—'

'Then I can't be mytho-bloody-logical, can I?'

'I'm terribly sorry,' said Norwood. 'I really didn't mean to—'

'And less of the "beast" as well, okay? I'm a Ligoatamos if you insist on calling me anything at all.'

The lion-head must have interpreted the blank-expressioned faces of the adventurers as a sign that further explanation was necessary and added, '"Li" as in lion. "Goat" as in... goat. And "amos" as in size-of-an-adult-hippopotamus except with "os" on the end because this is Greece.'

The etymology of the creature's name now established, Thestor, Horace, Norwood, Vesta and the Ligoatamos all adjourned into the cave so that the operation could be conducted in a marginally more sterile environment. It was agreed — entirely by Thestor himself — that to minimise any pain during the procedure, the Ligoatamos should first drink two earthenware jugs of his home-concocted-but-not-at-all-unpleasant liquid refreshment, and half an hour later, when the Ligoatamos had lapsed into unconsciousness, Norwood set to work with his Swiss Army knife's handy little tool for extracting foreign bodies from the feet of a giraffe. The operation went extremely well, and after the bone fragment had been removed, Thestor applied a generous coating of his "special balm" to the infected area, although as far as Horace, Norwood and Vesta could tell, it looked and smelt exactly the same as the old man's home-concocted-but-not-at-all-unpleasant liquid refreshment.

One unfortunate side-effect of the operation was that, whilst beginning to come round from Thestor's "anaesthetic", the Ligoatamos inadvertently rolled onto her back and irreparably crushed the goat's skull between the hard, stone floor of the cave and her enormous bulk. Upon fully regaining consciousness, however, the Ligoatamos showed little sign of remorse and even wondered aloud why she'd never thought of doing that before.

23

The living room of 27 Brooke Street was immaculately clean and tidy but looked as if nothing had been changed or added in three or more decades. Howard Peter Ledley was similarly immaculate in Tattersall check shirt, green woollen tie and a fully buttoned-up beige cardigan. Scrupulously clean-shaven and with neatly groomed white hair, Harper was sure she'd caught a whiff of Brylcreem as she'd stepped past him into the hallway when he'd eventually allowed her to cross his threshold. He'd been more than a little reluctant at first and had dismissed the notion that he was about to become the next victim of a deranged serial killer as "utter poppycock", but Harper had persevered and finally gained admittance by invoking the old standby, "obstructing the police in the execution of their duty". One concession she did have to make, though, was to take off her shoes as soon as she'd come through the door.

'And you seriously expect me to believe that if I'd opened this, I'd be out cold in seconds?' said Ledley.

'More than likely, yes,' said Harper without turning to face him. She was standing at the bay window at the front of the house, which afforded a clear view of the street in both directions, and she could see his reflection in the glass. He was sitting in a wingbacked armchair by the fireplace and holding a large, pale blue envelope close to his face and examining it with a magnifying glass.

'And I really wouldn't fiddle with it if I were you,' she added.

She watched him put the envelope up to his nose and sniff at it before carefully adding it to the top of a small pile of mail on the coffee table in front of him. At the same moment, a phone began to ring from somewhere out in the hallway. Ledley started to lever himself out of his chair.

'Best let it ring,' said Harper. 'It might be him checking whether you're unconscious yet.'

'Him?'

'The killer.'

'Pah!' said Ledley and collapsed back into the armchair. 'And you're going to protect me when — *if* — this maniac happens to show up, are you?'

'There's another officer in the car outside.'

Ledley grunted. 'Not another *girl*, is it?'

'No, sir, it's a man, and he's built like Sylvester Stallone and has more martial arts black belts than Jet Li and Jackie Chan combined.'

'Oh well, that's something, I suppose,' said Ledley, apparently impervious to her sarcasm.

Harper glanced down the street to see what Rambo Scatterthwaite was up to and wasn't a bit surprised to find that he was stuffing his face with some unidentifiable snack. He was at least looking in her direction, though, and he gave her an exaggerated wave that bordered on camp. Just then, her peripheral vision caught sight of the monk making his way back up the road, about twenty yards or so beyond where Scatterthwaite was parked.

'He's on his way,' she said, stepping back from the window.

'Who? The Stallone chap?'

This time, she turned to look at Ledley directly. 'The serial killer? The one who wants to add you to his list of victims?'

'Pah!'

Harper had already established that the only lockable room in the house was the bathroom upstairs, so she told him to get up there and lock himself in. Grudgingly, he obeyed, and as soon as he'd gone, she took up position behind a drawn-back curtain in the bay window so that she was invisible from the outside but could still keep an eye on what was happening at the front of the house.

As the monk came in through the gate, she focused on his feet, but she still couldn't be sure whether he was wearing Union Jack flip-flops or not. The doorbell chimed a simple "*ding... dong*", and even though she was expecting it, she flinched. A few seconds' pause and then the chime again. Another brief pause before the monk went back out through the gate and turned left up the street. So far, everything was going as Harper had predicted. The monk had rung the bell to check that the intended victim had opened the card and was now unconscious before making his next move. The alternative explanation of course would have been that nobody was home, but presumably this was a possibility the monk was prepared to accept.

Harper and Scatterthwaite had inspected the access to the rear of the house when they'd first arrived and found there was a narrow lane running the length of the terrace, which was backed onto by another row of houses. The lane was linked to the street by a series of pedestrian alleyways, regularly spaced after every tenth house, and there was little doubt that the monk was now on his way to the nearest of them. To make sure Scatterthwaite was still paying attention, Harper called him on her walkie-talkie, and after the initial static and some loud chomping noises, he answered through a mouthful of food.

'Maurice Scatterthwaite, ace detective.'

'Cut the crap, Scatterthwaite. Did you see the monk go down one of the side alleys?'

'Yep.'

'Well, keep watching the house and stay on your toes. He'll be round the back any second now.'

She put the walkie-talkie back in her pocket and hurried out of the living room. The short hallway led to a dining area with a kitchen extension at the back of the house and French windows leading onto a small, neatly kept garden. She crouched down behind the fitted sink unit in the kitchen area and waited, but less than half a minute later, she heard the anticipated rattling of the handle on the French windows. Next came a faint metallic sound, and Harper was in no doubt that the intruder was picking the lock. She felt the blood hammering through her veins and had to remind herself to breathe as the "*click*" of the lock was immediately followed by the slight creak of the French windows being opened. The barely audible slap of rubber flip-flops against bare soles, and the monk came into view. He stopped by the dining table with his back to Harper, but she could see he was wearing a pair of blue, disposable latex gloves and had a small, hessian bag slung over his shoulder. And with a strange mixture of relief and mounting anxiety, she could finally confirm that the flip-flops were very definitely of the Union Jack variety.

'Police!' she shouted, grabbing hold of the overhanging edge of the kitchen worktop and springing to her feet. 'Stay exactly as you are and put your hands behind your back.'

Wishing she'd had the sense to bring a gun with her, she pulled out a pair of handcuffs and took a couple of steps towards the monk. But she came to an abrupt halt when he failed to move so much as a muscle.

'Don't tell me you've taken a vow of deafness as well

as silence,' she said. 'Hands behind your back. Now.'

Still no movement, and Harper was about to issue the command again when the monk very slowly began to move his hands behind his back. Harper stepped forward, ready to snap one half of the cuffs onto his left wrist, but noticed that the voluminous sleeves of his habit had fallen below the tips of his fingers and completely obscured his hands. She reached out to pull up the sleeve, but as she did so, the monk's elbow jerked backwards and caught her a crunching blow to the bridge of her nose. Too dazed to be immediately aware of the pain, she staggered and fell to the floor. The monk turned and headed for the French windows, and Harper made a grab for the hem of his robe. But her grip on the coarse material wasn't strong enough, and he easily wrenched himself free.

By the time Harper had hauled herself upright, the monk was already through the gate at the bottom of the garden. She raced after him, the cold dampness of the grass instantly reminding her that she'd left her shoes behind. Too late to do anything about it now, she reached the narrow lane at the back of the house to find that the monk wasn't as far ahead of her as she'd expected. The flip-flops and the long skirt of his habit, which he held bunched up around his thighs, were clearly not designed for a fast getaway. But, as she quickly discovered, nor were bare feet on an uneven surface of soft mud and rough stone.

As she ran, she pulled out her walkie-talkie and managed to communicate to Scatterthwaite the bare details of what had happened through a series of jolting, breathless phrases and half sentences.

'Get going and... watch he doesn't... come out... side alley... street.'

The jarring motion of her running meant that it was difficult to keep the walkie-talkie close to her ear, so she

168

couldn't be sure what Scatterthwaite was saying in response, but she was almost certain she heard the sound of a car engine starting up. She thrust the walkie-talkie back into her pocket and quickened her pace, aware that she was already gaining on the monk and oblivious to the stabs of pain to the soles of her feet from the occasional sharp stone or shard of broken glass.

For the first time, the monk glanced back over his shoulder, but the shadow cast by the deep cowl of his habit made it impossible to distinguish any of his features. Then he turned down an alleyway on the left, in the opposite direction to where Scatterthwaite should have been looking out for him. Harper took out her walkie-talkie again.

'Parallel street' was all she had the breath to say — or the time. No sooner had she spoken the words and dived into the alleyway behind the monk than she caught a fleeting glimpse of him standing square on in front of her. He was holding something in both hands. A wooden plank?

The end of it hit her full and hard on the forehead, and she crumpled to the ground, instinctively throwing out a hand to clutch at anything that might break her fall. In the moments before she lost consciousness, she realised that she'd caught hold of the monk's shoulder bag, breaking its thin strap and pulling it down with her. She curled herself into a ball, hugging the bag close to her chest as the monk tried to wrest it from her grasp.

'Oi! You!'

The words echoed around her brain as if she were in a long, dark tunnel, and then the darkness faded to black.

24

'So, will you have to change your name now?' Norwood asked the Ligoatamos while she was recuperating from her second operation — the one to remove the now deceased goat from the middle of her back.

'How do you mean?' said the Ligoatamos.

'Well, now that you're minus the goat, I thought perhaps you might want to call yourself Liamos or Lipotamos or something.'

'Not my decision to make, I'm afraid. That's up to the gods who created me. Not that they could care less *what* I was called. As soon as they'd made me, they realised they'd made a big mistake, and I have to say I tend to agree with them. From what I heard, they'd all been drinking heavily, and it was one of those seemed-like-a-good-idea-at-the-time-but-not-so-clever-in-the-cold-light-of-day things, so I was the only Ligoatamos they ever created. End of the line when I'm gone, and I dare say the gods'll breathe a big sigh of relief when that happens. I'm a bit of an embarrassment, you see. Dog with three heads. Flying horse. Half man half bull. At least they make *some* kind of sense. But what use is a six-legged lion the size of a hippopotamus with a goat sticking out of its back?'

Nobody was able to answer this question directly, and the Ligoatamos descended into a gloomy despondency until Horace and his co-adventurers cheered her up by pointing out that the creatures she'd mentioned weren't entirely without design flaws themselves. For instance, a dog with three heads would have to be fed three times as much food and would therefore cost three times as much to keep as a pet than a normal dog. As for the half man half bull, how on earth would he ever find a motorcycle helmet to fit over those massive horns? Admittedly, no-one could come up with anything particularly negative to say about the flying horse, which they all thought seemed to be quite a good idea, but the Ligoatamos conceded that two design fails out of three wasn't bad and got on with her convalescence with a slightly lighter heart.

In fact, so rapid was her recovery that it was little more than a day later when she announced that she was fit enough to leave, and after many expressions of undying gratitude — and apologies to Thestor for almost having eaten him — she went on her way with a cheery wave of four of her six feet and a much happier non-mythological creature than when they'd first met her.

Towards the end of the Ligoatamos's convalescence, Thestor had once again raised the issue of how he might find his way back into royal favour, and Horace, Norwood and Vesta had suggested a variety of plans, but most of these had been abandoned for reasons of total impracticality or just plain silliness — or both. During one of the frequent lulls in this discussion to allow the participants time for quiet cogitation, Vesta had asked Thestor about the "quo" part of the "quid pro quo" that he'd mentioned when he'd first proposed the arrangement.

'Naturally, we'd be delighted to help you in any way we can,' she said, 'but I think what we're all wondering is... Well, what I mean to say is... is...'

'What will you get in return?' Thestor prompted.

Vesta, Horace and Norwood all nodded, but not too vigorously for fear of having their selfless benevolence cast into doubt.

'So tell me how I may be of service,' said Thestor.

The adventurers exchanged a series of glances, the last of which elected Horace as spokesperson.

'Snails,' he said.

'Snails?' Thestor repeated, raising one eyebrow to the very limit of its incredulity scale.

'Not just any old snails though. They have to be of a particular type.'

'You mean like the sort of snails that have hundreds of tiny holes all over their shells and are the main ingredient in a special kind of soup which bestows the gift of eternal youth on any who drink it?'

'That's the one.'

'But how did you know it was that kind of snail we're looking for?' Norwood asked.

Thestor shrugged. 'It's what most of you time traveller types seem to be after.'

'Oh?' said Vesta. 'And did they find any?'

'Oh yes. Loads apparently.'

'So how come there aren't any around in the future — in *our* time? Didn't they bring any back with them?'

'They all died, unfortunately.'

'The snails?' said Norwood.

'The time travellers. Or at least all the ones that were looking for the snails.'

Horace, Norwood and Vesta exchanged another set of glances, but this time they were of the shocked and horrified variety. When they eventually got round to looking back at Thestor, he explained that there was only one place in the whole of Ancient Greece — and as far as he knew, the whole of the Ancient World — where Holey Snails could be found and that they were guarded day and night by three of the most terrifyingly fearsome creatures known to mythology. They were three sisters called Gorgons, and one of them — Medusa — had a mass of writhing, venomous snakes where her hair

172

should have been, and anyone who dared to look at her hideous face was instantly turned to stone.

'So how does anyone know her face is hideous if you can't look at her without being turned to stone?' said Vesta.

'I don't know,' said Thestor, a trifle testily. 'I'm just telling you what I've heard, okay?'

But Horace was less concerned about whether the Gorgon sisters were plug ugly or raving beauties and rather more about their ability to inflict serious physical harm.

'Are you sure that's the only place you can find Holey Snails in Ancient Greece?' he asked.

'Oh yes,' said Thestor. 'You see, the gods are a jealous lot, and there's no way they're going to give up their monopoly on immortality in a hurry, so the last thing they want is for us mortals running around being eternally youthful. That's why they had all the Holey Snails rounded up and put in this one place so the Gorgons could keep an eye on them.'

'So why didn't the gods just destroy all the Holey Snails and have done with it?' said Norwood.

'Search me,' said Thestor. 'Maybe they wanted to keep some for themselves in case their own eternal youth started to get a bit flaky one day.'

'So even if we can get past these Gorgons and grab some of the snails, the gods aren't going to be too chuffed either,' said Horace.

'You kidding?' Thestor chuckled, and then his eyes darted upwards to the roof of the cave and he whispered, 'Between you and me, they're a wrathful bloody bunch. I mean, you wouldn't believe the kind of wrath they can dish out when they've a mind to it. There was this one bloke, for instance, about three hundred years ago. Prometheus, his name was, and all he did was nick a little bit of fire from the sun and give it to the mortals so they could keep themselves warm and have a nice hot dinner now and again. Well, Zeus, the top god, he got himself into a right old rage about it. Fuming, he was. And d'you know what he did?'

Horace, Norwood and Vesta shook their heads.

'He only goes and has this Prometheus chained to a rock way up in the mountains for the rest of his natural, and every day, this bloody great eagle — 'scuse my Latin — this eagle comes down and eats his liver.'

'Every day?' said Vesta.

'Yes, because each night, his liver kind of grew back again, so the whole sorry business could start all over again.'

'Eeeuw. Gross.'

'I'm beginning to wonder if we should maybe try another time period,' said Norwood. 'Holey Snails only became extinct in the twelfth century, so there's plenty to choose from between then and now.'

Horace wasn't at all keen on incurring the wrath of the gods and having his liver eaten on a daily basis, but tearing off into the unknown again quite so soon didn't hold much appeal either. Right now, a bit of judicious procrastination seemed to be the healthiest option.

'Let's not be too hasty, though,' he said. 'Perhaps we should at least check the place out first before we go tearing off into the unknown again quite so soon.' He turned to Thestor. 'Would you be able to take us to where these Holey Snails are?'

The old man's eyes popped. 'Are you out of your mind? I wouldn't go within a thousand leagues of that place for all the loincloths in pre-Christendom.'

'That's a pity,' said Norwood, 'because I think I've just had the most brilliant idea how you could get back into favour with the king.'

25

For once — for the first time ever in fact — Harper was actually grateful to DS Scatterthwaite. He may even have saved her life. Having been thwarted from committing his latest murder, the monk might well have decided that she would have to do instead. Not that she fitted the bill for his usual victims, but he would have had a different motive for killing her. Fear that she'd be able to identify him. As it happened, his face had been constantly in the shadow of his hood, so all Harper had to go on was that he was dressed in an off-grey habit and wore Union Jack flip-flops. But the monk wasn't to know that, and there was a good chance he'd have hedged his bets and finished her off if Scatterthwaite hadn't turned up when he did.

Not surprisingly, the sergeant's act of selfless heroism was already the talk of Nelson Street police station, the details having been lavishly embellished by the hero himself — particularly when describing the incident to the younger, female officers. Harper suspected she'd never get to know the true version of events, but the closest was probably the one he'd told her while she was waiting to have her wounds seen to at the A and E department of the local hospital. Reading between the lines, Scatterthwaite had been driving along the road with the intention of getting to the parallel street in time to cut the monk off as he came out of the alleyway, but he'd glanced down each alley as he went and that was when he'd spotted the monk laying into her with a plank.

175

He'd jumped out of the car and raced down the alley, shouting his head off and...

Well, according to Scatterthwaite, he'd then engaged the monk in life-or-death combat, but since the sergeant didn't have so much as a slight bruise, Harper was more inclined to believe that the monk had simply legged it as soon as he'd heard the shouting. Either way, she'd still thanked Scatterthwaite for his timely intervention, although she'd been careful not to overdo it. The last thing she wanted was for him to start strutting his stuff as her knight in shining armour, so a "Thanks for that" and a cup of tea and a King Size Snickers from the vending machines at the hospital had been more than adequate, she'd thought.

Two hours later, she'd despaired of ever getting any medical attention, so she'd discharged herself — and Scatterthwaite — and picked up some painkillers and a pack of plasters on their way back to the station. Even after swallowing twice the recommended dose of the painkillers, her skull felt like the monk was still whacking away at it with a plank, but at least her nose didn't seem to be broken. That was the good news. The bad news came as soon as she walked through the door of her office. The phone on her desk was already ringing, and she had a sinking, sixth sense feeling that it was going to be Superintendent Leopold.

'What the bloody hell is going on?' he barked before she'd even got the receiver as far as her ear.

'Well, sir, I've just got back from the hospital and—'

'Yes, yes, I know all about that. What I *don't* know is how you managed to make such a godawful cockup. Three poxy addresses you had under surveillance. Nobody shows up at the other two, and the one you're watching, the sodding murderer gets away scot bloody free. Scot. Bloody. Free.'

The throbbing in Harper's brain went into volcanic

176

eruption mode. She'd already established that there was more than one killer, and with only three people having seventieth birthdays that day, it had been odds on that all three would have been targeted. So why the no-show at the other two addresses? One possible explanation was that the monks *had* turned up but had spotted Sergeant Noble and co and decided to make themselves scarce. Not exactly a big surprise since, as she already knew, the words "discreet" and "covert" didn't even exist in Sergeant Noble's vocabulary. Perhaps that was why he and the other officers had been avoiding her calls when she'd been trying to find out whether they'd made any arrests. Not only incompetent but bloody cowards as well.

Harper held the phone further away from her ear to lessen the head-pounding effect of Leopold's ranting, which mercifully ended soon afterwards with some inevitable yelling about getting results "or else" and a loud bang as he slammed his receiver down.

'Bad news?' said Scatterthwaite as he breezed into her office with the self-satisfied smirk of the conquering hero he now believed himself to be.

Harper ignored him and picked up the hessian shoulder bag she'd taken from the monk, then emptied the contents onto her desk. A hypodermic syringe, almost completely full with a colourless liquid. A blackish-red lipstick, presumably for writing the symbols on the victim's chest. A pocket-sized copy of the Bible. Two snail shells, both lying on their sides. Harper brought her eyes down to the level of the desktop to get a closer look. Both shells were occupied, but she couldn't tell whether the snails were alive or dead, so she rolled them both the right way up with the tip of her pen.

'My bet's on the darker one,' said Scatterthwaite.

'What?'

'Put them side by side and we can race them. The one

177

that falls off the edge of the desk first is the winner. Fiver says it's the dark one.'

'I'm not going to do any such thing,' said Harper. 'And if you've got nothing better to do than race snails, you can bag up the rest of this stuff and get it checked for fingerprints. And have whatever's in the syringe analysed while you're at it.'

She took a pair of disposable latex gloves and a batch of clear plastic evidence bags from a drawer in her desk and handed them to Scatterthwaite. With a petulant scowl, he took his time pulling on the gloves while Harper checked inside the hessian bag to make sure she hadn't missed anything. She had. Inside was a folded sheet of A4 paper which had got caught up in the rough material of the bag when she'd tipped it out onto her desk. Taking another pair of gloves from the drawer, she unfolded the paper and read the few lines of print:

"FOR INCLUSION IN NEXT EDITION: TIRED OF SEEING GOD'S WILL FLOUTED? THEN JOIN US ON AN EXCITING SPECIAL CRUSADE. GENDER IMMATERIAL BUT MUST BE FIT AND HEALTHY AS SOME HEAVY LIFTING MAY BE INVOLVED."

There was no address for applicants to reply to, but Harper guessed the monk was planning to take the advertisement to some local newspaper and ask for replies to be sent to one of the paper's own PO boxes.

'Exciting special crusade, eh?' said Scatterthwaite, who had shuffled round behind her and was reading over her shoulder. 'What's that all about then?'

'I'd say our serial killers are looking for new recruits.'

'Yeah?'

It was clear from the inflection in just this one word that Scatterthwaite had no idea what she was talking about, so she swivelled round in her chair to face him.

'We already know that there's more than one killer out there, and if they're intent on murdering everyone with a seventieth birthday, they might be needing a few more. There's one day next week, for instance, when there's nine people turning seventy in this area alone.'

'So there'll be a whole bunch of 'em running amok?'

Harper shrugged. 'Maybe. Or maybe some of them commit more than one murder in a day. Either way, the ad might give us a useful lead, so check out all the local newspapers and find out if any of them are running it. Even if the monk hadn't placed the ad before the attempt on Ledley, he or one of his pals will probably have done it by now.'

'Is that before or after I get all this lot fingerprinted and the syringe analysed?'

'Just get on with it, Sergeant,' said Harper and glanced down at the desktop to see if the snails had shown any signs of life. One hadn't moved at all, but the other — the darker one — had left an inch-long trail of slime behind it.

'And when you've done that,' she added, 'nip to the canteen and fetch me some lettuce.'

Scatterthwaite was almost at the door, and he turned round with a wry smirk. 'Diet again, is it?'

'This one's still alive,' said Harper, ignoring the remark and nodding in the direction of the snail.

'Good thing you didn't take that bet then,' said Scatterthwaite and set off, tunelessly whistling his way along the corridor.

26

Brother Simeon was rushed off his little marmoset feet as he trundled his trolley up and down the surface of the huge mahogany table, trying to keep up with the demands for drinks, snacks and other delicacies from the throng of monks crammed into the subterranean meeting room. The stagnant air was thick with the scent of candle wax and cheese and onion crisps, and the babble of expectant chatter was easily loud enough to drown out the "*squeak squeak*" of the trolley's unoiled wheels. The squeaking became instantly audible, however, when Chairbrother Lemonsole banged his gavel and yelled above the din to call the meeting to order. But before he had a chance to say another word, he saw with a gnawing sense of dread that one of the brethren had his hand thrust high into the air and was clutching a slim sheaf of paper above his hooded head. Even though the shadow cast by the monk's cowl made it impossible to discern any features, Lemonsole could guess it was Brother Anchovy with one of his irritatingly pedantic points of order.

'Point of order, Brother Chairbrother,' said the monk to the accompaniment of assorted moans, groans and jeers from the assembled company.

'Yes, Brother Anchovy? What is it this time?'

'Well, according to our constitution,' said Anchovy, giving the slim sheaf of paper a bit of a flourish for emphasis, 'an emergency meeting can only be called if all members are given a minimum of two days' notice in writing.'

'I am aware of that,' said Lemonsole, 'but when the constitution was first drafted, the extreme... emergenciness of this particular emergency could not possibly have been foreseen.'

'Even so, Brother Chairbrother, this meeting is in direct contravention of the constitution as it stands and, therefore, any decision which arises from it must be deemed not only null but completely void as well. And if I may quote from Article Twelve, Sub-section—'

'No you may not,' Lemonsole interrupted before Anchovy had found the relevant page in the slim sheaf of paper. 'But if it'll make you feel any better, I'll have it minuted that an appropriate amendment to the constitution will be discussed at the next non-emergency meeting.'

This was greeted with several shouts of "Hear hear", "Well said" and "Zip it, Anchovy" while Lemonsole turned to the monk on his right and asked him to record the minute as he had specified. Brother Haddock dutifully dipped his quill pen into a silver inkpot and began scratching at the open page of the leather-bound tome on the table in front of him.

'Happy now?' said Chairbrother Lemonsole, directing the question to Brother Anchovy, but the response was indecipherably muffled within the cavernous depths of his cowl.

Obviously not happy at all, thought Lemonsole, glancing down at the minutes book and realising that he'd be even less happy if he knew what Brother Haddock had entered. Instead of a note about amending the constitution at the next meeting, he'd drawn a rather crude representation of a decapitated fish — presumably an anchovy.

'Very well then,' said Lemonsole, choosing to ignore the blatant misrepresentation. 'As you will all know by now, Brother Carp narrowly escaped capture by the local constabulary earlier today, and I have called this emergency meeting to discuss how such a potential catastrophe might be avoided in future. But first of all, I'd like to call upon Brother Carp for an account of the events which led up to what would undoubtedly have been a major setback to our just and holy cause.'

Brother Carp got to his feet, drained his can of fizzy drink and belched loudly before delivering his version of the morning's events. Well known to be a monk of few words, his report was brief and mostly to the point, and he concluded it with 'So when this other cop turns up yellin' his head off, I legged it.'

Chairbrother Lemonsole immediately proposed that all should bow their heads in silent prayer and give thanks to God for delivering their brother from the clutches of the police, and less than ten seconds later, his "Amen" was echoed around the room like a series of toppling dominoes.

When he was sure that the last "Amen" had been uttered, he planted his palms squarely on the tabletop and said, 'In addition to Brother Carp's narrow escape, Brothers Trout and Piranha have informed me that they were forced to abort their missions this morning when they spotted that the police were watching both of their targets' addresses. Since the police have clearly realised that all of our victims meet their ends on the day of their seventieth birthdays and that all they have to do is lie in wait for one of our number to appear, I would suggest that we make a slight alteration to our strategy so that, from now on, most eliminations will be carried out a day or two either side of the actual birthdays.'

As Lemonsole had expected, his proposal was greeted without so much as a murmur of dissent, so he drew the proceedings of the emergency meeting to a close and opened the floodgates for the usual torrent of "Any

Other Businesses". The significant highlights from the minutes are printed below:

AOB 1a — Brother Haddock sought clarification from Brother Carp whether he had managed to place the recruitment advertisement despite his unfortunate encounter with the police. Brother Carp responded that he had done so prior to the unfortunate encounter.

AOB 2b(1) — Brother Guppy pointed out that everyone above the age of seventy should be eliminated and not just those who were exactly seventy if the Society was to fully implement the will of God. Brother Haddock replied that this had been discussed at the previous meeting and was one of the chief reasons for their campaign to recruit more members as a matter of urgency. (Chairbrother Lemonsole reminded Brother Haddock that language such as "if you morons are too bloody idle to read the minutes" was highly inappropriate.) **ACTION:** All brethren should read the minutes of any meeting they are unable to attend.

AOB 2b(2) — Concerns were raised that the Society was only eliminating Septoes (septuagenarians) in a fairly small geographic area, and it was God's will that *no-one* should exceed three score years and ten, so need to expand coverage — nationwide and ultimately global. Brother Haddock pointed out that this had also been discussed at the previous meeting and was a further reason for recruiting more members. **ACTION:** As for AOB 2b(1).

AOB 4c — Brother Halibut reprimanded for not ensuring that Mr Barney Wadd lived alone before elimination procedure carried out. Brethren were reminded that sole occupancy was an essential prerequisite when selecting appropriate targets in order to avoid the complication of potential witnesses. **ACTION:** Issue of how to eliminate co-habiting Septoes to be addressed at future meeting.

AOB 6b — Discussion re Sixth Commandment, "Thou shalt not kill", and whether the Society's policy on septuagenarian elimination was in direct contravention. Unanimously agreed that the commandment was not intended to be taken literally and there were allowable exceptions (e.g. it was clearly God's will that a person should be prevented from exceeding his/her allotted lifespan of three score years and ten by any means available).

AOB 8c — Brother Turbot asked if there had been any news of Brothers Mackerel and Herring. Brother Pilchard informed him that contact was no longer possible since *Hawking 3* had travelled beyond its communications range of two thousand years.

AOB 10b — Brother Barracuda queried whether individual members of the Society were entitled to call themselves "serial killers" since they were all *collectively* involved in carrying out the elimination of Septoes. Chairbrother Lemonsole made a ruling that each individual member could term themselves a "serial killer" once they had performed a minimum of three eliminations.

AOB 12a — Brother Perch reported that the Society's snail stocks were running perilously low. **ACTION:** All brethren to be on the lookout for more snails to replenish stocks. Species immaterial.

AOB 14c — Motion to rename the "Society for the Murder and/or Assassination of Septuagenarian Heretics" (SMASH) to the "Brotherhood Of

Youthful Solidarity" (BOYS). Brother Anchovy argued that being seventy didn't actually make someone a heretic *as such*, and the word "heretics" was only included in the Society's name to make the acronym sound punchier than "SMASP" (Society for the Murder and/or Assassination of Septuagenarian People). Motion defeated by ten votes to two.

MEETING CLOSED AT 04.19.

27

Horace gently revved the engine of the camper van, having first made certain that the sink tap was securely in the "Off" position. This particular trip was to be in Normal and not Time Travel Mode, although, strictly speaking, it was very far from normal.

Thestor had guided the adventurers to the forest clearing where they were now parked, and then he'd walked on alone in search of the king, having first lent them his spare pocket sundial, which he'd synchronised with his own.

'How long now?' Horace called out through the open driver's window to Norwood, who was sitting on a tree stump in the shade.

Norwood stared at the pocket sundial in his hand, then frowned and shook it close to his ear.

'I think it's stopped,' he said.

'You might find it works better if you're not in the shade,' said Vesta, who was lying flat on her back close to the van and soaking up the sun. 'The clue's in the name.'

'Of course,' said Norwood, slapping his forehead with the palm of his hand. Then he got to his feet and strolled to a part of the clearing that was in direct sunlight.

'These things aren't terribly accurate,' he said after turning the sundial this way and that for several seconds, 'but I'd say we should be setting off in about one minute and eleven seconds from now.'

* * *

The rough track through the forest soon turned into something approaching a proper road of a compressed, gravel-like substance, and almost immediately, the arena came into view less than a mile ahead. As Horace drove the van slowly closer, he and his co-adventurers could see that the enormous edifice was constructed from huge blocks of grey stone formed into walls of about fifty feet in height. Already, they could hear the excited hubbub of thousands of voices from within, and the sound grew ever louder as they approached, reaching cacophonous din levels by the time they'd got to shot-putting distance of the main entrance. Horace stopped the van and pulled on the handbrake.

'Are we sure this is wise?' he said, his teeth seeking out anything that remained of his fingernails to chew on.

'Not entirely,' said Norwood from his position next to Zoot on the back seat.

Vesta twisted round in the passenger seat to face him. 'It was your idea, Norwood.'

'Even so,' he said. 'There's actually quite a good chance this could all go horribly wrong.'

There followed a lengthy pause, during which, each of

187

the adventurers considered at least a dozen different ways that the plan *could* go horribly wrong, several of them involving a variety of slow and unpleasant deaths.

'Still,' said Horace eventually, shaking his head to banish the image of the four of them (including Zoot) being boiled alive in a massive cauldron of white wine vinegar, 'we did promise Thestor we'd do it.'

'And a promise *is* a promise,' sighed Vesta.

'Quite,' said Norwood. 'And if we don't, he's not going to show us where the Holey Snails are.'

Horace briefly wondered quite how it would be possible to continue their quest for the Holey Snail once they'd been reduced to a pile of bones in the bottom of a cauldron of boiling vinegar but decided that this was neither the time nor the place for hair splitting. And so, disengaging the handbrake and also his fingernails from his teeth, he eased the van through the high, stone archway of the arena's entrance and along a narrow, stone alleyway.

By now, the cacophonous din from inside the arena had transformed itself into an almost deafening roar of yelling and chanting, but the van hadn't quite made it to the end of the alleyway yet, so the noise from the crowd couldn't have been to herald its arrival. Thestor had been more than a little vague about what was going to be happening at the arena that day, saying, "Just turn up and we'll take it from there", and Horace sincerely hoped it didn't involve lions and Christians until he remembered that Christianity hadn't been invented yet. Gladiators perhaps? But that could make for an equally unpleasant spectacle of blood and gore.

Oh well, it's too late to turn back now, he thought, as the van emerged in the middle of one of the two curved ends of the stadium, which was shaped like an elongated oval with two straight sides of about two hundred and fifty yards in length. At ground level, the whole area was filled with a flat surface of hard-packed earth, a low stone wall running down the centre and parallel to the sides. Row upon row of stone seating raked steeply upwards all around the arena, and twenty-five to thirty thousand spectators were up on their feet, some jumping up and down, others gesticulating wildly, and all of them shouting their heads off and apparently having the time of their lives.

Horace stopped the van again and looked towards a huge cloud of fast-moving dust which was following the curve at the opposite end of the arena.

'Can anyone see what's actually happening?' he said.

'Looks like a fast-moving cloud of dust to me,' said Norwood.

Moments later, the cloud of dust entered the far end of the straight to their left, and Horace squinted to try and make out what was causing it.

'Are they... horses?' he said.

Vesta and Norwood followed his squinting example.

'And... chariots?' said Vesta.

'And they appear to be coming this way,' said Norwood in a slightly falsetto, panicky sort of tone, which was hardly surprising since the van was straddled across what was apparently some kind of racetrack, and the fast-moving dust, horses and chariots would be upon them in seconds.

Horace slammed the van into gear and swung the steering wheel hard to the right.

'Now what?' he said as he accelerated away.

'I'd suggest we keep going and stay ahead of the...' Norwood hesitated. 'Are they really chariots?'

'Looks like it,' said Vesta, staring out of the passenger window and peering through the cloud of dust, which had almost reached the end of the straight. 'About half a dozen of them, I'd say. Four horses on each.'

As the van got to the halfway point along the opposite

189

straight, Horace glanced to his right to see a small, flat area recessed into the banked seating about a third of the way up. It was shaded from the sun by an awning of red, blue and gold, but even so, there was plenty of glinting from the necks and arms of the twenty-or-so occupants.

'Must be the VIP area,' he said.

'Is that Thestor?' said Vesta.

Horace slowed the van to a halt, and he and his co-adventurers fixed their eyes on the bony old man who was standing near the front of the VIP section and waving at them with a big, beaming smile that was just visible through his straggly grey beard. Judging by the gold crown, the rich blue robes and the enormous golden throne he was sitting on, the man next to him was the king, and he wasn't smiling at all. Instead, he poked Thestor in the ribs, and the old man bent down to hear what he was saying. Thestor nodded, then straightened up and gestured frantically at the occupants of the van with a straight-armed left-to-right movement which he repeated several times before pointing at something to the rear of the van.

'I think he's suggesting we should move,' said Vesta.

'Good idea,' said Horace, who had just glanced in the rear-view mirror and spotted the chariots about twenty yards behind and approaching rapidly.

Once again, he accelerated away, engulfing the VIP section in its own cloud of dust, and it was only then that he became aware of the eerie quiet that had descended over the stadium. An almost total silence that had swept through the crowd like the sonic equivalent of a Mexican wave since the van had first appeared on the track.

And thinking of which, Horace said, 'So do you think we should just head out the way we came in?'

'Thestor must have already done his prophesying bit to the king about a strange, horseless carriage turning up out of nowhere,' said Norwood, 'so I suppose we *have* fulfilled our side of the bargain.'

'I agree,' said Vesta. 'Let's get the hell out of here pronto.'

Horace put his foot down and sped up the back straight, slowing only slightly as the van entered the curve at the far end. But a second later, he and his co-adventurers detected a crucial flaw in their plan of escape. The alleyway by which they'd entered the stadium was now completely blocked with several rows of heavily armed soldiers.

'Oops,' said Vesta. 'Plan B, I guess.'

'Which is?' said Norwood.

Vesta shrugged. 'Keep going and stay ahead of the chariots until the end of the race?'

'Doesn't sound like much of a plan to me.'

'As far as I see it,' said Horace, 'the only other option is to shift into Time Travel Mode and vanish into thin air.'

'Yes,' said Vesta, 'but we're so close to finding the Holey Snails, it would be a shame to have to start all over again in some other time zone.'

'Well, if you put it like that, Plan B it is then,' said Norwood. 'After all, what's the worst that can happen?'

28

Harper Collins was sitting in her second office — the end cubicle of the women's toilets — and letting her mind wander over the most recent events in the seventieth birthday murders. As soon as she'd tracked them down, she'd grilled Sergeant Noble and the other officers who'd been staking out the other two addresses on her list, but as she'd expected, none of them had been able to provide her with even the merest scrap of useful information.

The contents of the monk's hessian shoulder bag had all been checked for fingerprints, but none had been found. Not even on any of the pages of the pocket Bible, which Harper thought was rather surprising. Either the monk had never even opened it or he'd read it while wearing gloves, and bizarre as it seemed, the latter must have been the case because the line about "the days of our years are threescore years and ten" in Psalm Ninety had been underlined in red ink. The liquid in the syringe had been analysed and, in common with the postmortems on the previous murder victims, was discovered to be potassium chloride. Also as expected, the birthday card sent to Ledley had contained a sufficient amount of a fentanyl-derived gas to render someone unconscious for up to thirty minutes.

Leopold was right. The whole operation had been a total disaster, and the fact that three murders had been averted did little to ease Harper's sense of frustration and bitter disappointment. The only potential new lead was the newspaper advertisement, but so far, all enquiries at the offices of local papers and magazines had drawn a blank. If they did strike lucky, then at least she had an idea of how they might use the information, but if they failed... Well, it didn't bear thinking about. On the next day alone, there were eight people who were due to have their seventieth birthdays and six more the day after that. Of course, she could always stake out another three addresses with her limited resources, but she considered it highly probable that the monks might lay low for a while after their narrow escape that morning. Maybe they'd even change their choice of victims. But that seemed unlikely, given that their motive was obviously and specifically connected with people who had just turned seventy.

Harper sighed and leaned back against the toilet's low-level cistern. To ease the throbbing in her head, which was made worse by too much thinking, she scanned the graffiti that filled almost half of the cubicle door. She'd barely noticed it before, despite the frequency of her visits, and she quickly realised she hadn't missed very much. Most of the scribblings were either tired old jokes or outright obscenities — some with explicit illustrations. She turned her gaze to the wall on her right in search of something that might at least raise a smile, and straight away, she got her reward. Someone with a modicum of artistic talent had drawn an almost perfect caricature of Superintendent Leopold and added a Hitler moustache and hairstyle, complete with Nazi salute. The rest of the wall held nothing of interest, the scribblings being mostly devoted to allegations of who was shagging who and which officer was a tosser — or worse.

The left-hand wall appeared to be slightly more promising as the first piece of graffiti that caught her attention wasn't the simple statement that "Jesus saves" but the addition that someone had scrawled underneath: "but Ronaldo scores on the rebound". It was a very old joke, but it still made her smile, and over the years, only the name of the scorer had changed. When Harper had first come across it in her early teens, it had been Maradona who'd put one past the Saviour.

The quality of the graffiti on the rest of the wall was extremely poor by comparison, many of the wannabe-but-no-hope Banksy's picking up on the religious theme with drawings and remarks that would have had them burned at the stake a few centuries ago.

Harper turned her head away to try and refocus her mind on how to solve the case in hand, but as she did so, her peripheral vision spotted another piece of graffiti low down and at an angle of about thirty degrees. A row of small black characters no more than an inch and a half in length and less than half an inch high with a neat diagonal line drawn through the centre. Exactly the same as they'd found inscribed on the chests of every one of the murder victims so far:

$$\text{III} \ast \text{XX} + \text{X}$$

It was as if an electric cattle prod had scored a direct hit on her frontal lobe. Who the hell had written it? These toilets were out of bounds to the general public, so it must have been a cop or one of the admin staff. But that was impossible. The killers were quite clearly monks. Or were they? The newspaper advertisement hadn't said anything about applicants having to be monks, so perhaps they were just ordinary people simply *dressed* in monastic habits and Union Jack flip-flops as some kind of quasi-religious uniform. But if that was the case, then at least one person who worked at the station was a serial killer. On the other hand, the symbols on the victims' chests were common knowledge around the station, so maybe somebody had just doodled them on the wall while they did what they had to do.

The pounding in Harper's skull had returned with a vengeance, and she reached inside her pocket for another double dose of painkillers. But her hand came up empty, and she realised that she'd left them behind in her office. She got to her feet and was about to unbolt the cubicle door when her mobile phone rang. She glanced at the display. Oh great, she thought, and had to force herself not to reject the call.

'Yes?' she said.

'You still in the bog?' said Scatterthwaite.

Harper didn't bother to answer.

'Well,' the sergeant continued, 'I thought you'd like to know that DS Maurice Scatterthwaite has triumphed yet again.'

'Uh-huh?'

'I've only gone and found where the monk placed the newspaper ad. Oh yes.'

Harper slid back the bolt on the cubicle door. Finally, she could begin to put her plan in motion.

'Tell me, Sergeant,' she said. 'Have you ever done any undercover work before?'

29

When Norwood had posed the question, "What's the worst that can happen?" back at the arena, neither he nor his co-adventurers could have envisaged that they'd wind up in a cold, damp dungeon on an even lower level than the very bowels of the royal palace. Strictly speaking, of course, it wasn't the *worst* that could have happened, but on the scale of "What's The Worst That Can Happen If You Seriously Annoy The King By Messing Up His Chariot Race", it was well within manacle-rattling distance of the top spot.

Horace had carried on driving around the track, keeping just ahead of the chariots until the race had ended, and then parked the van in front of the VIP section. A dozen heavily armed soldiers had immediately surrounded them and escorted them all — somewhat roughly — into the presence of the king. Thestor had remained close to the throne, and even through his straggly, grey hair and beard it was easy to see that his face had turned almost the same shade of white as his unusually clean loincloth, which he apparently kept for special occasions. Not only had he been beside himself with anxiety and fear, he'd also been beside the king, and Amnestios the Lenient had been beside *him*self with rage.

'What in the name of Hades do you mean by ruining my chariot race?' he'd blustered.

'Yes, sorry about that,' Horace had begun, 'but the thing is—'

'Silence!' the king had yelled and then turned his angry, black-bearded face to Thestor. 'And it's all very well you predicting the arrival of a horseless chariot, but you didn't say anything about it making a complete nonsense of the race, did you?'

'I think I did,' Thestor had mumbled, shuffling his feet and gazing down at them with feigned fascination.

'When?'

'When what, your majesty?'

The king had snatched the gold crown from his head and run his hand over his thinning black hair. 'When did you tell me about the horseless chariot making a nonsense of the race?'

Thestor had smacked his lips and stroked his straggly, grey beard while he'd thought about it. 'Now, let me see. That would have been right after I'd told you about the horseless chariot appearing as if from nowhere in a puff of smoke.'

The king had squeezed his eyes tight shut for a moment as if trying to recall this particular part of the conversation. 'Are you *sure*?'

'Oh yes,' Thestor had said. 'Perhaps your majesty didn't hear that bit.'

'Nothing wrong with *my* hearing. You must have been mumbling.'

Thestor had held up his palms in a you've-got-me-there-your-majesty gesture. 'One of my many faults, I'm afraid, sire.'

The king had stared at him for a full twelve seconds and then turned back to Horace and his co-adventurers. 'And not only did you ruin the race, you also cheated.'

'Excuse me?' Vesta had said with a heavy dose of indignation.

'Just because you crossed the finishing line first doesn't mean you won the race, so you needn't think for one moment that you'll be picking up the victor's prize.'

197

'Well, that's okay because we didn't actually—'

The king had held up a heavily-ringed hand to silence Horace and said, 'And don't try and tell me you were at a disadvantage because your chariot didn't have any horses to pull it. Dear me, no. That's no excuse for entering the race two laps after it started, is it?'

Norwood had opened his mouth to answer this patently rhetorical question, but the king had held up his other, equally bejewelled hand.

'So, in my book,' he'd continued, 'that amounts to a blatant and thoroughly unsportsmanlike attempt to win the race by means of trickery and deception, and since I'm the king, what it says in *my* book is what goes. Got it?'

On the basis that the king didn't have any other hands to hold up for the purpose of silencing him, Horace had begun to protest their innocence, but to no avail. Despite his lack of a third hand, the king had resorted to a different method to shut him up, and this had involved shouting at his guards to drag Horace and his co-adventurers (including Zoot) down to the deepest dungeon in the palace and keep them there until he'd decided on an appropriately unpleasant punishment.

That had been almost two hours ago, although it was impossible to know exactly how long since none of the adventurers had brought a watch with them, and the pocket sundial was utterly useless in the subterranean darkness of the dungeon.

'I didn't think places like this actually existed except in films,' said Norwood, casting his eye around what was just about visible of the damp stone walls, floor and ceiling of their cell and the massive iron door at one end.

'Yes, Norwood,' said Vesta, 'but this *is* the fourteenth century BC, you know.'

'Good point. I was forgetting that.'

Horace wasn't at all sure how Norwood could

possibly have forgotten, given everything they'd seen, heard and otherwise experienced since they'd arrived in Ancient Greece, but he decided to let the matter rest. There were far more important things to think about, such as:

    a) how long they'd be kept down in this damp, dark dungeon;

    b) what terrible punishment they'd have to endure when they did get let out;

    c) would the king turn out to be as lenient as Thestor had claimed?

'I must say,' he said, 'this King Amnestios doesn't seem to be quite as lenient as Thestor led us to believe.'

'Perhaps it's a "by comparison" thing,' said Vesta. 'You know. Maybe he's an absolute sweetie compared to the previous king. All that boiling alive in a cauldron of vinegar and being torn apart by wild horses. Ugh.'

She shuddered visibly, and not from the cold or the damp either, so Norwood suggested they should change the subject to something more cheerful. Play a game perhaps or sing a song to keep their spirits up. But after a less-than-convincing rendition of *Glad All Over* and a couple of lacklustre verses of *Jailhouse Rock*, followed by two somewhat pointless rounds of "I-Spy", the adventurers once again lapsed into silent and gloomy contemplation of the fate that might await them.

Try as he might, Horace had great difficulty in dislodging certain images from his mind, all of which entailed particularly brutal and long-drawn-out methods of depriving him and his co-adventurers (possibly including Zoot) of their precious lives. His least favourite of all — so far — was the one that made excruciating and highly imaginative use of a rotary clothesline, a cheese grater and a stainless steel nit comb. In a desperate attempt to convince himself that he would meet his end by some far less agonising means, he reasoned that not all, if any, of these implements had probably been invented yet. However, instead of contenting himself with this line of reasoning, he foolishly did a bit more reasoning and was ultimately forced to conclude that the Ancient Greeks were a pretty smart lot, and even though they might not have access to rotary clotheslines, cheese graters or stainless steel nit combs as such, it was a fairly safe bet that they'd have already invented items that were remarkably similar and would perform their fiendish, death-dealing duties equally as efficiently as their modern day equivalents.

He was on the point of asking his co-adventurers if either of them knew when the rotary clothesline was invented, but he only got as far as "Does anyone know" when he was interrupted by the unmistakable sound of a very big key being turned in the lock of the massive iron door of their dungeon and the clunking of several bolts being unbolted. This was immediately followed by an extremely loud creaking noise, which echoed around the damp stone walls for a good twelve seconds before Thestor popped his grizzled head round the door and said, 'Hello there' in what the adventurers considered to be an inappropriately bright and breezy tone of voice, given the circumstances.

Zoot, who alone had seemed largely unperturbed by his incarceration, was roused from his slumber at the sound and raced over to Thestor, sniffing excitedly at the old man's feet.

Thestor closed the door behind him and hopped from one foot to the other to try to avoid the worst excesses of Zoot's salivary greeting. 'So this is where you've been hiding,' he said.

This remark didn't fare too well on the appropriateness score either.

'You seem inappropriately cheerful considering it's because of you that we've been banged up in this awful dungeon,' said Vesta.

'Yes, I'm sorry about that but—' Thestor began but broke off when Horace raised his hand to silence him. (Apparently, you didn't have to be a king or have rings dripping from every finger to be able to use the gesture effectively.)

'Before you go any further,' he said, 'I need to ask you if you've ever come across such a thing as a rotary clothesline.'

'A what?' said Thestor, his brow furrowing into a ploughed field of slack, brown skin.

'Good enough,' said Horace. 'You were saying?'

'Only that it's a bit unfortunate you all ending up down here like this. I certainly didn't see that coming, I can tell you, but it's not entirely my fault.'

'Oh?' the adventurers chorused.

'I did tell you that timing was critical, and if you'd turned up before the start of the race instead of in the middle of it, you wouldn't be in the pickle you are now. That's why we synchronised sundials.'

Horace considered Thestor's use of the word "pickle" to be as inappropriate as his cheerfulness, spoken as it was in such close proximity to his recent speculation about being boiled alive in vinegar, but he let it pass.

'They're not exactly the most accurate of timepieces though, are they?' said Norwood, holding up the pocket sundial Thestor had lent them and pointlessly angling it this way and that as if trying to read the time in the gloom of the dungeon.

'You know what they say,' Thestor chuckled. 'A bad workman always blames his—'

The old man ducked just in time to avoid a nasty on-head collision with the pocket sundial, which Norwood had hurled at him with not inconsiderable force.

'Hey, watch out!' Thestor shouted. 'That could have really hurt.'

'You still haven't told us why you're quite so chirpy,' said Vesta.

Thestor picked up the pocket sundial and gave it a wipe on his Sunday-best loincloth.

'Ah,' he said, the grin smearing itself back over his face. 'It's because I have some good news for you.'

'They've run out of vinegar?' said Horace.

'What? No. Not that I'm aware of anyway. It's better than that.'

'The king's given us a free pardon and wants us to be his guests of honour at an enormous banquet before sending us on our way, laden with all manner of riches, the like of which we couldn't possibly imagine?'

Thestor hesitated. 'Not quite that good, I'm afraid, no.'

'The free pardon bit would do,' said Norwood.

'Um, not exactly a free pardon.'

'We have to *pay*?' said Vesta with obvious disgust.

'No, no, not at all.'

'It hasn't got anything to do with cheese graters, has it?' said Horace.

'Cheese what?'

'Or stainless steel nit combs?'

Thestor stared blankly at him until Norwood broke the awkward silence. 'Perhaps we should give up on the guessing games and you just tell us exactly what *is* going to happen to us.'

There was a pause while Thestor seemed to be choosing his words, and then he launched into a lengthy and detailed description of how the king was so furious with them for ruining his chariot race and their unsportsmanlike behaviour that he'd ordered the Royal Executioner to devise a far more agonising death than the "old hat" method of boiling people in vinegar and the "rather messy" tearing apart by wild horses. The adventurers gasped in horror, and once again, Horace queried whether a serious error had been made when the king had been named Amnestios the Lenient.

'To be fair,' Thestor said, 'he's usually pretty tame when it comes to dishing out punishments. If your crime hadn't been quite so serious, he'd probably have had you standing on one leg for twenty minutes or eating a bowl of custard with lumps in it. That sort of thing. But unfortunately for you, the one thing that really gets his goat is people messing up his chariot races.'

'So what *is* our punishment?' said Horace, failing miserably to control the wobble in his voice.

'Ah well,' said Thestor, 'luckily for you — and after many hours of cajoling, wheedling and fawning — I eventually managed to persuade the king that you hadn't deliberately intended to sabotage the race and that this was a perfect opportunity for him to demonstrate the leniency for which he's so renowned.'

Thestor paused, clearly expecting an outpouring of gratitude for his efforts on their behalf, but Horace, Norwood, Vesta and Zoot were suspending all forms of reaction until the old man had told them precisely the fate that awaited them. He cleared his throat, putting his hand over his mouth — ostensibly for the sake of decorum — and said something that was totally unintelligible.

'What was that?' said Norwood.

'Slaves,' Thestor blurted. 'You're all to be his slaves for the foreseeable future, so I've no idea how long that might be because, as you all know, I can't foresee the future any more than you can. But what's great about it is you won't be the sort of slaves who have to do all that awful stuff like breaking rocks or working in the sulphur mines. Not at all. You'll be house slaves. Quite a doddle really — and definitely a whole lot better than what the Royal Executioner had in mind.'

The huge grin that once again spread across what was

visible of his face was, Horace presumed, another indication that Thestor was anticipating a gushingly appreciative response. Instead, all that was forthcoming was a stunned and stony silence.

'Oh, I almost forgot,' said Thestor, clearly undeterred. 'The other piece of good news is that the king has reinstated me as Royal Soothsayer. And all because I predicted the spectacular appearance of your horseless chariot at the arena. How about that, eh?'

Horace scanned the ground around where he was sitting for something very hard and very pointy.

30

Harper leaned back in the chair behind her desk and gave Scatterthwaite the once-over. Not that she could tell that it really was Scatterthwaite just by looking. The hood of the dark brown monastic habit was deep enough to obscure his face completely, and only when he spoke could she be sure it was him.

'You sure this get-up is entirely necessary,' he said. 'It didn't actually say anything about already having to be a monk in the newspaper ad.'

'No,' said Harper, 'but you'll maybe stand a better chance of being accepted if you are.'

'Well, I feel like a right pillock. Makes me look like a Jedi Knight reject who's lost his lightsaber.'

Harper refrained from pointing out that he really was a right pillock regardless of what he was wearing and told him to lift the hem of his habit so she could get a look at his feet.

'You need to lose the flip-flops,' she said.

'Why? What's wrong with them?' said Scatterthwaite, staring down at the offending Union Jack footwear. 'It took me bloody ages finding these.'

'You could have saved yourself the trouble then.'

'It's what *they* all wear. The killers.'

'Precisely my point,' said Harper. 'There was nothing in the ad about recruiting serial killers, so how would an innocent, God-fearing monk like yourself know anything about the Union Jack flip-flops?'

Scatterthwaite thought about it, throwing back his

cowl and scratching his head. 'Yeah, I see what you mean.'

Then he scratched his left armpit, his chest and his groin area and added, 'Bloody itchy, this material.'

'I think it's meant to be,' said Harper. 'Sackcloth and ashes and all that.'

'Well, I just hope that whoever had it before me didn't have lice or some 'orrible skin disease.'

'Before you?'

'I got it from a fancy dress hire shop,' said Scatterthwaite and momentarily suspended his scratching. 'Which reminds me. I only rented it for twenty-four hours. You reckon that'll be enough?'

Harper shrugged. 'Depends if they take you on or not. And anyway, if they do, they'll probably kit you out in their own gear. Most of the ones we know about so far have all worn the same off-grey habits. That's when you'll get the flip-flops as well, I expect.'

Scatterthwaite nodded and resumed his scratching, paying particular attention to his groin area. 'One thing I wasn't sure about was whether monks wear underpants or not. You know, like if Scotch blokes wear anything under their kilts.'

'Scots,' Harper corrected. 'Oddly enough, I've never actually looked under a monk's habit before — or a Scotsman's kilt for that matter — but if I were you, I'd play on the safe side and go commando.'

'Yeah?'

'In case monks actually don't wear underpants and they decide to strip-search you.'

'Wha—?' Scatterthwaite's mouth froze in the open position before he'd got to the end of the word.

'I'm only saying it's a possibility,' said Harper, suppressing a grin at the mental image of the detective sergeant being subjected to a full cavity search by a bunch of monks. 'These people are serial killers after all, and they don't know you from Adam, so they might want to check that you're not wearing a wire or whatever.'

'Oh, great.'

Harper skim-read the letter on the desk in front of her, inviting Scatterthwaite — Brother Thomas — for interview. It had been checked for fingerprints, but nothing had been found other than a few useless smudges. On the other hand, the envelope it had arrived in was smothered in prints, but Harper was certain that none of them would belong to any of the monks. She checked her watch.

'You'd better get going,' she said and handed him the letter. 'Someone will meet you at two o'clock outside the Lost Soles Boot and Shoe Repair Shop in the High Street, and you're to carry a copy of *Practical Fishkeeping* so they can identify you.'

'Oh yeah, 'cos there's bound to be dozens of people dressed as monks hanging around outside a shoe repair shop,' Scatterthwaite scoffed and headed for the door.

'And may God be with you, Brother Thomas,' said Harper.

Scatterthwaite turned back to face her. 'Eh?'

She narrowed her eyes at him and waited for the penny to drop.

'Oh yeah,' he said at last. 'Brother Thomas. I'd better remember that, hadn't I.'

Harper didn't respond, but as soon as he'd gone, she planted her elbows on the desktop and buried her face in her hands. DS Scatterthwaite wouldn't have been the most obvious choice for undercover work, but she'd had very little option. Ideally, she would have gone herself, but there was too much of a risk that the monk she'd tangled with at Ledley's place would be there, and if so, he'd recognise her immediately. As for Scatterthwaite, he'd assured her he'd been too far away from the monk to be identifiable, which was interesting considering his earlier accounts of heroic hand-to-hand combat. He was also the most monk-like in appearance of the few other officers she had at her disposal. Despite the vast quantities of food he constantly shoved down his throat, he was remarkably thin, and his slightly gaunt, hollow-cheeked features gave him the look of someone who might well have shunned the material world and spent most of their life in quiet contemplation of matters spiritual. How ironic, Harper thought, but then it only went to prove the old saying about not judging a book by its cover.

She sat back in her chair again and stared up at the ceiling. Right now, she almost felt like praying herself. Something along the lines of "Dear Lord, please do whatever you can to make sure DS Scatterthwaite doesn't make a complete and utter balls of this". But what would be the point? There'd be nobody "up there" listening to her, and even if there was, they'd probably given up on Scatterthwaite as a lost cause years ago. They'd certainly given up on *her*.

As she continued to stare up at the ceiling, she realised with a wry smile that if she *had* offered up a prayer, it would have gone straight to Superintendent Leopold, whose office was directly above hers. About right, she thought, or at least as far as his own self-image was concerned. If his behaviour was anything to go by, he clearly believed that if God ever decided to retire, there'd only be him and Bono in the running to take over.

He'd had her up in his office earlier that day to give her yet another grilling about what, if any, progress she was making with the case. She'd told him about the newspaper advertisement she'd found in the monk's bag but that enquiries at the paper's offices had yielded nothing of any use. The monk had paid cash, and once again, the hood of his habit meant the woman who'd dealt with him was unable to give a description other than what he'd been wearing. As for Scatterthwaite's undercover operation, she'd decided not to even mention it. The fewer people that knew about it, the better, especially after she'd found the symbols written on the wall of the women's toilet.

After Leopold had dismissed her with the usual warnings and threats, she'd spent the next couple of hours coaching Scatterthwaite on his new identity and what he should say at the interview. Not surprisingly, he hadn't been the most diligent of students despite her frequent reminders that his life might very well depend on getting it right.

Now that he was on his way, another phrase from the Bible sprang into her mind: "like a lamb to the slaughter", and she hoped — not prayed — that this wasn't how it would turn out, and not just for the sake of the case. Scatterthwaite might be an almighty pillock and irritated the hell out of her most of the time, but she certainly wouldn't wish him dead.

31

'I really *really* don't see the point of this at all,' whispered Norwood. 'I mean, it's not as if he's exactly short of furniture.'

Norwood and Horace were side by side on their hands and knees on a cold, marble floor, Norwood supporting the king's thighs on his back and Horace the lower legs and feet, while the king sprawled back on a heavily cushioned marble throne. Horace cast his eyes around and confirmed for himself that his co-adventurer was correct. There was indeed a vast array of every conceivable type of furniture in whatever direction he looked throughout the enormous room, which was approximately 12.8 times more enormous than the enormous room where they'd first met their current employer, Mr Wellwisher. But that seemed such a long time ago now, which was rather odd because, strictly speaking, it wasn't "ago" at all but more than three thousand, three hundred years in the future.

'You're quite right,' Horace whispered back. 'There's all manner of furniture items that would serve perfectly well as footstools. Possibly even better.'

'So why use us instead?'

'Because he can?' suggested Horace with a shrug, which wasn't a good choice of body language in the circumstances as it brought an instant and sharp rebuke from the king, who told him to "Stop jiggling about, damn you, or I'll have you boiled alive in whatever alternative we have to vinegar, which unfortunately we ran out of the day before yesterday".

Horace and Norwood fell into a non-jiggling silence, believing that this was the best policy to adopt if they wanted to avoid being boiled alive in anything at all. During this time, Horace pondered their present predicament, which was admittedly far more preferable to being dead but decidedly unpleasant nevertheless. They'd been kneeling on this cold, marble floor for almost an hour, and his knees were killing him. He was also ravenously hungry. "Thin gruel" was a phrase he'd often read in Victorian novels — mostly ones by Charles Dickens — and he now had first-hand experience of the awful slop because all that he and his co-adventurers (including Zoot) had been given to eat so far was a very small bowl of the stuff.

He wasn't at all keen on the outfits they'd all (excluding Zoot) been forced to wear either. Sleeveless white frock affairs that ended a few inches above the knee. Not that Horace was in any way fashion conscious, but apart from being decidedly unmanly, they were also distinctly draughty, especially around the nether regions when on all fours as a human footstool. He had to confess, however, that Vesta looked particularly fetching in hers.

He turned his head slightly to try and catch sight of her but failed. As far as he knew, she was still where he'd last seen her, just before he and Norwood had been ordered to assume the footstool position. She was to be the king's personal Keeper of the Peanuts, which meant that she had to stand close to where he was sitting and offer him an enormous gold platter of peanuts whenever he clicked his fingers three times. This was to avoid confusion among the other slaves who were responsible for keeping him supplied with wine (one click), truffles (two clicks) and toothpicks (four clicks).

Thestor had also been in close attendance, now

resplendent in an immaculately clean and sharply pressed red and blue loincloth with gold tassel fringe. Although he too was outside Horace's limited field of vision, he could still hear the old man occasionally as he flattered and fawned over the king like the weaselly sycophant he was. A couple of times, the king had asked him a question about what the future held in store regarding a particular concern of his. The first such question had been about when the Royal Vinegar Vats were likely to be replenished, and Thestor had blathered something about having to consult his cosmological almanac before he could come up with a definitive answer. On the second occasion, the king had asked if his name would be remembered in a thousand years from now, and Thestor had said, 'Not only remembered, your majesty, but you will be revered for all time as the kindest and most generous of all monarchs in your treatment of soothsayers.'

'How much longer are we going to have to stay like this, do you think?' whispered Norwood.

Horace was about to shrug but stopped himself just in time.

'No idea,' he said, 'but if the awful stink that's been coming from his direction is anything to go by, I'd say the king'll be needing a visit to the Royal Lavvy before very long.'

'Tuh,' tutted Norwood. 'It's all right for you. I'm the one who's got my head damn near up the man's backside. — Oh, good grief. There's another one.'

'Must be the peanuts.'

'Or the truffles. More likely the truffles. I don't think peanuts have ever affected *me* like that. How about you?'

'I wouldn't know. I'm allergic. And I don't think I've ever eaten truffles in my life, so I wouldn't know about them either.'

'I don't think *I've* ever eaten truffles, come to think of it.'

'Very expensive apparently.'

'So I believe, yes.'

'Vesta might have had them. On account of her uncle being so rich, that is.'

'Perhaps we should ask her later.'

'Yes, perhaps we should.'

'Whenever "later" might be,' Norwood sighed. 'I'm not sure my knees can stand much more of this. And what if we have to do this every day? I didn't sign up for this adventure to end up being crippled for the rest of my life.'

'Nor me,' said Horace.

'Maybe we should start giving some serious thought to how we might escape. Perhaps we could bribe someone — the king himself even.'

'What with, though? As far as I know, we don't have anything we could—'

'A Swiss Army knife?'

Horace almost choked. Bizarrely enough, they had all been allowed to keep their personal possessions, which had surprised them at the time, although they'd surmised that the guards would never have seen a Swiss Army knife before and would therefore have no idea about the vast array of handy little tools and gadgets they contained. But to give up even one of their precious multi-tools would be bordering on sacrilege, and Norwood's suggestion appalled Horace to the core.

'You can't be serious,' he said in a hoarse whisper.

'It would be an enormous sacrifice, I grant you,' said Norwood, 'but think of it this way. If the king would settle for just one of our Swiss Army knives, we'd still have two left between us. And if it means we don't have to be human footstools any more and we can get on with our quest for the Holey Snails, I reckon it'd be a price worth paying.'

Horace thought about it. Norwood had a point of course, and it was certainly true that he would have done almost anything right now to relieve the excruciating pain in his knees and the gnawing hunger in his stomach, but surely this was far too high a price. It also occurred to him that giving the king such a sophisticated multi-tool as the iconic Swiss Army knife might very well change the course of history itself. At the very least, poor old Mr Swiss, the Hungarian knitwear importer, would be robbed of his fame as its inventor three thousand years in the future. It wasn't a matter to be taken lightly, and Horace expressed this concern to Norwood.

'You don't believe in that load of old twaddle about this so-called Mr Swiss, do you?' Norwood snorted. 'Of the two main theories concerning the invention and development of the Swiss Army knife, that's by far the least plausible by a million miles.'

DIGRESSION THREE: ON THE INVENTION AND DEVELOPMENT OF THE SWISS ARMY KNIFE

Unfortunately for researchers into the history of the now ubiquitous multi-tool, precise details of the invention and early development of the Swiss Army knife have been lost in the mists of time. Many theories have been put forward, but only two have ever gained a significant level of support within the multi-tool research community.

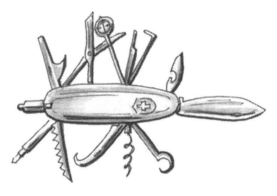

The first, and less popular of the two, has come to be known as the "Van Driver Theory" after its creator, Gustav van Driver, Emeritus Professor of Multi-Tool Mechanics at the Polytechnic of Eastern Gdansk. After many years of painstaking research into how the Swiss Army knife came to be invented and its early development, Van Driver finally published his findings in a three-volume treatise, *Everything You Ever Wanted*

to Know About the Invention and Early Development of the Swiss Army Knife.

To summarise briefly, Van Driver discovered that the earliest known prototype of the Swiss Army knife was produced in 1783 by a Hungarian knitwear importer called Joseph Swiss, who had a curious obsession about scissors. According to his diaries and a variety of other documents, including letters, diagrams and artists' impressions, which Van Driver had unearthed, Mr Swiss believed that the secret to a long and healthy life was to keep all forms of bodily hair and nails immaculately trimmed at all times. But because Mr Swiss insisted on always using the right tool for the right job, he had to carry with him several different types of scissors — a pair for eyebrows, another for nose hair, one for armpit hair, separate scissors for thumbnails and fingernails, and so on. He even had a special pair for trimming any hairy moles he might have. In all, Mr Swiss took with him a minimum of fifteen pairs of scissors every time he left his house since he never knew when he might discover an unruly eyelash or wayward chest hair. However, as he transported all of the scissors in the pockets of his trousers — and despite taking extreme care — he received frequent wounds in the upper thigh area from the tip of one scissor blade or another.

Not surprisingly, Mr Swiss grew tired of being jabbed in the legs almost every time he sat down or ran to catch the mail coach, so he urgently sought a solution to the problem. But every method he devised resulted in failure. His first idea was to put a wine bottle cork onto the tip of each blade, but this made the scissors far too bulky for all of them to fit into his trouser pockets. Another scheme was to line his pockets with lead to reinforce the regulation cotton, but this proved to be impractical due to the additional weight causing his trousers to fall down around his ankles whenever he stood up or walked anywhere.

Finally, he hit upon the notion of mounting all of the pairs of scissors together inside an open-sided metal box so that each pair could be hinged out from the container as required. The invention was far larger than the Swiss Army knife we know today and still much too big to fit into a standard-sized trouser pocket but was nevertheless made easily portable by strapping it to the upper arm with two thin strips of leather.

Delighted with his creation, Mr Swiss paid a local scissor factory to produce hundreds of copies in the belief that people would flock to buy such a useful invention. Sadly, however, not a single one was sold during the entire first year that the multi-scissor was on the market, very probably because no-one on the planet — apart from Mr Swiss himself — was of the opinion that keeping all forms of bodily hair and nails neatly trimmed was the secret to a long and healthy life. So heavily had he invested in the manufacture of his invention and so non-existent were the returns that Mr Swiss was on the point of bankruptcy when he was approached by a multi-national cutlery manufacturer who offered to buy the patent. It was a generous offer, and Mr Swiss had little choice but to accept, although he was deeply saddened when the "new improved" version of his invention first appeared in the shops.

Of the fifteen pairs of specialist scissors, only a single general purpose pair now remained. The rest had been replaced with a range of tools and gadgets, none of which would be of any use at all for such essential tasks as the trimming of ear hair or the paring of toenails. Mr Swiss was also aggrieved that the new owners of the patent had broken — or at least fudged — a condition of the sale that the product should continue to bear its original name of "Mr Swiss's Arm Scissors". Mr Swiss therefore sued the company for breach of contract, but the court ruled against him, accepting the defendant's arguments that Mr Swiss's handwriting was so bad, they thought he'd written "Swiss Army Knife" and that, in any case, "Mr Swiss's Arm Scissors" just sounded silly.

It is said by some that Mr Swiss died soon afterwards of a broken heart, but according to the postmortem report discovered by Professor Van Driver, the cause of death was given as "a sudden and violent attack of sneezing which resulted in the accidental impaling of the brain with a pair of long-bladed nasal hair scissors".

The second theory on the invention and development of the Swiss Army knife is considered by many in the multi-tool research community to present a far more plausible explanation than Professor Van Driver's and is based in large part on an in-depth analysis of the Swiss psyche. It is well known of course that Switzerland has always maintained its neutrality in military matters, which stems not from a morally ethical adherence to pacifism but from an ethnologically innate inability to make decisions. Such indecisiveness dates back to the very creation of Switzerland as an independent nation state when its founding fathers failed to agree on a name for the country when completing the application form for the IRN (International Registry of Nations). A compromise was finally reached after several days of dithering and indecision, and it was agreed that the newly born nation would henceforth be known as "Switzerland", which is the ancient Siculo-Hurartian word for "whatever".

It is also no coincidence that Switzerland has not one but four official languages. Faced with yet another choice, the founding fathers eventually whittled down the options to French, German, Italian and Romansh, but no-one could reach a decision on which to select, so in the end, it was left to the Swiss people themselves to decide what language they wanted to communicate in.

Almost from the moment the new country was established, opposing sides in a variety of nearby wars begged and pleaded with Switzerland to join with them and become their ally in their "heroic battle against evil". (They all said that, regardless of what side they were on.) However, the Swiss government could never make up its mind which side to fight on because it couldn't decide which was telling the truth about fighting evil and which was actually the evil one itself. Consequently, the Swiss always ended up by declining to participate on either side, and over the centuries, insisting on their neutrality became a habit rather than the result of any rational analysis of the particular situation, so nobody bothers asking them to be their ally any more.

Switzerland's neutrality also explains why the Pope employs Swiss soldiers to guard the Vatican. Not because His Holiness is under the totally misguided belief that Swiss troops are the crème de la crème of military achievement or that they are fiercer warriors than any other soldiers, but simply because they are incredibly cheap. Given that Switzerland has quite a large standing army but never goes to war, there's nothing much for their troops to do, so the Swiss government lends some of them out to the Pope, who pays them little more than the Vatican's minimum wage. It's an arrangement that suits both parties very well and is rather like a professional football club lending a player to another team. The lending club still has ownership rights over the player but doesn't have to pay his wages while the club which borrows him gets the temporary use of a player who's usually a lot better than most of the dross it already has in its team.

Yet despite this mutually beneficial arrangement with the Vatican, Switzerland's continued insistence on its neutrality meant that the vast majority of its troops remained at home with little else to do than hold endless parades and repeatedly whitewash every inanimate object in the grounds of their barracks. Consequently, after many decades of not being allowed to kill anyone, it became apparent that morale among the Swiss military had sunk to a dangerous level, and mutiny was not beyond the realms of possibility. As a result, the No-War Office ordered some of Switzerland's top boffins to design a completely new "weapon" that was useful rather than warlike in order to keep the troops occupied and therefore distract them from their growing desire to "get out there and do some serious killing".

Many months passed before a prototype of the "weapon" was delivered to the No-War Office, and, in essence, it was the earliest known version of the Swiss Army knife. Small enough to fit into a standard, army regulation trouser pocket, it contained no less than twenty-seven handy little tools and gadgets including, for example, a tool for extracting stones from the hooves of regimental goat mascots, a gadget for finding the ends of regimental Sellotape, and a small brush for the application of verruca ointment. Even though the No-War Office had asked for one "weapon" only, the reason why the boffins had created twenty-seven "weapons" in one was purely because none of them could decide which of the twenty-seven "weapons" to choose, so they'd compromised by including them all.

And thus, the Swiss Army knife was born, and it is Swiss indecisiveness that we have to thank for the wonderfully handy multi-tool we cherish today — unless of course you happen to believe Professor Van Driver's ridiculous guff about some Hungarian scissor freak and his utterly bonkers "Arm Scissors". In *three* volumes? Get real, Prof. You should get out more.

31

(Continued)

Horace and Norwood continued to argue over the two main theories on how, when and why the Swiss Army knife came to be invented and whether giving one of these precious multi-tools to King Amnestios the Less-Lenient-Than-He-Used-To-Be would fundamentally and irrevocably alter the course of history. Unfortunately, the argument became so heated that the shoulders of both Horace and Norwood began to shake with the heightened emotion, which didn't please King Amnestios at all.

'I warned you before about jiggling about!' he yelled. 'Guards! Take them both back down to the dungeon and do unspeakably unpleasant things to them until I've made up my mind as to the precise manner in which they will meet their horrifically agonising deaths.'

Rough, soldierly hands immediately hauled Horace and Norwood to their feet, and the guards were about to drag them away when the king held up a heavily bejewelled hand to stop them. Clearly, he still had a bit more ranting to do.

'You have the recently reinstated Royal Soothsayer to thank for my leniency before,' he said, 'but you've gone too far this time. Cajole, wheedle and fawn though he might, this time you really will get your fatally grisly comeuppance. In fact, because of you, I'm seriously considering changing my name from Amnestios the Lenient to Amnestios the Inappropriately and Excessively Brutal.'

'Oh, please don't go to any trouble on our account,' said Norwood. 'Amnestios the Lenient has a much nicer ring to it.'

The king's face flushed redder than a baboon's backside, and his mouth pulled all manner of shapes as he battled to regain the power of speech. At the same moment, there was the crash and rattle of precious metal against marble, and Horace and Norwood shifted their gaze a few degrees to the right to see where Vesta stood open-mouthed and goggle-eyed in horror. Close to her feet, the enormous gold peanut platter wobbled and clattered where it had landed, and several hundred peanuts lay scattered in every conceivable direction.

The king spun his head round so fast that his crown was taken unawares and ended up skewed over one eye. Adjusting it to its rightful position, he surveyed the cause of the sudden din, then fixed Vesta with an anything-but-lenient glare.

'And take her too!' he yelled.

Two more guards stepped forward, and each took hold of one of her arms, but scarcely had the soldiers begun to frogmarch the three adventurers towards the door than a high-pitched caterwauling stopped them in their tracks. Captors, captives and everyone else in the room all turned to see Thestor wailing and moaning like a demented banshee, his head thrown back, his eyes closed, and his scrawny arms outstretched above him and flailing wildly at the air. His entire bony body quivered and shook so violently that Horace feared he might lose his loincloth at any moment.

'What in the name of almighty Zeus is the matter with you, man?' roared the king, who, judging by his tone, was not in the mood for any more disturbances to his peace.

'I think he's going into a trance,' said the Keeper of the Toothpicks.

'Shut up,' snapped the king. 'When I want any advice from a slave, I'll—'

'Noooo. Noooo. This cannot beeee,' Thestor wailed, his voice sounding as if he was at the far end of a very long and echoey tunnel.

'What cannot beeee?' said the king.

But Thestor didn't answer. Instead, he did quite a lot more arm flailing and generalised wailing and moaning before suddenly collapsing to the floor in an untidy heap of skin and bone. Twelve seconds passed, and when Thestor still hadn't stirred, the king ordered the Keeper of the Wine to revive him, which she duly did by pouring half a jug of Chateau Neuf d'Acropolis over the old man's head. Instantly, he jackknifed into a sitting position, spluttering like a half-drowned Yorkshire Terrier and snatching strands of wine-sodden hair and beard from in front of his eyes and mouth.

'What did you do that for?'

'Never mind that,' said the king. 'What was all that nonsense about just then?'

'Nonsense, your majesty?'

'All that wailing and arm flailing.'

'Oh yes,' said Thestor, staring at the marble floor between his knees as if he were struggling to remember. 'Seems like I went into a bit of a trance.'

'Told you,' muttered the Keeper of the Toothpicks.

'And?' said the king.

Thestor slowly raised his eyes to meet the king's. 'Oh dear.'

'"Oh dear" *what*?'

'It's not good news, I'm afraid, your majesty.'

'What isn't?' said the king, shifting uncomfortably on his throne.

'About the future. The very *near* future unfortunately.'

'Yes, yes. I think I already gathered it was some sort

of prophecy.'

There was a brief pause as Thestor held the king's gaze, seemingly rehearsing the words in his head before he spoke.

'Plague, pestilence and famine, your majesty. But not necessarily in that order.'

'I thought plague and pestilence were much the same thing,' muttered the Keeper of Truffles, but no-one took any notice.

'Oh yes,' Thestor added, 'and there'll also be a mighty earthquake and a massive volcanic eruption, the combined forces of which will obliterate the whole of the city and a lot more of your kingdom besides.'

'But there isn't a volcano within two hundred leagues of here,' said the king.

Thestor pursed his lips. 'Okay, so maybe not the volcanic eruption then, but the earthquake and the other stuff are a racing certainty.'

King Amnestios slammed his fists down onto the arms of his throne. 'But this cannot be,' he moaned.

'That's what *I* said,' said Thestor, 'but with a much longer "eeee" sound.'

'But can there be no salvation? No escape from all these plagues and pestilences and whatnot?'

'Same thing,' muttered the Keeper of Truffles, but everyone ignored him again.

'Well...' said Thestor, making this one syllable sound three times longer than it needed to be and pensively stroking his still damp beard, which was far more than three times longer than it needed to be.

'Out with it, man,' barked the king. 'Is there any hope or not?'

'According to my spirit guide,' said Thestor after a few more strokes of his beard, 'your majesty has severely angered the gods, and as everyone knows, it's no easy matter getting *them* to forgive and forget once they've got the hump about something. Oh dear me, no.'

'Oh, for goodness' sake. *Now* what am I supposed to have done?'

Thestor waved a skeletal arm in the general direction of Horace, Norwood and Vesta. 'Well, you see, the gods do tend to expect their special envoys on Earth to be treated with rather more courtesy and respect than—'

'*Them*?' said the king, jumping to his feet and also waving an arm towards the three adventurers. 'Special envoys of the gods?'

'Uh-huh.'

The king took his time while he studied each of the adventurers from top to toe and back again, his upper lip twisting into a snarl of scornful disbelief.

'Is this... true?' he said at last.

Horace, Norwood and Vesta exchanged the briefest of glances and then nodded vigorously in unison.

'Certainly,' said Horace.

'Absolutely,' said Vesta.

'Yes indeed,' said Norwood.

'So what exactly is it the gods have sent you to *do*... as "special envoys"?' said the king.

Each of the three adventurers opened their mouths to speak, although Horace for one had no idea how to answer. Fortunately, Thestor already had it covered.

'Top secret, I'm afraid, your majesty,' he said, tapping the side of his nose. 'If they told you, they'd have to kill you.'

The king spun round and shot him a glare so fierce that it rocked the old man back on his heels.

'Just kidding, obviously,' said Thestor with the merest of unconvincing chuckles.

'This is hardly the time to play the jester, Thestor.'

'Of course not,' said Thestor, lowering his head as if suppressing a giggle.

'And besides, you haven't answered my question

about how we might escape these plagues and pestilences and whatnot.'

The Keeper of Truffles got only as far as the word "Same" when the king struck him hard in the face with the back of his hand without even looking in his direction.

'Is there no way we might appease the gods?' he added.

'Hmm,' said Thestor with a bit more beard stroking. 'There is *one* way from what my spirit guide told me, but I don't think you're going to like it.'

'Well?'

'Release the three of them immediately and let them be about their envoying business.'

'And that will do it, will it?'

'Ah,' said Thestor, clicking his fingers as if suddenly remembering something. 'Apparently, the gods did say that, by way of apology for your appalling treatment of them, they should first be your guests of honour at an enormous banquet and you should then send them on their way, laden with all manner of riches, the like of which they couldn't possibly imagine.'

And that, as they don't necessarily say, is precisely what happened. Despite his obvious scepticism about Thestor's prophecy and, in particular, that Horace and his co-adventurers could indeed be celestial envoys, King Amnestios decided that the risk factor of incurring the wrath of the gods far outweighed their usefulness as slaves. On the contrary, they were three of the worst he'd ever owned, and he'd come across a fair few duffers in his time, so, truth be told, he was heartily glad to see the back of them. A lot less satisfactory, however, was having to part with quite such a large amount of gold, silver and jewellery from the Royal Stash, not to mention the vast quantities of food and drink they and their damned dog had gorged themselves with at the banquet.

32

DS Scatterthwaite felt faint from the lack of sustenance. Not a single morsel of food had passed his lips in almost two hours. He'd deliberately arrived at the Lost Soles Boot and Shoe Repair Shop a few minutes early for his appointment and nipped into a nearby mini-market with the intention of filling his pockets with as many chocolate bars, pasties and assorted snacks as they could hold, but as soon as he'd left the shop, he'd discovered to his horror that the habit he was wearing was entirely devoid of any pockets at all. Deciding that it might be bad form to turn up at the interview clutching a carrier bag stuffed to the brim with gluttonous intent, he'd crammed the whole lot inside the hood and sleeves of his habit. This worked perfectly while he was sitting still on the bench outside the shoe repair shop with his arms folded, but the slightest movement had been accompanied by the telltale sound of crinkling crisp packets and chafing chocolate wrappers. Worse still, the moment he stood up, turned his head or uncrossed his arms, most of his emergency supplies cascaded to the ground in a heap of brightly coloured packaging.

In despair, he'd decided to stoke himself up with as much of the food as he could manage, and when two monks on a motorbike and sidecar had pulled up alongside him ten minutes later, his chin was heavily streaked with chocolate, and his mouth was so stuffed with pasty and crisps that he was barely able to speak.

'Brother Thomas?' the pillion passenger monk had

asked.

Scatterthwaite had nodded, making a conscious effort not to move his mouth and hoping that his food-stuffed cheeks didn't make him look like a jazz musician with mumps, attempting to hit double high C on the trumpet. To divert the monks' attention while he quickly chewed and swallowed, he'd handed them the letter inviting him for interview. They'd obligingly perused it long enough for him to reduce the bulge in his cheeks to less hamster-like proportions and then instructed him to climb into the sidecar, blindfolding him with what looked a lot like a Millwall FC scarf as soon as he was seated.

'I'm sorry about this,' the pillion monk had said, 'but the location of our headquarters must remain a secret to all who have not yet been admitted into the Society. — Is that chocolate on your chin by the way?'

The trip had taken about twenty minutes, and Scatterthwaite had had no way of knowing whether the two officers Harper Collins had ordered to tail them had managed to keep up. But given the speed the motorbike had been travelling at and, from what his ears had told him, the occasional narrow alleyway they'd passed through along the tortuous route, he very much doubted it. By the time the bike came to a halt and the driver switched off the engine, he himself had had no idea whether he was two miles or fifteen from where he'd been picked up. Still blindfolded, the two monks had taken an arm each and guided him through a large, creaking door, along a short corridor that echoed to the sound of two pairs of flip-flops and one pair of size nine Doc Marten shoes, and then down a long flight of stone steps.

When the scarf had been removed from his eyes, Scatterthwaite had found himself in a small, windowless room with stone walls and a flagstone floor, and even though the only illumination was from four candles on a table in the centre of the room, he'd blinked against the sudden shift from almost complete darkness. As his vision adjusted itself, he'd seen that there was a wooden pew-like bench along one wall, and sitting on it were two men in monks' habits and a young woman wearing a traffic warden's uniform. He'd taken up the only vacant space next to them on the bench, and all had waited in silence for their turn to be interviewed. Since then, the woman and one of the monks had each been ushered through a sliding oak door into an adjacent room and had come back out into the waiting room half an hour later and left without a word. No other candidates had arrived after Scatterthwaite, so he sat alone on the bench, waiting for the second monk to reappear. Then it would be his turn.

He stood up and paced an oblong route around the table, mentally rehearsing answers to what he might be asked. It wasn't that he was particularly anxious about the interview — although the possibility that he might be strip-searched still weighed heavily on his mind — it was more an attempt to distract his taste buds' craving for a ham, cheese and pickle sandwich. By the time he'd completed the second circuit of the room, the strategy had been partially successful but only to the extent that he'd forgotten all about the ham, cheese and pickle sandwich and was now desperate for a generous slice of Black Forest gateau with extra squirty-cream.

The minute this is over, he promised himself, I'm heading straight for the nearest—

But his gastronomic aspirations were interrupted by the squeak of the sliding door. His pacing had brought him almost directly in front of it, and Monk Number Two brushed against him as he passed.

'Brother Thomas!'

The voice from inside the room was deep and husky and sounded like it belonged to someone who didn't appreciate being kept waiting.

'Close it behind you,' said the voice as Scatterthwaite stepped through the doorway.

He did as he was told and quickly surveyed the room. Stone walls and curved stone ceiling. Like a stone railway carriage but slightly wider and about half the length. An enormous mahogany table filled almost the entire room. High-backed wooden chairs all around it, three of them at the far end occupied by monks in off-grey habits, the hoods pulled well forward so that their faces were hidden in shadow.

'Please take a seat,' said the monk who sat at the head of the table, his chair a little bigger than all the others.

The Head Monk, Scatterthwaite guessed, and sat down on the nearest chair at the foot of the table.

'I'm Chairbrother Lemonsole,' said the Head Monk. 'On my left, Brother Whitebait, and on my right, Brother Haddock.'

He gestured vaguely towards each monk as he spoke their name, and both gave a slight nod in response. Or maybe they didn't. It was hard to tell under their hoods.

'That's quite a coincidence, isn't it?' said Scatterthwaite cheerily, partly to get the ice broken as soon as possible and partly to demonstrate from the start how quick on the uptake he was.

'Pardon me?' said Lemonsole.

'You all having the names of fishes. What are the chances of that, eh?'

The Head Monk paused momentarily before answering. 'Ah, no. It is a tradition of the Society that all members are given the name of a type of fish during their initiation.'

'Cool,' said Scatterthwaite. 'And do we get to choose our own?'

'Well, it's the normal practice that we—'

''Cos there are some fish names I really wouldn't

want to be saddled with, if you know what I mean. Like "Minnow", for instance, or "Flounder". And "Sperm Whale" would be a complete no-no of course. Although now I come to think about it, maybe "Sperm Whale" wouldn't be so bad after all.'

'I believe you'll find that whales are in fact mammals and not fish,' said Brother Haddock.

'Get outta here,' said Scatterthwaite, genuinely surprised. 'So Brother Sperm Whale's out then. How about Brother Shark or Brother Swordfish? Something with a bit of... attitude, yeah?'

'I think we may be getting ahead of ourselves here, Brother...' Lemonsole glanced at a sheet of paper in front of him on the table. 'Brother Thomas.'

'No worries,' said Scatterthwaite. 'I'm in no hurry, so you blokes take your time, yeah? Although I wouldn't say no to a cuppa and a bun if you happen to have the wherewithal.'

'I'm afraid it's Brother Simeon's day off today,' said Lemonsole.

'Simeon? That a kind of fish, is it?'

'Actually, he's a monkey, but—'

'Oh, I see. Like he's not a full monk, you mean. Sort of... "monky". As in... I dunno, when a colour's kind of yellow but not quite, so you say it's "yellowy".'

'Ah no,' said Brother Whitebait. 'Brother Simeon is a mon-*key*. With an "E". M - O - N - K - *E* - Y. A marmoset in fact.'

'Yeah?' said Scatterthwaite, struggling to picture a monkey dressed in a habit and cowl. 'A monkey monk. How weird is that?'

There was a brief pause while Chairbrother Lemonsole and his colleagues exchanged glances that might well have been furtive, but again it was hard to tell.

'It's complicated,' said Brother Haddock.

'And I really think we should crack on with the interview,' said Lemonsole, who was beginning to sound quite grumpy.

'Fair enough,' said Scatterthwaite, sitting back in his chair and crossing his legs. The stone walled room was a touch on the cool side, and there was an almighty draught sweeping up the inside of his habit and causing an unpleasant chill in his commando region. Still, at least they didn't seem to have any plans to strip-search him, which was a major boost to helping him relax, and so far, everything appeared to be progressing nicely. He felt particularly pleased with the way his ice-breaking strategy had turned out, and he was confident that the interview itself would simply be a formality before he was admitted into membership of the Society.

'First of all,' said Chairbrother Lemonsole. 'What is your order?'

Scatterthwaite thought this was rather a strange question, considering he'd already told them, but he answered it anyway. 'Er, cup of tea and a bun, but I thought you said—'

'No, no,' snapped Lemonsole. 'What *monastic* order do you belong to?'

'Oh, right.'

It was a question that Harper Collins had felt sure would come up, and Scatterthwaite scoured his brain cells for the answer she'd given him. Order of the Bath? Order of the Garter? No, they were something else altogether. Oh God, what the hell was it? Something to do with that film about monks that Sean Connery was in? Not sure, but it'll have to do.

'The Order of the Rose,' he said with as much feigned pride as he could muster.

The three monks went into a huddle of unintelligible whispering, and then the Head Monk said, 'We don't appear to be familiar with that particular order.'

'We're quite new actually.'

'And does this... "order" have any specific vows?'

Scatterthwaite pursed his lips while he thought about it. 'Er, well, vow of silence is one.'

The statement was met with a silence of its own, which gave him a clue to his error.

'Oh, except when we're being interviewed of course,' he added quickly. 'We're allowed to speak then, obviously. It'd be a bit daft otherwise, wouldn't it. You asking me all these questions and me just sat here like a constipated clam.'

A heavy sigh forced its way out of Lemonsole's hood. 'Any other vows?' he said wearily.

'Um, yes. That other one I can never remember the name of. You know. The one about not doing rumpy-pumpy. Selly-something-or-other.'

'Celibacy?'

Scatterthwaite clicked his fingers. 'That's the one. Celibacy.'

There followed another brief huddle of whispering, during which Scatterthwaite sat back in his chair and smiled to himself. This was all going pretty well, he thought. Compared to some of the interviews he'd had in the past, this one was turning out to be a piece of cake. But as soon as the metaphor had entered his head, the image of a generous slice of Black Forest gateau swept back into his consciousness, and he suddenly remembered he was very very hungry indeed.

33

There was scarcely room for everyone to fit into the camper van once it had been loaded up with all manner of gold, silver and jewellery, the like of which none of them could ever have imagined, so they'd had to stow as much of it as possible into every available cupboard space (and even the oven) before they could set off. Thestor had been most reluctant to accompany them at first, insisting that he ought to remain at the palace to further consolidate his newly restored position as Royal Soothsayer, but the adventurers had painstakingly explained the concept of "welching on a deal" and forcefully reiterated their need of his assistance in finding the exact location of the Holey Snails. And after all, they'd added, it was the least he could do after the hell they'd been put through in helping him to get his old job back. What had finally swung it, though, was when they'd told him he could keep enough of the gold, silver and jewellery to ensure that he'd never again have to live the life of a hermit once the king discovered — as he surely would — that he was totally rubbish at predicting the future and banished him for good.

They'd been on the road — or more accurately, dirt track — for almost two hours, and Horace had already had to pull over three times for Thestor to be sick. He was still looking a bit on the queasy side now.

'Are we nearly there yet?' he said in a quavering might-be-about-to-throw-up-again kind of voice.

'That's rather difficult to say,' said Vesta,

'considering you're the only one who knows where we're going.'

Thestor groaned. 'I'm not used to this sort of travelling. I've only once in my life even been on a horse-drawn cart, and that was only for a couple of leagues.'

There then followed a lengthy silence until Horace spotted Thestor in the rear-view mirror suddenly sitting forward on the back seat. He was about to pull over to the side of the track again when Thestor, in a rather more animated voice than before, said, 'If this is a time machine, why don't we just jump forward a few hours? You know. Get where we're going in a minute or two without having to put up with this constant bumping and jiggering about.'

'The controls aren't that accurate, I'm afraid,' said Horace. 'We could end up in a completely different century.'

'Not to mention different part of the world,' Norwood added.

Horace somewhat resented his co-adventurer's slur on the efficiency of his van, given that the geographical settings were far more reliable than the temporal ones, but he let the matter pass. Something else that then passed was another lengthy silence, which was several times longer than the previous one. Strictly speaking, though, neither of the silences were *completely* silent because of the constant clattering and clanking of pots, pans, crockery, cutlery, gold, silver and jewellery as the van lurched and shuddered its way along the rough dirt track. Also clearly audible were Thestor's incessant moans and groans and Zoot's Richter-scale snoring. "No-one spoke a word for quite a long time" would therefore be a more appropriate description, and this period of no-one speaking lasted until Vesta said, 'It'll be getting dark soon. Maybe we should park up for the night and carry on in the morning.'

Not surprisingly, Thestor was the first to agree to Vesta's suggestion, followed by Norwood and then Horace. He was beginning to feel bone-achingly tired, and even though Vesta or Norwood could have taken a turn with the driving, he was always a little reluctant to let anyone else take command of his precious van. Besides, they were getting low on fuel, and an overnight stop would be the perfect opportunity to produce some more.

One of the great things about all vehicles capable of time travel was that they didn't run on any of the standard motor fuels but on a synthetic liquid called XR-964(b). To replenish the fuel tank with XR-964(b), all you had to do was add three drops of one specially formulated chemical and two drops of another, then flick a switch on the inside of the filler cap and wait for the chemical reaction to do its job. How long you had to wait depended on the size of the fuel tank of course, but in the case of Horace's van, six hours was usually enough to refill it to the brim from empty.

The chemicals involved in creating XR-964(b) were extremely cheap to produce since they were derived entirely from a specific mixture of naturally occurring herbs and wildflowers, but the precise formula was an incredibly closely guarded secret. Unsurprisingly, the multinational oil company which had developed the new wonder-fuel was more than a little reluctant to make public a method of producing fuel which every motorist on the planet could achieve with a children's chemistry set and a few hours of botanical scavenging. As luck would have it, however, the chief executive of the company happened to be a keen time travel enthusiast himself and was also president of The Worldwide Association for Travelling Through Time and Space (TWATTTS). A deal had therefore been struck which allowed only full members of the association to purchase the XR-964(b) chemicals on the strict, contractually enforced condition that they never so much as breathed a word to anyone about even the very existence of the wonder-fuel.

'This looks like a good spot,' said Norwood as the van emerged from a densely wooded area and the crystal clear waters of an almost perfectly round lake appeared before them.

Horace swung the van off the dirt track, and even before he'd come to a complete halt, Thestor flung open the sliding side door and leapt out, a bony hand cupped over his quivering mouth.

34

Brother Herring took a couple of steps back to better appraise the quality of his handiwork. It wasn't a perfect job by any means, but at least *Hawking 3* was no longer covered in quite so many layers of dust. He'd paid particular attention to the motorcycle's saddle and also the seat inside the rocket-shaped sidecar to avoid further soiling of his and Brother Mackerel's habits when they had to set off along the dirt track once again, and both were spotless. In fact, they would probably have been gleaming if the sun had still been out, but it was already dark and there was little more than a fingernail of moon to see by.

'It's not perfect by any means,' he said, 'but at least the seats are a lot cleaner now.'

'Well done,' said Brother Mackerel without turning to face him. She was far too busy watching the activity a hundred yards away on the far side of the lake through a pair of night vision binoculars.

'Anything happening?' said Herring, sitting next to where she was lying face down on a small patch of dead, brown grass.

'Not much. They've got a fire going, and it looks like they're roasting something on a spit.'

'Here for the night then, I guess.'

'Seems that way.'

Herring pulled his hood even lower over his face and thrust his arms into the opposite sleeves of his habit.

'Getting a bit chilly,' he said. 'Maybe we should light

a fire too.'

'Too risky,' said Mackerel. 'There's no way they wouldn't see it, and they'd know we were here then.'

'Yes, but they wouldn't know *who* we were, would they? Wouldn't know we were following them, like.'

'But what if they came to investigate?'

She was quite right of course, thought Herring. The last thing they needed was to get rumbled now after all the effort they'd put into keeping tabs on them. All the same, if it was this chilly at this time in the evening, it was going to get an awful lot colder as the night wore on.

'I wish I'd worn my underpants now,' he said.

'Too much information,' said Mackerel.

'Sorry. I didn't actually mean to say that out loud.'

Mackerel laughed. 'That's okay. We're all God's children under the skin.'

'That's true,' said Herring even though he had no idea what that had to do with whether you were wearing underpants or not.

He stood up again and paced out an almost perfect circle in the dust, roughly ten feet in diameter. Round and round he went, sometimes speeding up, sometimes slowing down, sometimes hopping, and occasionally switching from a clockwise to an anti-clockwise direction (and vice versa) to prevent himself from getting dizzy. It was an activity that kept him a degree or so warmer, but it was also something to do to alleviate the boredom and try to take his mind off his worsening hunger pangs. The ham, cheese and pickle sandwiches they'd brought with them had been tasty enough, but he could really have done with a good hot meal. Without a fire, though, this was obviously out of the question. He almost wished he was back home in the twenty-first century with his feet up in front of a roaring blaze and tucking into a generous helping of steak and kidney

239

pudding — preferably in a cosy little pub that served Fuller's London Pride on draught.

On the other hand, he always enjoyed these occasional forays through time. Well, maybe not always. On the last trip, for instance — to Paris, smack in the middle of the French Revolution — he'd had to endure more than a week of Brother Pilchard and his constant prattling in Latin, which had driven him almost to the brink of insanity. This was different, though, and it was a definite bonus to have some female company for a change. Herring had an idea that Brother Mackerel was actually rather pretty, but it was hard to know for sure since he'd only ever glimpsed part of her face a couple of times when the cowl of her habit had slipped back. Not that it particularly mattered whether she was pretty or not of course. As with all the other members of SMASH (the Society for the Murder and/or Assassination of Septuagenarian Heretics), he'd taken a solemn vow of celibacy when he'd first joined up.

Truth be told, this was one of several reasons why Herring often wondered if he was really cut out for the monastic lifestyle. He'd been extremely partial to unbridled hedonism in his youth, paying for his pleasures out of the paltry wages he earned working at a factory which made Swiss Army knives. The job itself had been mind-numbingly tedious and consisted of spending seven hours a day hunched over a conveyor belt and attaching the little gadget for unpicking the end of a roll of Sellotape to every new multi-tool that came his way. (Approximately one every six and a half minutes.) He wouldn't have minded quite so much if his employers had varied the job a bit and, say, allowed the assembly line workers to fit a different little tool or gadget on a week-by-week basis to alleviate the monotony. Sellotape unpicker one week, nasal probe the next, and so on until you'd gone through the lot and started at the beginning again.

He'd even suggested this to the management, but they'd abruptly dismissed the idea on the grounds that this would involve an unjustifiable increase in the time and expense necessary for retraining. Herring had argued that an improvement in job satisfaction would have a highly beneficial effect on worker morale, which would almost certainly result in a dramatic increase in productivity, but his employers had disagreed and sacked him the following day for "quasi-anarchistic tendencies incompatible with the manufacture of the Swiss Army knife and the associated attaching of its handy little tools and gadgets".

Utterly disillusioned with the multi-tool manufacturing industry and gainful employment in general, he'd immediately decided to become a monk. With minimal understanding of what this might entail, however, he'd soon discovered that being a monk was even more boring than working at the Swiss Army knife factory, and as a career choice, it left a lot to be desired. Not only that, but he'd quickly realised that he had almost no aptitude for the job or any of its day-to-day tasks. His singing voice was atrocious, his attempts at calligraphy were completely indecipherable, and somewhat less importantly according to most of the other brethren, he was a committed and devout atheist.

After only a few weeks, he'd been on the point of hanging up his habit for good and heading off to look for more suitable employment when he'd heard about SMASH from a fellow monk who'd recently joined up. Their activities were all supposed to be top secret, but Brother Mullet, as he was now called, had dropped a couple of hints about the three-score-years-and-ten stuff, which Herring thought sounded right up his alley. Not that he was a natural born killer or had any psychopathic tendencies to speak of, but he'd decided that bumping off a few wrinklies would add a bit of spice to his otherwise mundane existence. The time-travelling part of the job had come as a totally unexpected but thoroughly welcome bonus, even though it sometimes meant having to freeze his butt off and existing on a diet of ham, cheese and pickle sandwiches for days on end.

He stopped his circular pacing and wandered back to where Brother Mackerel was still lying face down on the ground.

'Anything?' he said.

'Sitting around feeding their faces.'

'Maybe we should just kill them all now and have done with it.'

Brother Mackerel slowly lowered her binoculars and twisted her head round to look up at him. 'For one thing, it isn't God's will that we go round murdering people willy-nilly. Only the Septoes, remember?'

Herring shuffled his feet in the dirt. 'Well, what about the old bloke then? The one in the loincloth thing. He's gotta be eighty if he's a day.'

'But that's not what we're here for, is it? The whole point of our mission is to stop them bringing back any Holey Snails.'

'So if we kill them now, it's job done, isn't it?'

'Our orders are to follow them until they find what they're searching for and then destroy all the snails so they become extinct much further back in time than they were already.'

'And *then* we kill them.'

'No,' Mackerel snapped. 'We simply immobilise their time machine to stop them finding any snails even further back in time.'

'So they'll be stuck here forever?'

'I imagine so, yes.'

'I could think of a lot better time periods to be stranded in than this,' Herring said with a snort. 'I

242

reckon if I were them, I'd *rather* be killed by us.'

'That's as may be,' said Mackerel, once again training her binoculars on the small group of adventurers at the far side of the lake, 'but orders are orders and we've got a job to do.'

Herring grunted and was about to resume his circular pacing when there was a soft pinging noise and a small cloud of dust burst upwards from the ground less than a foot in front of his Union Jack flip-flops.

'What the—?'

Another "*ping*" and another explosion of dust — even closer this time. Mackerel threw down her binoculars and jumped to her feet.

'Jesus,' said Herring. 'I think we're being—'

He was interrupted by a third "*ping*" and a burst of dust at the exact midpoint between his flip-flops.

'—shot at,' said Mackerel, finishing his sentence for him, and the two monks flung themselves headlong into the cover of the time-travelling motorbike and sidecar known as *Hawking 3*.

* * *

Kenny Bunkport fired half a dozen more shots, most of which pinged off the motorbike and sidecar the monks were cowering behind.

'Damn cowards,' he muttered and lay his enormous gun down on the hard-baked earth.

He left the silencer fixed to the barrel in case he got another chance to take out the two interfering monks who were more than likely going to screw up his mission if he didn't deal with them now that he had the opportunity. From his position on the top of a small hill overlooking the lake, he had a perfect view of the monks and also the bunch of goons with the camper van. With the aid of the telescopic night sight on his gun, he'd been able to identify the two guys he'd followed to Wellwisher's house and the woman who'd pole-axed him with a single karate chop. Him. Kenny Bunkport. Ex marine, built like a tank, and being roughed up by a *woman*.

He winced at the shame of it, and his fists clenched into twin weapons of mass destruction at the memory of being tied hand and foot and dumped into the middle of hell knows where. It had taken him hours to free himself and trudge through miles of open countryside, often up to his knees in thick, sucking mud, until he reached some dumbass little village which had at least a passing acquaintance with civilisation — and a payphone. And during every minute of all those hours, he had had only one thought in his head and one thought alone. Revenge.

Oh, how his trigger finger had itched when he'd caught up with those three and had each of them fixed in the cross-hairs of his telescopic sight. The goddamn woman in particular. But that would have to wait. First, he had to carry on tailing them until they'd found these Holey Snails his employer was so desperate for.

A faint smile crept across his face, skewing the deep scar which ran from just below his left ear to almost the middle of his chin.

'That's when we'll have our reward, my sweet,' he said, picking up his gun again and stroking it as tenderly as if it were a newborn kitten (which he wouldn't actually have done if it really was a cat because he was seriously allergic).

A momentary glint of light caught his eye from somewhere close to the motorbike and sidecar, and he fired off another half dozen rounds. He listened intently, but there wasn't even the slightest yelp or groan to indicate that he'd so much as winged either of the monks. Judging by the number of times it sounded like he'd hit the bike, though, it was well on the cards that this particular machine wouldn't be travelling through time *or* space any time soon.

But maybe that would be the perfect solution. Bunkport didn't have anything personal against these two monks — or monks in general, come to that — so stranding them here might be all he needed to do to keep them out of his way. And besides, putting bullet holes in holy people was bound to be worth at least triple points when it came to totting up the scores on whether you'd go to hell or not when you croaked. Not that this was a particular issue where Kenny Bunkport was concerned. He knew full well that he'd reached the "Do Not Pass Go" point a long time ago.

He swivelled his gun through ninety degrees and focused in on the chunky black dog, which was barking its dumb head off at the edge of the wood a dozen or so yards up from the lake. A few degrees down, and there was the scrawny old guy in some kind of diaper — whoever the hell *he* was. A slight shift to the right, and he had the blonde chick slap bang in the centre of his cross-hairs. 'Boom!' he said quietly and then, with a determined effort, eased his finger from the trigger.

Later, he told himself. She'll get hers when you're good and ready. A pity in a way though really. She's pretty damned stunning in the looks department, and in any other circumstances—

Bunkport interrupted his own lascivious train of thought as he swung the telescopic sight back and forth around the immediate area of the camper van, frantically trying to spot the two other men from the group. He extended his search by thirty or forty yards to either side, but there was no sign of them anywhere.

'Damn me if they ain't goddamn vanished into thin goddamn air,' he said aloud and then slammed three more rounds into the motorbike and sidecar, simply because he felt like it.

35

Harper Collins got up from her chair and went round to the front of the desk to get a closer look as DS Scatterthwaite lifted the hem of his habit to reveal the shiny new pair of Union Jack flip-flops.

'Cool, eh?' he said through a mouthful of individual chicken and ham pie.

'So you're in then?' said Harper, scarcely believing that he'd actually managed to pass the interview.

'Absolute doddle. Hit it off with them right from the start.'

Harper thought this was highly doubtful unless his interview technique was very far removed from his everyday persona. Still, he'd achieved the objective of infiltrating the group, which should prove to be a major step forward in cracking the case wide open.

'So what have you learned so far?' she said.

'Well, for a kickoff, they call themselves SMASH, which apparently stands for "Society for the Murder and/or Assassination of Septuagenarian Heretics", and they've all got fish names.'

'Sorry?'

'Every new member gets given the name of a kind of fish. Not sure why exactly, but it's one of the rules. I'm Brother Bream from now on.'

'Uh-huh.'

'It was going to be Brother Chubsucker, but I wasn't havin' none of that.'

Harper sat back down behind her desk. 'Anything

else?'

'Er... oh yes. They say it's okay to wear underpants.'

'Oh, that *is* a relief,' said Harper, but Scatterthwaite failed to pick up on the sarcasm.

'Bloody sight more of a relief that they didn't strip-search me, I can tell you.'

Harper counted to ten while he tossed the empty tinfoil tray of his pie into the wastebin and then rummaged in the bulging carrier bag by his feet for a tube of sour-cream-and-onion Pringles.

'What I actually meant when I said "anything else",' she said, 'was did you find out anything that might be useful to our investigation?'

'Um...'

'What about the place where they interviewed you? Is that where they're based, and would you be able to find it again? The officers I got to tail you lost you when you went down some alley or other.'

'I'm pretty sure it's their headquarters, but I haven't got a clue where it is. They blindfolded me as soon as they picked me up — with a bloody Millwall scarf of all things.'

'Have they said anything to you about the murders yet?'

'A bit, yeah, but they told me I'd have to do some training first and also help out in the office till I was ready.'

'Doing what?'

'Putting those birthday cards together — the ones that knock the old geezers unconscious when they open them,' said Scatterthwaite and then, grinning sheepishly, added, 'Mind you, I did get the first one a bit wrong and ended up spark out on the floor for a few minutes.'

Unlike her sergeant, Harper didn't find this in the least amusing, so she simply folded her arms and waited for him to continue.

Scatterthwaite's grin instantly faded as even he couldn't fail to take the hint. 'Then there's filing, making the tea and putting together lists of all the seventieth birthdays coming up. They've got this database on their computer with the names and addresses, whether they live alone, elimination dates. All that kind of thing.'

'Elimination dates?'

'When they plan to do the killings. I overheard a couple of 'em talking, and apparently they've got a bit twitchy since we nearly collared one of their blokes. They've obviously figured out that all we have to do is find out who's got a seventieth birthday on what day and then just wait for them to turn up, so now they're not always gonna do the killing on the actual day.'

'And you'll be drawing up these lists yourself?'

'The basic details, yeah, and then they tell me what elimination dates to put in.'

Harper slapped both her palms onto the top of the desk so hard that it made her empty coffee cup rattle on its saucer. 'But this is brilliant news. I had a feeling they'd try and fool us by shifting the dates of the murders, but if you can feed us the information in advance, we'll know exactly which addresses to watch and, more importantly, when.'

She stood up and came back round to Scatterthwaite's side of the desk. She almost felt like hugging him, but it was an urge she had little difficulty in suppressing. Instead, she patted him lightly on the shoulder and said, 'Good work, Sergeant. You've done well.'

Scatterthwaite instantly stopped chomping, and a hint of red brought a flush to his food-stuffed cheeks. For once, he seemed lost for words until he waved the tube of Pringles under Harper's nose. 'Pringle?'

She shook her head. 'When are you back with them again?'

'They're picking me up at the same place tomorrow at

nine.'

'Okay, that's great, but from now on we should meet in secret so you can keep me updated. You keep turning up here dressed as a monk every day is way too conspicuous.'

'Yeah, sure. Maybe by the old bandstand in the park?'

'That'll do for starters, yes, but we'll need to keep changing the location in case they're keeping tabs on you.'

'We could both wear a red carnation or something,' said Scatterthwaite with mounting enthusiasm, and then glanced down at the top of his habit. 'Except I don't have a buttonhole in this thing. — Folded newspapers then. And I could say... "The butterflies are nesting early this year", and then you say "Yes, but not as early as the hedgehogs".'

Harper couldn't resist a chuckle. 'Let's not get too carried away, Sergeant. I really don't think we'll have too much trouble recognising each other, do you?'

Scatterthwaite's features collapsed into a pout of disappointment, and she almost felt the faintest pang of guilt. After all, idiot though he was, it was because of him that she could at last be on the verge of bringing these murdering monks to justice.

'Perhaps just the folded newspapers then,' she said.

'The pink ones would be good,' said Scatterthwaite, his eagerness returning in a flash. 'Financial whatsit. *Financial Times*.'

Harper wasn't convinced that the *FT* would be high on the list of most monks' preferred reading material, but she decided not to argue the point.

36

The cries for help became gradually louder as Horace and Norwood left Vesta, Thestor and Zoot to finish their meals by the van and inched their way cautiously through the thick, dark wood which began a dozen yards or so from the edge of the lake. So dark was it, in fact, that without the handy little torches in their Swiss Army knives, the two adventurers wouldn't have been able to see their hands in front of their faces. Not that they wanted to see their hands in front of their faces (either their own or each other's). This would have been counterproductive in helping them to see where they were going, so instead, they used the torches to focus on all the low and overhanging branches which threatened to smack them in the face at almost every step.

It was Zoot who had first heard the cries for help, and although he hadn't actually recognised the sounds as cries for help, he'd pricked up his ears, raised his hackles and started barking excitedly in the direction of the wood. Horace, Norwood, Vesta and Thestor had all listened intently to try to identify the source of the dog's alarm but hadn't been able to hear a thing over all the barking.

Since Horace and Norwood had finished their dinners and Vesta and Thestor hadn't, it had been agreed (by Vesta and Thestor) that Horace and Norwood should be the ones to volunteer to go and investigate. Norwood had argued that he had no wish to be accused of either sexism or ageism and that he would therefore be more than willing for Vesta or Thestor to go in his stead, but Vesta had countered that finishing her meal while it was still hot took precedence over slavish adherence to the principles of political correctness. Thestor, on the other hand, had had no idea what either of them were talking about and had simply carried on eating in silence.

As for Horace — and despite his ingrained aversion to all that "feel the fear and do it anyway" nonsense and an overwhelming preference for a "feel the fear and run like hell" approach to life — the last thing he'd wanted was to appear in the lovely Vesta's eyes as a cowardly wuss with the backbone of an amoeba, so he'd set off into the wood without a word of dissent.

'What if it's some kind of mythological monster?' Norwood whispered as he stooped to avoid a nasty facial wound from yet another low and overhanging branch. 'You know, like that Ligoatamos creature.'

'Just sounds like some bloke to me,' said Horace even though his mind had already conjured up a variety of images, most of which involved multitudes of enormous razor-sharp teeth, massive blood-drenched claws and the ability to projectile vomit searing blasts of flesh-sizzling fire at will.

'Do you mean like a really really big bloke or a really really small one?' said Norwood.

'Oh, really *really* small, I'd say. Almost tiny in fact.'

'Yes? Well, I just hope you're right, that's all.'

So do I, thought Horace, but I very much doubt it.

And after another twelve trees and numerous low and overhanging branches further into the wood, he realised that, whilst his doubts had not been entirely unfounded, the teeth/claws/flesh-sizzling fire scenario had mercifully been overstated. There in front of them was a man who, though not tiny by any means, was only a few inches above average height and, quite frankly, a touch on the puny side. Not at all scary as such, and nor were

251

the thick, black beard which tapered to a sharp point nearly a foot beneath his chin or the matching mane of coarse, black hair. What *was* somewhat alarming, however, was the enormous pair of black wings that sprouted from his shoulders.

Horace and Norwood stepped warily towards him to get a closer look — but not too close — and gave him a thorough scanning with the beams of their handy little torches. Rather than standing stock still with his back pressed against the trunk of a tree, as they'd first thought, it soon became clear that he was bound to it with a length of heavy iron chain wrapped several times around his body and the treetrunk. His cries for help, which had escalated into furious roars for help, ceased as soon as he spotted the two adventurers, and he fixed them with a piercing stare that gave Horace the shivers. Even more shiver-inducing was the way the colour of his eyes alternated every few seconds between tar black and the fiery red of molten lava.

'Take that bloody light outta me eyes, will yer?' the creature yelled, his voice a peculiar blend of squawking raven and operatic castrato.

'Sorry,' Horace and Norwood chorused and immediately diverted their handy little torches in a slightly more downward direction.

'Who the Hades are you anyway?'

'Um, well, my name's Horace Tweed,' said Horace, 'and this is my friend and co-adventurer Norwood Junction — although that's not actually his real name. His real name's not very easy to pronounce, you see, so we decided to—'

'Shut up!' the creature shrieked. 'I don't give a flying fart what your names are. What I wanna know is where'd you spring from all of a sudden.'

'That's rather a long story,' said Norwood, 'but perhaps I might enquire as to your own identity.'

'What?'

'My co-adventurer wants to know who *you* are,' said Horace.

'Well, if it's any of your business,' said the creature and puffed out his not very impressive chest, 'I am a daemon, and since we're all being so incredibly bloody polite, my name's Thanatos.'

Norwood took a step back. 'You're a demon?'

'*Dae*-mon. You deaf or what?'

'So there's a difference, is there?'

'Course there's a bloody difference. Demon's spelt with an "E", whereas daemon's got a diphthong in the middle.'

'No, I mean is there a difference between a *de*-mon and a *dae*-mon?'

The creature sighed as if this was the gazillionth time he'd been asked this question. 'Daemons are kinda like demigods, whereas yer demons are just plain bloody evil.'

'I see,' said Norwood, but judging by his deeply furrowed brow, probably didn't.

'Anyroad,' said Thanatos the daemon, 'much as I'd love to carry on our little chat, how's about you get me outta these bleedin' chains so I can get on with me work?'

'Oh, so daemons have jobs, do they?' said Horace, who had no more knowledge of daemons than Norwood.

'Depends.'

'On?'

'On what line of daemonry you happen to be in. Me, for example, I'm in what you might call the logistics business.'

'Oh yes? And what does that involve exactly?' said Norwood.

'Basically takin' people to the underworld when it's their time to snuff it.'

253

'You mean like the... like the... Grim Reaper?' Horace stammered.

'The what?'

'The, er, Bringer of Death, sort of thing.'

'Yeah, I guess that about sums it up. Although I ain't the one what decides when somebody's gotta croak. I get me orders from upstairs, see? Then all I do is cart the stiffs off to Hades.'

'Upstairs?'

'The gods.' Thanatos's eyes then glowed an even more fiery red than before. 'And now you know all about me, are you gonna get me outta these chains or what?'

He wriggled slightly, which was about as much as the tightness of his chain would allow.

'Yes, of course,' said Norwood and had taken half a step forward when Horace grabbed him by the arm.

'Hang on a minute,' he whispered. 'If this guy is really who he says he is, we've no idea what we might be letting ourselves in for once we set him free. And why's he been chained to a tree in the first place? Smells a bit fishy if you ask me.'

'Good point,' Norwood whispered back. 'Perhaps we should ask him.'

So that's what Horace did, and it was immediately apparent that Thanatos wasn't at all happy about being questioned on the subject.

'That's on a need to know basis,' he said.

'Yes,' said Horace, 'and we need to know so we can make a properly informed decision on whether to let you go or not.'

'Ye gods, give me strength,' Thanatos muttered heavenwards but seemed to recognise that he was in no position to argue. 'Well, all right, but this goes no further than you and me, okay?'

The two adventurers nodded their agreement, and

Thanatos told them how Zeus had sent him to find a particularly nasty piece of work by the name of Sisyphus and drag him off to the underworld pronto. But, the god had warned him, this Sisyphus was a slippery little devil, so he'd better take something along to tie him up with to stop him escaping. Now, it just so happened that Hephaistos, the gods' blacksmith, had recently invented a brand new kind of padlock which he claimed to be more secure than any lock previously known to man or god, so Thanatos had decided that this would be ideal for the job at hand, and armed with the new lock and a good length of heavy, iron chain, he'd set off in pursuit of his quarry.

It hadn't taken long to track him down to the very wood in which they now stood, and Sisyphus had recognised the daemon straight away.

'Oh, hello,' he'd said, 'and who is it you'd be after this time, Mr Death?'

'That'd be you, Sisyphus. Time's up, I'm afraid,' Thanatos had replied and begun to uncoil the length of chain.

'Sorry, old boy, you've got the wrong chap. My name's *Sos*yphus. Never heard of this Sisyphus fellow.'

Thanatos was not to be taken in by such a blatant lie, and nor had he fallen for any of Sisyphus's subsequent attempts to argue and plead his way out of his imminent death. Instead, he'd carried on preparing the chain and checked the lock was working properly before ordering Sisyphus to stand still and put his hands behind his back. Much to Thanatos's surprise, he'd obeyed the instruction without further argument, but as the daemon had come towards him with the chain in one hand and the lock in the other, Sisyphus's eyes had fallen on the gleaming new padlock with evident glee.

'I say,' he'd said. 'Is that one of those fancy new locks I've heard so much about? The "Hephaistos Ultra 23"?'

'It is, as a matter of fact.'

'How absolutely fascinating. Mind if I take a look?'

Knowing Sisyphus's well-deserved reputation for worming his way out of awkward situations, Thanatos had hesitated at first, but Sisyphus had eventually won him over with a series of not entirely unreasonable arguments, the last of which was 'Surely you wouldn't refuse a dying man his one last request?'

'Well,' said Thanatos, back in the present, 'to cut a long story short—'

'Don't tell me he tricked you into demonstrating the lock on yourself?' Horace interrupted, having by now formed a pretty good idea of how the story *did* end.

Thanatos's head drooped and his enormous black wings twitched uncomfortably. By now, the fire had been completely extinguished from his eyes and their colour reduced to a solemn black of excruciating embarrassment.

'You did, didn't you?' said Horace, unsuccessfully attempting to stifle his laughter to spare the daemon's shame.

'Yeah, okay, you can laugh,' said Thanatos, 'but if this ever gets out, I'll be out of a job quicker than you can say "Death, where is thy sting?".'

'Or *Chain of Fools*,' said Norwood, apparently finding it harder to suppress his giggling than Horace.

'Whatever. Just undo this damned chain and we can all be on our way as if nothing had happened.'

'Not so fast, Mr Thanatos,' said Horace with uncharacteristic assertiveness. 'Now that we've heard your explanation, my co-adventurer and I will need to discuss the possible ramifications of giving you your freedom.'

'Rami *what*?'

Horace and Norwood began to walk away so that they would be out of earshot of the daemon, but Thanatos shouted after them, 'Listen, you idiots, do you realise that all the time I'm chained up 'ere, nobody can actually die?'

The two adventurers turned back to face him, and Norwood said, 'But surely that's a good thing then. A reason *not* to set you free.'

Thanatos muttered some expletive or other under his breath. 'You really don't get it, do you? For a start, there's this god Ares — god of war, he is — and he's doing his nut 'cos there's been all these battles since I've been stuck 'ere, and not a single soldier has died in any of 'em.'

'Also a good thing, I'd say,' said Horace.

'Oh yeah? So how'd you like to have *your* head lopped off and be lying there in all the muck and blood and not be able to die? Or your arms and legs hacked off, or split up the middle with all your—'

'Yes, yes, I think we get the picture,' said Horace, beginning to feel distinctly queasy.

'And it ain't only the battles either. Think of all them poor sods with some 'orrible incurable disease or whatever, writhing in agony and praying for death to release them from their terrible suffering. *Praying* for it,

257

I tell you.'

As a staunch supporter of the right to die campaign, this was certainly an argument which struck a chord with Horace, but he still had misgivings about setting the daemon free.

'But if we do unchain you, what's to stop you killing *us* the minute you get loose?' he said.

'For gods' sakes, I'm not a bloody psychopath. I told you before, it's not up to me who gets croaked. That's for them upstairs to decide, and as far as I know, you two ain't on their list.'

'As far as you know?'

The daemon closed his eyes, which had been rapidly reverting to a fiery red once again. 'All right, I'll tell you what I'll do. Even if you are on the list, I promise I won't kill you, okay? Cross my heart and hope to— Well, you get the idea.'

Horace considered the proposition briefly and then looked at Norwood, who tilted his head from side to side several times and then nodded it somewhat tentatively.

'Very well,' said Horace, 'as long as you promise.'

'Yes,' said Thanatos irritably. 'Just get on with it, will yer?'

Horace and Norwood stepped cautiously forward to get a better look at how the daemon's chain was fastened, skirting round to the back of the tree that he was shackled to and giving him a very wide berth in the process.

'Pah!' snorted Norwood when he spotted the shiny but elementary padlock which held the ends of the chain together. 'Call this more secure than any lock previously known to man or god? A blind gerbil with the brain of a tapeworm could open this in two seconds flat.'

'Oh yeah?' said the daemon. 'So how much longer is it gonna take *you*?'

'Any more of that and you can stay exactly where you

are, matey.'

'All right, all right. Gods almighty, can't you people take a joke?'

Neither Norwood nor Horace bothered to respond. Instead, Horace pulled out his Swiss Army knife and said, 'I think we have a handy little tool or gadget for precisely this occasion.'

'Indeed we have,' said Norwood and watched as his co-adventurer selected the handy little tool in question and had the lock open in a fraction over twelve seconds.

Then the two adventurers each took an end of the chain and circled the tree in opposite directions to unwrap it, glad to be getting further and further from Thanatos with every circuit. When they had done, they dropped the heavy, iron chain to the ground, and the daemon flexed his enormous wings.

'Ooh, that's better,' he said. 'You can't imagine how stiff these things get if you don't at least give 'em a bit of a flap once in a while.'

'You're welcome,' said Norwood snootily.

'Gimme a chance,' said the daemon. 'I was gonna say "thank you" soon as I got me flappers sorted out. But just as a matter of interest, how *did* you get the lock open so quick?'

'With this,' said Horace, brandishing his Swiss Army knife with evident pride and then displaying some of the handy little tools and gadgets for Thanatos's perusal.

'Wow, that's awesome,' he said. 'I could well do with one o' them. Any chance you could—?'

'No!' said Horace and Norwood before he could finish the inevitable question.

The daemon shrugged his wings. 'Okay, keep yer hair on. I was only askin'. Anyway, I can't stand around chatting all day. Places to go, stiffs to cart off to the underworld. There's gonna be a right old backlog as it is.'

With that, he began to flap his wings faster and faster in apparent preparation for takeoff, beating them so hard that Horace and Norwood were almost blinded by the huge cloud of dust created by the turbulence. But before the daemon's feet had even parted company with the ground, the two adventurers turned and ran for what they still believed might be their lives.

37

Scatterthwaite was late as usual, so Harper sat on a pew near the middle of the empty church and, for want of anything better to do to pass the time, picked up a hymn book and started flipping through the pages. She was surprised at how many of the hymns she still recognised. *All Creatures of Our God and King*, *Immaculate Mary* and *Love Divine, All Loves Excelling* were all pretty much a given of course, but *Be Thou My Vision*? She even remembered the tune and hummed it silently inside her head while she carried on turning the pages, stopping abruptly when she came to *For All the Saints* and the verse which began with:

"*Oh may thy soldiers, faithful, true and bold,
Fight as the saints who nobly fought of old*".

Was that how the monks saw themselves? Like some kind of army, perversely believing they were doing God's will by going round killing people purely because of an overly rigid interpretation of a couple of sentences in the Bible?

Christ knows, she thought, snapping the book shut and picking up another. This one was about the same size as a pack of playing cards and was clearly intended to educate and inform the non-Catholic members of the congregation on how to behave at a wedding ceremony. Each page gave basic details of every part of the service from the opening hymn to the "Thanks be to God" bit at the end. Most helpfully, in the top outside corner of each page was a small picture of a stick figure in profile, standing, sitting or kneeling, to indicate which of these positions the congregation should adopt at any given moment during the proceedings. Harper quickly realised that by flicking quickly through the pages, the little stick figure rapidly alternated between the three positions like an animated cartoon character with Saint Vitus Dance, and she put her hand over her mouth to stifle a childish giggle.

'Yes, people often find that amusing.'

Harper spun round and looked up at a smiling, ruddy-cheeked face with a double chin and a dog collar beneath.

'I'm sorry, Father,' she said, getting to her feet. 'I didn't mean to—'

'As I said,' the priest interrupted, his smile even broader than before, 'you certainly aren't the first to have had a chuckle over that, and I very much doubt that the Lord would be in the least offended.'

'Well, that's a relief,' said Harper with unintentionally heavy sarcasm.

The priest didn't seem to notice and glanced at his watch. 'I'm sorry, but I'm afraid you're a little early for confession, although if you'd like to—'

It was Harper's turn to interrupt. 'That's okay, Father,' she said, vigorously shaking her head. 'I'm not actually here to make confession. I'm, er... supposed to be meeting a friend.'

The priest raised a dark, bushy eyebrow.

'He's been going through a rather difficult time of it lately,' she explained, 'and he asked me to come here to pray with him.'

'I see,' said the priest with a hint of a frown. 'And you're content to help your friend in this way even though you've lapsed?'

Harper was genuinely taken aback. 'You can tell?'

'Sometimes. Might I ask for how long?'

'Well, I'm really not sure I want to...' She hesitated over finishing the sentence, reluctant to give offence by, in effect, telling him to mind his own damned business. But fortunately, she was saved, not by a bell but by the loud "*clunk*" of the church door's heavy iron latch being lifted. Both she and the priest turned to see who had entered, and Harper wasn't entirely surprised when a monk in Union Jack flip-flops and with a folded copy of the *Financial Times* under his arm slip-slapped his way up the aisle.

Noticing that his boss wasn't alone, Scatterthwaite stopped dead in his tracks, paused for several seconds and then continued on his way in the direction of the altar. As he passed, the priest gave him a slight nod and said, 'May God be with you, Brother.'

Scatterthwaite didn't break stride or even look at the priest when he said, 'Yeah, you too, vicar', and a couple of paces further on, he took the newspaper from under his arm and gave it what he presumably intended to be an unostentatious flourish.

'How very odd,' muttered the priest as if unaware that he was speaking the words aloud. Then, as Scatterthwaite took a seat several rows in front of them, he switched his attention back to Harper. 'I'm sorry. You were saying?'

'Um, that's actually the friend I was telling you about. He's terribly shy, and also his order forbids him to even *talk* to a woman. That's why he pretended not to recognise me.'

'I see,' said the priest with another raising of a bushy eyebrow. 'Well, don't let me keep you. But if you ever want to talk anything over with me — your faith or whatever else — you know where to find me.'

Harper made a brave attempt to mirror his genial smile. 'Thank you, Father. I'll bear it in mind.'

'Please do,' he said and set off up the aisle, giving

Scatterthwaite a surreptitious sideways glance when he drew level with the end of his pew.

Harper followed and sat down next to Scatterthwaite, watching the priest as he passed the altar with a bow of his head before disappearing into the vestry.

'Vicar?' she whispered. 'He's Catholic, for God's sake.'

'So?'

'So you call him "Father". Jesus Christ, you're supposed to be a bloody monk.'

'Yeah, well, I haven't been at it that long.'

Harper sighed and got to her feet. 'Anyway, we should probably get out of here in case he comes back.'

'Yeah, and he might have bugged the place,' said Scatterthwaite, apparently in all seriousness, and picked up his *Financial Times* from beside him on the pew.

'And I told you the other day when we met up in the park that we don't need the damn newspapers.'

The sergeant shrugged and dropped the paper back on the seat, then followed her out into the open air.

'So, what have you got for me?' Harper said as soon as he'd closed the door behind them.

It was as if a lightbulb had suddenly pinged on inside his head. 'Ah,' he said, then opened the door again and headed back inside the church.

'Where the...?' She didn't bother to finish the question but strolled instead to the edge of the extensive graveyard which bordered the church on three sides.

While she waited, she scanned the lettering on some of the headstones until one of the epitaphs in particular caught her eye. The grave was of a girl who'd died two years earlier at the age of four.

'And he was going to ask me why I'd lost my faith,' she said softly.

'What you say?'

Scatterthwaite was hurrying towards her, breathing

heavily and brandishing his *Financial Times*.

'Nothing. Just thinking out loud, that's all.'

'Oh, okay.'

'Well?'

'It's all in here,' he said, opening up the *FT* and taking out a single sheet of A4 paper that was folded inside it.

Harper took it from him and walked towards the far side of the graveyard while she started to read. It was a table in four columns, printed on both sides of the paper and divided into sections, each of which was headed with a date. The first column consisted of a list of names, and next to every name was an address and telephone number. The final column was headed "Confirmed Lives Alone?" and contained a tick by each entry.

'So these are all the people who they're going to—?' she began, but got no further when she turned to see Scatterthwaite six yards behind her with the front of his habit hoisted up almost to his neck. Fixed to his bare chest with strips of silver duct tape were several rows of assorted chocolate bars, individual pies, packets of peanuts and a variety of other snacks.

She watched in stunned silence as he peeled back the end of one of the strips of tape and removed a small packet of pork scratchings.

'No bloody pockets,' he said by way of explanation and let the habit fall back to its rightful position. 'Good job they let me wear underpants though, eh?'

Harper couldn't have agreed more, but she was too much in shock to speak.

'What do you think then?' said Scatterthwaite, ripping open the packet and shoving a couple of pork scratchings into his mouth.

'Eh?'

The sergeant nodded towards the paper in her hand. 'The next lot of victims.'

Harper shook her head slightly to try and rid it of the

image of an almost naked Scatterthwaite and looked at the list again. 'What's the date today?'

'Er... sixteenth, isn't it?'

'So all of these people are due to be murdered next week.'

'Uh-huh.'

For all his numerous faults, Scatterthwaite had actually come up with the goods. This list was precisely the kind of breakthrough she'd been hoping for when she'd first had the idea of infiltrating the group. Armed with this information, she'd be able to warn all of the potential victims, but just as importantly as saving so many lives, she'd be able to focus all of her limited resources on one address instead of three. This time, there'd be no way the monk could escape and, caught red-handed, there was an excellent chance he'd be more than willing to cough the lot in exchange for a lighter sentence. Case closed and another feather in DCI Harper Collins's promotion cap. Even Leopold wouldn't be able to deny her another rung up the ladder after that.

'Good work,' she said and drew back her hand just in time to stop it from patting Scatterthwaiite on the back.

'Thanks, boss,' he said and held out the almost empty packet of pork scratchings. 'Want one of these?'

Harper easily declined the offer and at the same moment, spotted the priest coming out of the church and heading in their direction.

'Time we weren't here,' she said. 'Let's say we meet again four o'clock on the day the first murders are scheduled for. It should all be over by then. The museum in town by the "Footwear Through the Ages" exhibits.'

She waited only long enough for Scatterthwaite to say 'Okay, cool' and then hurried off towards the graveyard exit, quietly humming the tune to *All Creatures of Our God and King* before suddenly realising what she was singing and switching to a rather more spirited rendition of REM's *Losing My Religion.*

DIGRESSION FOUR:
A BRIEF ACCOUNT OF HOW
RELIGION GOT INVENTED

Although the precise date and time when religion was invented are unknown, it is commonly believed to have been soon after the dawning of the Borassic Period. As for *where* it was invented, this is universally agreed to have been at a community of cave dwellings on the outskirts of Cardiff, which was home to one of the largest tribes in the area. The tribe's leader was a woman called Gogg, who, as well as being highly charismatic and immensely strong, was very well endowed in the grey matter department. This was in stark contrast to the vast majority of her tribe, who knew nothing much about anything except how to fight with other local tribes and the best ways of hunting and killing weird-looking animals for food. And it was entirely due to Gogg's superior intellect that she managed to prevent a full-scale revolt during the second year of her rule.

At about this time, there was a major drought and a serious famine throughout the land of Yakki-Dah, which was approximately the area we now know as "South Wales". Weird-looking animals had become extremely scarce through over-hunting, edible roots had been all but obliterated by a virulent attack of Edible Root Blight, and the normally abundant supply of blackberries had failed to materialise.

As is usually the case when people's standard of living suddenly plummets so dramatically, Gogg's tribespeople began by blaming other tribes in their vicinity for their catastrophic plight, and, for a while, all the ranting and finger-pointing did at least take their minds off the fact that they were starving to death. But the respite lasted only briefly until they realised that scapegoatism — although great fun and an excellent way to promote (mostly male) bonding within one's own tribe — did nothing to put food in their mouths or water in their wells. The only recourse left open to them, therefore, was to turn to Gogg and demand that, as their leader, she should act immediately to relieve them from their suffering.

Now, Gogg was no magician, but, as mentioned earlier, she had a brain on her the size of a rather large turnip. (Given the size of the human brain in the Borassic Period — and the size of most turnips — this was relatively massive.) And after thinking long and hard for almost an entire sun-cycle, she finally hit upon the idea of creating a wholly fictitious land in the sky which she called Lisvane and another deep beneath the ground called Splott. She then summoned all of her tribespeople together and, since a proper language hadn't yet been invented (not even Latin), Gogg conveyed her message by means of some elaborate miming and quite a lot of grunting. Loosely translated, this is what she said:

'Never in the field of troglodyte existence has so much gone so horribly wrong for so many. But, I say to you, do not be alarmed. Even though our lives here in Yakki-Dah are pretty bloody miserable right now and many of us will perish for lack of food and water, there is still hope for a new life after we die that'll be a whole lot nicer than this one.'

Gogg then went on to explain how everyone who died would be whisked off to a place in the sky called Lisvane to spend the rest of eternity in peace and tranquillity and little golden wings. In Lisvane, there'd be an abundance of delicious things to eat and drink,

269

amazingly useful stuff like fire and the wheel (neither of which had yet been invented) and even electricity. So skilfully did Gogg sell the idea of life after death that her tribespeople came to believe that all their suffering and misery wasn't so bad after all and they'd happily put up with it now they knew what joys awaited them "on the other side".

As a further stroke of genius, Gogg also made it clear that only those who behaved themselves would be allowed in to Lisvane, and those who didn't toe the line would end up in Splott, where all kinds of really nasty stuff awaited them. And thus did Gogg quell any thoughts that had been brewing within her tribe that their currently desperate situation was somehow her fault, and all talk of rebellion was banished forever. On the contrary, from that moment on, the whole tribe bore their suffering without any further complaint, and although most of them did actually succumb to starvation very soon afterwards, at least they died with a smile on their faces.

Emboldened by her success, however, Gogg began to develop delusions of omnipotence and started to make all kinds of extraordinary claims about herself that would have totally defied logic nowadays but which seemed perfectly reasonable in the Borassic Period. (Admittedly, this was partly due to the fact that logic — like so many other things at that time — hadn't been invented yet.) For example, her most astonishing claim by far was that she herself had single-handedly created the entire Universe (although, to be fair, this wasn't quite such an outlandish claim back then since it was generally believed that "the entire Universe" consisted solely of the land of Yakki-Dah itself).

Even so, all of her tribespeople accepted this without so much as a murmur of dissent. All, that is, except for one man by the name of Boff, who, at the age of thirty-four was one of the oldest members of the tribe. (Life expectancy in those days was really rather poor.) Night after night, he would sit around a campfire (actually just a pile of sticks) and tell anyone who would listen that the Universe existed long before Gogg herself came into being.

'My father once told me,' Boff would say, 'that there was no such thing as Yakki-Dah until one day he heard what could only be described as a "big bang", and then suddenly everything appeared, totally out of the black.'

Not surprisingly, word soon reached Gogg's ears about what Boff had been saying, and she reasoned with him by having him instantly stoned to death, thereby inventing the hitherto unknown concepts of blasphemy and heresy.

In the meantime, news of Gogg's success in keeping her tribespeople in order had spread near and not particularly wide, and the leaders of other local tribes soon began to emulate her strategy. One such leader was a man called Ugg, who began to develop his own "system of belief" along almost identical lines to Gogg's except for a handful of very minor but significant differences. For instance, his version of Lisvane was called "Hisvane" and instead of being up in the sky was just off the coast at the approximate location of what is now known as Barry Island. Perhaps more controversially, whereas Gogg had clearly stipulated that coveting your neighbour's blackberry bush would almost guarantee you a one-way ticket to Splott, Ugg decreed that such coveting was perfectly acceptable so long as the covetor was standing on one leg at the time. Most inflammatory of all to Gogg and her followers, however, was that Ugg commissioned wall paintings in every cave in his territory of scenes depicting him — and him alone — as the sole creator of the Universe.

But Ugg was not the only tribal leader to have

diverged from what Gogg would have called "the true path" if she hadn't been restricted to a series of grunts and some often incomprehensible miming. Many other leaders in the Yakki-Dah region developed their own "religions" (as they much later came to be known), some of which were also remarkably similar to the one that Gogg had invented, but again with minor but significant differences. For example, one of the new religions was almost indistinguishable from Gogg's except that, whereas Gogg decreed that the Stegosaurus was sacred and should not be hunted, this other religion insisted that it was the Stegoceras that was sacred and that the Stegosaurus was fair game when it got to dinnertime.

Other religions were, however, almost unrecognisable as originating from the same source, and unusually at the time, there was one tribal leader who told her people that *all* of the weird-looking creatures in Yakki-Dah were sacred and none should be harmed on any account. Sadly, though, this particular tribe was completely wiped out by weird-looking animals that were desperate for food.

Another, relatively minor, religion is also worthy of mention because its adherents believed that the creator of the Universe and everything in it was someone called Fodd, who lived somewhere in Yakki-Dah, although they didn't know exactly where. They therefore spent their entire time going round in pairs, wearing identical animal skins, and visiting cave after cave, asking "Have you found Fodd?". Generally considered to be harmless, they were often subjected to mockery and ridicule, but more often than not, the cave-dwellers who received a visit from the "Foddites" pretended not to be at home.

But whether the differences between the various religions were great or small, in a relatively brief period after Gogg came up with the idea, the tribes of Yakki-Dah had another reason to wage war against each other.

Previously, battles had been fought almost exclusively over territorial rights, but differences in religion now became the root cause of many of the conflicts. Instead of each tribe contenting itself with the belief that it was their own leader — Gogg or Ugg or whoever it might be — who created Yakki-Dah and everything in it, they felt somehow compelled to try and coerce other tribes into believing in the same leader as they did, often with horrific and bloody consequences.

Thank God — or whoever it might be — that people are much more sensible and tolerant now than they were when religion was first invented back in those far distant days at the dawning of the Borassic Period.

38

'May the gods be praised,' said Thestor and let out a huge sigh from the back seat of the van as Horace applied the handbrake and switched off the engine.

'Are you sure this is the right place?' said Horace, peering through the windscreen and the lashing rain that was being driven almost horizontally by the brutal, howling wind.

'Absolutely,' said the old man and then with rather less conviction, added, 'At least, I hope to Hades it is. I couldn't face another minute bouncing around in this damned chariot of yours.'

For the last dozen miles or so, the track had been far rougher and bouncier than anything they'd encountered so far, and at the same time, the weather had also deteriorated, both instantly and dramatically. At one moment, there'd been a cloudless blue sky with bright sunshine and the gentlest of breezes, and the very next moment, a raging, thunderous tempest where the foreboding blackness of the unremitting cloud was illuminated only by the frequent flashes of dazzling sheet lightning. The landscape too had been transformed from sun-scorched fields and dense woodland to a vast expanse of utterly barren, grey-black rock as suddenly as if a line had been drawn in the earth between the two.

In front of them now stood a sheer, towering cliff of the self-same rock, so high that it was impossible to tell where the precipice ended and the blackness of the sky began. About fifteen feet up from its base, the gaping mouth of a cave was just about visible through the incessant, driving rain.

'Well, it certainly looks like the sort of place where monsters would hang out,' said Norwood.

'Maybe we should wait until the weather clears a bit,' said Vesta.

Horace squinted upwards through the windscreen of the van as yet another sheet of lightning lit up the sky. 'Doesn't look like that's going to happen any time soon. And in any case, we'll be out of the rain once we get inside the cave.'

The silence which greeted this remark was hardly surprising since Horace hadn't the slightest doubt that his co-adventurers were no more keen to get "inside the cave" than he was. After what Thestor had told them about this Medusa and her Gorgon sisters, the very prospect of coming face to face with them sent spasms of terror throughout every part of his anatomy. Come to think of it, if they *did* come face to face with Medusa, they'd be instantly turned to stone, so that was to be avoided at all costs of course. On the other hand, the van was rocking wildly from side to side in the wind, and Thestor was beginning to look decidedly queasy again.

'Perhaps we should just have a bit of a recce to start with. Have a little peek inside and see what's what.'

'Well, all right then,' said Thestor. 'Anything to get on solid ground again.'

Horace looked at Norwood and Vesta in turn, and each nodded their reluctant agreement.

And so it was that a few minutes later, and each having donned a hooded anorak or an oilskin cape — both shunned by Thestor and neither offered to Zoot — the three adventurers, the dog and the old man ran as fast as they could over the rough terrain towards the cliff. After some difficult slithering and scrambling up a slippery and uneven ramp of fallen boulders and grey-black rocks at the base of the cliff, they at last reached the relatively dry sanctuary of the mouth of the cave. "Relatively" because, although sheltered from the torrential rain, the air was heavy with a bone-piercing dampness, and water dripped constantly from the rocky ceiling thirty feet above their heads.

'What's that awful smell?' said Vesta.

'Rotten eggs?' said Norwood.

'Very old fish?' said Horace. 'Or both?'

'Or very possibly the decaying corpses of hundreds of the Gorgons' victims,' said Thestor.

The old man's companions did their best to ignore this comment but with minimal success, so they all told him to shut up and keep his gory thoughts to himself or they'd all take turns at punching him in the face.

'Ssh!' Vesta hissed suddenly, even though nobody was speaking at that particular moment. 'What was that noise?'

Four foreheads creased into concentration as their owners channelled all of their senses into the one responsible for listening intently. But apart from the incessant drip drip drip of water which echoed eerily around the walls of the cave, there was absolute silence.

'I think you must be imagin—' Horace began but was cut short by another 'Ssh!' from Vesta.

'There it is again,' she said, and this time, the sound was clearly audible to all. A kind of muted sobbing that disappeared and then returned every few seconds. It seemed to be coming from somewhere at the far end of the cave where the roof and walls curved rapidly downwards and inwards to converge at a narrow opening less than six feet high.

'Well, I'd say that's probably enough of a recce for now,' said Norwood and turned to make his way back the way they'd come.

'But we've only just got here,' said Vesta, placing a

276

gently restraining hand on his arm. 'And I really think we should find out what's making that noise.'

Norwood sighed and lifted his gaze towards the roof of the cave, only for an especially large drip of water to score a direct hit on his open right eye.

'The last time we went to investigate a strange sound,' he said, wiping his eye with the sleeve of his anorak, 'we ran slap bang into the Grim bloody Reaper himself, so I'm not exactly keen on repeating the same mistake twice.'

'But what if it's somebody in distress? Somebody who needs our help,' said Vesta.

'Oh yeah? And what if it's this Medusa, lurking in the shadows and champing at the bit to turn the lot of us into stone?'

'To be honest,' said Thestor, clearing his throat, 'from everything I know about Medusa and her sisters, I don't think they're much given to a lot of sobbing. They're far more the demonic cackling sort of monster really.'

'Okay then,' said Norwood, 'if you're so confident, why don't you go and check it out?'

Thestor gave him a withering scowl. 'Listen, Junction. I never wanted to come on this trip in the first place, and the only reason I *am* here is as a guide and not as some Hades-or-glory hero type with suicidal tendencies and a penchant for spending the rest of eternity as a stone statue of his former self.'

By the time Thestor had finished speaking, his voice had increased in volume by several decibels, and his face would have been directly in front of Norwood's if he'd been at least a foot taller.

'The only reason you're here?' said Norwood, staring down at the top of the old man's head. 'So nothing to do with the absurdly large amount of treasure we promised you then?'

'That's got nothing to—'

Horace had heard enough and was particularly concerned that all this shouting would alert the Gorgons to their presence, so he was about to interrupt when someone else did the job for him.

'Hello?'

As a unit, they all turned to see who it was that had spoken, and framed in the small opening at the far end of the cave was a heavily armoured young man who was so tall that he had to stoop to avoid scraping the top of his helmet on the rock.

'I thought I heard voices,' he said and stepped cautiously through the opening, but only as far as where he could pull himself up to his full and impressive height. Besides the helmet and the armour, he carried a large, round shield in one hand and an enormous, gleaming sword in the other.

'I'm terribly sorry if we disturbed you,' said Horace.

'No, not at all,' said the warrior, or so he appeared to be. 'I was just, um... I was only, er...'

'Was that you that was sobbing?' asked Vesta in a gentle, almost motherly tone.

'Who, *me*?' said the young man, his armour clanking as he pointed at his breastplate.

'Oh, I'm sorry. I didn't mean to—'

'Don't you know who I am?'

'Er...' Vesta scanned the faces of the others for some indication that they had any idea, but Horace and Norwood's expressions were a total blank, and so too was Thestor's until inspiration seemed to strike and he clicked a bony finger and thumb.

'You're not that, um...?' he faltered. 'Oh, what's his name? — Ah, I know. That hero chap, Theseus.'

'Are you kidding me? *That* lily-livered buffoon of a mummy's boy?' the warrior sneered.

'Lily-livered?' said Thestor, clearly taken aback. 'But wasn't he the one that slew the Minotaur?'

The young man waved a dismissive hand. 'Yes, yes, whatever.'

'*And* rescued Andromeda from a sea serpent? And wasn't he involved with the Golden Fleece thing where he—?'

'Look, I'm not bloody Theseus, okay?'

'All right, all right. Keep your helmet on. So if you're not Theseus, then—?'

'I,' said the man, who less than a moment ago had looked very angry indeed, now pulled himself up to even taller than his already impressive height and puffed out his breastplated chest. 'I am... Perseus!'

He paused, maintaining the pose while he appeared to be waiting for a round of applause or at least a gasp of admiration. Instead, the three adventurers exchanged quizzical glances, and even Thestor was at a loss this time.

The pose wilted.

'Perseus?' said Perseus, repeating the name as if this might jog their memories. 'Son of Zeus? Set adrift in a wooden box on the open sea with his mother?'

The response was complete silence, accompanied by four pairs of pursed lips and quite a lot of head shaking.

'Sorry,' said Thestor. 'You got us there, I'm afraid.'

'Oh, for f—' Perseus hurled his shield to the rocky ground and stamped a golden-sandalled foot.

'Ah, wait a minute,' said Vesta, who was always good in these situations (and not just because she was a woman either). 'Now I remember. *Per*-seus. That's right. Weren't you the one who, er...?'

Perseus's armour clanked heavily again as he leaned forward towards her, his eyes brightening with eager anticipation. 'The one who was sent to kill Medusa and chop off her head. That's the one, yeah.'

Excellent, thought Horace. So all we have to do is wait for him to do the deed, and hopefully he'll deal with

Medusa's sisters at the same time. Then we can just stroll in and collect as many Holey Snails as we need without any risk to ourselves. Unless of course he's already killed the monsters, in which case, we might as well get straight on with collecting the snails.

'So have you done it yet?' he said. 'Chopped off Medusa's head, I mean.'

Perseus made a big show of inspecting each of his hands and the rocky floor around him. 'You see a severed head with dozens of writhing, venomous snakes where the hair should be?'

'No, but—'

'Well, there's your answer then.'

'Any thoughts on when it might happen?' Horace asked tentatively.

'And what business is that of yours?'

Horace made a quick visual check of his co-adventurers to make sure that it was okay with them and then gave a very brief account of their quest for the Holey Snail. While he was speaking, Perseus's demeanour lightened visibly, and by the time Horace had finished, the young warrior was positively aglow with what appeared to be a mixture of delight and relief.

'But that's wonderful,' he said, clapping his hands together. 'To be perfectly honest, I wasn't at all keen on tackling these Gorgons alone, but now that you're here—'

'Whoa there, Persy-boy,' Norwood interrupted. 'Who said anything about us helping? Killing the monster's your job.'

Perseus's chin sank slowly towards his chest. 'Please?'

'I thought you were supposed to be some kind of hero,' said Norwood.

'Who, me?' the young man snorted. 'That's a laugh. In fact, that's the only reason I'm here at all. Because I made some damned silly joke and the bloody king only went and took me seriously, didn't he?'

'What king?'

Perseus then explained how a certain king called Polydectes wanted to marry Perseus's mother, but Perseus was dead against it on the grounds that Polydectes was a seriously nasty piece of work with all the charm of a viper with haemorrhoids. So the king had hatched a plan and pretended he was going to marry someone else — some princess or other from across the sea — but he needed to give her father a whole load of fancy presents before he'd agree to the match. So, calling all the young men of the area to a meeting, Polydectes had told each of them to scour the four corners of the known world and bring back the most exotic and unusual presents they could find.

'What about a really nice pair of socks?' one of them had suggested.

'Or a beer mug with his initials engraved on it,' said another.

'How about a cloak with "The World's Best Ruler" printed on it?' had been one idea.

'You can't go wrong with aftershave,' someone with an enormous bushy beard had said.

Perseus had scarcely been able to control his laughter at the sheer naffness of most of the suggestions, and unable to contain himself any longer, had blurted out that if the king wanted a gift that was *really* exotic and unique, then something like the head of Medusa on a plate would be far more likely to impress than any of the other tat which had been suggested so far.

'It was the first thing that popped into my mind,' said Perseus, 'and I obviously didn't mean it to be taken seriously.'

'But the king *did* take it seriously,' said Vesta.

Perseus nodded sadly. 'Wanted me out of the way,

didn't he? For good, most likely, and if I go in there and start mixing it up with these Gorgons, that's exactly what's going to happen.'

For several seconds, the only sound that could be heard was the dripping of water from the roof of the cave onto the rocky floor beneath and an occasional sniffing noise from Perseus's direction. The relative silence was eventually broken when Vesta proposed that she and her co-adventurers should discuss the matter in private, and even though neither Horace nor Norwood believed that there was anything that needed to be discussed, they reluctantly followed her to the entrance of the cave with Thestor tagging along behind.

After six and a half minutes of argument and counter-argument, it was finally agreed that helping Perseus to slay Medusa was probably their best chance — maybe their *only* chance — to fulfil their quest for the Holey Snails without their own grisly and agonising deaths getting in the way. Thestor, however, exercised his right to abstain from the show of hands at the end of the discussion, repeating his assertion that he was only there as a guide and no way was he going to get involved with no monster beheading.

Perseus was beside himself with joy when they informed him of their decision, and without further ado, he set off through the small opening at the far end of the cave, closely followed by Horace, Norwood, Vesta and Zoot with Thestor bringing up the rear, several paces behind. Instantly, the stench of rotten-eggs-or-very-old-fish-or-very-possibly-both intensified to retch-inducing proportions, and before them lay a narrow, natural tunnel through the rock, its walls oozing with an unidentifiable green slime. On the plus side, however, the slime itself gave off a strange, eerie glow by which they were able to see their way without recourse to the handy little torches of their Swiss Army knives.

282

After thirty or forty yards, and frequently having to stoop to avoid cracking their heads open when the height of the tunnel suddenly reduced to stooping level, they came to a T-junction with each of its arms leading off in an almost perfect right-angle from the main tunnel. Just visible in the eerie green glow of the slime were two wooden signs fixed to the wall in front of them. The one on the right bore a roughly drawn, right-pointing arrow and the words "THIS WAY TO THE HOLEY SNAILS". The sign on the left bore a roughly drawn, left-pointing arrow and the words "THIS WAY TO THE GORGONS AND AN INSTANT GRISLY DEATH".

39

Harper Collins had no interest whatsoever in what people wore on their feet at various stages throughout the history of cobbling, but she'd already inspected every exhibit in the museum's "Footwear Through the Ages" section at least three times. Scatterthwaite was hardly known for his punctuality, but he was now almost an hour late for their appointment. All she wanted to do was to hear what he had to say and then get off home and close the door on what had been one of the shittiest and most disappointing days of her career.

She'd been up since soon after dawn, having hardly slept more than a couple of hours, full of excited anticipation for the day that lay ahead and, in particular, the look on Superintendent Leopold's face when she informed him of her triumphant success. The element of surprise would make that moment all the more glorious, so she'd deliberately kept him in the dark about her plan, and she hadn't even told him about the list of victims that Scatterthwaite had given her. Besides, there'd been no point in asking him for any additional manpower for the stakeout, and given that she had far more specific intelligence than for the previous surveillance operation, four officers should have been easily enough to get the job done. Two outside in a car keeping watch while she and the other two waited inside the target's house, ready to grab the monk the moment he stepped through the door. This time, with three onto one and another two as backup, it was all but guaranteed that the killer would have no chance of escaping. That had been the theory anyway.

Of the five names on Scatterthwaite's list that had been scheduled to be killed that day, Harper had taken her time in making her selection. Three she'd dismissed on the grounds that the addresses were in similar areas to Howard Ledley's house. Terraced streets with too many back alleys and cut-throughs for the killer to get away if he happened to slip through their clutches as he had on that occasion. That had left two possible candidates, but after she'd discovered that one of these was currently in hospital for a heart bypass operation, her eventual choice had been a Mr Keith Donovan, who lived in a two-bedroomed bungalow near the end of an upmarket cul-de-sac on the edge of town. As a plus point, there was no outside access to the small garden at the rear of the property, so the killer would have had to scramble over a six foot wooden fence to make his getaway.

Harper had of course warned the others on the list to make sure they vacated their premises on the day, and she'd then visited Mr Donovan to explain the situation and brief him on what she proposed to do. He'd been infinitely more cooperative than Ledley and had even told her that he was looking forward to having their company and "a bit of excitement for a change". And when Harper and her two officers had knocked on his door very early that morning, he was already in the process of cooking a full English breakfast for them all. She herself had been far too pumped on adrenalin to eat more than a couple of mouthfuls, but Sergeant Noble and PC Barnes had more than made up for her lack of appetite.

At Ledley's house, the first stage in the intended murder had been shortly after eight o'clock when the monk had posted the doctored birthday card through the letterbox, but by nine, all that had dropped onto

Donovan's mat was a newspaper and a small bundle of mail delivered by the postman. Another hour had passed and then another, and still no monk had appeared. More and more frequently, Harper had got on her walkie-talkie to check with the officers in the car whether they'd spotted anything even slightly out of the ordinary, but apart from the paperboy and the postman, the cul-de-sac had been all but deserted from the moment they'd arrived.

By the time Mr Donovan had said that he always had lunch at one o'clock and asked if Harper and her colleagues would like him to rustle up something for them too, she'd begun to wonder if Scatterthwaite had cocked up as per usual.

Lunch had come and gone, and this time, Harper hadn't been able to manage even a single bite. Tea and cake in the middle of the afternoon had been enthusiastically welcomed by Noble and Barnes, but as soon as they'd finished, they'd begun to fidget in their seats and mutter about the current freeze on overtime pay. Harper had been almost on the point of giving up in despair herself, so she'd told them to knock off for the day and tell the other two in the car to do the same. And even though she'd been forced to admit to herself that the operation had been a complete washout, she'd stayed on at the bungalow in the faintest glimmer of hope that the monk might finally make an appearance. She'd no idea how she'd cope on her own if he did, but it was a million to one chance that the situation would arise anyway, so she'd sat it out until there'd been only just time to make it to her appointment with Scatterthwaite at four. But now it was starting to look like her sergeant was going to be the second no-show of the day.

Realising that she'd been staring at a glass cabinet full of little scraps of leather — which apparently dated from Roman times — for a great deal longer than they actually merited, she tried his mobile again. As with the previous dozen attempts, the call went straight to voicemail. She checked her watch. The museum would be closing soon, so she slowly made her way towards the exit, resolving to wait for Scatterthwaite outside the main entrance for another half hour before giving up on him.

Moments later, and just as she was passing through the museum's "Exotic Thimbles Through the Ages" section, her mobile phone rang. And as if a total disaster of a day couldn't get any worse, it was yet more bad news. Another seventy-year-old had been found murdered in his home, laid out in the usual cruciform shape and with the usual symbols scrawled across his chest. With her free hand clasped tight against her forehead, Harper asked the detective constable on the other end of the line to tell her the victim's name. As she'd feared, this was the fifth murder victim that day, and not one of them had appeared on the list that Scatterthwaite had given her.

40

Even though a dog's sense of smell is said to be about a thousand times more sensitive than a human's, the appalling stench of rotten-eggs-or-very-old-fish-or-very-possibly-both didn't seem to be bothering Zoot in the slightest. On the contrary, he appeared to relish every lungful, which he took at frequent and apparently blissful intervals while Horace, Norwood, Vesta, Thestor and Perseus all stared at the two signs on the cave wall in front of them with their hands firmly clasped over their noses.

'How very thoughtful,' said Norwood. 'If somebody hadn't put up these signs, we'd never have known which way to go, and there's at least a fifty-fifty chance that we'd have turned left and headed straight for...' He leaned forward and read from the sign. '"The Gorgons and an instant grisly death".'

'Yes, but who do you think put the signs there in the first place?' said Vesta.

'I don't know. Maybe there's some kind of local tourist board or—'

'You think it could be a bluff?' Horace interrupted.

'Or even a double bluff,' said Vesta.

Horace considered the possibility of a triple bluff but decided not to mention it on the grounds that the conversation could become endlessly repetitive and ultimately pointless. Instead, he plumped for 'Bit of a conundrum which way to go then.'

'We could always split up into two groups,' Vesta

suggested. 'One goes left and one goes right.'

Horace was about to say that he didn't think this was a terribly good idea when there was a loud clanking noise from immediately behind them. Perseus was holding up a heavily armoured arm as if about to make a point of order.

'If I might interject,' he said. 'It was my understanding that you'd agreed to help me slay Medusa in return for helping you to collect these Holey Snails that you seek.'

Norwood muttered something about short straws, and Horace reluctantly confirmed that this had indeed been the arrangement.

'In that case,' said Perseus, 'it doesn't really matter which way we go first because we'll have to go both ways in the end anyway. And besides, if we happen to go in the snails' direction first, the Gorgons will almost certainly hear us and come and investigate. That's their job after all. Stopping people like you from stealing the snails.'

There followed a lengthy pause while the adventurers pondered his analysis of the situation, and when they'd finished pausing, all were forced to concede that the point had been well made. There was, however, further discussion concerning whether it was better to sneak up on the Gorgons or have the Gorgons sneak up on them, but since it was impossible to tell if the two signs were telling the truth or not, the decision was completely out of their hands. Even so, it took several more minutes before a consensus was reached that the signs were probably – or perhaps possibly – intended as a double bluff (or maybe even a quadruple one). Of the five of them, only Thestor failed to contribute anything to the debate, having repeated at the outset that he was only there as a guide, so it mattered little to him which way they went as he would be staying right where he was and keeping watch.

'Keeping watch for what exactly?' asked Norwood.

'For anything... unusual.'

'Unusual? We're about to come up against a bunch of vicious, psychopathic monsters who are guarding a caveload of snails that possess the secret of eternal youth, and you think you're going to come across something "unusual" by stopping here?'

'You never know,' the old man said lamely but then turned to Perseus and, with rather more confidence, added, 'And if you take my advice, you'll ditch the helmet and the rest of the metal stuff before you go any further. Clank clank clank. It's a wonder the Gorgons haven't heard us and turned us all into stone already.'

'But this is all the protection I have against the evil Medusa and her sisters,' Perseus complained.

Thestor shrugged. 'Suit yourself, chum, but you'll be putting everyone else in danger as well as yourself. Of course, if you want to be selfish about it...'

He let the sentence hang, and after a short deliberation, Perseus said, 'Oh, very well then. But the helmet doesn't clank. I can keep that, can't I?'

'Makes an awful grating noise when it scrapes against the rock in a low part of the tunnel.'

Perseus made a disgruntled grunting sound and with more than a passing resemblance to a petulant adolescent, removed his helmet to reveal a shock of curly, blonde hair and dazzlingly blue eyes. His various bits and pieces of armour followed until he stood in nothing more than a knee-length crimson tunic and his golden sandals.

'I'm keeping the sword and the shield though,' he said defiantly.

'Fair enough, but just make sure you don't clank them on anything,' said Thestor, donning the discarded helmet and strapping the breastplate to his own bony chest.

'Safe keeping,' he added when he caught Perseus's open-mouthed stare upon him. 'It'll be a lot quicker getting this lot out if we have to make a run for it.'

* * *

As it turned out, the entire discussion about which of the two tunnels to follow at the T-junction had been a complete waste of time and breath. Presumably bored with all the chit-chat and lack of action, Zoot had suddenly taken it upon himself to hurtle off down the tunnel marked "THIS WAY TO THE HOLEY SNAILS", and Horace, Norwood, Vesta and Perseus had had little option but to go after him. Their pace was considerably slower than Zoot's, however, and the reek of rotten-eggs-or-very-old-fish-or-very-possibly-both became more and more overpowering the further they went.

'I hope it's not the Gorgons who smell like that,' said Norwood. 'Because if it is, we must be getting closer to them with every step.'

'Maybe it's the snails,' said Vesta. 'I don't think I've ever smelt a snail close up before.'

'Just so long as it's not dead snails,' said Horace. 'Mr Wellwisher made it very clear that the snails we brought back must be very much alive.'

After it seemed like they'd been walking and stooping for about 3.67 miles in a gradual downward direction and negotiating more twists and turns than on an Escher-designed bobsleigh run, the tunnel suddenly descended sharply down a long, steep flight of naturally formed steps in the rock. Reaching the bottom of these, Perseus and the three adventurers stood in silent awe at what lay before them. A vast subterranean chamber, lit with a rather brighter greenish glow than the tunnel, and at its centre, a pool of mirror-smooth water the colour of polished jade. Everywhere about them were enormous, green-tinged stalagmites and stalactites, some so huge that they met in the middle, giving the appearance of huge columns supporting the roof of the cave sixty feet above.

'Impressive,' said Norwood.

'Wow,' said Horace.

'Magical,' said Vesta.

'Ow!' said Perseus, who had taken a step forward into the cave and fallen face down onto the rocky floor.

So awestruck had he been with the enchanting splendour of the cavern that he'd failed to notice the foot high strip of wood which had been fixed across the bottom of the steps. On the adventurers' side of the plank were scrawled the words "YOU ARE HERE" in the same rough hand as the signs back at the T-junction.

'Very helpful,' said Norwood, stepping over the low barrier to help Perseus to his feet. 'I mean, why couldn't they just say whether— Oh, hang on a minute. There's something on this side too.'

Easing himself down onto his knees, he peered at the board, and almost immediately, his features rearranged themselves into the broadest of smiles.

'What's it say?' said Vesta.

'Come and see for yourselves,' said Norwood, so his co-adventurers hopped over the plank and knelt down beside him.

The inscription on the wood consisted of a large red circle with a diagonal red line through it, and in the centre of the circle was a black, one-dimensional representation of a snail in profile. To the left of this symbol, and also in red, were the words "NO SNAILS PERMITTED BEYOND THIS POINT — OR ELSE!".

'You know,' said Horace chirpily, 'I think we've actually made it.'

'At last,' said Vesta with a similar amount of chirpiness.

'Only thing is...' said Norwood, sounding a lot less chirpy and rather more uneasy. 'I don't seem to see any snails.'

The others followed his gaze as he scanned the floor of the cave in every conceivable direction and confirmed for themselves the awful truth. There wasn't a single snail in sight. Zoot was also conspicuous by his absence, although Horace was confident he'd show up once he'd grown tired of exploring. The snails, however, were quite a different matter.

'Perhaps they're hiding,' he said.

'Or asleep,' said Vesta.

'But Thestor said there were supposed to be thousands of them,' said Norwood. 'Surely even in a cave this size, we'd be bound to see at least a few.'

'Unless...' said Perseus, who now sported a rather nasty graze on his forehead where his helmet would have been. 'Unless the snail sign on the plank is another bluff, and this is actually where the Gorgons hang out.'

'I don't know,' said Norwood. 'Is it possible to bluff a snail?'

'I think he means it's for potential snail thieves,' said Horace. 'Us, in fact.'

'Oh crikey,' said Norwood.

After a rapid exchange of generally terrified glances, it was decided to conduct a quick preliminary search for the snails to ascertain whether the sign was a bluff, a double bluff or not even a bluff at all. And so, keeping a sharp eye out for any Gorgons that might be lurking, they all set off in such a tight formation that they were in constant danger of tripping over each other's feet.

Despite the damp chill in the air, Horace was sweating heavily, and his insides felt like they were rushing to rearrange themselves into entirely different positions from the anatomical norm.

'Do you think we ought to have some kind of strategy worked out in case the Gorgons do show up?' he whispered, unsuccessfully trying to control the tremor in his voice.

'How about run like hell?' said Norwood.

'Main thing is not to look them in the face,' said Perseus, 'although I think it's only Medusa that can turn you to stone if you do.'

'Yes, we know all that,' said Norwood testily. 'Won't be a problem if we're running away though, will it?'

'But Perseus still has to kill her and lop off her head,' said Vesta, 'and we did promise to help him.'

Norwood grunted and tripped over Horace's foot. Relatively unscathed, he picked himself up and eyeballed Perseus. 'So, did you have a plan how you were going to do the deed — before we turned up, I mean?'

'Not exactly, no, although I was rather hoping my special shield would come in handy.'

'Oh yes? And what's so special about it?' said Norwood as the three adventurers cursorily examined what appeared to be a perfectly ordinary round shield, the like of which they'd all seen many times in movies such as *Alexander the Great, Gladiator* and *Asterix and the Vikings*.

'It's got a big mirror on the inside,' said Perseus, turning the shield so that everyone could see their own slightly distorted images in the fractionally concave surface. 'The idea, in theory, is that I'll be able to do battle with Medusa without having to look directly at her.'

'In theory?' said Horace.

'Well, the thing is, I've been practising with it quite a lot, and to be honest, it hasn't been going terribly well. Fighting backwards is actually much harder than you'd think.'

'Oh, that's very reassuring,' said Norwood. 'You mean to tell us that—'

But he got no further with what was probably building into a tirade of sarcastic abuse, interrupted as he was by a loud crunching noise from beneath his left foot. Placing a hand on Horace's shoulder to support himself, he lifted the sole of his shoe and, embedded in the deep tread, found fragments of crushed shell and the slimy remains of what was unmistakably a very dead snail. They'd been so busy discussing Perseus's shield and how best to deal with Medusa and her sisters that they'd failed to notice the large natural alcove set into the wall of the cave on their right. Previously invisible from the foot of the steps, the alcove now appeared behind a row of impressively huge columns of conjoined stalagmites and stalactites, its floor almost entirely carpeted with a thousand or more snails.

'Eureka!' said Vesta.

'Pardon?' said Perseus.

'Sorry. After your time, I think.'

With the greatest of care, Horace bent down and picked up one of the snails between forefinger and thumb.

'It's the right sort, is it?' said Norwood.

Horace held the snail to within a few inches of his eyes, but it was impossible to make out any detail in the green glow of the cave, so he pulled his Swiss Army knife from his pocket and switched on the handy little torch. The snail was about half as big again as any he had come across before, and it had already withdrawn its head and neck into its shell. Seen from the side, this was a tightly coiled spiral that was bright purple in colour with thin black stripes running parallel to the curve of the spiral and giving it the appearance of a mint humbug with near fatal amounts of E-numbers.

'Does it have holes in its shell?' said Vesta.

It was hard to tell in the artificial light, so Horace asked her to extract the handy little magnifying glass from her Swiss Army knife and take a look for herself while he kept the torch trained on the shell.

'How many holes are there supposed to be?' she said as she moved the magnifying glass to and fro until the shell was in focus.

'I don't think your uncle specified a precise number,' said Horace, 'although I do have a vague recollection he said there were quite a lot.'

'Well, this one's got hundreds,' said Vesta. 'Tiny little holes all over its shell.'

Immediately, the three adventurers began to congratulate each other and clap each other on the back while Perseus looked totally bemused and pointed out that it might not be a bad idea to keep the noise down a bit. Horace, Norwood and Vesta then whispered to each other to ask if anyone had brought something to collect the snails in, but it quickly became apparent that none of them had.

'Well,' said Norwood, putting forward the case for their mutual defence, 'we were only intending to recce the place this time. We weren't actually expecting to *find* any snails, were we?'

'Anyone remember how many Mr Wellwisher wanted us to bring back?' said Horace.

Neither Norwood nor Vesta could, but they both agreed that he'd stipulated there should at least be several pairs that were capable of breeding.

Vesta took the specimen snail from Horace and turned

296

it upside down, closely examining its underside with the aid of the magnifying glass. 'Any idea how you can tell the sex of a snail?'

'Not at all,' said Norwood, 'although now I come to think about it, I'm fairly sure some kinds of snails are hermaphrodite.'

'Herma what?' said Horace.

'It means they've got... you know... both *bits*.'

'Bits?'

Norwood ran a palm over his bald scalp, wiping away the beads of sweat that were beginning to form. 'It's like... like if they're hermaphrodite, they can kind of... make baby snails all on their own.'

'Yeah?'

'Yeah.'

'Weird,' said Horace. 'So they wouldn't be able to pretend they had a headache if—'

'But just in case these snails *aren't* hermaphrodite,' Vesta cut in, 'we'd better stuff as many as we can into our pockets and hope for the best. The odds are that if there's enough of them, some'll be male and some female.'

Her co-adventurers acknowledged that this was probably the only option open to them since nobody was about to volunteer to go back to the van and fetch a suitable container, but no sooner had they stooped to begin collecting the snails than they froze rigid at the sound... Of what? It was like a low, deep-throated growl but with a touch of a hiss about it, and it seemed to emanate from somewhere on the flight of steps which led down into the cave.

'Uh-oh,' said Vesta. 'I think we may have been rumbled.'

41

'I think he may have been rumbled,' said Harper. 'He didn't show up for our appointment yesterday afternoon, and as far as I can gather, he hasn't been back to his flat since two days ago.'

Superintendent Leopold had his elbows planted squarely on the top of his desk, his chin resting lightly on the tips of his steepled fingers. 'Perhaps he's just gone AWOL. Bit of a loose cannon, isn't he, this er...?'

'Scatterthwaite, sir. Well, yes, he can be, but this is a different matter altogether. He's working undercover with the monks — the serial killers — and he—'

'Undercover?' said Leopold, collapsing his steeple and sliding his elbows off the desk. 'You never told me about that.'

'Well, sir, I—'

'And please don't tell me he's actually *killing* people.'

'Of course not, sir, but—'

'And what makes you think he *has* actually been "rumbled", as you so eloquently put it?'

Harper told him about the list of potential victims that Scatterthwaite had passed on to her and how none of the monks had shown up at the address she'd targeted for surveillance. On the same day, however, five other seventy-year-olds had been murdered, and not one of the victims' names was on the list. And the only conclusion she'd been able to come up with was that SMASH maybe suspected Scatterthwaite of being a mole and wanted to check him out.

'So they fed him disinformation, you mean,' said Leopold.

Harper nodded. 'And carried out their own surveillance to see if we turned up at any of the addresses on the bogus list.'

'It's a theory, I suppose.'

'It's rather more than a theory, sir, and it would certainly account for Scatterthwaite suddenly disappearing like that. And if I'm right and they find out he's not only a mole but a police officer as well, I really don't give much for his chances.'

'I'm not sure his being a policeman would make any difference. As far as I'm aware, these SMASH people recruit from all walks of life. You don't already have to be a monk to join, you know.'

'Oh?' said Harper, surprised that he seemed to be so well informed, considering he had shown little interest before, other than to bang on about getting a result and constantly moaning at her about having to face the press without an ounce of anything positive to report.

'Don't sound so shocked, Chief Inspector. Although you might think I spend my entire life sitting behind this desk, pushing paper around and counting paperclips, I still happen to be a policeman, and a policeman who likes to keep at least one finger on the pulse of what's going on under my command.'

Yeah, thought Harper, the finger that runs down the list of crime statistics every week to check whether you're going to be in for a bollocking from the Deputy Chief Constable for "disappointing clear-up rates".

'So, tell me,' Leopold went on. 'What precisely do you want me to do about the situation? Always assuming of course that this Scatterthwaite has indeed been "rumbled".'

Harper took a deep breath and talked fast. 'Escalate the whole case to top priority. Put every available officer onto it until we find these monks and where they hang out. The way I see it, it's the only way we're going to break this case and, far more importantly, get to Scatterthwaite before he ends up like all the other victims – if we're not already too late, that is.'

Leopold passed a weary palm across his face. 'Christ almighty, Collins, how many times do I have to tell you? My resources are stretched well beyond the limit as it is. Much as you'd obviously like me to, I can't just—'

'With all due respect, sir,' Harper interrupted with blatantly perceptible irony, 'we're talking about the life of a fellow officer here.'

'Don't you *dare* start lecturing *me* on morality,' Leopold fumed. 'I'll have you know that in all my years on the force—'

This time, the interruption came from the strident ringing of one of the two phones on his desk, and he stabbed at one of the buttons next to the receiver with a long, skeletal finger.

'Which bit of "not to be interrupted" did you not understand?' he yelled before his secretary had had a chance to say a single word.

'I'm terribly sorry, sir,' came the voice over the speakerphone, 'but I thought you'd want to take this. It's the Deputy Chief Constable, and he says he needs to speak to you as a matter of great urgency.'

'Ah, I see,' said Leopold, his tone instantly ditching several decibels. 'Well, you'd better put him through then.'

Without so much as a glance in Harper's direction, he picked up the receiver and pushed another button.

'Ronnie,' he said, all syrup and hail-fellow-well-met. 'And what can I do you for?'

Harper got up from her chair, and keeping half an ear open in case she might pick up anything useful, she meandered over to the window and stared out over the rooftops at the rapidly darkening bank of cloud. From what she could glean from Leopold's side of the phone conversation, the matter of great urgency was exclusively concerned with arranging a round of golf for the following morning and then lunch at an expensive, fancy restaurant in the town.

Growing tired of seeing her own mood reflected in the blackness of the clouds, she switched her attention to a different reflection – the one of Leopold's smugly grinning face in the glass of the window, yakking on about par threes and nineteenth holes and other golfing bullshit. Harper could hardly bear to look at him any longer, and her eyes strayed downward to the bulging Waitrose carrier bag on the floor next to his chair.

Yes, of course, she thought. On his pay scale, he can afford to shop at Waitrose. I wonder what he's hunter-gathered this time. Most likely a stackload of ready meals for one since his wife left him — smart woman.

It was difficult to get a clear view of the contents of the bag in the reflection, so she casually turned away from the window and walked slowly back to her side of the desk, passing closer to the bag than was strictly necessary. But what she saw almost stopped her in her tracks, and she had to force herself to keep going. There, and only just visible near the top of the bag, she caught a flash of red, white and blue which looked very much like the toe-end of a Union Jack flip-flop.

42

The hissing, growling sound grew steadily louder, and as it did so, the three adventurers and Perseus withdrew further and further into the snail alcove.

'Now what do we do?' whispered Norwood.

No-one answered because no-one had the slightest idea. So excited had they been at discovering the Holey Snails that they'd forgotten all about the need to formulate a strategy for dealing with the Gorgons, so that particular issue had never been resolved. Horace had rather hoped that Perseus would take the lion's share of the responsibility, considering it was him who was supposed to kill Medusa and chop off her head, but here he was, cowering in the shadows with the rest of them.

'Time for din-dins, my little ones.'

The voice was surprisingly mellifluous for a monster and more like a slightly higher pitched Alan Rickman.

'Din-dins?' said Norwood. 'Does she mean *us*?'

'Maybe she's just come to feed the snails,' said Vesta. 'I don't see anything around that they could actually eat.'

'And anyway,' said Horace, 'she's hardly likely to eat us if she's turned us to stone.'

'Oh, that's a relief,' said Norwood.

'Of course, it might not be Medusa herself,' said Vesta. 'It could be one of her sisters.'

'That's not really helping,' said Norwood.

'Lots of lovely lettucey things for mummy's little slimers.' The voice was a little louder now and reverberated almost soothingly around the walls of the cave.

'I think you've got your answer,' Horace whispered to Norwood, 'but it would rather suggest that she's coming this way.'

'Perhaps somebody should have a look-see and find out whether it really is Medusa,' said Vesta. 'At least then we'll know if we're likely to get turned to stone or not.'

A brief silence followed, during which, Vesta, Horace and Norwood all stared at Perseus, who immediately stared down at the rocky floor between his feet.

'Well, you're the one with the shiny shield,' said Norwood.

Perseus slowly raised his head. Was that a look of sheer unadulterated terror on his youthful features? Yes, it was.

'I really don't mind if someone else wants to borrow it,' he said.

The three adventurers didn't respond but continued to stare at him until finally he made a harrumphing kind of sound and edged his way towards the entrance to the alcove. Reaching the corner, he turned his back to the main cave and, inch by inch, eased his shield out from the cover of the rock, but no sooner had he done so than he let out a very un-hero-like gasp-cum-whimper and snatched the shield back in again.

But it was too late. The hissing sound instantly increased in volume by a multiple of twenty-four, and the Rickmanesque voice almost purred when it said, 'And who have we here, come to visit us? A pretty, young boy with golden locks and—' All of a sudden, the seductive purr switched to the grating screech of a bad-tempered seagull. 'Will you bloody snakes pack it in for *one* second! I can hardly hear myself think.' The hissing ceased abruptly, and the soothing tone returned. 'Don't be shy, pretty boy. Come out here where I can get a

303

proper look at you.'

By now, Perseus had scuttled back into the alcove to join the others. 'It's her all right.'

'Medusa only wants to say hello to her handsome young guest,' cooed Medusa.

'No you don't,' shouted Perseus. 'You want to turn me to stone. That's what you want to do.'

'Oh, you don't want to believe that silly old myth. Turn you to stone? I'd much rather be turning your knees to jelly — if you catch my drift.'

'Sounds like she's getting nearer,' said Vesta. 'We need to do something — and fast.'

Perseus thought for a moment, then raised his sword and yelled out, 'Any closer and the snails get it!'

There was a short pause before Medusa answered. 'Excuse me?'

'Nice try,' said Norwood, 'but I'm not sure she's going to fall for that one.'

No sooner were the words out of his mouth than a dozen snakes' heads appeared round the corner of the alcove.

'Quick,' said Horace. 'Everyone turn and face the wall.'

As they did so, he whipped out his Swiss Army knife and opened out the largest of the blades from amongst the array of handy little tools and gadgets. Holding it at eye level, he angled it this way and that until he could see Medusa's reflection, the snakes on her head now hissing again for all they were worth, and beneath them a face like the business end of an overused battering ram.

'Ah, I see you are not alone, my pretty one,' she said, combing a set of viciously sharp talons through her serpentine hairdo and causing at least a couple of the snakes to let out a shriek of pain. 'But didn't your parents teach you that it's rude to turn your back on a lady?'

'And turning people to stone is considered the height of politeness, is it?' said Norwood.

Medusa's sigh was like an asthmatic locomotive letting off steam. 'How many more times do I have to—?'

A greenish-tinged flash swept across the reflection in Horace's blade as Perseus slashed his sword wildly behind him, missing Medusa by a good two feet. Again and again he struck, but each time, the hideous creature avoided the blows with ease, laughing at every forlorn attempt.

'Not going too well, is it?' said Norwood, who, like Vesta, had followed Horace's example and was watching the reflection in the blade of his Swiss Army knife.

'I told you it was difficult,' Perseus panted and continued to hack and slash at the air behind him until a particularly energetic swipe overbalanced him and brought him crashing to the ground. But Medusa, instead of seizing her opportunity, simply waited patiently while he clambered back onto his feet. Evidently, she was enjoying the young man's humiliation and wanted to prolong it for as long as possible.

'I think he could do with some help,' said Vesta.

'Any suggestions?' said Horace.

'How about this?'

Vesta retracted the blade of her Swiss Army knife and switched on its handy little torch, which she set to maximum power. Then, taking hold of Norwood's wrist and angling his blade to give her a clear view of Medusa's face, she pointed the multi-tool back over her shoulder and aimed the powerful beam of light directly into the creature's eyes. Medusa's head twisted sharply to the side and a taloned hand flew up to shield her from the glare. At the same moment, another wild sweep of Perseus's sword missed its target completely and slammed hard into the wall of the cave, shattering the blade into a thousand pieces.

Sensing the need for some additional input, Horace positioned himself so that he could also see Medusa's reflection in Norwood's blade and mounted the second of a two-pronged attack with the beam from his own Swiss Army knife. The creature's other taloned hand shot up to protect her eyes, but the snakes on her head were afforded no such defence, and they squirmed and writhed like never before in dazzled panic. So much so that their rapidly shifting weight wrenched Medusa's head in ever-changing directions, severely affecting her balance and her ability to remain upright.

Presumably alerted by all the noise, Zoot suddenly returned from his no-scent-unsniffed exploration of the cave and — whether as a deliberate act or not — positioned himself directly behind Medusa's ankles so that, as she staggered backwards, she tripped over him and toppled to the ground with a terrifying shriek and a loud thud as her skull bounced off the rocky floor. There she lay, motionless and silent except for the thrashing and hissing of the still conscious snakes, which Zoot took obvious pleasure in tormenting by barking at them and then jumping back just out of reach of their fangs as they struck at him.

It was several seconds before Vesta was the first to dare to turn and look at Medusa directly. 'Hard to say whether she's spark out or dead,' she said. 'But either way, her eyes are closed, so she's not going to be turning anyone to stone right now.'

One by one, the others shuffled round to follow Vesta's gaze.

'Hurry up and cut her head off then, Perseus,' said Norwood. 'If she's not dead, she could come round any minute.'

'And how do you suggest I do that?' said Perseus, holding up the hilt of his sword and the inch and a half of blade that still remained.

'Oh, terrific.'

'We could always lend him one of our Swiss Army knives,' said Horace.

'The biggest blade's not much bigger than what's left of his sword,' said Norwood, 'but if he wants to go plunging his hand into a whole bunch of seriously pissed off snakes, that's up to him.'

By the look on Perseus's heavily sweating face, it was perfectly clear that he wasn't in the least bit keen on the prospect.

'I think there's a hacksaw back at the van,' said Horace.

'Oh yes?' said Norwood. 'So who's going to volunteer to go and fetch it? Don't forget there's the other two Gorgon sisters somewhere around. Who knows if they might be on their way here right now?'

'You're quite right of course,' said Vesta. 'We need to get out of here as quickly as we can, but we did agree to help Perseus, and he hasn't finished the job yet.'

'Okay, I've got an idea,' said Horace. 'If Medusa's actually dead, I'm sure that between us it won't be too hard to drag her back to the van so Perseus can... do what he has to. But if she's only unconscious, we can get her to follow us under her own steam when she comes to.'

Norwood's eyes popped. 'Are you *completely* insane? Get her to follow us and then what? Start all over again even if we do make it back to the van? Persy here doesn't even have a sword any more.'

'Ah, but that's the second part of my plan. As soon as we've got her back to the van—'

Horace broke off at the sound of a strange noise that was somewhere between a groan and a rumbling volcano. It was coming from the prone and slightly twitching body of Medusa.

307

'Er, I don't want to worry anyone,' said Perseus, 'but I don't think she's dead after all.'

'Right, that settles it,' said Horace. 'Everyone stuff their pockets with as many snails as they can.'

Norwood gave a somewhat less volcanic groan of his own. 'Oh dear. Why do I think this is all going to end in tears?'

43

Harper had spent well over an hour in her "second office", thinking. There was a lot to think *about*, so she'd taken a notepad and pen with her to jot down the salient points:

1) *Were they really Union Jack flip-flops in Leopold's bag?*
2) *If so, are they his?*
3) *If not, whose are they?*
4) *If they* are *his, does this necessarily mean he's a member of SMASH? A serial killer himself???*

At this point in her jotting, she sat back on the toilet, leaned her back against the cistern and closed her eyes. True, Leopold was a total shit, but was he really capable of murder? As far as she was aware, he wasn't in the least bit religious, so why join up with a bunch of fanatical fruitcakes like SMASH? On the other hand, he'd seemed very well informed about the kind of people they recruited, almost to the point of defensive. And what about the three-score-years-and-ten symbols she'd found in the women's toilets? Could it have been him that had written them? But if he had, what was he doing in the women's loos?

She opened her eyes again and, in capital letters, wrote *"EVIDENCE LEOPOLD A MEMBER OF SMASH"*, underlined it and added:

1) *Knowledge of SMASH. Defensive?*
2) *Refused to allow extra resources to solve case.*
3) *Flip-flops??*

4) *Symbols in women's toilet???*
5)

She tapped the tip of the pen repeatedly against the paper while she considered the meagre list and the second item in particular. Even if his being a member of SMASH was the reason he hadn't made extra resources available, surely he'd also have tipped them off about the first surveillance, so the monk would never have turned up at Ledley's house at all — unless of course he only became a member *after* that. But when? Before or after Scatterthwaite went undercover? Either way, she'd kept Leopold out of the loop on that one, so he wouldn't have been able to expose him as a mole. Otherwise, SMASH wouldn't have had to go to all the trouble of feeding Scatterthwaite with disinformation.

And what about Scatterthwaite himself? For all she knew, he could be dead already, but if he wasn't, it was surely only a matter of time. But what was she supposed to do about it? She'd no idea where SMASH had its base or even how to go about finding it.

She looked down at her notepad again and re-read the four solitary pieces of evidence she had against Leopold. Evidence? They were nothing more than pure conjecture and nowhere near enough to confront him with. And as for going above his head and reporting her suspicions, she'd be laughed all the way to her P45. A search of his office — or, better still, his home — might produce something a bit more solid, but she hadn't a hope in hell of getting a search warrant, especially without his knowledge, and breaking and entering wasn't her style. In Harper's book, two wrongs didn't make a right, whatever might be at stake.

She closed her notepad and sat back again. There was really only one legitimate option open to her. Follow Leopold and hope he'd give himself away somehow and provide her with some real evidence against him. Ideally, he might even lead her to wherever SMASH happened to hang out, and pray to God — or something — that DS Scatterthwaite hadn't already scoffed his last Twix bar.

* * *

It was a little after eight o'clock in the evening when Superintendent Leopold pulled out of the police station car park in his top-of-the-range, silver-grey Range Rover, and Harper was ready and waiting for him in a side street almost directly opposite. She was fairly certain he wouldn't recognise her own car, but to be on the safe side, she'd borrowed an unmarked Skoda from the station's vehicle pool. Keeping at least two cars between them, she had little difficulty following him through the moderately busy streets of the town, but when he hit the open countryside, the lack of other traffic meant that she had to exercise considerably more caution.

Half a dozen miles further on, he pulled into a small roadside services for fuel, and Harper parked at a discreet distance, but in a spot where she had a clear view of most of the building. After he'd been into the shop and paid, Leopold drove the Range Rover off the forecourt and pulled up around the corner, close to the doors of the Ladies' and Gents' toilets. Getting out of the car, he reached over to the back seat and took out a bulging Waitrose carrier bag. Harper was as sure as she could be that it was the same one she'd seen in his office and snapped a couple of photographs with her mobile phone before he disappeared into the Gents'.

Five minutes later, Leopold reappeared wearing a monk's habit and Union Jack flip-flops. The hood hung down his back, so his face was clearly visible as Harper fired off as many shots as she had time for before he got back into his car and slammed the door.

'Gotcha,' she said aloud and waited until he'd left the services and rejoined the main road before starting up her engine.

* * *

Harper knew next to nothing about golf, but she'd never heard of it being played under floodlights or with luminous balls, and since it was already dark when Leopold turned in through the big iron gates of Bellwood Park Golf Club, she doubted he'd come to get a round in. It was also unlikely that an almost floor-length monk's habit and a pair of flip-flops would do a lot to improve his swing.

She gave him a couple of minutes and then carefully observed the ten-mile-an-hour speed limit as she second-geared the car along a newly asphalted driveway, which ran dead straight for nearly half a mile and then suddenly elbowed to the right. Two hundred yards in front of her, and tastefully lit from below with ground level spotlights, a long two-storey building loomed out of the darkness. Mock Tudor and about the size of a modest mansion. The clubhouse, Harper presumed.

She slowed the car to a crawl and drove off the road onto a narrow patch of bare earth which was obscured from the clubhouse by a small thicket of trees. Taking a torch from the glove box, she kept well away from the drive and followed the edge of a dog-legged fairway on foot until she reached the putting green near the left-hand end of the clubhouse. The car park was almost full, mostly with cars she could never even dream of affording, and roughly in the middle, Leopold's Range Rover.

Doesn't look like these monks believe in taking a vow of poverty then, Harper thought, but immediately, a little voice in her head told her that she might be being a bit too hasty in jumping to conclusions.

Surely this couldn't be where they had their base. As far as she could tell, this was a fully operational golf club, and a bunch of monks trooping in and out every day would be bound to raise some disgruntled eyebrows amongst the nineteenth hole brigade. Unless SMASH actually owned the place of course? But then she remembered the sign at the gate which listed some of the club's major attractions, including "CONFERENCE FACILITIES AVAILABLE". Maybe that was it. The monks had simply rented a function room for the evening. Some sort of convention perhaps. If that was the case, there'd probably be a sign up inside the main entrance with a big arrow and saying something like "THIS WAY TO THE SERIAL KILLING MONKS' ANNUAL CONFERENCE". Or something a little less obvious perhaps. But there was no way she was going to risk marching in through the front door to find out. At the very least, it was certain there'd be some toffee-nosed jobsworth sitting behind a big desk in the foyer asking awkward questions, and she'd no intention of making her presence known until she was good and ready.

Stooping low and keeping as close to the clubhouse wall as possible, she edged her way to the near side of the open main door, then retraced her steps and completed a circuit of the entire building, peeking in at each window as she went. But there was nothing of interest in any of the rooms that were occupied and definitely no Leopold or anyone else dressed as a monk.

'Upstairs then,' she said to herself and hurried back to the metal fire escape staircase she'd passed halfway along the back of the clubhouse.

Almost on tiptoe to avoid making any more noise than necessary, she reached the wood-framed glass door at the top of the steps and tried the handle. The door opened inwards, and Harper persuaded herself that since it wasn't locked, she couldn't be accused of breaking and entering.

A short, carpeted passageway led at right-angles to another corridor which ran the length of the upper floor. There were doors at irregular intervals on either side, but all of them were closed. She looked in both directions and noticed that the door at the far end of the corridor to her left was considerably nearer than the one at the opposite end.

Assuming that the room behind it must be the biggest on the floor — and therefore the most likely to be a function room — she made her way past framed oil paintings (mostly of old men) and photographs of golfers about to play a shot, golfers just having played a shot and golfers with supercilious, toothy grins holding up some trophy or other. Every so often, the occasional glass cabinet containing actual trophies and other golfing paraphernalia, and everywhere the rich, deep scent of wood polish.

Further along the corridor, she began to hear the beat and bass notes of music, which seemed to be coming from behind the door she was heading for. Bit odd for a conference, she thought, but all the political parties played rousing tunes at theirs these days, so why not the unholy brethren? Gregorian chanting might have been rather more appropriate than Elvis Costello's *Watching the Detectives* perhaps, but there was a certain irony in that too.

Six feet from the door, the hubbub of voices was audible above the blare of the music. Definitely a lot of people inside, but what to do next? She could hardly just burst in and arrest a roomful of serial killers single-handed. Her best bet now was to get herself back outside and call for backup. But before she got half the local constabulary out here with a team from the armed response unit, she'd better make certain she'd read the situation correctly first.

Crouching down, she closed one eye and had just brought the other to within two inches of the keyhole when a solid, firm hand gripped her by the shoulder.

'Looking for something?'

44

'I wish you'd tell us the second part of your plan,' said Norwood.

'All in good time,' said Horace mysteriously, although, in truth, the real reason for his reluctance to tell the others the second part of his plan was that he wasn't at all convinced that it would actually work.

This was the third time they'd had to wait for Medusa to catch up, presumably because she was still a bit groggy after her concussion, but Horace, Norwood, Vesta and Perseus (and probably Zoot as well) were all quite happy to take the occasional break from their exertions.

'Here she comes,' said Vesta as the unmistakable hissing of Medusa's snakes came into earshot once again.

When they finally reached the T-junction with the left- and right-pointing signs, they found Thestor sitting with his back against the rocky wall, snoring loudly and still wearing Perseus's helmet and breastplate. Zoot ran straight up to him and began to lick the part of his face that was still exposed, and the old man sat bolt upright, flailing every one of his bone-thin limbs at the cold, damp air.

'What — no — not me — I never — it was... Oh, it's you.'

'Do try and curb your delight that we're all still alive,' said Norwood. 'You'll be making me blush.'

After a brief struggle, Thestor eventually managed to

free himself from Zoot's enthusiastic attentions and stretched his scrawny arms out in front of him. Taking this as a silent appeal for assistance, Horace and Vesta each grabbed an elbow and hoisted him up onto his feet.

'So what about Medusa then?' he said. 'She dead or what?'

'That'd be a "what",' said Norwood and theatrically cupped his hand to his ear. 'In fact, judging by that loud hissing noise, she'll be here any moment.'

Thestor's mouth hung open as if he himself had been turned to stone, which clearly wasn't the case because, two seconds later, he was scurrying as fast as he could go towards the mouth of the cave. The others followed hot on his heels, and by the time they got to the van, any part of them that wasn't protected by anorak or oilskin was thoroughly soaked by the still relentless torrential rain.

Horace glanced back over his shoulder to check that Medusa was still behind them, and as soon as everyone was safely inside the van, he fired up the engine and switched on the lights.

'Don't anybody look round,' he said, staring fixedly into the rear-view mirror at the image of Medusa staggering towards them.

Beads of sweat began to mingle with the rivulets of rain that ran from his hairline as he repeatedly revved the engine and waited. The timing didn't have to be especially precise, but he needed to judge the moment as closely as possible.

Forty yards — thirty yards — twenty yards —

Horace rammed the van into reverse gear and stamped on the accelerator. Too hard. The wheels spun uselessly on the rain-sodden earth, so he eased off slightly on the throttle until the tyres found some traction. He checked the rear-view mirror again as the van hurtled backwards, uncertain now that he'd be able to pick up enough momentum to—

There was a loud bang and an abruptly curtailed scream as the rear wheels of the van jolted upwards and sent each of the passengers bouncing up out of their seats. A fraction of a second later, the front wheels produced exactly the same effect, and Horace slammed on the brakes. Breathing heavily, he rested his forearms on the top of the steering wheel and peered through the rain-smeared windscreen at the twisted, lifeless body of Medusa, clearly visible in the beam of the headlights. Or at least he sincerely hoped she was lifeless because if she turned and looked at him now, he was a goner.

'Is she... dead?' said Vesta, also peering through the windscreen from the passenger seat beside him.

'Better give her a couple of minutes to see if she moves,' said Horace and switched on the windscreen wipers to get a clearer view. 'In the meantime, we ought to get these snails out of our pockets before they all get squashed.'

Norwood produced a plastic bucket from a cupboard beside him at the back of the van, and having contributed his own haul, passed it forward to Horace and Vesta as if he were taking up a collection — which he kind of was really.

'Not bad at all,' said Vesta when they had finished and the bucket was almost full to the brim with Holey Snails, 'although we ought to find somewhere better to keep them so the ones at the bottom don't all suffocate.'

'*Can* snails suffocate?' said Horace.

'No idea,' said Norwood, 'but the last thing we want is them pegging out on us after all the trouble we've gone to getting the damn things. And speaking of pegging out, d'you reckon it's safe to check on old snakehead by now?'

Horace and Vesta both peered through the windscreen again.

'Doesn't look like she's moved at all,' said Horace. 'And as far as I can tell, the snakes are all dead too. Must have run right over them with one of the wheels.'

'Right then,' said Norwood. 'Off you go, Persy.'

'Uh?' said Perseus.

'You need to cut her head off, don't you? The sooner you do that, the sooner we can all get the hell out of here.' He opened the cupboard where he'd found the bucket and took out a large hacksaw. 'There you go.'

Perseus gingerly took the saw from him and gave it a thorough examination. 'I don't think I've ever come across one of these before.'

'I'd lay bets on it,' said Norwood, 'but it's really very simple. That's the bit that does the cutting, and you just run it back and forth across the... the... the thing that you're cutting until you're through.'

Perseus ran his finger carefully along the blade. 'Not very sharp, is it?'

'It'll do the job, I promise you.' Norwood stood up and opened the sliding door of the van. 'Now can we please just get on with it?'

With obvious reluctance, the soon-to-be-hero forced himself upright. 'I don't suppose anyone'd like to...'

'Come with you?' said Norwood

Perseus's eyes lit up, and he nodded enthusiastically, but everyone else shook their own heads with a similar vigour, so Perseus stepped out of the van like an Ancient Greek Neil Armstrong and sidled over to Medusa's crumpled body.

Horace and Vesta deliberately turned their gaze away from the windscreen and towards the back seat of the van where Norwood, Thestor and even Zoot were intently studying the floor in front of them. Nobody was in the least bit curious to watch Perseus sawing his way through skin, flesh, sinew, gristle and bone, producing all manner of gore and spurting jets of blood which

319

splattered his tunic with glistening streaks of sticky crimson, so they didn't bother to look.

A few minutes later, there was a knock on the side of the van, but no-one had any interest in seeing what had caused it. It wasn't hard to guess that Perseus was very probably standing in the open doorway with an irritatingly self-satisfied smirk and holding Medusa's head by the dead snake hair stretched out in front of him, a steaming torrent of blood gushing from the neatly severed neck.

'Got it?' said Horace.

'I most certainly have,' said Perseus, the tone of his voice confirming that he really did have an irritatingly self-satisfied smirk on his face. 'This weapon you gave me is a thing of great wonder.'

'Actually, we'll be needing that back, I'm afraid,' said Norwood, keeping his eyes averted as he passed him a piece of old cloth. 'Perhaps you could give it a bit of a clean first though. And you might like to pop the head in here while you're at it.'

As well as the cloth, he handed Perseus an empty carrier bag, and after a protracted rustling sound consistent with stuffing a severed head into a plastic bag, Norwood peeked through his fingers to check that the coast was clear.

'All clear,' he said, and his co-adventurers and Thestor (and even Zoot) breathed a collective sigh of relief.

'Well then,' said Perseus, 'I'd better be getting this back to King Polydectes before he goes ahead and marries my mum.'

'Can we offer you a lift anywhere?' said Horace, more out of politeness than any wish to delay their own homeward journey for any longer than was strictly necessary.

'No thanks. I think these will get me there a lot

quicker than this horseless chariot of yours.'

Perseus pointed down to his golden sandals, and what had previously appeared to be elaborate patterning on the sides of each suddenly sprang outwards to form two pairs of golden wings.

'Fair enough,' said Horace, realising that there was very little that could still surprise him.

And so it was that after Perseus had given back the hacksaw and Thestor had reluctantly returned his helmet and armour, the young hero — for so it seemed he now was — thanked them all for their help and took half a dozen paces back from the van. Then, the tiny wings on his sandals beat faster and faster until they became a literal blur of activity, and Perseus shot skywards and vanished into the swirling mass of deep black cloud.

Horace felt a twinge of regret that none of them had stepped outside the van to get a better view of Perseus's dramatic departure, but the rain was still hammering down, and besides, he was desperate to set the van's time travel controls and launch them on their way back home. However, as he got to his feet and turned towards the rear of the van, he spotted Thestor sitting next to Norwood on the back seat. They could hardly take him with them, but what else were they going to do? Drive him all the way back to the court of King Amnestios?

'Thestor,' he began, wondering quite how he was going to phrase the question, but he got no further than uttering the man's name.

"Krrakkk!"

The explosive blast was a hundred times louder than any of the thunderclaps they'd heard so far and only a few decibels short of a sonic boom.

Five heads (including Zoot's) spun round to look out of the side windows of the van, and at the same moment, a brilliant white flash of lightning lit up the slightly less than enormous figure of a man dressed in a broad-brimmed, dark black hat, an almost floor-length, dark black coat and red and white baseball boots.

'Is that who I think it is?' said Norwood.

'The American chap at Wellwisher's house?' said Horace.

'The one I floored with a single karate chop to the back of the neck?' said Vesta. 'Kenny Bunkport?'

'Who?' said Thestor.

"Krrakkk!"

The slightly less than enormous figure fired a second shot up at the sky and then slowly — very slowly — arced the muzzle of the enormous gun downwards until it was pointing directly at the van.

Another flash of lightning, and the deep scar which ran from just below the American's left ear to almost the middle of his chin contorted itself around the leer of a twisted grin.

45

The grip on Harper's shoulder eased off, and she straightened up, expecting to see the shadowy, hooded face of a serial killing monk. But the man was bareheaded and wore a maroon blazer with an embroidered crest on the top pocket.

'Private party, madam,' he said with a sideways nod at the closed door. 'Do you have an invitation?'

There was an unmistakable tone of "of course you bloody don't" in his voice, ably supported by the faint curl of his upper lip. Harper decided that attack was the best form of defence.

'No, but I do have this,' she said and flashed her warrant card under his nose.

It might as well have been a gun the way the man took a step back and looked as though he was about to put up his hands in surrender. But he recovered himself instantly, took the ID from Harper and studied it minutely.

'Detective Chief Inspector Harper Collins,' she said as if she doubted that his reading skills were up to the task. 'And you are?'

He handed the warrant card back. 'Anthony Holroyd. Assistant Manager.'

'Well, Tony, I'm here on official police business, and what I'd really like to know is whether there's a roomful of monks behind this door.'

'Monks?'

'Yes. You know. Hoods, habits, Union Jack flip-flops?'

'Union Jack flip-flops?'

Harper gave him a flicker of a patronising smile. 'You don't seem to get quite how this goes, do you? Me, chief inspector. You, assistant manager. Chief inspector asks the questions, not assistant manager, okay?'

Holroyd glared back at her, clearly not happy about being spoken to as if he were a five-year-old with attention deficit disorder, so Harper carried on.

'So, let's start again, shall we? What exactly's going on inside this room here?'

She delivered her own sideways nod at the closed door, but at the same moment, it opened inwards and the combined din of up-tempo pop music and raised voices flooded out into the corridor, immediately followed by Napoleon Bonaparte. Well, not *the* Napoleon Bonaparte obviously. He was far too tall for a start and hadn't even the slightest trace of a French accent when he said, 'Excuse me, but where might I find the gents' toilet?'

'And in answer to your question, Chief Inspector,' said Holroyd when he'd sent the Emperor on his way to the third door on the left, 'it's the golf club's annual fancy dress party.'

Harper's heart sank like a tenth-storey lift that had just had its cable cut, and she stared in through the still open doorway at the throng of revellers inside. Darth Vader was making a lame attempt at shakin' his booty on the dance floor with either Marie Antoinette or little Bo Peep. It was hard to tell which she was meant to be. Close by, Julius Caesar was gettin' down and dirty with Wonder Woman's much older sister, and Albert Einstein/Doctor Who was rashly attempting a hitherto unknown version of the twist with an open bottle of wine clutched in his mitt.

Around the dance floor, an impressive range of the famous and infamous chatted, drank and ate at large round tables or stood in small groups around the edge of the room. Charlie Chaplin, Elwood (or Jake) Blues and Captain Jack Sparrow were all laughing their socks off at some joke or other that the Pope had apparently been telling, while a little further away, two other Jack Sparrows (one of them female) were deep in serious conversation with Elvis Presley and Queen Victoria. To Harper's left and about twenty feet away, Marilyn Monroe, Cowardly Lion and a highly unseasonal Christmas cracker were clinking glasses with a monk in Union Jack flip-flops.

Time I wasn't here, thought Harper, but before she moved so much as an inch to make her escape, the Christmas cracker must have noticed her staring at them, and her garishly red lips moved up and down a few times as she pointed a tinsel-wrapped finger. Too late to flee, Harper held Leopold's open-mouthed gaze while she frantically kickstarted her brain into trying to concoct some sort of plausible explanation for what the hell she was doing there. But by the time the superintendent was upon her, all she'd come up with was a rough approximation of a sycophantic smile and a sickly sweet 'Good evening, sir. Having a good time?'

The assistant manager was still hovering, so Leopold dismissed him and waited until he was out of earshot before firing his opening salvo.

'What in God's name are you *doing* here, Collins?'

Harper's mind raced. She could hardly tell him the real reason now that it seemed he was perfectly innocent.

'The thing is, sir, and I'm terribly sorry to disturb you while you're, er... while you're...'

'Get on with it, for Christ's sake.'

'It's just that we had a report in that a... um...'

'A what?'

'A monk in Union Jack flip-flops had been spotted in the vicinity, so I decided to follow it up myself.'

Leopold took a second or two to figure it out. '*I* was spotted, you mean?'

'So it would appear, sir, yes.'

Of course, there was always the possibility that Leopold might check to see if there really had been any such report, but somehow she doubted he'd want to raise his head above the parapet any more then he had to on this one. Could a superintendent be charged with wasting police time? Unlikely, but if the pink tinge to his cheeks was anything to go by, he'd be keen to keep this particular incident as quiet as possible. Harper gave herself a metaphorical pat on the back, and to compound his embarrassment still further, made an ostentatious show of running her eyes over his costume from hood to flip-flops and back again.

'Interesting choice, sir?' she said, subtly phrasing the words more like a question than a statement.

Leopold's face flushed a couple of shades redder. 'Yes, well, I er... thought it might be... amusing. Ironic even. Most people here will know about the case, and there's a fair few on the force themselves. The Deputy Chief Constable came as Count Dracula in fact—'

He broke off abruptly, presumably aware that he was blathering to a subordinate who, in the normal course of events, he wouldn't have spoken two words to unless it was to yell at her and tell her what a crap job she was doing. No doubt he'd also become aware of Harper's barely suppressed expression of gloating amusement at her boss's squirming humiliation.

'Yes, well, probably not the best choice of costume in the circumstances,' he muttered.

'Positively distasteful... some might say,' said Harper with a deliberate beat of a pause.

Leopold's deep-set eyes narrowed at her, and it wasn't difficult to read the message: "So far but no further".

Harper decided to quit while she was ahead. 'Well

then, sir, I guess there's no reason to detain you from your party any longer.'

'Indeed.' He hesitated momentarily and then took half a step closer to her. 'Perhaps we could keep this little matter between ourselves, Chief Inspector?'

She let him stew for a couple of seconds while she pretended to consider her response. 'Technically, of course, I'd have to write up a report.'

'Yes, I realise that, but—'

'In fact, you yourself are usually quite a stickler for that sort of thing.'

Oh, how she was loving this. The image in her head was of a pinball machine with the points notching up so rapidly they were almost a blur. Apparently, Leopold had a similar image in his own mind because his cheeks glowed redder than ever. Heightened embarrassment or escalating anger? Best not to find out.

'However,' she said, 'perhaps we could forget about the rule book on this occasion.'

Leopold gave her the slightest of nods, and his eyes noticeably failed to contribute to the semblance of a smile.

Harper was less than half way back along the corridor when her elation at having got one over on the arrogant shit of a bully suddenly evaporated. Talking her way out of a tight spot and humiliating Leopold in the process were all very well, but the fact remained that she was no further forward in cracking the case and, even more pressingly, how to find Scatterthwaite before it was too late. It was already over twenty-four hours since he'd failed to turn up for their appointment, so the chances that he was still alive were minimal to say the least.

46

Kenny Bunkport walked slowly towards the van, curtains of rain cascading from the brim of his dark black hat, and tapped the muzzle of his enormous gun against the passenger window. Vesta hesitated, but only for as long as it took the American's twisted grin to transform itself into a blood-chilling scowl of malevolent intent. She wound down the window, and the twisted grin instantly reappeared.

'Hi, guys. Remember me?'

No-one answered.

''Cos I certainly remember you.' He glanced at the back seat. 'Except, who's the old-timer in the diaper?'

Thestor bristled even though he probably had no idea what a diaper was. 'My name is Thestor. Royal Soothsayer to the—'

'Yeah, yeah. I really ain't that interested, Grandad, so what say you zip it, okay?'

Thestor grunted and sat back in his seat, his stick-like arms folded across his ribcage of a chest.

Norwood leaned towards him and whispered, 'He's American.'

'But what I *am* really interested in,' Bunkport went on, 'is this fine lookin' mess o' snails you have here.'

Vesta clutched the bucket of snails closer to her chest. 'They're not for sale.'

Bunkport's laugh was like the distress call of a Canada goose with whooping cough, but it ended as abruptly as it had begun. 'Now, you listen here, funny girl, and you listen good. You ain't my favourite person in the world right now, so if I was you, I'd quit with the wisecracks 'fore I blow that purty little face clean off that purty little neck o' yorn.'

'I wasn't actually joking as a matter of fact.'

'Oh, as a matter of fact you weren't, were you? Well, here's another little matter of fact for you, Miss Cutiepie. If you ain't all got your goddamn sorry asses outta this ole jaloppy by the time I count to five, me and Edwina here are gonna start havin' ourselves a whole lotta fun.'

He brought the stock of the rifle up against his cheek and took aim at Vesta's "purty little face", but she shifted her head slightly and looked past him into the driving rain.

'Edwina your wife, is she?' she said.

'What?' Bunkport lowered the stock by a fraction of an inch. 'No, Edwina ain't my goddamn wife. Edwina is my little honey of an enormous gun here. And for your information, I ain't even married, see?'

'Huh,' Vesta snorted. 'And why does that not surprise me?'

The American huffed, puffed and generally worked himself up into such a mouth-foaming rage that the part of his brain responsible for producing meaningful language failed him completely, so he let Edwina do the talking for him and fired a single ear-ringing shot into the air directly above his head. Then, he pointed the rifle back at Vesta and began counting.

'One.'

Vesta turned to Horace, who responded with a slight shrug and a look on his face that said "I really don't think we have an awful lot of choice in the matter, given the circumstances".

'Two. And y'all come outta this side door here, one after the other. I don't want any o' you sneakin' out no other way and disappearin' off, okay?'

Horace glanced round at Norwood, who also shrugged and responded with a remarkably similar look to the one Horace had given Vesta a moment ago. Thestor didn't respond at all, either because he hadn't the faintest idea what a gun could actually do to him or because he was still sulking about the recent insult to his choice of apparel.

'Three. And bring the goddamn snails with you.'

Horace briefly weighed up the odds against all of them escaping unscathed if he slammed the van into gear and hit down hard on the throttle, but since he knew he couldn't hope to achieve nought to sixty in anything less than forty-five seconds, he dismissed the plan as barkingly insane.

'Four. I ain't kiddin' now.'

Horace heaved a sigh of bitter resignation.

'I suppose we'd better do as he says,' he said and clambered between the two front seats into the back of the van.

'You do realise of course,' said Norwood, 'that we're all going to get soaking wet again.'

Nevertheless, he forced himself upright and stepped out of the van behind Horace. Vesta followed with the bucket of snails and then Thestor. Bunkport backed off half a dozen yards and told them to line up side by side with their backs against the van.

'Okay, missy,' he said when they'd all positioned themselves to his satisfaction. 'You just bring them there snails over toward me, but make it slow, okay? And no funny business or I'll put a goddamn hole in you as big as... as... as the biggest goddamn hole you ever see'd in your life.'

Vesta looked along the row at Thestor and her co-adventurers as if to check that she was indeed the "missy" that Bunkport had referred to.

'And what exactly do you intend to do with them

when you've got them?' she said.

'Well, ain't you the little Miss Curiosity That Killed the Cat,' sneered the American. 'And not that it ain't none o' your business, but I'll tell you, seein' as how you ain't gonna live to—'

'That's rather ambiguous, isn't it?' Norwood interrupted. 'I mean, "not that it ain't none o' your business" is actually a double negative — almost a triple negative in fact — so the listener could easily be misled into believing that it *is* in fact their business and therefore—'

Bunkport rounded on him with venom in his eyes and the enormous gun aiming straight at his chest. 'You sassin' me, fella?'

'Certainly not. I was merely trying to point out that—'

'You wanna hear me out or not?'

'Of course,' said Vesta. 'You were saying?'

Bunkport cleared his throat and took a moment to muster his thoughts. 'Okay, so as I was saying, I'm being paid a shitload o' dough by this guy who's gonna make an even bigger shitload o' dough turning these little babies into some kinda potion that stops people gettin' old.'

'Worsthorne Pharmaceuticals, you mean,' said Horace, remembering back to the business card they'd found in Bunkport's pocket at Mr Wellwisher's house.

'Hey, you cotton on fast, dontcha, cowboy. But as much as I've enjoyed our little chat, it's high time we concluded this here business of you handing over the snails before Edwina here starts gettin' twitchy again.'

He swung his attention and his gun back towards Vesta, but she stood her ground, meeting his gaze with steady defiance and said, 'You're going to kill us all whether we give them to you or not.'

'Ah, shucks, honey-pie. Whatever gave you that idea?'

'You did. Just now. The bit about you telling us why you wanted the snails because we weren't going to live to tell the tale anyway.'

'Ah yes, but I never got to finish the sentence, did I?' said Bunkport, beaming smugly at his own cleverness.

'It was what you were *going* to say though, wasn't it?'

'Er...' The smug grin quickly dissolved. 'Just bring the goddamn snails here, will yer?'

'You know, I really don't think I can be bothered,' said Vesta and set the bucket of snails down at her feet.

Horace wasn't at all convinced that Vesta's recalcitrance was going to do them any favours vis-à-vis not being killed and was about to point out that compliance might at least buy them a few more seconds of life when he spotted two shapes approaching fast through the gloom and the rain.

'Suit yourself then,' said Bunkport, once again bringing the stock of the enormous gun up against his cheek and taking aim at Vesta's head. 'But I'm gonna save you till last, sweetpea, on account of I wanna take my time watchin' you die a slow and pertikerly painful death.'

So saying, he swung the barrel of the gun to aim it at Norwood's head instead. At the same time, a spectacular flash of lightning revealed the true hideousness of the two shapes scampering towards them less than ten yards behind Kenny Bunkport's back. Only marginally less ugly than Medusa herself, the Gorgon sisters were possessed of the same vicious-looking talons but sported long dark hair in place of a writhing mass of hissing snakes. The other more crucial difference was that you didn't turn to stone when you looked at them.

'Oh — my — God,' said Horace, sincerely hoping that one of Bunkport's bullets would carry him off before these two got their claws into him.

"Krrakkk!"

A burst of flame from the muzzle of the gun and the shrill whistle of a bullet passing inches above Norwood's head as one of the Gorgons performed a flying, waist-high rugby tackle that brought Bunkport crashing to the ground. Winded and dazed as he clearly was, she had little difficulty in rolling him onto his back before squatting heavily on his chest, a knee planted firmly on either side of him, while her sister pinned his arms down so that he formed an almost cruciform shape. Another bolt of lightning, and the massive talons gleamed as the Gorgon on his chest raised her hand high in the air. But just as she was about to bring the flesh-ripping claws sweeping downwards and presumably removing most of Bunkport's face with one mighty blow, her sister yelled, 'Wait, Stheno!'

Stheno stayed her hand, frozen in mid air, rain dripping from the tips of her razor-sharp talons.

'What?' she snapped. 'It's not your turn, and you know very well it isn't.'

'Take a look at him, will you?'

Stheno took a look at him.

'So, tell me,' said her sister. 'Is he or is he not a bit of a hunk?'

'Yes, I see what you mean,' said Stheno and brought her face to within a few inches of Bunkport's to examine him more closely.

The American twisted his head to the side, very possibly to avoid the full frontal assault from the creature's fetid breath, which reeked of rotten eggs and very old fish.

'Can't say I'm a big fan of this scar though,' Stheno added, tracing its length from ear to chin with the tip of a talon.

'Oh, I don't know. I think it's quite sexy in a pugnaciously rugged kind of way. But in any case, he's the best looker we've had round here for many a long while, and I really don't think we can afford to be quite that picky.'

Stheno gave it some thought and then slowly nodded her head. 'Okay — but don't forget I've still got first dibs with the talons on the next ugly one that shows up.'

'What about those four over by that big box thing on wheels then? They're not exactly what you'd call "ugly", I know — apart from the old one of course — and the woman's really rather stunning in fact, but we really ought to wreak some kind of vengeance for our dear departed sister before we have our fun, don't you think?'

Apart from the hammering of the rain on the roof of the van and a couple of claps of thunder, a fearful silence descended as both the Gorgons turned their evil gaze on Horace and his companions, all of whom had stopped breathing and put their hearts into a state of suspended animation.

'You're right of course,' said Stheno at last. 'I don't think we'd ever forgive ourselves if we let Medusa's death go unavenged. But who's going to keep an eye on Scarface here while we tear this other lot to shreds?'

'I tell you what,' said her sister. 'How about you stay with him while I do the first two, and then we can swap?'

Once again, Stheno took her time to consider the proposition. 'Seems fair, I suppose. Just don't get carried away and slaughter all four of them before I have my go. You know what you're like, Euryale.'

'Trust me,' said her sister, but before she'd taken three steps towards the objects of her gruesome intentions, Zoot chose that precise moment to hurl himself out of the van, where he'd been recovering from his earlier exertions, and attacked the Gorgons with a deafening volley of frenzied barking.

Euryale stopped dead. 'What in the name of Zeus almighty is *that*?'

'Some kind of... dog?' said Stheno.

'You ever see a dog with only one head before?'

'Can't say I have, no.'

'Weird or what?'

The two sisters continued to stare at Zoot as he upped the volume of his verbal assault.

'To be honest,' said Euryale, 'I'm really not sure I want to tangle with something like that. I mean a three-headed dog is one thing, but there's something seriously evil about this monstrosity.'

'Straight from Hades by the look of it,' said Stheno. 'Maybe we should just... you know... head back to the cave with Scarface and call it a day.'

'What about avenging our beloved sister though?'

'"Beloved sister"?' Stheno tutted. 'Good riddance to the old cow, I say. Her and her bloody snakes writhing and hissing all over the place and keeping us awake every night. Not to mention hogging the bathroom for hours while she tried to arrange them into something that vaguely resembled a respectable hairdo.'

'And still come out looking like she'd been dragged through a snakepit backwards,' her sister chuckled. 'But what about the snails they've stolen?'

'Bugger the snails. Now you've got me all fired up over Scarface here, I don't want to waste any more time getting stuck in.'

'Fair enough,' said her sister and grabbed hold of one of Bunkport's arms.

Stheno took the other, and between them, the two Gorgons hauled him to his feet.

'Get yer goddamn hands offa me, you filthy old hags,' yelled the American, but despite his bulk and his frantic struggling, he was no match for the deceptively powerful Gorgon sisters as they dragged him kicking and screaming towards their cave, all the while making lewd and unprintable remarks about what they were going to do with him once they'd got him inside.

One by one, Horace and his companions began to breathe again, and as soon as their hearts had resumed active service and the blood in their veins started to flow normally once more, Zoot was rewarded for his act of selfless heroism with an appropriately lavish amount of praise. And probably more importantly as far as the dog was concerned, Horace promised him extra rations for at least the rest of the week.

'I think perhaps we should leave before the Gorgons change their minds,' said Vesta when Zoot seemed to have grown tired of all the head patting and taken himself off back into the van for a well deserved rest.

Everyone agreed that this was a strategy that couldn't be faulted, and as soon as they were all safely seated back inside the van, Horace fired up the engine and released the handbrake.

'Don't you need to set the time travel controls?' said Norwood.

'Not yet,' said Horace. 'First, we need to get away from here and then... we need to talk about Thestor.'

The van shot forward, bouncing over Medusa's headless corpse (which Horace had forgotten lay directly in their path), and even over the din of the torrential rain and the crashes of thunder, it was still just possible to hear Kenny Bunkport's anguished screams of torment echoing from the mouth of the Gorgons' cave.

DIGRESSION FIVE: THE DISCOVERY OF AMERICA AND A BIT ABOUT WHAT HAPPENED AFTERWARDS

Americans live in a very big place called "America", which was so named after a man called Amerigo Vespucci because a lot of people believed he'd discovered it even though he hadn't. In reality, America was first discovered by the people who already lived there, and since they were "Indians", they called it "India" after themselves. But unbeknown to them at the time, there was already a country called India, and they were told to come up with a different name because having two countries in the world called India was likely to get very confusing. To differentiate between the two, it was suggested that the Indians could call themselves "*Red* Indians" and rename their country "Red India", but this was immediately rejected on the grounds that most Indians were not at all happy about the implication that they were all communists.

Consequently, the International Registry of Nations (IRN) [see also Digression Three on the naming of Switzerland] then took it upon itself to impose a name of its own choosing, and the most logical option was to name the country after the first non-Indian to have discovered it. On further consideration, however, it was decided that neither "Hieronymos" nor "Sprayberry" seemed particularly appropriate. "Hieronymosland" and "Sprayberryland" were also quickly dismissed, and as for giving the country its full title of "The United States of Hieronymos" or "The United States of Sprayberry", there was a clear mismatch between these names and what would later become known as the "land of the free and the home of the brave".

And so it was that the good people of the IRN randomly selected a copy of *Italian Births, Deaths and Marriages 1500-1550* from a bookshelf and, eyes closed, flicked through some pages and stuck in a pin. "The United States of Vespucci" didn't get any votes at all, but everyone agreed that "The United States of Amerigo" had quite a nice ring to it. Even so, some members of the New Countries Naming Committee expressed their concern that "Amerigo" sounded a bit too much like a fairground attraction, and it took only a subtle shift in pronunciation before "The United States of America" was duly named. Concomitant to this, every one of the country's indigenous population received a letter informing them that they were no longer "Indians" but were henceforth to be known as "Native Americans".

Hieronymos Sprayberry was understandably distraught when he discovered that his discovery was not to be named after him after all, even though he'd never intentionally set out to discover anything in his life, let alone the New World, and had only come across it by pure chance. (The "New World", incidentally, was the name given to America when its very existence had only been guessed at and was named after a range of kitchen appliances that were particularly favoured by explorers.) Hieronymos had simply been enjoying a day's fishing in his homemade canoe off the southwest coast of Cornwall when a mighty storm had suddenly whipped up as if from nowhere and capsized the flimsy vessel. He'd managed to cling on to the overturned hull until the storm eventually abated, but by now, his only paddle had vanished and he was completely at the mercy of wind and current, which were predominantly westward at the time. (In those days, the Gulf Stream flowed in the opposite direction to what it does today.)

For months he drifted helplessly, barely surviving on a diet of Fisherman's Friends and the occasional handful of rainwater. As close to death as anyone can be without actually *being* dead, his battered canoe finally reached land, and he dragged himself up onto the beach, where he was soon discovered by a small group of young Indians who'd come down to the sea for a spot of body-surfing.

'Hey, dude, where'd you spring from all of a sudden?' one of them asked, having apparently failed to notice the battered canoe or that Hieronymos was drenched from head to foot.

But the accidental explorer was too near death to even open his mouth to speak, so the Indians carried him back to their village and gradually restored him to health with a constant supply of buffalo burgers and the ministrations of a local witch doctor. During this period of convalescence, the tribal elders held meeting after meeting to try and decide what to do with this strange, badly sunburned creature who had emerged from the sea as if by magic, and it was eventually agreed that he must be the god, Tonto, whose coming had been foretold for many generations past. So, as soon as Hieronymos had fully recovered, Indians flocked from far and wide to bring him wonderful gifts and do all kinds of other things generally associated with worshipping a deity.

Pleasant as all this worshipping was, however, Hieronymos became more and more homesick and longed to return to his native land and a decent bowl of mulligatawny soup. The Indians tried everything to persuade him to stay, but there was no shifting him from his resolve, and because he was a god, they even obeyed his command to repair and improve the battered old canoe he'd arrived in. But before he set sail, he had a flag made up which roughly resembled the Union Jack, and planting it firmly in the earth, he shouted, 'I claim this land in the name of the King of Britain' and then added a little more quietly, 'or Queen, in case there's been a change of monarch since I've been away.'

Several months later, he at last reached British shores and immediately notified the relevant authorities of his discovery of The United States of Sprayberry, as he believed it should now be called. The Queen of Britain (for there had indeed been a change of monarch in his absence) then wasted no time in dispatching a fleet of her biggest ships to do a proper job of colonising the place so that a really big area of pink could be officially added to the *Atlas of the Known World So Far*.

The Indians strongly objected to British people taking over their lands and making them go to church every Sunday, but they were especially incensed at being forced to drink a minimum of six cups of tea every day. So, by way of protest, the top Indian chiefs invited the top British chiefs to a tea party in Boston where they deliberately infuriated the latter by adding the milk *after* the tea instead of putting the milk in the cup first.

When the Queen of Britain was informed of this outrage, she immediately ordered General Custer — the commander of the British forces in America — to "rid the country of these turbulent Indians". This he duly did by inflicting a heavy defeat on the Indians at the now famous Little Battle of the Big Horn where many braves met their deaths. Those Indians who survived — probably the less brave ones — were then rounded up and sent to live in places where nobody in their right mind would actually choose to set up home. As Big Chief Sitting Red Bull remarked when he was coerced into signing the Contract of Unconditional Surrender, 'Okay, we'll go and live in these awful dumps but not without reservations.'

After that, things went pretty smoothly for quite a few

years until a man called George Washington published a dictionary of what he called "American English" in which he deliberately altered the spellings of hundreds of *British* English words so that, for example, "colour" became "color", "centre" became "center" and, somewhat bizarrely as it hadn't even been invented yet, "aluminium" became "aluminum".

By now, there was a king on the British throne, and he was as furious about this dictionary as his female predecessor had been over the whole Boston Tea Party incident, especially when he heard that Washington hadn't just tinkered with the word "football" but had transformed it beyond all recognition into the word "soccer". As a result, he ordered the commander of the British forces in America — General Custer, Junior — to start the American War of Lexicography. But the war went badly for the British, partly because General Custer, Senior's son wasn't nearly as good as his dad in the commanding department and partly because there were an awful lot of British, Dutch, Germans, Polish, Italians and other nationalities who now called themselves Americans and were willing to fight for the right to spell words in whatever way they wanted.

Almost inevitably, therefore, the Americans emerged victorious, finally routing the British at the Battle of the Fourth of July. They immediately renamed the war "The American War of Independence", declared the country a republic and drew up a constitution which included such new freedoms as "the right to bare arms". (Under British rule, it had been strictly forbidden for any man, woman or child to roll up their sleeves in public.) And as occurred in the aftermath of the Little Battle of the Big Horn, things once again settled down quite nicely until the people in the north of America told the people in the southern states to stop bringing people from Africa against their will and making them do all the unpleasant jobs they didn't want to do themselves. The southern Americans refused, and a big fight broke out, which was eventually won by the northern Americans, and all the people from Africa were set free under an agreement signed at a now unknown address in the town of Gettysburg.

However, although all the people from Africa were now free, they didn't have an easy time of it at all. It was only after they invented "blues music" that non-African-Americans began to take them seriously and started to let them do jobs that they really wouldn't have minded doing themselves. Eventually, an African-American was even allowed to become President of the United States, although opinion is divided over whether that's a job that people would quite like to do or not.

47

Detective Sergeant Maurice Scatterthwaite bit down hard on the second finger of his last Twix. Of all the chocolate bars in all the world, the mighty Twix was far and away his all-time favourite, so he'd saved the best till last. Bizarrely, the monks had allowed him to keep the variety of sweet and savoury snacks that they'd discovered taped to his chest when they'd thrown him into the dank cell deep in the bowels of their headquarters. Perhaps they'd considered this to be the equivalent of the condemned man's final meal and would therefore save them the bother of actually preparing one themselves. But whatever their motive, Scatterthwaite's snack stash was now utterly exhausted apart from this one last delicious stick of chocolate-coated caramel and biscuit.

Before he'd unwrapped the twin fingers of heavenly delight, he'd told himself that he should savour every mouthful, taking several minutes — hours even — to first lick away all of the synapse-tingling milk chocolate and then luxuriate in the ambrosian nectar of the caramel to finally lay bare the slender firmness of the biscuit beneath. But the moment he'd got the wrapper open, he'd torn off a good half of the first finger with his teeth and voraciously chomped his way through it within a matter of seconds. Deferred gratification? Sod that for a lark, he'd thought. If whoever makes Twixes wanted you to eat the three parts separately, they'd have sold them in three different packets.

Now that he'd eaten all but the very last inch, however, he held what remained delicately between forefinger and thumb and pondered his future — or, more precisely, what little of it he had left. The head monk — Chairbrother Lemonsole — and a couple of his hench-monks had interrogated him for hours at a time, demanding to know every detail of the police investigation and how much they'd found out about SMASH and its activities. Considering they were serial killers, their interrogation techniques had been remarkably tame. Attaching an electrode to each of his big toes would have been infinitely more effective as an instrument of torture if the other ends of the cables had been connected to some kind of power source, and as for being forced to listen to a constant stream of Justin Bieber songs at a moderately high volume, this had been seriously annoying but hardly likely to get him to spill the beans. But spill the beans he had, given that the little he had to tell them scarcely amounted to a tiny *pile* of beans, never mind a hill. Of course, they hadn't believed him when he'd told them that the police knew next to nothing about SMASH and the investigation was going nowhere, so they'd carried on inflicting him with mild inconveniences and bombarding him with pointless questions.

Chairbrother Lemonsole had finally accepted that he wasn't going to get any more out of Brother Bream, né Maurice Scatterthwaite, so he'd had him taken down to the cells, but not before he'd warned him of the grisly and agonising death that awaited him.

'To be perfectly honest, it's the sort of death I wouldn't wish on my own worst enemy,' he'd said, and then with an evil smirk, added, 'But then again, I suppose you *are* my own worst enemy at the moment, so it's really rather appropriate.'

Scatterthwaite, however, had no intention of meekly

accepting his fate lying down — or sitting, or standing, or on all fours, or whatever other position Lemonsole had in mind for meting out his untimely and excruciatingly painful death — so, scoffing what he hoped would not be his last bite of Twix on this earth, he set about putting his plan into action.

First, he gathered up all of the strips of silver duct tape he'd used to secure his supply of snacks to his chest and rolled each one lengthways as tightly as he could to create eight thin cords. Then, he took one of these and measured it against the heavy wooden door of the cell. Two would be plenty, he decided, so he tied four pairs of the cord end to end to double their length and plaited them together to make a single rope. Fixing one end to a sturdy-looking nail which protruded from the left-hand door frame about eight inches above the floor, he stretched the rope across to a nail on the opposite upright and tied it off. He stepped back to check his handiwork, and although the duct tape wasn't quite parallel to the ground, he was confident that it was strong enough to do its job when the time came — and that could be any minute now.

Scanning the brightly coloured array of food wrappers strewn in all directions across the stone-flagged floor of the cell, he quickly spotted the one he was looking for. He snatched up the empty packet of Whopping Wotsits and peered inside. Not quite empty after all, he realised, and upended the packet to tip the last residual crumbs into his mouth.

The second item he needed was somewhat harder to find, and he dropped down onto his knees to sift through the debris. Pasties never tasted quite so good without tomato ketchup, so when he'd taped his snack stash to his chest, he'd made certain he'd included half a dozen of the individual mini-packs, and it had taken a great deal of willpower to eat one of the pasties *au naturel* in order to preserve one of the servings for precisely this occasion. And there it was at last, nestling on a bed of chocolate wrappers and beneath a scrunched-up bag of smoky bacon crisps.

He tore open the little plastic pack and squeezed out a small amount to create a trail of ketchup from the corner of his mouth to his chin and slightly beyond. The rest he smeared as liberally as possible over the area of his left breast, bare as it was since the monks had stripped him of his habit when they'd thrown him into the cell, leaving him naked except for his Marks and Spencer's underpants.

Back over by the door, he blew into the empty Whopping Wotsits packet, then held the neck of the bag shut, trapping the air inside. With his face close to the small, iron-barred opening near the top of the door, he shouted, 'Help! No! Please don't! No! Help me!' Smacking the palm of his hand sharply against the bottom of the bag and producing a fairly impressive "*bang!*" as it burst, he added, 'Aaargh!' and backed quickly away from the door. He lay down and arranged his arms and legs in awkward positions — not unlike the limbs of a corpse's chalk outline at a murder scene — and made sure that the ketchup stains on his face and chest were clearly visible from the cell door.

He didn't have to wait for long.

'Brother Bream? Are you all right in there?'

It was Brother Halibut, the monk who had been assigned as his gaoler, and fortunately for Scatterthwaite, he wasn't by any means the sharpest knife in the drawer.

'Oh, my goodness,' muttered the monk. 'What on earth has happened?'

Several seconds of silence were followed by some more muttering, the jangling of keys and the clunk of the door being unlocked. Two heavy iron bolts clanked, and Scatterthwaite peeled open an eyelid to the merest of slits at the metallic grating sound of the door's hinges.

'Brother Bream? Are you—?'

But the monk got no further with his question since, in his haste to check on his prisoner's wellbeing (or otherwise), he'd failed to notice the duct tape tripwire and went sprawling face down onto the stone floor. Scatterthwaite leapt to his feet and rolled the stunned monk onto his back.

'Sweet dreams, Brother Halibut,' he said and delivered an expertly judged uppercut to the monk's jaw.

There was an abruptly truncated gasp, a low groan, and Brother Halibut's head flopped to the side.

'Excellent,' said Scatterthwaite and hastily stripped him of his habit and Union Jack flip-flops.

No longer naked except for his Marks and Spencer's underpants, he ripped the tripwire from the open doorway and tied the monk's hands securely behind his back. A short piece of duct tape, which he'd kept back for the purpose, made a perfect gag, and as soon as he was done, Scatterthwaite hurried out of the cell and locked and bolted the door behind him.

Pulling the cowl of the habit as low over his face as he dared, but not so low as to arouse suspicion, he set off along the rough stone passageway towards the flight of steps at the far end. As he walked, he began to wonder whether he should write to whoever made Whopping Wotsits and tell them how their delicious product had literally saved his life. Come to think of it, why not write to the people who made Twixes and all of his other favourite snacks as well? No doubt about it, he was bound to get boxloads of freebies in return.

But just as he began to salivate uncontrollably at the very idea of a free-of-charge snack fest, he heard voices and the slip-slap of at least two pairs of flip-flops coming his way from the top of the steps.

48

There was a flash of intense violet — or possibly even ultraviolet — light, an explosively loud "*bang!*" and a sound that was not unlike the clanging bells on a pinball machine, which exponentially decreased in volume and rapidity of clangs until there was almost complete silence.

'Is that it then?' said Thestor from the back seat of the van as he removed the woollen Peruvian hat (with ear-flaps), which is all they'd been able to find for him in the way of protective headgear.

'What do you mean, "Is that it"?' said Norwood from the seat beside him.

'Three thousand, three hundred and thirty-eight years in less time than it takes to say "Is it too late to change my mind?" and without me needing to throw up even once? You have *got* to be kidding, right?'

'Well,' said Horace as he switched off the engine, 'I can't be *absolutely* certain that we're back in the present — or at least not at the exact same time that we first set off — but it looks about right.'

He and the others all peered through the van's windows at the vast expanse of fields and open land that stretched all the way to the horizon in every direction.

'I'm not sure how you can tell,' said Norwood. 'I mean, this could be almost anywhere and any period in time.'

Horace had to admit that Norwood was right, but it definitely *felt* like England. As for the period, the

348

patchwork of fields ought to provide a clue. Was it the Enclosure Acts when they started walling them off? He thought it probably was but couldn't remember when the Acts were introduced, so it wasn't a terribly helpful clue at all.

'Hang on a minute,' said Vesta, who was sitting in the passenger seat next to him. 'What's that?'

She pointed out of her side window, and the others followed her gaze. Horace couldn't see anything except the same fields and open countryside, but Norwood said he thought there was something just this side of the skyline and grabbed a pair of binoculars from the cupboard at the back of the van.

'Got it,' he said after a few seconds' twiddling the focusing ring.

'And?' said Horace.

'Any idea when Stonehenge was built?'

'Stone *what*?' said Thestor.

'I've got an idea it was somewhere between two and three thousand BC,' said Vesta.

'Oh, so we might in fact have gone *back* in time instead of forward,' said Norwood. 'I thought you said the time travel controls on this thing were at least accurate when you wanted to get back to the present.'

Horace had certainly *believed* this to be the case, but perhaps this had been a simple matter of wishful thinking.

'Is there a fence round it?' said Vesta.

'A what?' said Norwood.

'A fence.'

Norwood picked up the binoculars again and refocused. 'Looks like it, yes.'

'That was put up in the late seventies, I think, so that means—'

'We could be nearly four decades too early.'

'Still,' said Horace, 'at least we know *where* we are if

not exactly *when*. We'll find out on the way.'

'On the way?' queried Thestor, a note of alarm in his tone. 'Where to?'

'To deliver the snails,' said Horace 'Getting on for a hundred miles, I reckon.'

Thestor looked blank.

'About twenty leagues or so,' Vesta explained.

'Oh no,' Thestor groaned. 'Not more bumping and lurching for hours on end.'

Vesta laughed. 'I think you'll find the roads are much better now than they were in your day.'

'Not always,' said Norwood as he turned the sink tap off to switch from Time Travel Mode to Normal Mode.

'And it shouldn't take more than about three hours,' said Horace and fired up the engine. 'Depending on traffic of course.'

'Traffic?' said Thestor with more than a hint of anxiety.

'We did tell you that there'd be an awful lot of new stuff you'd have to get used to if you came with us,' said Norwood.

In fact, Horace, Vesta and Norwood had gone to great lengths to try and persuade Thestor that the twenty-first century would be too much of a culture shock for him and that he'd be far better off staying in his own time period. (They'd also impressed on him that wandering around dressed only in a scruffy loincloth would be seriously frowned upon in some quarters and could quite possibly result in his rapid acquaintance with the mental health services.) But Thestor had insisted that his prolonged absence from court would not have endeared him to King Amnestios, and besides, it would only be a matter of time before the king discovered that his claims to be able to foretell the future were entirely fraudulent. 'And whatever your twenty-first century has got to throw at me is likely to be infinitely preferable to being boiled alive in a cauldron of vinegar.'

The three adventurers had then taken turns to enlighten him about various aspects of the twenty-first century which the old man would find difficult to come to terms with and several that he would consider utterly abhorrent. These included reality TV shows, films about loved-up vampires, flatpack assembly instructions and excessive packaging, but in the end, they'd had to agree that, on balance, even these horrors were marginally more bearable than being boiled alive in vinegar.

* * *

The trip to Mr Wellwisher's house took considerably longer than the three hours Horace had estimated. This was partly due to essential roadworks on the M3 near Basingstoke and partly because of the frequency of having to stop so that Thestor could throw up. (Apparently, the smoother roads did little to alleviate his travel sickness.) They'd also taken a short break at a motorway services where they'd checked the date and discovered that, although the van's geographical accuracy had been a little off-target, its sense of time had been remarkably close to the mark. And so it was that when they finally pulled up outside Wellwisher's house, it was less than two weeks since they'd set off into the past.

'Quite a relief really when you think about it,' said Norwood as they all clambered out of the van. 'I mean, if we'd arrived back *before* we'd set off, we'd have had to start the whole thing over again from the beginning.'

'But at least we'd know exactly where to find the Holey Snails this time,' said Vesta.

'Ah, but would we though? Would we have any memory of something we'd already done in reality but hadn't *actually* done according to the passage of time?'

351

They all considered the point for several seconds until Horace broke the silence and said, 'All very complicated this time travel business, isn't it?'

The conundrum of the practical implications of time travel satisfactorily resolved, Horace, Norwood, Vesta and Thestor crunched their way across the gravel forecourt and climbed the twelve stone steps to the massive oak door at the front of the house. (Horace had decided to leave Zoot in the van to avoid upsetting Wellwisher's imaginary white cat, which, not unlike its owner, had seemed somewhat bad-tempered and cantankerous on their previous visit.) But before any of them had even begun to reach for the huge brass knocker in the shape of a giraffe's head, the door swung slowly inwards with a Dracula's-castle-type creak.

Framed in the doorway stood the impressively enormous figure of one of Wellwisher's aides and general factotums, Enormous Figure One.

'Hello, Enormous Figure One,' said Horace. 'Is Mr Wellwisher at home?'

'He is, yes,' said Enormous Figure One but instead of

stepping back to usher them inside, began to close the door.

Horace realised he needed to be more specific, and quickly. 'May we come in and see him then?'

'*See* him? What, as in you want to come in and *look* at him?'

'Well, no,' said Horace with an embarrassed chuckle. 'Obviously, we'd like to speak to him as well.'

Enormous Figure One pondered the proposition before answering. 'Okay then.'

Fully opening the door again, he stepped back and ushered them inside, then led the way across the highly polished marble floor, past a huge double staircase and down a very long corridor before coming to a halt by the fourteenth door on the right.

'Come in.'

The deep and somewhat muffled voice from beyond the door was unmistakably Mr Wellwisher's.

Enormous Figure One knocked lightly but firmly on the door, waited for 4.7 seconds and then opened it. Nothing in the vast expanse of the room had changed since their previous visit except that, instead of being ensconced in his high-backed crimson armchair as before, Wellwisher was now standing with his back to the roaring flames of the inglenook fireplace and warming his hands behind him. One other difference was that his ginger toupee (if indeed he was wearing it at all) was completely obscured by the cowl of an off-grey monk's habit, the hem of which reached to within two inches of the Union Jack flip-flops on his feet.

49

'And because everybody goes round with their hoods low over their faces, hardly anybody knows what anyone else looks like, so I just walked right out of there without being challenged even once.'

'Remarkable,' said Harper, genuinely impressed — but also astonished — at Scatterthwaite's ingenuity when he'd finished telling her of his miraculous escape from a certain and highly unpleasant death. 'I'd never have thought you had it in you.'

'Not just a pretty face, y'know,' said Scatterthwaite, leaning back in his chair on the other side of Harper's desk, his hands clasped behind his still-hooded head.

Harper allowed him a few more seconds of self-congratulation before cutting into it with a call to action. 'Right then, we need to get a move on. They're bound to know you've escaped by now, and my guess is that they'll be clearing out before we can get to them.'

'There's quite a lot of them,' said Scatterthwaite. 'We're going to need plenty of backup.'

'Oh, I don't think that'll be a problem this time,' said Harper, fleetingly producing a smug grin of her own.

'Yeah? How come?'

'Let's just say that the superintendent and I have reached... an understanding.'

Scatterthwaite shrugged and got to his feet. 'Okay, cool.'

'And lose the monk's outfit, yes? We don't want you getting arrested by mistake.'

'I'll just swing by the vending machine first. All this excitement's making me peckish all of a sudden.'

Is there anything that *doesn't* make you peckish? thought Harper, but she could hardly begrudge him since his snack addiction was probably the only reason he was still alive.

She picked up the phone and tapped out Leopold's number, relishing the prospect that, for once, her request for extra resources was unlikely to be met with the customary ear-bashing.

50

Apparently satisfied that his hands were sufficiently warm from the roaring flames of the inglenook fireplace, Wellwisher sat down in his high-backed crimson armchair, and following Vesta's lead, Horace, Norwood and Thestor seated themselves on the vast settee opposite him.

'Expect you're wondering what happened to the cat,' said Wellwisher.

The remark took Horace by surprise since he'd merely *noted* the absence of the imaginary white cat, which could hardly be described as *wondering* about it.

'Ruddy thing bit me once too often,' Wellwisher went on with a wry grin and a peculiar kind of twitch which resulted from his attempt to wink at them with the sightless eye socket behind his monocle.

As far as Horace could recall — and he was almost certain he was right — the last time they'd seen Mr Wellwisher, he'd worn his black-rimmed monocle over the empty socket where his right eye should have been. Now, however, it seemed that his right eye was fully functioning, and the empty socket and monocle were on the left. Strange enough as this was, the monocle still bore the inscription "THIS ONE, IDIOT!", but the large red arrow that was painted on it now pointed in the opposite direction from before to indicate the eye that was in service. This meant that Wellwisher must have had two monocles that were identical except for the direction of the arrow, and which one he wore depended on which side the working eye was on.

'Actually, Uncle,' said Vesta, 'I think we were wondering less about the cat and more why you're dressed as a monk with Union Jack flip-flops.'

Wellwisher threw back the cowl of his habit, revealing a heavy frown and a rakishly dislodged ginger toupee. 'Vesta? Is it really you?'

'Uh-huh.'

'Yes, I thought you seemed familiar. And how the devil are you after all this time?'

'Fine, thanks, but I was asking you about what you're wearing.'

Wellwisher glanced down at his off-grey robe. 'Rather suits me, wouldn't you say?'

'I was more interested in *why* you're wearing it.'

'All in good time, my dear. All in good time. But far more importantly, did you get the *helix pertusa* — the Holey Snails?'

Realising that Wellwisher had suddenly entered what might well turn out to be a very small window of lucidity, Horace seized the opportunity and launched into an extremely brief account of their ultimately successful quest.

'How splendidly splendid,' said Wellwisher, leaning forward and slapping his palms down hard on the arms of his chair. 'And where are the little blighters now?'

'Outside, in the van,' said Norwood.

'The van?'

'The time travel machine.'

Wellwisher sat back again with a rarely witnessed expression of joy. 'Malachy will be delighted.'

'Malachy?' said Vesta.

'Yes indeed. Malachy Worsthorne himself.'

'Worsthorne?' said Horace. 'As in Worsthorne Pharmaceuticals, you mean?'

'Wouldn't trust the conniving old dodge-merchant with my Great Aunt Jemima's piddle bucket most of the time of course, but you know what they say. You can take a horse to water, but you can't paint it pink. Or something like that anyway.'

After a spirit-crushing amount of prevarication on Wellwisher's part and some stalwartly determined badgering and cajoling on the parts of Horace, Norwood and Vesta (but not really Thestor, who had very little idea of what was going on), Wellwisher was finally persuaded to explain his involvement with the owner of Worsthorne Pharmaceuticals.

Shortly after their departure in search of the Holey Snails, he'd received an unscheduled and unwelcome visit from Malachy Worsthorne, who was accompanied by a couple of extraordinarily large men with guns and a psychopathically belligerent approach to life. Not even Enormous Figure One or Enormous Figure Two had been any match for them, and Wellwisher had had no choice but to listen to the proposition that Worsthorne had proposed.

Worsthorne knew all about his quest for the Holey Snails and had sent one of his men — a certain Mr Kenny Bunkport of Wellwisher's previous and deeply unpleasant acquaintance — back through time to grab the snails from Wellwisher's people if they succeeded in finding them. However, in the meantime, he'd come to the conclusion that he needed a backup plan in the event that Bunkport might fail in his mission, and he was therefore prepared to offer Wellwisher a deal which would be to their mutual advantage.

'From what I've heard,' Worsthorne had said, 'you only want these snails for your own personal use, but can you imagine how much money there is to be made by selling a potion on the open market that guarantees eternal youth?'

Wellwisher had replied that he could imagine it quite easily, so Worsthorne had explained the specifics of the deal he had in mind.

'So, if Bunkport screws up and your lot make it back with the snails, you hand them straight over to me, and my company starts churning out the eternal youth potion by the barrel load. In return, I'll provide you with as much of the stuff as you want for free. And on top of that, I'll give you enough shares in Worsthorne Pharmaceuticals to make you such an obscene amount of cash that you won't be able to spend it fast enough.'

There was a stunned silence in the room from the moment Wellwisher finished explaining the deal he'd made with Worsthorne until Norwood said, 'You do realise that Bunkport was going to kill us all as soon as he'd got the snails?'

'Ah yes,' said Wellwisher, 'but there was no way I could get in touch with you to warn you and no way Worsthorne could call off his American chappie. Still, all's well that ends well, eh? Tea, anyone?'

51

Harper had been right. By the time they'd got to SMASH's headquarters and had it completely surrounded, most of the monks had already fled, and those that remained were busily destroying evidence. In one room, the remains of half a dozen computers lay strewn around the floor, their hard drives smashed almost beyond recognition, and in a small yard at the back of the building, two monks were dumping boxloads of documents onto an enormous bonfire. Surprisingly, the armed response unit that had stormed the headquarters had met with very little resistance, and it hadn't been long before all the monks had been rounded up and Harper, Scatterthwaite and twenty other officers were safe to enter and start making arrests.

'Which one is Lemonsole?' Harper asked Scatterthwaite when the monks had been lined up side by side in front of her.

'I'm not entirely sure,' he said. 'What with the hoods and that, I never got a proper look at his face. We could always try asking, I suppose.'

Harper was doubtful that anyone would own up to being the ringleader of a bunch of serial killers, but she decided to give it a go anyway. 'Okay, so which one of you is Chairbrother Lemonsole?'

The expected silence lasted for more than a minute before her patience ran out, and she came to the conclusion that her best course of action was to have them all carted off down to the station and interview them individually. But no sooner had she opened her mouth to give the order than one of the monks near the middle of the row slowly raised his head, took a step forward and said, 'I'm Chairbrother Lemonsole.'

'Okay, so that wasn't so difficult, was it?' said Harper, but as she began to walk towards him, a second monk stepped forward and said, 'No, I'm Chairbrother Lemonsole.'

Then a third. '*I'm* Chairbrother Lemonsole.'

A fourth. 'I'm Chairbrother Lemonsole.'

Oh Jesus, thought Harper, not the old "I am Spartacus" routine.

Soon, the room was filled with the din of all eighteen monks repeatedly claiming to be Chairbrother Lemonsole and getting louder and louder with each repetition until Harper could stand it no longer.

'Shut — up!' she yelled at the top of her voice, but, if anything, the monks' chanting grew louder still, and it was only when she ordered the uniformed officers to draw their batons that the racket gradually subsided until order was finally restored, albeit with a few mutterings about police brutality.

'There's definitely a few women amongst this lot by the sound of it,' said Scatterthwaite, 'and Lemonsole's definitely a bloke.'

Harper had the monks remove their hoods so that their faces were clearly visible and pulled six women out of the lineup. One of them she recognised as a junior from the admin department at Nelson Street nick, so at least that explained the three-score-years-and-ten symbols in the women's toilet.

'He was pretty tall as well,' said Scatterthwaite, and seven monks of average or less than average height joined the women at the far end of the room.

Scatterthwaite walked up and down in front of the five remaining monks, taking his time to study the features of

361

each one before moving on to the next.

'Sorry, boss,' he said at last with a doleful shake of his head, 'but it could be any one of them.'

'Oh well,' said Harper. 'We'll see what we can get out of them back at the station.'

While the monks were being handcuffed and formally read their rights, Scatterthwaite tore open a Twix packet and bit off the end of the first finger. He chewed it for a few seconds, then swallowed, and was about to take a second bite when a hitherto elusive memory flashed into his mind.

'Hang on a minute though,' he said and went back over to the five possible Lemonsole candidates. 'Right, you lot, roll up your sleeves.'

With excruciating slowness, the monks hitched up the long, loose sleeves of their habits to reveal their hands and forearms, and Scatterthwaite examined the right hand of each in turn.

'Gotcha,' he said, grabbing the wrist of the fourth monk in the row and holding up the hand for all to see. 'I got a glimpse once and noticed the tip of his little finger was missing.'

Harper covered the space between her and the monk in three strides and stood almost toe-to-toe with him. He stared back at her, his pale grey eyes unblinking and his thin lips set into a sneering grin.

'Find something amusing?' she said.

'You think you've won, don't you?' said Lemonsole. 'You think because you have me and some of my brethren, that'll be the end of it, but you have no idea how many of us are still out there, dedicating their every waking moment to doing God's holy work and—'

'God's holy work? Systematically murdering innocent people just because they happen to have turned seventy?'

'"The days of our lives are three score years and ten". It says so quite clearly in the Bible.'

'It also says that people might live till they're eighty. And since you seem so keen on interpreting the Bible quite so literally, how about some of the other stuff, like not coveting your neighbour's ox, for instance? It's even one of the commandments. So how come you're not taking it on yourselves to enforce that one?'

Lemonsole's grin widened. 'Many passages in the Bible are open to interpretation of course and—'

'"Thou shalt not kill"? Heard of that one, have you?'

'As I say. A matter of interpretation.'

'And what's with shoving snails down the victims' throats? Something about that in the Bible as well, is there?'

'"The days of our lives are three score years and ten",' Lemonsole repeated.

Harper had an almost overwhelming urge to slap the irritating grin off his face and see how he interpreted the bit about turning the other cheek, but instead, she ordered the monks to be removed and held in the cells back at the station until she was ready to interview them.

Lemonsole was the last to be led away, and as he went, he called back over his shoulder. 'God's work will be done, and he alone will be my judge when that day comes.'

'Yeah?' Scatterthwaite shouted after him. 'Well, if that's the case, then there'll definitely be deep-fried Lemonsole on the menu that night.'

He looked round at Harper as if to check that she'd fully appreciated the biting wit of his remark, but as he did so, his eyes lit up at the sight of something over her shoulder.

She turned to see what it was that had so enthralled him, and entering through a door at the opposite end of the room was a little marmoset monkey dressed in its own scaled-down version of a floor-length hooded robe and wheeling a three-tiered trolley that was laden with all manner of drinks and snacks.

'Wow,' said Scatterthwaite. 'How cool is that?'

52

Thestor had nodded off at one end of the vast settee and was snoring loudly, so Norwood jabbed him in the prominently protruding ribs with his elbow. The spluttering commotion that erupted from the old man's abrupt awakening instantly drew Wellwisher's attention.

'And who in the name of all that's seriously undernourished is the bone-bag in the underpants?' he said, glowering at Thestor and apparently noticing his presence in the room for the first time. 'Don't tell me you've brought Gunga Din back with you. Or is it Karl Marx on a diet? He's not a ruddy communist, is he?'

'It's rather a long story,' said Vesta, 'but while we're on the subject of inappropriate clothing, you still haven't told us why you're dressed as a monk and wearing Union Jack flip-flops.'

'Also a rather long story, my dear,' said Wellwisher and immediately launched into his second major explanation of the day.

Not long after Vesta and her companions had set off on their quest for the Holey Snail, he'd begun to hear horrifying reports about monks in Union Jack flip-flops going round murdering people on their seventieth birthdays, and because he himself was due to turn seventy in just a few short weeks, he'd understandably become increasingly alarmed. Initially, he'd tried to convince himself that once he had the snails — and therefore the eternal youth which they would bestow upon him — the monks might be fooled into believing

365

he wasn't anywhere near being seventy years old and would pass him by without a second glance. However, he couldn't be sure that the quest for the Holey Snail would be successful or whether the monks would base their assessment on appearance rather than date of birth, so when he'd spotted an advertisement in the newspaper, he'd guessed that it was these very same monks on the lookout for new recruits.

'Thought I'd hedge my bets, so to speak. After all, it'd be a bit of a rum do if SMASH started bumping off its own members, eh?'

'SMASH?' said Horace.

'Society for the Murder and/or Assassination of Septuagenarian Heretics,' said Wellwisher somewhat testily. 'Where have you *been* for the last couple of weeks?'

'Er, Greece in the fourteenth century BC?' said Norwood.

'Ah yes. Good point.'

'So you mean to tell me you've joined a group of monks that murder people just because they're seventy?' said Vesta.

Wellwisher waved a dismissive hand. 'Not done any of that sort of thing myself of course. But there's more to it than that, and I'll tell you if you stop keep interrupting.'

He paused for a moment until he was satisfied that he had their complete attention and then continued with the "more to it than that" part of the explanation.

Having applied to become a member of SMASH, he'd been duly invited for interview, and although he himself had been sceptical that they would even consider someone who "let's face it, is hardly a spring chicken any more", they'd welcomed him with open arms. However, about five minutes into the interview, the real reason for such an enthusiastic welcome had become disturbingly clear. The head monk told him that they knew all about his quest for the Holey Snail and that he and the other top monks assumed that he'd seen the terrible error of his ways and wanted to join SMASH as an act of contrition.

'Utter balderdash of course,' said Wellwisher, 'but what was I to do? I mean, there am I sitting at the end of this great long table with these three nincompoop God-botherers banging on about how it was God's will that no-one should exceed their three score years and ten and how the Holey Snail was the spawn of the Devil himself because of the whole eternal youth malarkey. Cheating God, they said. The heresy of heresies, they said. And do you know what? That's why they always leave a couple of snails when they bump someone off. One by the body and one shoved down the poor bugger's throat. Supposed to be a warning to others that the word of God should not be ignored. Pah! Totally bonkers, the whole ruddy lot of them.'

Wellwisher's head dropped and he stared down at his lap, absent-mindedly stroking the imaginary white cat, which really was imaginary now because it wasn't there at all.

'So what did you do?' prompted Vesta.

Wellwisher looked up, a dazed expression lasting for several seconds until he remembered where he'd got to in the story.

'What did I do?' he said. 'I did a deal of course. After all, they made it pretty damn clear what the distinctly unpleasant consequences would be if I didn't atone for my so-called ruddy sins. Told me I'd have to make the ultimate sacrifice, and in return, they'd make me an honorary member of SMASH and I'd get immunity from being eliminated.'

'What sort of "ultimate sacrifice"?' said Vesta, anxiously sitting forward on the edge of the vast settee.

'The buggers said that if you did make it back with the Holey Snails, I'd have to destroy the lot of them. Every last one. And they wanted to watch me while I did it.'

'Destroy them?' Horace couldn't believe what he was hearing.

'After everything we've been through to get the damn things?' said Norwood.

'And what about the other deal?' said Vesta. 'The one you did with Worsthorne.'

'Well, obviously I'm not going to destroy the real thing,' said Wellwisher. 'Worsthorne will still get the *helix pertusa*, but I've had Enormous Figure One and Enormous Figure Two out collecting as many garden snails as they could find, and Mrs Gaviscon's been in the kitchen all morning jabbing lots of little holes in their shells. Ruddy monks can do what they like with those ones.'

'And you really think that'll fool them?' said Vesta.

'We'll soon find out because Enormous Figure Two telephoned them as soon as you arrived, and if I'm not much mistaken, that'll be them at the front door now.'

Less than a second later, the sound of the giraffe's-head brass knocker being banged against the massive oak door echoed boomingly through the house. Wellwisher dispatched Enormous Figure One to go and let their guests in and Enormous Figure Two to fetch the bogus Holey Snails from Mrs Gaviscon and a large hammer from the cupboard under the stairs.

While they waited, no-one spoke. Horace, for one, was too much in shock to think of anything sensible to say. From the sound of it, these monks were ruthless, cold-blooded killers, and it didn't take a genius to work out what they'd do to Wellwisher if they discovered that he'd double-crossed them. Not only that, but they probably wouldn't want to leave any witnesses alive to tell the tale. So much for the "without risk of personal physical harm" clause that he'd clearly specified in his advertisement. He'd lost track of the number of times he and his co-adventurers had faced gruesome and grisly deaths since the quest for the Holey Snail had begun, and familiarity with the experience had done little to make him feel any easier about the prospect.

'Ah, welcome, gentlemen,' said Wellwisher as Enormous Figure One ushered four figures into the room who were considerably less enormous than he was. All were dressed in the same off-grey habits and Union Jack flip-flops as Wellwisher himself, but unlike him, wore their cowls forward so it was impossible to see their faces.

'"Brethren" is the correct form of address,' said one of them, and judging by the pitch of the voice, was evidently not a gentle-*man* at all. 'You should know that by now, Brother Flounder.'

'Brother Flounder?' said Vesta.

Wellwisher turned towards her with an almost apologetic facial shrug. 'It's complicated.'

'So where are these 'Oley Snails then?' said one of the other monks, the voice indicating that he was very much a man, but whether he was gentle or not remained to be seen.

Right on cue, Enormous Figure Two entered the room bearing a very large hammer and a silver salver, upon which lay a dozen or so garden snails with some rather unevenly distributed holes in their shells.

'Is this all?' said one of the two monks who hadn't yet spoken and was also a man.

'They're breeding pairs,' said Wellwisher.

'So how do you tell which ones are boy snails and which ones are girl snails?' asked the fourth monk (and the second female one), picking up one of the snails and inspecting it thoroughly.

'Trained eye and all that,' said Wellwisher, tapping

his monocle with the tip of his finger, 'but essentially, you just let them get on with it and you'll find out soon enough.'

'And these are definitely the real thing?' said the first female monk. 'Holey Snails that you make a potion from to get eternal youth?'

'The very same.'

'You wouldn't be trying to pull a fast one, would you now? Pull the wool over our eyes, eh?'

'As opposed to your hoods, you mean?' Wellwisher let out a guffaw of laughter, but nobody else made the slightest attempt to join in, so he nipped the guffaw in the bud and said, 'Certainly not. Genuine Holey Snails, every last one of them.'

'Very well then. But you know what'll happen if we find out you've been lying.'

Wellwisher nodded his head so vigorously that his precariously perched ginger toupee fell from his head completely, and hastily replacing it, he said, 'Would you like to do the honours or shall I?'

'Honours?' said the first of the male monks.

'You know. Smash the little blighters to smithereens.'

'What? Are you serious?'

'Well, yes. I thought that was the whole point of the deal.'

'Not any more it ain't. Not since the cops raided our HQ and Chairbrother Lemonsole and a bunch of the others got busted.'

'Oh?'

'SMASH is screwed, mate, so now that me and the brethren 'ere 'ave been relieved of our responsibilities, so to speak, we 'ad a bit of a think, and we thought, "Holey Snails? Eternal youth? Yeah, we'll 'ave some o' that. Too bloody right".'

Even before he'd finished speaking, he and the other three monks each pulled a semi-automatic pistol from somewhere within the sleeves of their habits and aimed them at the rest of the assembled company. Then the first female monk took the silver salver of snails from Enormous Figure Two, and they all backed out of the room, their guns still at the ready to shoot anyone who was stupid enough to try and stop them.

Seconds later, at the sound of the massive front door being slammed shut with an almighty bang, Wellwisher clapped his hands together and said, 'Well, I'd say that all went rather swimmingly, wouldn't you?'

53

'Right, that oughta do it,' said Brother Herring, stepping back from *Hawking 3* and wiping oil and grease from his hands on the front of his already grubby habit.

'You think?' said Brother Mackerel, exuding minimal confidence in Herring's ability as a mechanic.

Not that her doubts were at all unfounded. Ever since the time-travelling motorbike and sidecar had been peppered with bullets back at the lake, it had consistently failed to perform satisfactorily in either Normal Mode or Time Travel Mode. Even though the tracking device was still functioning correctly, their attempt to follow the camper van in Normal Mode had been an unmitigated disaster. Every dozen or so miles, *Hawking 3*'s engine had spluttered and abruptly died, steadfastly refusing to be coaxed back to life again until Brother Herring had spent several hours tinkering, fiddling and adjusting.

By the time of their twelfth unscheduled stop, it had become clear to them that there was very little chance of catching up with the van if they carried on like this, and the only alternative was to try out the machine in Time Travel Mode. If this was working properly, they could leap forward through time and space and be hot on the heels of their quarry within a matter of moments.

As a theory, it was perfectly sound, but as is often the case with theories, it had turned out to be hopelessly wide of the mark in practice. Having checked their tracking monitor for the precise location of the camper van, they'd entered the coordinates into *Hawking 3*'s on-board computer so that it could calculate the necessary time shift. Unfortunately, however, and unbeknown to Mackerel and Herring, the computer's motherboard had taken a direct hit from at least one bullet and was so severely damaged that it would have struggled to work out the square root of nine, never mind the really complex stuff involved in accurately computing time travel parameters.

And so it was that after a great deal of whirring, clanking, clinking, clonking and some other disturbingly grating metallic noises, Mackerel and Herring had found themselves somewhere on the Indian subcontinent in an unknown time period but during a heatwave that was so intense that their Union Jack flip-flops had begun to melt. Working feverishly and sweating profusely, they'd overridden *Hawking 3*'s computer system and manually entered what they hoped were the appropriate space/time coordinates — or at least anything that would get them out of there before they fried to death.

But out of the frying pan into the fire, as the saying goes, they'd next found themselves on the edge of some kind of market square that was thronged with people in medieval-looking clothes who were jabbering excitedly in Italian. All of them had their gazes fixed on the middle of the square, some of them on tiptoe, craning their necks to get a better view of whatever was going on. By standing on the saddle of the motorbike, Mackerel had been able to see over their heads and discovered to her horror that the object of their attention was a group of three huge piles of wood with a hefty wooden pole protruding upwards from the centre of each. Securely tied with their backs to these poles were three men in monks' habits and with tonsured heads. All of a sudden, the three wood piles had burst into flames, and a mighty cheer had gone up from the crowd.

'They don't seem very keen on our sort round here,'

Mackerel had said, jumping down from the motorbike and rapidly resetting the time travel controls with barely a thought as to where or when they might end up.

Where and when they did end up was right here and right now, slap bang in the middle of fifteen or so covered wagons that had been drawn into a circle. Fortunately, the two brethren had been able to avoid the necessity of explaining their sudden arrival and mode of transport because no-one appeared to have noticed. All of the people on the inside of the circle were far too busy firing their guns at the vast horde of Native Americans who were careering round and round the outside of the circle on horseback and firing their own guns and bows and arrows at the people on the inside.

Once again, Herring and Mackerel had realised that a hasty retreat was called for, but they'd also come to the conclusion that there was very little hope of ever catching up with the time-travelling camper van, so they'd decided to abandon their mission altogether and, if possible, head back to the present.

But Brother Mackerel still harboured the gravest of doubts. 'I mean, who's to say that the Back To The Present setting will work any better than all the other time travel controls we've tried so far?'

'Well,' said Brother Herring, 'it looks like that part of the circuitry hardly took any damage at all apart from a couple of wires and the doodah on the centrifuge accelerator thingy, but I reckon I've fixed those, so we should be fine.'

Doodah? Thingy? I reckon? Mackerel's confidence was waning by the nano-second, but given that at least half of the wagons were now ablaze, she was forced to recognise that the hard place was probably preferable to the rock on this occasion, and she clambered into the sidecar while Herring sat astride the bike and hit the Start button. Thick clouds of black smoke belched forth from the twin exhaust pipes, and the whole of *Hawking 3* vibrated so violently that Mackerel feared the sidecar was about to detach itself entirely from the bike at any moment. But no sooner had the thought entered her head than there was a loud screeching noise which got so high in pitch that only dogs would have heard it, and then a retina-searing flash of light which quickly dissolved into impenetrable darkness.

Mackerel couldn't be sure whether she'd passed out or not, but when the darkness began to clear and the vibration was suddenly curtailed with a spine-jarring jolt, she was amazed to find that *Hawking 3* had delivered them safely, if not comfortably, back to the small yard at the rear of SMASH's headquarters. The strong smell of burning, she presumed, was simply an indication that the severely damaged and overstressed time machine was about to give up the ghost entirely, but when she turned her head, she saw two monks in Union Jack flip-flops dumping boxloads of documents onto an already enormous bonfire.

Incredible, she thought. Not only the right place but must be about the right timeframe as well.

Eighteen seconds later, however, she rapidly revised her opinion about it being the *right* timeframe when half a dozen armed police in helmets and flak jackets stormed into the yard and screamed at Mackerel, Herring and the other two monks to lie face down on the ground with their hands behind their heads.

Time travel can be a fickle mistress sometimes.

54

'I wasn't too keen on the cut of *his* jib, I must say,' said Horace as he, Norwood, Vesta and Thestor climbed back into the camper van outside Wellwisher's house.

Zoot was fast asleep on the back seat and fleetingly peeled open an eyelid before letting it drop back into place again.

'Worsthorne, you mean?' said Vesta.

Horace nodded. 'Shifty *and* greedy. Bad combination in my book.'

'I must admit I was a bit surprised that Uncle Alexander had done a deal with him over the snails.'

'Especially as it was Worsthorne who nearly had us all killed,' said Norwood. 'And now he's going to reap the benefits.'

'And you can bet your life he's going to charge a small fortune for the potion, so it'll only be the very rich that'll be able to afford it,' said Horace. 'And now I come to think about it, why should *anyone* have access to eternal youth? It's just not... natural, is it?'

'You know,' said Vesta with a heavy sigh, 'I almost wish we'd never gone on this quest in the first place. I mean, I adore my uncle, and I'd do anything for him, so I didn't have a problem when we were just getting the Holey Snails for *him*, but selling the potion for profit's a different matter altogether.'

'Wonderful thing, hindsight,' said Norwood, 'but we can hardly turn back...'

He didn't bother to finish the sentence. He didn't need

to. The others knew exactly what he'd been about to say, and everyone lapsed into silence as they considered the implications. For his part, Horace wasn't at all sure that he wanted to go time-travelling ever again, and there were also practical considerations that couldn't be ignored.

'Can't be done, I'm afraid,' he said eventually with a ponderous shake of his head. 'The time controls aren't that accurate, as you know, so it's highly unlikely we could ever make it back to the same time or—'

'Does that matter though?' Vesta interrupted and leaned forward in her seat. 'As long as we could get the snails back to some period or other before they became extinct, we could—'

'Slight flaw in that plan,' said Norwood, taking his turn at interrupting. 'We don't actually *have* the snails any more.'

'You could always buy them back,' said Thestor, who until now had seemed not to have been taking any interest in the discussion whatsoever. Instead, he'd been busying himself with a detailed examination of the interior of each of the van's cupboards, all of which were crammed full with the gold, silver and jewellery that had been reluctantly given to them by King Amnestios three thousand, three hundred and thirty-eight years ago. Then he crouched down to open the door of the oven, which was also stuffed to bursting with gold, silver and jewellery, and as a complete non sequitur, added, 'Why's this one different to all the other cupboards?'

'What?' said Horace. 'Oh, that's the oven. It's for cooking food in.'

'Yes, I do know what an oven is, thank you,' said Thestor. 'It's just that I've never seen one like this before. Where does the wood go for the fire then? Underneath somewhere?'

'It runs on gas, and you control how hot it gets with

377

that dial thing on the front.'

'Gas?'

Horace's brain struggled to come up with a brief and coherent explanation, and he scanned Vesta and Norwood's faces in a silent appeal for help. None was forthcoming, and as he turned his attention back to Thestor, he noticed that the old man was repeatedly rotating the oven's temperature control back and forth with an expression of utter bewilderment adding even more creases to his heavily wrinkled brow.

'And please don't fiddle with that,' Horace snapped, even though he was trying not to sound snappy at all. 'In fact, could you just sit down and not fiddle with anything?'

Thestor grunted and slumped down on the back seat next to Vesta and Zoot.

'Thestor's got a point though,' said Vesta. 'I don't know what Worsthorne reckons he'll make from the Holey Snail potion, but all this loot we got from Amnestios must be worth an absolute fortune.'

'It's a possibility, I suppose,' said Horace, secretly hoping they'd be able to keep back enough for him to buy the latest version of the Swiss Army knife, which was due on the market any day now and had all kinds of handy little tools and gadgets it didn't have before. 'But what if Worsthorne doesn't want to sell?'

'Well, in that case, we could always steal them back,' said Norwood. 'After all, if we can take them from right underneath the noses of old snakehead and her sisters, Worsthorne'll be a walk in the park.'

The memory of their near-death encounter with the Gorgons brought sweat to Horace's palms, a shiver to his spine and his severely depleted fingernails to his mouth. Norwood was probably right that stealing the snails from Worsthorne was unlikely to result in their grisly and excruciatingly painful deaths if they were caught, but even so, the option of simply *buying* them back sounded infinitely preferable. However, he had no desire to go straight back in and confront Worsthorne with their proposal — especially not in front of Wellwisher — so any negotiations would have to wait till morning.

'How about we sleep on it and see how we feel tomorrow?' he said, always a firm believer in the angels' attitude to rushing into anything.

'Sleep?' said Norwood. 'But I'm starving. And it's not that late anyway, so why don't we go and find somewhere to eat?'

'Not French though,' said Horace as he started up the van's engine and set off up the driveway. 'In fact, nowhere that's likely to have snails on the menu. And we'd better stop off somewhere to get Thestor some decent clothes first.'

'I wonder if they accept Ancient Greek gold at T K Maxx,' said Vesta.

'Urgh, that's disgusting!' Thestor shouted.

'T K Maxx or eating snails?' said Norwood.

'No, the damn dog just dribbled all over my hand.'

'Yes, he does that,' said Horace. 'I think it's a sign of affection.'

'Disgusting,' Thestor repeated, jumping to his feet and flipping open the hinged worktop above the sink. He stared blankly at the white plastic mixer tap. 'So now what do I do?'

As Vesta explained and Thestor turned on the tap full blast, Horace glanced at the van's speedometer. Twenty-seven-point-three miles per hour.

'Oh my God, no!' he yelled. 'Turn it off quick or we'll—'

But he didn't get to finish the sentence, suddenly interrupted as he was by a sound that was not unlike the clanging bells on a pinball machine, which exponentially increased in volume and rapidity of clangs until there was an explosively loud "*bang!*" and a flash of intense violet — or possibly even ultraviolet — light.

Then everything went black.

* * *

DCI Harper Collins braked sharply to avoid... To avoid what? The big empty space that had been occupied a fraction of a second earlier by the elderly VW camper van she'd been stuck behind for the past five minutes?

'Did you see that?' she said.

'See what?' said DS Maurice Scatterthwaite, his words barely intelligible through the large chunk of Ginsters pasty that filled his mouth to overflowing.

Harper glanced across at him, far more important matters on her mind to be repulsed by the thin trickle of tomato ketchup oozing down one side of his chin as he looked up from brushing flakes of pastry from his lap.

'The camper van that was in front of us,' she said. 'Vanished into thin air. Just like that.'

Scatterthwaite shook his head. 'Sorry, no, I wasn't watching,' he said — or something that sounded very much like it.

'This isn't the first time it's happened either,' said Harper, 'and I'm almost certain it was the same van as before.'

The only response she got was some loud chomping noises, so she drove on in silence, wondering if her mind had been playing tricks with her. It wouldn't be surprising of course. The stress she'd been under lately was enough to have driven anyone round the bend, and she made up her mind there and then that as soon as this case was wrapped up, she'd be taking some very substantial and long overdue leave. Somewhere hot. Somewhere like Greece perhaps. She and Jonathan had never been, and they'd always said they'd have a holiday there one day. Great weather, beautiful beaches and all those amazing places like the Acropolis, Ancient Olympia, the Temple of Apollo, and the cave where Medusa and her Gorgon sisters were supposed to have lived.

Yes, that'll do nicely, she thought, and a smile crept across her face for the first time in a very long while.

EPILOGUE

There was always the same smell in this office. Always unpleasant and yet always impossible to fathom exactly what it consisted of or where it emanated from. It had a kind of rotten eggs and very old fish stink to it, but there were other elements that Cordelia Thornton-Gayle had never been able to put her finger on. Nor had any of the other civil servants or admin staff at the Ministry for Work and Pensions, but since this was the only room in the entire building that the smell could be detected, many of them had concluded that it must be coming from the Minister himself. Cordelia had never subscribed to this theory personally, believing instead that it resulted from some form of virulent rot within the office's elegant but ancient wood panelling. Even so, she always dreaded a summons from the Minister and on each occasion took the precaution of having with her a handkerchief that had been heavily doused with cologne.

She dabbed at her nose with it now as she sat patiently waiting for the Minister to finish watching the recording of the morning's main news bulletins. For the past thirty seconds or so, the images on the TV screen had been exclusively devoted to the efforts of dozens of firefighters to douse the flames which still erupted from the remains of a once substantial factory building. Sometimes in the foreground and sometimes off camera, the young male reporter had been explaining that Worsthorne Pharmaceuticals' laboratories and main production centre had been all but obliterated by a massive explosion some time during the early hours of the morning.

The fire chief in charge of the operation had already been interviewed and had given his opinion that, although it was too early to make a precise assessment, there appeared to have been at least five simultaneous explosions, and from the evidence available so far, these had been caused by a series of large and reasonably sophisticated bombs.

Now, the reporter was beckoning to somebody off camera, and a short, ruddy-faced man in his mid to late sixties shuffled into shot.

'Mr Worsthorne,' said the reporter, 'I understand of course that you must be utterly devastated by what has happened here tonight, but I wonder if I might ask you a few quick questions.'

Worsthorne nodded bleakly, and the reporter continued. 'Although it's apparently too soon to know for certain, it seems that the destruction of your factory was a deliberate act. Have you any idea at all who might have been responsible?'

Worsthorne's mouth moved, but even with the microphone shoved under his nose, it was impossible to hear what he was saying.

'I'm sorry, Mr Worsthorne,' said the reporter, 'but could you speak up a little?'

'Bloody monks,' said Worsthorne, spitting out the words and glaring directly into the camera.

'Monks?'

'Bloody mental cases in their bloody Union Jack flip-flops. Hanging's too good for them lot, I tell you, and if I ever get my hands on—'

'Yes, indeed,' interrupted the reporter. 'You're obviously deeply upset about this tragic—'

'Upset? Upset? I was just about to start a new project that would have made me one of the richest men on the planet, and now this. Every last one of them blown to bits.'

'Them?'

'The holey bloody snails of course. Every bloody one.'

'Still, looking on the bright side,' said the reporter, failing miserably at a conciliatory smile, 'none of your employees were in the building at the time, so at least no *people* were hurt.'

There followed a lengthy pause while Worsthorne eyeballed the reporter, and then he drew back his fist and punched him hard in the face. The camera kept the reporter in shot as he crumpled to the ground, and as the blood began to flow from both of his nostrils, the viewer was hastily returned to the news anchor in the studio.

'I think I've seen enough now, thank you, Cordelia,' the Minister said, getting up from his chair and strolling over to the nearest window, his hands clasped behind his back as he stared out into the middle distance. 'So was it them? SMASH, I mean.'

Cordelia picked up the remote and clicked off the TV. 'My information is that Lemonsole found out that the Holey Snails were at Worsthorne's laboratory and managed to get word out to order the bombing after he'd been taken into custody.'

The Minister grunted. 'A bit on the extreme side even for him, but that's always going to be an issue when you jump into bed with a fruitcake.'

Cordelia was fighting to keep this bizarre image from entering her mind when the Minister suddenly rounded on her.

'Are we absolutely sure that Lemonsole's the only one who knows about our... arrangement?'

'Well, Minister, we can't be *absolutely* sure that he didn't tell any of the other SMASH members.'

The Minister chewed at his lower lip for a few

moments while he considered the implications. 'I suppose it's no great matter even if he did. I can't see anyone believing any of the foot soldiers who've been arrested, and from what you've told me, the rest of them have pretty much gone to ground.'

'Apart from the ones who bombed Worsthorne Pharmaceuticals, yes, but I expect they'll be keeping a very low profile from now on.'

'Either way, Lemonsole will have to be dealt with of course. Can't have *him* shooting his mouth off, what?'

'Indeed not, Minister.'

'Set it in motion, would you, Cordelia? You know the drill.'

Cordelia made a brief note on the pad on her lap and stood up from the leather-bound settee. 'Will that be all then, Minister?' she said, taking what she hoped was an inconspicuous sniff of her scented handkerchief.

'Pity about SMASH though really,' said the Minister, totally ignoring her question. 'Served our purposes rather well. Or would have done once they'd expanded to cover the whole country.'

'Yes, Minister.'

'I assume you've already cut their funding?'

'Of course, Minister.'

The Minister sighed heavily. 'Oh well, *c'est la vie*. I suppose we'll just have to think up another scheme for keeping the pension payments down. Tweaking the euthanasia legislation might be one option of course. Have a look into that when you've got a spare moment, would you, Cordelia? Maybe set up a meeting with some of those bods from the right to die campaign. Top secret though, yes?'

'Certainly, Minister.'

'Good girl.' The Minister clapped his hands together and gave her a beaming smile. 'Right then, off you pop. No rest for the wicked, eh?'

Cordelia was halfway out of the door when the Minister called after her. 'Is it my imagination or is there a ruddy awful stink in this office?'

Without turning to face him, Cordelia Thornton-Gayle took another unobtrusive sniff of her handkerchief.

'Your imagination, I think, Minister,' she said and closed the door quietly behind her.

THE END

OTHER BOOKS BY
ROB JOHNSON

LIFTING THE LID
(Book One in the 'Lifting the Lid' series)

There are some things people see in toilets that they wish they hadn't. What Trevor Hawkins sees might even cost him his life…

It was simply a matter of a broken flush, so how come he's suddenly a fugitive from a gang of psychopathic villains, a private detective, the police and MI5? 'Lifting the Lid' is a comic thriller with more twists and turns than an Escher-designed bobsleigh run.

"A superb adventure-comedy." - Jennifer Reinoehl for *Readers' Favorite*

"It's brilliant!" - Samantha Coville for *SammytheBookworm.com*

"The story is just so much FUN!" - Joanne Armstrong for *Ingrid Hall Reviews*

HEADS YOU LOSE
(Book Two in the 'Lifting the Lid' series)

The assignment in Greece might have been the answer to Trevor and Sandra's problems except for one thing. Someone was trying to frame them for murder... with a watermelon.

Trevor and Sandra's detective agency is almost bankrupt when they take on the job of looking after the ageing Marcus Ingleby at his villa in Greece. It's easy money until someone tries to frame them for murder, and Ingleby gets a visit from two ex-cons and a police inspector from his murky past.

 "A highly entertaining, well-constructed screwball comedy." - Keith Nixon for *Big Al's Books and Pals*

"Masterfully planned and executed... It tickled my funny bone in all the right places." - Joanne Armstrong for *Ingrid Hall Reviews*

Shortlisted for a Readers' Choice Award 2015 (*Big Al's Books and Pals*)

ABOUT THE AUTHOR

'You'll have to write an author biography of course.'

'Oh? Why?'

'Because people will want to know something about you before they lash out on buying one of your books.'

'You think so, do you?'

'Just do it, okay?'

'So what do I tell them?'

'For a start, you should mention that you've written four plays that were professionally produced and toured throughout the UK.'

'That was quite a while ago now.'

'They're not to know that, and besides, it wasn't your fault that theatre funding dried up almost overnight.'

'So should I say anything about all the temp jobs I had, like working in the towels and linens stockroom at Debenhams or as a fitter's mate in a perfume factory?'

'No, definitely not.'

'Motorcycle dispatch rider?'

'You were sacked weren't you?'

'Boss said he could get a truck there quicker.'

'Leave it out then, but make sure they know that *Quest for the Holey Snail* is the third book you've written.'

'It's very different from the other two.'

'Doesn't matter. But make sure you put in something that shows you're vaguely human.'

'You mean this kind of thing: "I'm currently in Greece with my wife, Penny, working on a fourth novel and a couple of screenplays. I've also been producing a series of short, hopefully humorous podcasts (with background barking sounds provided by our five rescue dogs)".'

'It'll have to do, I suppose, but don't forget to finish off with your website and social media stuff.'

'Oh, okay then.'

- visit my website at
  http://www.rob-johnson.org.uk

- follow **@RobJohnson999** on Twitter

- check out my Facebook author page at
  https://www.facebook.com/RobJohnsonAuthor

REVIEWS

Authors always appreciate reviews – especially if they're good ones of course – so I'd be eternally grateful if you could spare the time to write a few words about *Quest for the Holey Snail* on Amazon or anywhere else you can think of. It really can make a difference. Reviews also help other readers decide whether to buy a book or not, so you'll be doing them a service as well.

AND FINALLY...

I'm always interested to hear from my readers, so please do take a couple of minutes to contact me via my website at:

http://rob-johnson.org.uk/contact/

or email me at:

robjohnson@care4free.net

I look forward to hearing from you.

33942212R00229

Printed in Great Britain
by Amazon